About the author

Tessa Duder worked as a journalist and raised four daughters before becoming a full-time writer. Her thirty-five books include the multiple award-winning novels of the *Alex* quartet, the *Tiggie Tompson* trilogy, and a portrait of Margaret Mahy. Among her awards are the Margaret Mahy Medal and the 2003 Meridian Energy Katherine Mansfield Fellowship to Menton, France. She lives in Auckland.

For more information, see www.tessaduder.com

TESSA DUDER

IS SHE STILL ALIVE?

Scintillating stories for women
of a certain age . . .

HarperCollins*Publishers*

For Tina

The author gratefully acknowledges the support of
Creative New Zealand and the 2003 Meridian Energy
Katherine Mansfield Fellowship to live and work in Menton,
France, where she began writing this collection of stories.

National Library of New Zealand Cataloguing-in-Publication Data
Duder, Tessa.
Is she still alive? / Tessa Duder.
ISBN - 978-186950-710-7
I. Title.
NZ 823.2—dc 22

First published 2008
Reprinted 2009
HarperCollins*Publishers (New Zealand) Limited*
P.O. Box 1, Auckland
Copyright © Tessa Duder 2008
Tessa Duder asserts the moral right to be identified as the author of this work.

ISBN: 978 1 86950 710 7
Cover design by Matt Stanton, HarperCollins Design Studio
Cover image courtesy of Getty Images
Internal text design and typesetting by Janine Brougham
Printed by Griffin Press, Australia

70gsm Bulky Book Ivory used by HarperCollins*Publishers* is a natural, recyclable product
made from wood grown in sustainable forests. The manufacturing processes conform to
the environmental regulations in the country of origin, New Zealand.

Contents

Introduction

Sometime in my fifties I came across a magazine piece by Ursula Le Guin about crones, menopause and space travel.* Who, she asks, would be the best single human being to go on a long space journey, 'an exemplary person' to tell alien beings about the nature of the human race? Wouldn't most say, 'a fine, bright, brave young man, highly educated and in peak physical condition?'

I remember this piece fondly, because Le Guin's choice would be an old woman, a grandmother, over sixty, perhaps found in the local Woolworths or the local village marketplace. She was 'never educated to anything like her capacity, and that is a shameful waste and a crime against humanity' but possesses 'a stock of sense, wit, patience, and experiential shrewdness.'

Trouble is, writes Le Guin, 'she'd be reluctant to volunteer, and it will be hard to explain to her that we want her to go because only a person who has experienced, accepted, and acted the entire human condition — the essential quality of which is Change — can fairly represent humanity. "Me?" she'd say, just a trifle slyly. "But I never did anything."'

A few years later, I found myself happily living for seven months in Menton, on the Côte d'Azur, as the 2003 Katherine Mansfield Fellow. It seemed like a good time and place to have a crack at a short story, and, new for me, one unquestionably for adults. One experimental story about an ordinary 'older woman' at the formal reading of her late husband's will was followed by another, about two bejewelled old crones observed on a Riviera beach, and another, about an Italian immigrant being buried in a windswept Wellington cemetery after a lifetime of servitude.

* 'The Space Crone' (1976), included in *Dancing at the Edge of the World* by Ursula Le Guin, HarperCollins, 1992.

Three seemed like the start of a collection, all stories about ordinary, older women's lives: change, loss, laughter. I finished at thirteen only because the word count had got to book length, knowing that many more could be written.

And yes, some of these stories do owe their origin to anecdotes told and retold in my family (and as in all other families) about the women of one, two or three generations back; mind you, *only* their origin, since the fun of writing fiction is to take the spark of an idea or an event and leap off with this torch to throw light on some new and unexplored place. So none are in any way strictly biographical, nor, for that matter, autobiographical.

The stories are set variously in New Zealand and Europe, but I believe parallel the female experience in other Western countries, particularly those with a colonial past. Most of the women were born into the period around World War II and the twenty years after. Surely no generation of women in history has seen greater change: from the comparative orderliness of the 1950s, to the 60s revolutions, 70s feminism (here to stay at last), then the 80s return to the workplace, the 90s political upheavals, the millennium. What a ride it's been!

And through it all, ordinary middle-class women coping, reaching cronehood with, quite often, thwarted personal ambitions. If there is a common thread to these stories, an underlying theme, it is lack of personal fulfillment. This was not my intention; I simply seemed to be echoing an all-too-familiar experience for the mid- to late-twentieth-century older women I knew, heard or read about.

So these stories are by way of three cheers for the crones that Ursula Le Guin would send into space — those who can stand and sing along with Stephen Sondheim's marvellous serenade to age from *Follies*: through all the good times and the not-so-good times, 'I'm still here.'

Is she still alive?

They had agreed by email to meet for an early lunch before going on to Joyce's party.

Isobel had a breakfast meeting in Hamilton but could easily get back in time and had given herself the rest of the day off, Stevie had cancelled her golf and Thea would drive up from Thames. They would meet at the Viaduct Basin (and since they all could, unlike some, still manage the stairs), at this upstairs fish restaurant which had a nice view of the big yachts and was a bit apart from the noisy hoi polloi below. Isobel would book a veranda table for noon.

Thea allowed three hours from Thames and arrived first, finding herself horrified at what she'd had to pay in the parking building and recalling yet again some psychologist stating that it was the lonely people who always arrived first. It was true that since her separation, she usually arrived early. Isobel, the high-octane, fully working grandmother, despite her otherwise superb time management, was nearly always running five or ten minutes late. Stevie was, as in everything, unpredictable. She ordered a latte from the aproned girl waitress (French from near Marseilles, she established, on her gap year), and got out her book, an iconoclastic new history of Europe post World War II, relishing the prospect of twenty minutes' quiet reading in a sunny, nearly-empty restaurant. Too early yet for Aucklanders who lunched. With the windows shut to a brisk June southwesterly, the noise from the crowded bar below was tolerable.

'Darling Thea!' The girlish voice, the high heels approaching across the tiled floor and the advance waft of her favourite Chanel No 5 were all undoubtedly Stevie's. 'Always so *punctual*!' she cried.

'Early, actually,' said Thea, closing her book, feeling just a little cheated. But here was one of her oldest, best-preserved and most fun friends; what was the matter with her? 'Don't you look wonderful! Very . . . cheering.' As indeed Stevie did on this crisp winter's morning, in a stylish waist-defining suit, high-heeled Italian boots, both in shades of deep Venetian red, and a cheeky black beret; despite three children, she'd kept her dark hair, firm jawline and figure without too much apparent effort and all her life had never looked less than a million dollars. Which she did in fact have: several millions cannily invested in property and shares by her Australian ex-grazier husband who'd died of prostate cancer a year earlier. Thea would have been astonished to know that Stevie, generally regarded as flakey, now enthusiastically monitored the sharemarkets almost daily with her financial consultant.

'Don't say a word!' Thea added quickly before Stevie could start mounting reciprocal but insincere platitudes about her own appearance. Compared to Stevie's bold and elegant statement in designer-label red, she knew she presented a sartorial mess (her trousers and jacket were different blacks, her boots were eight years old and she rarely bothered to change her greenstone earrings). That she no longer had a waist to define, or that her daughter had been overheard describing her to friends as dumpy, had long since ceased to worry her, though she considered her thick pepper-and-salt hair rather nicer now than the unremarkable brown it had once been. 'I look well enough for the wrong side of seventy. Do you want to sit in the sun?'

No sooner had they exchanged embraces, and Stevie had fondly wiped her scarlet Dior lipstick from Thea's leathery cheek, than Isobel roared into view.

'Good God,' said Thea. 'Isobel, you're never early. Not even close. You must have flown.' They all knew that Isobel drove a top-of-the-range silver Audi and drove it fast. It was also inhuman that this slim-line, power-suited, famously well-organised woman, who must have risen from her bed before 5 a.m., driven a hundred ks to bang a few hospital managers' heads together and driven the hundred ks back, should look so fresh and unscathed. More than one politician and bureaucrat chief had learned the hard way not to patronise Isobel; she'd added an MBA to her MSc (Chemistry, First Class Honours) while her youngest was still in nappies and pursued a career in the health sector with subtle determination. What you saw with Isobel — pretty, her bobbed hair tastefully silver-streaked, pale olive-green suit softened by flowery scarf and much gold jewellery — was not what you got.

'I finished with the Waikato boys early,' cried Isobel, delighted to have the best part of three hours truly relaxing and catching up with her oldest friends, before the more grim business of fronting up to Joyce. 'No traffic to speak of. Here I am!'

The blonde French waitress, picking her moment to offer iced water, dips with Turkish breads and the wine list, watched these three old crones, who clearly knew each other very well, exchange fulsome greetings and compliments on their dress and general well-being as they settled themselves at their window table. A loner herself, she would have been surprised, and perhaps a little envious, at their fully sixty-five years of friendship, still more that they had gone through the same kindergarten and schools in the same class since the age of four.

'Well, girls! Here we are, ready for the fray,' said Isobel, having chosen the Kumeu River pinot gris they would all drink, and Italian-style antipasti for starters. The wine arrived to cries about the excellent service, and was poured within nanoseconds. 'Don't you love screw tops, so quick, so little fuss. Think of all the cork trees saved. Oh, it's so good to be here. I've been looking forward to this all week. Don't you love the décor in this place — Italy meets Polynesia — yes?'

Stevie and Thea, also swirling the wine around their fashionably very large glasses before enjoying those first sublime sips, looked around and murmured agreement. In the corner by the bar a young man was setting up an electronic keyboard and its associated gear, and another slender young Maori, her music stand.

Stevie said, 'Nothing quite like live music, is there? That is one gorgeous young man, the pianist, I guess.' She grinned at the others, knowing of her long-standing reputation as a flirt with anything in trousers. 'He could come up and tickle my keys any time.'

'Stevie, you are incorrigible,' said Isobel affectionately.

'Hopeless,' said Thea.

'Just honest,' said Stevie. 'Got to get your kicks somehow.'

'Now, let's be serious for a moment,' said Isobel. 'I assume we all received the same extraordinary invitation from our dear friend?'

'A royal command,' said Thea. 'Four o'clock and don't be late. No presents.'

'I got a pot plant anyway,' said Isobel. 'I simply can't go to a party *sans* present. It's a rather spectacular yellow begonia.'

'Darling Joyce was always a tad imperious,' said Stevie. 'I was always just a little scared of her, even at school and I was nearly a year older.' She raised her giant wineglass. 'She was my minder my very first day, bless her! She was taller, full of bounce, and she knew *everything*. To Joyce!'

'To Joyce,' they cried, touching glasses gingerly across the table. 'To her three-score-years-and-ten! To such *good* memories! To darling Joyce. *Bonne chance*!'

The pinot gris was super, they agreed, consigning the ghastly prospect of Joyce's retirement-village birthday party a notch further into the background.

It was Thea who broke the short silence, voicing the unmentionable. 'And anticipating we meet again at a funeral in less than three months.'

'This rare wasting-disease thingy,' Stevie said, remembering how she'd felt quite sick reading the nearly illegible handwritten letter. They had been such a jolly quartet of chums at school and through much of university, friends for life through thick and thin. Barring accidents, it seemed Joyce would be first to go. 'It sounds quite horrendous.'

Thea said, 'When someone writes to warn you . . . well, so dispassionately, not to get a shock but she looks more like she's ninety-five, we'd better believe it.'

'Our dear friend was always a little austere,' said Isobel. Her BlackBerry rang — an insistent snatch of Rossini — and she dealt with it briskly, though did not, Thea noted, turn it off. 'Sorry about that. I saw her only, oh four months ago. I thought she looked so tired.'

Stevie said, 'She's been out of circulation for years now. Any old mates I bump into ask, is she still alive?'

'Sounds like she's still got her marbles, though,' said Thea. 'Most of them. I thought you'd taken the afternoon off, Isobel.' Thea looked pointedly at the BlackBerry on the table, but Isobel was busy writing something in her diary.

'I feel so guilty,' burst out Stevie. 'It must be a year since I saw her, two years since she went into that place. No excuse, none whatsoever. My mother's in there too, as you know, which makes it worse. It's all very gracious, gorgeous curtains — Thai silk, that gorgeous colour we used to call Ming blue, big bold checks — and such nice people, but somehow — I just couldn't face it for a while, not since . . .'

'Since what?' prompted Thea, knowing Stevie shared Isobel's admirable reluctance, at least when sober, to speak ill of anyone, even the not-very-likeable person that Joyce had become.

Stevie giggled slightly. 'The last time I saw her I took her this huge great purpley chrysanthemum, as you do, honestly the biggest one I've ever seen. It cost a bomb, just smothered with flowers and zillions of buds — thinking well, it couldn't fail to cheer her up. She took one look and said, sounding for all the world like the Queen, "Take it away, I can't possibly have that, oh do take it *away*."'

Isobel and Thea laughed benevolently; wasn't Joyce a trick? Silly outsized glasses holding apparently piddling amounts of liquid, thought Thea, were very deceptive. That had hardly touched the sides. She poured another all round, emptying the bottle, and signalled the watchful French girl for a second as Stevie continued on.

'So, I took it round to the front desk and said straight, "I bought this for Joyce in Room 12 but she doesn't want it, so please give this to someone who doesn't get many flowers and might appreciate a bit of colour." The desk person gave me such a funny look. I hope your spectacular begonia doesn't suffer the same fate, Isobel.'

'I would have shoved it up her jumper,' said Thea.

'It's just her expatriate past,' smiled Isobel, whose saint-like, Christchurch-born mother had trained her from childhood always to look for positives in people, no matter how strange their little ways. 'Running a big house, organizing servants, she loved all that. We passed through KL once and I could see she was right in her element. I remember how she loved having us driven round in a High Commission car with a New Zealand flag on the bonnet.'

'That only happened with important visitors,' said Thea. 'You and Brian fitted the bill — wasn't Brian something high in the Manufacturers' Association then?' Isobel nodded. 'But she was only in KL for a couple of years, surely, and I don't recall too many servants floating around. Mostly, it was London, as we all appreciated from time to time.'

'Oh yes we *did*,' said Stevie. 'Wasn't it wonderful to have her there, so generous with hospitality, when London's so horrendously expensive? The exchange rate simply doesn't bear thinking about. Fourteen dollars for a cup of tepid coffee!'

'Speaking for myself, personally,' said Thea, 'I only ever asked her for a bed if it was just one or two nights. It was lovely to see her, of course, but Dennis wasn't exactly scintillating company.'

'Well, I thought she was a perfect saint,' said Stevie, 'coping with that man. He was always on his best behave with visitors around, but she once got a bit tiddly and told me that most days for as long as she could remember he'd come home from the office, and drink pink gin, a good Bordeaux and neat Glenfiddich till he passed out on the floor. She used to just put a rug over him and go to bed.'

'Really?' asked Isobel. 'That's terribly sad.'

'And he treated her like a servant,' added Stevie.

'I knew he had a drink problem, but not that early or that bad, poor darling,' murmured Isobel, surprised at these revelations and the level of her second pinot gris already.

'It was *bad*,' said Stevie.

Isobel's BlackBerry rang again. 'Sorry, really should turn it off, shouldn't I, hate the jolly thing.' Nevertheless, she gave the caller a phone number, before continuing smoothly with the multitasking skill for which she was renowned. 'I always wondered why they didn't stay longer in KL. Marvellous life especially if you didn't have children, great shopping even then, badminton, swimming, bridge and mah jong, golf, *amazing* food and a hop, step and jump by air to practically anywhere.'

'All that incredibly cheap grog wouldn't have helped,' said Thea. 'Though I understood they weren't much on the diplomatic cocktail circuit.'

'Dennis wasn't a great success in KL, apparently,' said Stevie, whose extensive social network even as a widow included diplomats, lawyers and newspaper owners. 'Something to do with Trade and Industry, wasn't it? I heard he finally got out before he was pushed; people were amazed he lasted as long as he did in either KL or London. So they weren't that long overseas being grand.'

'Dear Joyce,' murmured Isobel. 'Always so generous with presents, almost embarrassingly so. Beautiful scarves from Liberty. And let us not forget that she was very active with Unicef, for years and years, secretary or something worthy. How's your mum, Stevie? Ninety-seven not out! Isn't that amazing?'

'She would say, "too jolly old, darling". She's tired, worn out, sick of living, basically. Sleeps most of the time, propped nearly bolt upright on one of those triangular pillows so the congestive stuff doesn't build up in her lungs and drown her. Occasionally they give her oxygen. She looks about 192 and takes twenty-one pills a day, would you believe?'

'Yes, I would,' shuddered Thea, whose own Very Aged P down in Thames was one of the two principal reasons she moved there when she finally got her National Super and no longer felt safe or effective at a large state school where insolent students increasingly assumed the right to swear at her and text messages in class from under their desks, and their 'caregivers' blamed the school when their progeny's exam results stated Not Achieved. Enough was enough. The other was simple lack of money to continue in super-costly Auckland after an acrimonious separation ending thirty-five years of marriage, during which she and a talkative but inept woman lawyer (she now knew) had found themselves taken to the cleaners.

'The old man, Thea — does he keep well?' asked Isobel, renowned among her friends for never forgetting birthdays, children's milestones, new grandchildren, parents' health, anniversaries even. Both her own parents had sadly died before the age of sixty-three (one quite swiftly of breast cancer, the other shortly thereafter in a car accident) and she was secretly mortified that stories about other people's seemingly indestructible ninety-year-olds brought forth most unworthy thoughts. 'Isn't his ninety-sixth coming up soon?'

'Spot on — October. And yes, thanks, he's OK,' said Thea shortly, relieved that the sleek French girl chose this exact moment to take their orders.

She looked at the clever menu's many varieties of fish and several methods of cooking on offer and, suddenly a little ashamed at her abruptness with such old and dear friends, decided to add, 'That's if I don't let it get to me. Actually, he doesn't know me any more.'

Isobel and Stevie both impulsively reached out to stroke her gardener's hands.

'Oh Thea, that's so hard,' whispered Stevie.

'You poor darling,' sighed Isobel, dealing a third time to her BlackBerry with her left hand. Momentarily, while Isobel spoke with a minion in her clipped professional voice, Thea pondered why some women should go a lifetime and not ever push back an uneven cuticle, and others favour high-maintenance talons of gleaming burgundy with little white weekly pushed-back moons.

'Confusion has taken over, utterly,' Thea continued, still mesmerized by Stevie's several diamond and ruby rings and ten perfect shining ovals — perhaps they were falsies, she wouldn't know — hovering so close to her own dull yellowed squares and knobby fingers. She had never bought a bottle of nail polish in her life. 'He had the *sans* eyes and *sans* teeth, and how would you know about the *sans* taste, but now it's the *sans* virtually everything.'

She decided to keep it simple and relatively cheap. 'I'll just have the flounder, poached, thanks, with a plain green salad, no chips.'

Three women sympathizing with each other's particular parental situation, while simultaneously placing their orders, certainly tested the young waitperson's English, but eventually it was done.

Isobel was having the South Island salmon, lightly grilled; Stevie, the Okarito whitebait fritters with loads of lemon; plus, to share, some roasted winter vegetables and a Greek salad. By the handing back of the menus, the good things about even extreme old age — the companionship, wisdom, tradition and continuity for grand- and great-grandchildren — had been unflinchingly placed against the good things of earlier, quicker departures — being spared the anguish of watching a loved parent daily humiliated by incontinence, frustration and helplessness after a lifetime of autonomy and achievement. Sudden was hard; lingering was equally hard; neither scenario, they agreed, was much fun. They would, as far as the fates decreed, try not to repeat patterns which placed the same burdens on their own children and grandchildren.

'Even if you choose to put stones in your pockets and walk into the sea, that leaves your family with all manner of guilts,' said Stevie. 'A friend of my mother's did just this, into that lake over on the Shore. She had bowel cancer, terminal. They didn't find her body for two weeks, floating among the weeds and goose shit. Or what was left of it, after the eels had . . .'

'Unbelievably selfish, I call it,' said Thea.

'One school of thought would say the opposite,' said Isobel, 'that it's actually very brave, from a genuine desire to release your family from . . .'

'I think that's all hogwash,' said Thea. 'What if the family don't *want* to be released? It's just swapping one set of horrible problems for another.'

'In your sleep would be nice,' said Isobel. 'After a good opera. *Butterfly*, I think. Sad but uplifting.'

'Indian men have the answer,' said Thea. 'They say their family goodbyes and go walkabout towards a sacred river and peg out unknown to anyone, of starvation or some progressive disease or a blessed accident. Then they get thrown on a fire, like a bag of rubbish.'

'It's not quite that callous,' ventured Isobel. 'I saw the burning ghats in Varanasi once. There was something rather spooky and beautiful . . . though I do remember tiny malnourished children rummaging in the ashes for valuables . . .'

'That's spooky,' said Thea. 'Nearly as hideous as Tibetans who chop up their bodies into little pieces before leaving them out on a rock for the birds. Can't you turn that damn thing off, Isobel?' she said testily, as the 'William Tell Overture' rang out again. 'Isn't there a better choice of music than that?'

Isobel mopped up the last of the tapenade, answering her PA's further fussing queries in monosyllables and pushing aside the suspicion that she was beginning to feel a mite light-headed; she knew about the dangers of early starts and a breakfast solely of one flat white, and she'd downed three slices of ciobatta and a large glass of water already for that very reason.

'That PA has got to go,' said Isobel, snapping the BlackBerry shut, and smiling sweetly at her friends. 'I must admit, in our own cultural practices, I do hate the moment at the crematorium at the end . . . you know, when they push the button and the coffin slowly goes down out of sight? All very tasteful, but . . . perhaps there's something more honest about the burning pyre out in the open, the smoke rising, the ashes going somewhere useful, the primitive sense of closure . . .'

'The ashes polluting the rivers,' said Thea. Much as she loved and admired Isobel, every now and again her Pollyanna tendencies got a bit much. 'Would you still feel the same if that pyre was burning up your husband or parent?'

'I didn't let them push the button on Don,' said Stevie, fully aware that she was the only one present who had buried a husband. 'I sat with him for a while, and then I left him right there. What they did after that I didn't want to know. I let the children do the ashes thing, out in the gulf off his beloved boat.'

The brief, sympathetic gap in the conversation was filled with long reflective sips of pinot gris, and murmured agreement that the live music now being heard was so much nicer than canned; 'Everybody loves somebody' and 'New York, New York' had taken them right back to their youth, really hit the spot. All were trying to forget that realistically, as far as loving family was concerned, there was actually no optimum time nor method of departure.

They ordered another bottle of wine, the famous hard-to-get Cloudy Bay sauvignon blanc this time. Stevie's shout, for a little treat.

Isobel led the conversation around to the more pleasurable, safer topic of grandchildren. Small albums bearing print-outs from the absolute miracle of emailed jpegs were dug out of Florentine leather handbags and shared around — Stevie's six and Isobel's nine. All were lovely happy children, handsome and well-dressed like their parents, pictured sharing fun on the slopes at

Coronet Peak, snorkelling in Fiji or at home with their favourite 'drop-in granny' on her last flying visit.

Both were aware and thoughtful enough to let Thea tell them as much as she chose about her two adult children's current situation — they knew the life stories of both so far had at best been described as complicated. It seemed Andy was back on his feet, working in IT in London after his earlier bankruptcy in Whangarei, some failed business venture which, Thea said, she understood that with only marginally more luck would have done every bit as well as TradeMe. Frances was living in Sydney with her partner, the father of Thea's two gorgeous grandchildren: these were the latest images of her two part-Vietnamese moppets. Stevie and Isobel both thought there was much sadness there, as well as pride; Thea hadn't seen them for nine months, and neither party on either side of the Tasman could afford to travel. She said bluntly, without self-pity or resentment, that savings were currently being soaked up by private hospital charges, even with some Government help. Stevie and Isobel bit their tongues, and cursed the memory of the dud lawyer who'd abandoned his wife of thirty-four years and two teenage children for a younger, prettier model; it got worse: the lying hound had found an equally crooked mate to help him screw her for every last cent and then some. They had watched this messy divorce and the effect on Thea and her children with horror; they had failed to convince her that Eric was a worse rat than even in her worst nightmares and she needed better legal advice than she was getting. How she ever came to marry the scumbag in the first place was a great mystery.

Privately, never voiced, each thought that there was just a whiff of the hair-shirt about Thea, an ingrained reluctance which not even the assertiveness classes they all did in the seventies had taught her to say what she wanted in life. Of all of them (Isobel and Stevie would have agreed), Thea had been the least enthusiastic to embrace the 1970s feminist imperative for wives to re-train, if that's what it took, and get back to the workplace and the incalculable pleasure of earning and spending one's own money. Stevie's wealth meant she could happily disdain a return to physio for the greater joys of motherhood, entertaining and good works, and Isobel had always been either full-time student or working mum, but Thea had seemed disinclined to use her good Second Class Honours MA in History and enter the teaching jungle again, until she had to.

Stevie, taking the last of the marinated artichoke hearts before the French lass took away the antipasto platter, made up her mind to suggest to Isobel later that they share a return airfare across the ditch, so their dear friend could spend a week or so with her lovely pigtailed moppets.

'Imagine not having grandchildren,' she cried. 'I can't understand these young things who say they don't want children. Today they're all so busy with their careers and partners, breaking through the glass ceiling. Or they have their sprogs so jolly . . .'

'I do so hate that word . . .' intercepted Isobel softly, but Stevie was used to Isobel pulling her up on her colourful language.

'. . . late, their own parents are past it or dead. You, my sweet—' Stevie raised her glass to Isobel '—are living proof that you don't have to give away motherhood for a successful career, not these days.'

'Grandmother-hood, neither,' said Thea.

'I do rather feel for the parents,' said Isobel. 'I know you don't have children simply to please your parents, that would be quite wrong . . . all the same, wouldn't it be hard to know you could never look forward to grandchildren, not even one? I get more pure joy from my nine than anything else in my life.'

'She might have done noble work for Unicef, but Joyce never wanted children of her own,' said Thea. 'She always said breeding was incompatible with a nursing career.'

'Well, so it was in the sixties, when they still had nurses' homes and curfews at eleven,' said Stevie. 'Unthinkable, now. Today's young folk wouldn't put up with it.'

'Joyce was a wonderful godmother,' reminded Isobel. 'As one of each of ours knows. Birthdays, Christmas, little billets-doux . . .'

'For the first few years,' said Thea. 'Once they hit double figures, that was it.'

'Isn't that the point?' asked Stevie. 'Insurance against parents of the very young getting wiped out in car crashes.'

'A Catholic relic of the Roman persecution of early Christians,' intoned Thea, 'and also pre-industrial England, when mothers regularly died in childbirth. Dependable grand-mothers were scarce in those days, when females were lucky to hit fifty, or even forty. Menopause was hardly known about. Joyce just didn't like children.'

'Well, she was a very good nurse,' said Isobel. 'Several prizes, as I remember. She was the first of her peer group promoted to charge nurse.'

'Yes, and had she stayed on,' continued Stevie, 'can't you just see her as one of those starched fifty-something matrons, marching in full sail along the green lino corridors and through the wards terrorizing patients and junior doctors.'

'Oh yes,' muttered Thea.

'But she went and married that pratt Dennis in a registry office and ended up with neither career nor children.' Stevie drained her glass of fortifying liquid, and thoughtfully rubbed at the smears of Dior on the rim. 'She did have an abortion once, she told me.'

'She *what*?' asked Thea.

'Joyce? You can't be serious,' said Isobel.

'I am too,' said Stevie, a little defiantly. 'While she was doing midwifery. Second or third year, I can't remember. She was about nineteen.'

'*Joyce*? You're not thinking of . . .' asked Isobel, still incredulous.

'Alzheimers hasn't got to me yet, Isobel. I remember exactly when and where — we were lying on Mission Bay beach on New Year's Eve, it would have been about 1957, '58. She'd had it done the previous week.'

'Well, I never,' said Isobel. 'Poor dear Joyce.'

'*Au contraire*, she wasn't miserable at all. Chipper actually. She said midwifery had put her off having babies for life,' said Stevie. 'She couldn't bear the thought of anyone, especially male doctors in white coats, peering up her twat.'

Isobel's face was a picture. Stevie continued, 'Forceps! Stirrups! Noise and pain! Getting stitched up with twine like an old laundry bag, and walking round the nursing home with your legs apart. So there was no question of having it, and adoption.'

'How did she do it?' asked Thea. 'Half a bottle of gin? Or a knitting needle in a back street? There wasn't abortion on demand then.'

'There isn't now,' said Isobel softly. She looked at her elegant watch. 'We should keep an eye on the time.'

'Eighteen thousand a year?' said Thea. 'All suffering from "mental illness" and life-threatening distress? Pull the other one, darling.'

'All legal and certified, though I'll give you that law's been around thirty years and needs reviewing.'

'Does it heck,' said Thea. 'When you live in a small town you get to know how easy it is, which doctors to turn to. When I run out of conversation with Dad, which is about five minutes into every daily visit, I talk to the nurses.'

'We're working on it,' Isobel said lightly. Rossini intervened. 'Oh sorry, I thought I'd turned it off. But I'd better . . . duty calls . . .' Stevie and Thea looked at each other in exasperation as Isobel took yet another call, smiling and gesticulating apologetically.

'I'm an adoption sort of person, myself,' said Thea, when Isobel was finished, and determined to ram her point home while she had the chance. 'We're all old enough to remember those days when it was the norm. They weren't all bad. In fact, in many cases, for the kids, a damn sight better than a single parent with no money and not the faintest idea about parenting — or your little life ending before the first trimester, sucked out with a vacuum pump.'

Oh, wasn't she being brave today, taking on the redoubtable Head Prefect Isobel in this gradually filling restaurant, with the winter sun on her back, the live music just right and the lovely attentive French girl bearing down with their mains and a young man with more good wine.

'Actually,' said Stevie, feeling a mite excluded and wanting to bring the political back to the personal, 'it was quite civilized, as abortions go. The other party was a naughty registrar, so it was quite easy to arrange a specialist chum to do a quiet D and C.'

'Of course,' said Thea, deciding she felt strong and relaxed enough to drop another little bombshell of her own, but being overwhelmed by the artfully constructed main dishes now being reverently placed in front of them, to murmurs of delight and admiration. Compliments to the chef! Works of art, begorra! Amazing what can be done, they agreed, with such simple everyday ingredients, so fresh and beautifully arranged. And weren't Japanese-style square plates so very attractive, the perfect background for such good food?

'I read some chef claiming that lemon and parsley are the iconic staples of New Zealand cuisine,' said Stevie, using the little plastic gizmo provided to squeeze the juice out of the lemon halves. She attacked the generous pile of whitebait fritters with gusto. 'Like pasta for Italians, crêpes and cream sauces for Frogs.'

'Not cream since the enlightened days of nouvelle cuisine,' said Isobel, watching more Cloudy Bay being carefully poured into her glass by an elegant young man who knew the approved way to hold the bottle, by the base, the left hand behind the back, the stance reverent, like so. He reminded her of a boyfriend, long ago. 'But for us, I'd have thought something more along the lines of pavlova and lamb chops. Mmmm, this salmon fair melts in the mouth. Better than anything we ever had in Canada, or even Scotland. Scrumptious!'

'Don't discount the pink lamingtons and asparagus rolls we'll probably get later today,' said Stevie. 'Should leave some room for those, girls, don't forget.'

'Yeah, right,' said Thea, grappling with her flounder's delicate backbone, a lot of work for titbits of white flesh so subtle as to be close to boring. She rather regretted she hadn't gone for the brilliant orange salmon steak lying invitingly on Isobel's plate, but oily fish was not the best choice for people prone to recurring gout. As she picked away the flesh from plentiful tiny bones and grey skin, she said, 'Joyce wasn't the only respectable girl in those days to have a D and C for dodgy reasons, you know.'

'Tell us more,' said Stevie. 'Who else was a naughty girl?'

'I'm still staggered about Joyce,' said Isobel. 'Of all people, the least likely. She wasn't slow in voicing her disapproval of people who didn't play by the rules.'

'Perhaps that's why,' muttered Stevie.

'Would you believe, talking about abortions, me?' asked Thea, pleased that both Stevie and Isobel looked up from their square plates with astonishment writ large in their eyes. 'It was easy enough to find a doctor who'd play ball. So to speak.'

Stevie, who had a fine ear for innuendo, spluttered over her wine.

Isobel recovered first, saying smoothly, 'Isn't that rather a "When was the last time you saw your father?" question, don't you think? You wouldn't have done it lightly, I know that for a fact. If it was the right thing for you at the time, Thea, and you have no regrets, that's all that needs to be said.'

'No regrets at all. Not a sausage.'

'You never breathed a word!' cried Stevie. 'You poor darling, going through that all alone.'

'I was deeply ashamed and desperate,' said Thea calmly. 'Eric wanted to have a third, God knows why except to sink me deeper into shitty nappies, but as we all know there's a big difference between two and three. Bigger house, bigger car, for starters. I said I didn't want any more. I think the scumbag deliberately put a hole in his condoms. Not that we were at it every night. Far from it. Did you know the average across the board for married couples is only two to three times a week?'

'Weren't you on the pill, in those days?' asked Stevie. 'I was.'

'Me too,' said Isobel. 'Doesn't it seem a *lifetime* ago?'

'I just hated the thought of long-term medication, so no, I wasn't,' said Thea. 'Those days — even now — nothing is ideal for women, is it? Chemical or just . . . mechanical, they're all bad in some way. I had a diaphragm for a while . . .'

'Ghastly things,' said Stevie. 'So rubbery and unreliable.' She clapped the musicians' fairly standard rendition of Stevie Wonder's 'You are the Sunshine of my Life' and sighed deeply. 'Don't you just love that song? Weren't we all so young and innocent then? Was Eric furious when you told him?'

'I never told him I was pregnant. I just said the gynaecologist advised a D and C for irregular periods. Two months later I had my tubes tied.'

'Didn't we all, eventually,' said Stevie, wondering if Thea had taken this final step without Eric's knowledge or assent, but unusually for her, hesitant in asking.

Thea said, 'I have a real problem with people who claim that women suffer terrible everlasting guilt and grief for the child they've "murdered in utero".' She had that infuriating habit, thought Isobel, of using her fingers to make speech marks in the air; plenty in the public service did likewise, and it irritated the hell out of her. 'That might be true of some. It wasn't true of me, and I suspect, many many others. Perhaps most.'

'A male patriarchal thing, perhaps?' said Isobel.

Thea looked at her in surprise. She'd long thought Isobel might be a closet feminist behind all that nice girl/neutral bureaucrat image. 'Of course it was,' she said.

'And the Catholic lobby, boots and all,' said Stevie. 'Do you remember SPUC? Remember Patricia Bartlett?'

'I try not to,' said Isobel.

Thea said, 'Well, I knew it was the right thing for me, and for the two I already had.'

'Forgive me, darling,' said Isobel, 'but wasn't that abortion on demand?'

'Yes it was, but I was "happily married", ostensibly in what we now call a "secure relationship". Believe it or not, I was actually rather desperately trying to preserve that relationship. How many of your 18,000 today are married? Most of them are young things aged twenty to twenty-four, right?'

'Correct. I can't recall the married figure offhand.'

'It would be tiny, yes? Marriage being soooo out of fashion.'

'You sound like Paris Hilton and her ilk. Probably.'

'To think of you making all those decisions alone,' said Stevie, dismayed at the asperity creeping into the conversation. Thea and Isobel always had the best brains of the four. They'd vied for top of the class all the way through school. It was such a shame that darling Thea's choice of spouse had turned out to be less than wise, and she hadn't used her abilities to quite such good effect. She could've done as well as Isobel if she'd put her mind to it, her shoulder to the proverbial wheel. Stevie took a long draught of mineral water; she was perhaps a little pissed. She said, 'That's so *sad*.'

'I survived,' said Thea. 'Even if my marriage didn't.'

'And we so understood why, my dear friend,' said Stevie, reassuringly. 'You gave it your very best shot for a very long time. We understand.'

'Well, Joyce didn't,' said Thea. 'I think she felt that if *she* could suffer the daily martyrdom of an alcoholic and pompous arse of a husband, I should be able to put up with the dreaded Eric. She disapproved. How she disapproved.'

'Like my bloody mother,' put in Stevie. 'I know about disapproval. I have lived my whole life with disapproval. I am sixty-nine years old and I am *still* living with disapproval. I will go "disapproved of" to my grave, before mother, probably.'

'Did she ever say anything?' asked Isobel. 'Joyce, I mean.'

'Didn't need to. Her body language was enough. It is every wife's duty to endure to the bitter end, long as it takes. Just because being married to Dennis was marginally better than retraining and going back to nursing. She could endure, so everyone else should be able to also. Anyway, she stopped sending little Christmas presents and invitations for lunch and made excuses on the infrequent occasions when I suggested a coffee. I could see she barely tolerated my company, at reunions and such, after I became single. Girls, it would be kinder if I didn't come this afternoon.'

Faced with this sudden betrayal, Stevie and Isobel quickly and loudly reassured Thea that if only for old times' sake, she simply *must* come to the party, no question. There was safety in numbers, in a united front, Stevie said forcibly. They should get another bottle of that lovely sav blanc to fortify their joint resolve. If it meant a taxi to the retirement village in Parnell, so be it. Isobel could call for a taxi on her BlackBerry, which, as if to prove a point, rang yet again.

'Sorry, *sorry*,' Isobel sang. 'It's my PA, she's having a wee crisis, just need to . . .' She gave out a phone number from her BlackBerry's Search function, then assumed a thoughtful pose. 'Can we see where Joyce was coming from? Seeing you so much happier since you separated probably was an uncomfortable reminder that she too could have known some of the same happiness, had she not been so dutiful and faithful to her marriage vows. I suppose deep down she very much regretted that she'd not followed the path taken by many of our generation and refused to put up with it any more — just listened to her inner voices and followed her heart.' As a skilled and practised monitor of every word she uttered professionally, Isobel was acutely aware that wine in the middle of the day made her prolix and preachy, then sleepy. Normally, weekdays, she never touched a drop, even when being lunched by her team leader, a known *bon vivant*, or worse, her minister, an old soak from way back who could drink anyone under the table. 'To Joyce, the single Thea was a constant . . . remonstrance? I think there's such a word. It sounds most peculiar.'

'Specially when her own bloody mother died and they moved into that huge great family home,' said Stevie. 'Dennis wanted to play lord of the manor, I expect. They rattled around something terrible. It wasn't as if she'd have needed to go back to work.

She could've ditched the house and ditched Dennis and had a gay old time.'

'Not a PC word, gay,' reminded Thea. 'It has a different meaning these days.'

'Couldn't give a flying fuck,' said Stevie. 'It still means merry and gay. Merry and gay!' The Maori singer, immersed in a soulful version of Bacharach's 'Close to You' found herself checking out the increasingly noisy table of three by the window. 'Anyway, after Dennis breathed his last she could've reinvented herself, you know, like Oscar Wilde saying about the widow whose hair turned bright gold with grief — but no, she just rattled around and banged out letters for Unicef on an old Remington and never had any visitors from one week to another. And she got completely paranoid about being burgled by someone with a kitchen knife and murderous intent. Honestly, the house was like Fort Knox. Her bedroom had triple locks on everything.'

'She was burgled once,' said Isobel.

'No-one would dare,' said Thea.

'Not long after Dennis died.'

'I never heard about any actual burglary,' said Stevie.

'She hears a noise in the night,' said Isobel, enjoying her sole proprietorship of this particular Joyce story, 'and decides to do exactly what we're told not to do — creeps downstairs in the dark, listens to the breathing and the scuffling, decides which room he's in and throws the light on.'

'Ta-da,' sang Thea, raising her hands like a gospel singer. 'The grand entrance, typical. As an only child, Joyce always expected to be heard and noticed. I am here! Pay attention now!'

'Recipe for disaster,' said Stevie gloomily. 'I'm still not used to sleeping alone in the house, never will be. I'd tell them what to take and show them the way out. Order them a taxi. Pay for it even. Joyce is an idiot. How did she know there weren't several of them in the house?'

'Well, this is what our friend does. She throws on the chandelier and standing there blinking is a young, fat, unemployable Poly . . .' Just where, Isobel thought, did *that* come from? She was always so scrupulous about correct, non-judgemental ethnic terminology: Polynesian or P.I. were acceptable, but *never* Poly, and you weren't allowed to call anyone fat these days. '. . . a young Samoan, jobless, of course, with a marijuana habit to support, standing there stoned to the eyeballs and confronted by this very angry small woman in a yellow candlewick dressing gown.'

'Like Medusa,' said Thea. 'Though perhaps not the candlewick or the hair.'

'She wasn't over-endowed in the hair department,' agreed Stevie. 'Oh, look, there's one of the America's Cup boats going out. I've always meant to go on that. Never got around to it.'

'Too cold, this time of year,' said Thea. 'It'd be bloody freezing.'

'He has a bag half-filled of stuff, silver and whatnot, but she doesn't ask him to hand it over while she calls the police. No, she just stands there and over the next ten minutes tears a strip off him for being a bad bad boy, letting down his parents, betraying his noble ancestors and his kaumatua, or the Samoan equivalent thereof, betraying his entire race. Like something out of Dickens, the crabbiest old schoolteacher you can think of.'

'Like Mr Bumble from *Oliver Twist*?' said Thea. 'No, perhaps that's going a bit far.'

'He wouldn't have stood a chance,' said Stevie.

'She took a huge risk. How do you know all this?' asked Thea, amused not only by the story but the rare sight of Isobel slightly pissed.

'She told me. Proud she was. She simply disarmed him — did

I say he was holding a knife? — by sheer force of personality. Then, having ordered him to hand over the weapon and the bag, she offers to make him a cup of tea.'

Stevie had started laughing, and continued to chuckle while Isobel checked and returned a further text message on her BlackBerry, to Thea's evidently increasing exasperation. She wondered how long Thea would hold out.

'By this time,' continued Isobel, undeterred, 'this huge Samoan kid is weeping and wailing, begging forgiveness. Like putty in her hands. Before she sends him on his way, she's invited him back to help her in the garden once a week. Which he did, for two years. She even helped him get a proper job. Now isn't that a story with a happy ending!'

'Brave, give her that,' said Thea, smiling despite herself, and deciding that Isobel was probably rather more than slightly pissed. Also that if the lady's BlackBerry rang one more time, swear to God, she'd toss it down into the rigging of the second America's Cup boat below. That she kept forgetting to turn it off was probably a measure of how pissed she was; Isobel being normally so considerate, courteous, ultra-polite, never putting a foot wrong. 'So why did she become paranoid if she'd proved to herself she could be so brave?'

'She said she'd used up her supply of courage that night.'

'Nonsense,' said Thea.

'And she was lucky Joseph was basically a misguided immature puppy, not a hard-core young crim who might have done unspeakable things . . .'

'Enough already,' said Stevie. 'You don't sleep alone, Isobel. You have the faithful Brian ready to leap out of bed and defend his wife, his hearth and home. Are we having pudding?'

'Why not?' said Thea, feeling unsatisfied and reckless after her flounder.

'*Brian* leap out of bed?' Isobel laughed raucously, earning a further glance from the singer and pianist, now singing about the sorrows of leaving their heart in San Francisco. 'Let's see — instant agonizing spasm of cramp in his thigh, which he gets often, usually around 4 a.m.—'

'Don used to get cramps,' said Stevie. 'He'd stand there gasping, crying with the pain.'

'—or a stroke from the too-sudden elevation of the brain from prone to upright position. Cardiac arrest from fright, the burden of responsibility. Risk of doing his back, yet again. Risk of doing something drastic to his knee replacement. Risk of dislocating his ten-year-old hip replacement — his doc's already talking about replacing the replacement. Wetting his Marks best winter flannel pyjamas because it's nearly two hours since he stood dribbling in front of a toilet pan.'

Isobel smiled at her intrigued friends. 'Leap out of bed to repel boarders? I don't think so!'

She beamed up at the startled French girl, now removing their square plates with their detritus of fish bones. 'That was just lovely, thank you. Wonderful, all round, don't you agree, girls? Best fish restaurant in town, please tell your boss. Even though *Metro* misguidedly says Hammerheads, what would they know? *Eh oui, merci, nous voudrons le menu pour les desserts, s'il vous plaît.*'

'So poor Brian's now an old crock, basically?' asked Thea, dabbing at her mouth with the linen napkin, and wondering how Stevie could so confidently put on lipstick without a mirror. Practice, clearly.

'He's pushing eighty-five, for God's sake,' said Isobel. 'That's what happens when you marry someone fourteen years older. Seemed like a good idea at the time.'

'It was, it was!' cried Stevie. 'He's been a wonderful husband to you, Isobel. You've never had to want for anything, travelled to practically everywhere on the planet, patrons of the opera, artworks on your walls, a bach at Taupo, a boat at Westhaven, gorgeous kids, all this plus a career of your own.'

Isobel gave her the sort of look she usually reserved for opponents across a polished teak table, but standing her ground, Stevie soldiered on: 'Make the most of it, darling one, while he's around. I'd have my Don back tomorrow, warts and all. Well, all except the last six months spent succumbing to prostate cancer, which were hideous. Sorting out the will, dealing with lawyers and stockbrokers, calming down the kids, all that was a mission. Dreadful. I was bewildered by it all, most of the time. Widowhood's not all it's cracked up to be, believe me.'

Isobel, topping up her glass, said decisively, 'I will enjoy it. When it comes.'

'Yes, perhaps you will,' said Stevie, not entirely charitably. 'Well, I for one get very lonely at times. Paralysingly, mind-numbingly *lonely*. Early evenings are the worst; that's when he came home from the office, and I had the slippers and Johnnie Walker at the ready. That's why I always watch the six o'clock news — it's better than emptiness and silence and no-one to talk to except the cat. You get lonely, Thea?'

'Not much. Sometimes,' Thea lied. 'I miss the touching from the early days, the back rubs, the foot rubs. Eric had his uses — I miss the sex.'

Isobel and Stevie, choking on their wine — *Thea* missed sex? — looked up at Mademoiselle standing above them with the dessert menus and knew she understood this bit, at least. She was French, after all. At least one nearby table was also looking at them with more than momentary curiosity.

'That was one thing the feminist movement taught us,' Thea went on implacably. 'That you don't have to wait for a man to have yourself some pleasure. And you're not going to go blind. Don't you think "self-pleasure" is so much a better word than . . .'

'Thea!' said Isobel sharply, kicking Thea's sensible boot under the table as she remembered doing as embarrassed schoolgirls sixty years ago, with monstrous and unlikely visions of the mature Thea holding a . . . what did you call them, agitators, motivators . . .? 'There's mokopuna around! Things they don't need to know.'

'She's right, though,' said Stevie dreamily. 'Don and I didn't have proper sex for years, just . . . you know. That was before Viagra. Two old things, fiddling . . . Well, it was better than nothing, don't you know.'

'*Le pannacotta pour moi, merci bien,*' said Isobel desperately, taking charge. *Vibrators!* 'They do one of the best in town, totally authentic. Stevie, what are you having?'

'The chocolate mousse with blueberry coulis, thanks,' said Stevie, smiling up at the Mademoiselle. 'Manna from heaven. Blueberries keep the antioxidants and death at bay. And let's have a sticky for old times' sake, girls.'

'Thea?' asked Isobel. Some diminishing shred of normality prompted a look at her watch. 'Talking of time passing . . .'

'Tiramisù for me, what the hell,' said Thea cheerfully. 'My sugar count can only go through the roof, never mind the cholesterol. What's that? What's a sticky?'

'Dessert wine, late harvest, sweet as,' said Stevie. 'Isobel, do the wine-list thingy, you've got the best eyes, one of mine is waiting for a rebore. Cataract. Out with the old, in with the new, clever little silicone discs these days. I've already had one done. Marvellous, I give thanks every day, no more driving glasses. Haven't seen so well in decades. Order a sticky, Isobel, I dare you.'

While Isobel pondered the wine list, Thea watched Stevie applying lipstick an unnecessary second time. Her aim being a little less steady, her bright new top lip was a touch crooked. 'Are you a closet diabetic, Thea, all this talk of sugar counts? My doc says my cholesterol level isn't what it should be either. That OK, Thea? Haven't overstepped the mark?'

'Just fine,' said Thea, smiling with secret joy at a Stevie *maquillage* slightly less than salon-perfect. 'There's good and bad cholesterol, you know, and you're as slim as a reed. But since you ask, type two. Elderly onset, as they charmingly call it. I haven't shouted it abroad, why should I?'

'How boring for you,' said Stevie. 'My bloody mother's type two, and it's so fucking *dreary*. She bangs on about low GI foods, high GI foods, till I could scream. Don't eat potato, white bread or short-grain Chinese rice, my dear, they're bad for you. She's ninety-four and fat as butter and who gives a toss at this stage what she eats. They've got insulin, soon you won't even have to stick a needle in your belly, they've got pills for Africa. May as well go out eating Belgian truffles and happy, I say.'

'You can get sugar-free chocolate,' said Isobel. Having ordered the Villa Maria sticky and telling herself firmly to focus on the job in hand, she confirmed in rusty French the three desserts and macchiato coffees all round. Macchiato for the purpose of not going to sleep in the taxi. She sat back and vigorously led the scattered clapping for the lovely singer and her blackly handsome pianist, the spitting image of a young Harry Belafonte. Back on safer ground, she was thinking with relief, and they *must* keep an eye on the time, allow for paying the bill and using the loo etcetera, but she reckoned without Stevie, now getting to her feet.

'Requests, girls?' she cried, setting herself on course for the musicians in the corner diagonally across the large room. 'I'm going to ask for "Que Sera Sera", if they know it. Remember cute little Doris Day in her gingham pinny! Anything else, while I'm there?'

'Stevie, you can ask the waitress to . . . or send a note . . .' began Isobel, but it was too late. She and Thea watched as Stevie walked with exaggerated care across the tiles through the tables, saying 'excuse me' and 'sorry' at regular intervals, to engage the pianist in a smiling discussion, even as his fingers were rippling over the fortunately undemanding accompaniment to 'This Masquerade'.

'I wish she'd sit down,' said Thea, as Stevie's animated talking soon elicited only smiling nods from the preoccupied pianist, while the singer, though obviously aware of the intrusion, soldiered gamely on; what else could she do? 'God help us if she starts singing. Isobel, go and get her.'

'That might make it worse,' said Isobel. 'But hasn't she got rather a lovely mezzo voice? Or had, once. Didn't she sing solos in the school choir?'

She didn't much like the expression on Thea's face, but neither did she want to exacerbate the situation into a scene worthy of a paragraph in a gossip column. Who knew what vipers were in the room? She could go to the loo, and sweep Stevie up *en passant*, and both of them get rid of some of the alcohol in their systems, but actually she didn't quite feel like trusting her legs to carry her all that way under such curious public scrutiny. To her enormous relief, Stevie soon relayed her message, reached across the keyboard and squeezed Harry Belafonte on the shoulder, allowed the back of her bejewelled hand to float softly down one soft boyish cheek, and unsteadily accomplished the journey back.

'Even more divine up close,' she said loudly, collapsing back into her stainless-steel chair. 'Bone structure to die for, complexion like milk chocolate. Sex on legs.'

'Stevie, shut up, will you?' said Thea, as a substantial tiramisù materialised in front of her. A slim bottle of sticky and the smaller glasses for the drinking thereof also appeared. The service was quick in this place. Although the flounder had made for a light lunch so far, she was feeling slightly sick. 'I can't eat all that.'

'You're not likely to lapse into a hyperglycemic coma?' asked Isobel anxiously.

'Oh no, never done that, ever. Trust me. The meter gizmo only goes up to about ten per whatsits, at worst eleven. Your hard-core diabetic on insulin goes to twenty or more. I'm allowed a treat, every once in a while.'

'And I'm still allowed to lust after a beautiful youth,' said Stevie. 'No law against window shopping, girls. And that is a very desirable piece of goods. Plays piano quite well too.'

'Keep your voice down,' said Isobel.

'*Que sera sera* . . .' Stevie started in her rich mezzo. 'Whatever will be, will be . . . They didn't know it. Too young.' This reminded her of another song. 'They used to say we were too young . . . Too young to really be in love . . .'

'Stevie, you're embarrassing us,' muttered Isobel, noting the pianist and singer, now taking a break, glance over with a look that she interpreted as part amusement, part pity. As were other looks coming from tables around them.

'Speak for yourself, darling,' said Stevie, looking at her chocolate mousse in rapture. 'Do you remember how black men and even chocolate-brown men were off limits to nice gals in the sixties and seventies?'

'That looks like a perfect mousse, Stevie,' said Isobel. 'My pannacotta is wonderful. I said they were the best in town.'

'Not like now, ladies,' continued Stevie. 'Multicultural is in!

Not that a little thing like society pressure, pure bigotry really, naked racism when all said and done . . . not that all that stopped someone I know.'

Isobel said, distractedly downing the late harvest riesling in one gulp, 'Shouldn't we be thinking of calling a cab? Are we all in the parking building at vast cost? Joyce is expecting us at four, remember.'

'Isobel?' wheedled Stevie, enticingly as to a grandchild slyly hiding something behind its back. 'A certain trip to Fiji?'

'I've often been to Fiji,' said Isobel loftily. 'One visit merges into another after a while.'

'Would you believe, Thea,' Stevie whispered across the table, her tongue lasciviously licking at the teaspoon of chocolate mousse, 'a certain conference in Nadi, a certain ambitious bureaucrat just going to her first Pacific health conference?'

'Stevie, you're . . . hallucinating,' said Isobel, but Thea was looking at the beginnings of that truly rarest of sights: Isobel struggling for words and blushing.

'She's arrived at this conference very upset, this lady who shall not be named, because she's only just found out her darling hubby is having an affair with his secretary at the Manufacturers' Association — isn't that such a cliché? — and she's wondering what to do about it. Leave the jerk? Be more like the civilized French and ignore it, and have her own little fling? Be grateful hubby is not like many Italians and ambidextrous?'

'Stevie!' croaked Isobel, her classic features flushed beetroot. 'You're pissed!'

'So she's having quiet little flirts around the bar with some of the other delegates, but knows in her heart she's just not the type for one-night stands. She suspects that all the men have decided she's untouchable, off limits. Until, that is . . .'

'Out of order, Stevie. You're talking pure fantasy.'

'Isobel, I've never ever *ever* seen you blush,' put in Thea gleefully.

'An offer,' continued Stevie, 'comes from the most unexpected quarter . . .'

Isobel, head down, scraped desperately round her dainty white pannacotta bowl. 'This, Thea, is an early sign of Alzheimers, making up stories, muddling one person with another . . .'

'Not this babe,' said Stevie implacably. 'A statuesque well-educated Fijian employed as a liaison officer for the seminar and clearly with a good eye for quality . . .'

'Quality in the Jane Austen sense,' said Thea.

'If you say so, Thea. Once a schoolteacher, always a schoolteacher, you know?' she added chattily to Isobel. 'Anyway, this black god chats after a seminar, asks quietly for her room number and could the door possibly be open around 2 a.m.? It is. I draw a discreet veil over the rest. Isobel, my pet, you're looking a little flustered.'

Beside Isobel's plate, the William Tell overture rang out into the silence.

'Oh *dear*,' said Thea, grabbing the offending mobile before Isobel could. 'What an inconvenient moment! What to do, chaps? Turn it off as it should have been two hours ago, or toss it into the drink?'

She looked meaningfully at the superyachts and gin palaces parked in the yacht basin below. The America's Cup boat was just manoeuvring itself back into its berth. 'I don't suppose you want to know who it is, Isobel?'

'Ah . . . no,' said Isobel huskily, her head bowed. 'Just . . . turn the damn thing off.'

'Right,' said Thea, peering at the possible keys on Isobel's BlackBerry. 'With pleasure. Your PA person can go hang, crises or no. No-one is indispensable, my friend.'

She found the *Off* key and leaning over, put the BlackBerry pointedly into Isobel's black suede handbag. 'Is that it, Stevie?'

'More or less. The story has a happy ending. No-one was hurt, no babies were conceived, hubby never played around again, wifey certainly didn't, with a black man or anyone else, the marriage survives. Only one person was ever told.'

'Who has now . . . I think I should leave.' Isobel straightened up with the impassive glare which her staff knew meant she was gathering her forces. She heard herself stating, as spookily pompous and inarticulate as the deadbeat minister she answered to, 'Stevie, you have touched the very depths of my shame, dragged up guilty feelings I've been trying to . . . undiminished by thirty-five years . . . betraying a confidence is . . .'

Thea said, 'If you think it's so shameful, Isobel, then aren't you being racist as well as melodramatic? So you had a one-night stand. Big deal. So he was big, black and beautiful. Who cares?'

'I care. *Not* about his colour, you must believe me . . .'

'I believe you,' said Thea. 'You were young and lusty and feeling unloved, and just about twenty years ahead of your time, that's all.'

'I can't help it, I felt deeply ashamed then and I still do.'

'Isobel, it's only us,' said Thea, reaching out a soothing hand. 'So you have feet of clay. You're vulnerable like the rest of us. I'm actually rather relieved, little Miss Perfect. And allow me to say . . .' More bravery, she should get the Victoria Cross! '. . . that you're in danger of taking yourself a bit too seriously. If that's the worst secret you've kept for seventy years, you're still more of a saint than most of us. Don't they say we've all got one dirty little story locked up and the key thrown away?'

Isobel swallowed. 'The worst of it was . . . it was all so unfeeling, so clinical, no sense of conquest or even pleasure. I'd spent the last eight hours trying to decide whether to unlock the door. Or not. He just walked in, didn't knock, didn't switch on the light, lay down on top, you know, missionary position, no foreplay, no condom . . .'

'Jesus,' said Thea. 'Imagine . . .'

'. . . no talking, put it in, came, pulled it out, tied his lavalava and left with barely a word. Just wanted an uncomplicated bonk, nothing more or less. Like an animal, and I swear to God that's got nothing to do with his . . . ethnicity. Left me lying there, thinking . . . what was *that*? Any pleasure I might have got . . .'

'Selfish bastard like all the rest,' snarled Thea.

'Brian and I hadn't so much as touched a hand or a knee in bed never mind anything else in over a year. I was thirty-four and exhausted and frantic for the comfort of a human touch and too proud to ask for it. Well, I didn't get it that night, either. Ten minutes start to finish, if that. God, did I feel used.'

'Brian told me around that time you were too tired to be fun any more,' said Stevie.

'He discussed our sex life with you?' cried Isobel.

'No he did not! An MBA and raising three kids didn't exactly mix, was all he said. He was worried about your health. He wondered if you were having a midlife crisis.'

'If I was, he never cooked a meal or hung out a nappy to help, though he found time for his floosie,' said Isobel. 'Do you know Brian is the only man I've slept with, apart from . . . Stevie, I will never forgive you . . .'

'Yes you will. Lighten up. What's a little intimate reminiscing between friends? Thea will be as silent as a tomb, won't you my sweet?'

'Why did you . . .?'

'I am slightly pissed,' said Stevie, her dignity intact, confident that this state of affairs explained everything. 'As are we all. And haven't we laid a few old ghosts today! Such fun! We must do it again. Here's to Joyce — oh the bottle's empty, day-yam.'

'We are *not* getting another,' said Isobel.

'That would make two of us to cross off her visiting list, if she only knew,' said Stevie mischievously.

'Stevie, you will promise here and now,' began Isobel, 'on your mother's grave . . .'

'I wish,' said Stevie.

'Two what?' said Thea.

'Two of whom she disapproves. Don't worry, my sweet Isabella, only joking. My lips are sealed.'

'I should call a cab,' said Isobel, bending down to find her BlackBerry. 'We can't be late.'

'Why not?' said Thea, looking at her empty plate in astonishment. 'Did I eat all that? I must have. Well, it's only Joyce.'

'Only Joyce?' cried Stevie. 'Darling, she's seventy and she's fucking dying!'

'And she can go to her grave "disapproving"—' Thea's fingers fluttered in the air '—all she likes. So bloody what? I don't know quite what she thinks she's got to be so hoity-toity about.'

'*In vino veritas*,' said Stevie.

'She's only able,' declared Thea, 'to be in the poshest old folks' home in Auckland because she inherited a house from her hardworking Scottish immigrant parents. No thanks to Dennis's less than brilliant career, or anything she achieved.'

'It's so sad,' said Isobel. 'She wasn't always like that. Good fun, once, so witty and fun. And nursing usually makes people more humane, not less. I can't find my BlackBerry. Where did you put it, Thea?'

'She only nursed for about seven or eight years,' said Thea. 'Then she took to playing *memsahib*. That's what did it. I bet she's got a few stories worthy of Somerset Maugham herself under lock and key, apart from getting preggers at nineteen.'

'I did hear Dennis left the diplomatic corps under a bit of a cloud,' said Stevie. 'Not just his drinking. Creative accounting, I heard, nudge nudge, wink wink. Did you know she was his second wife? First one left him because of his drinking.'

'There you go,' said Thea. 'I always thought he was a manipulative prick. And mean as buggery. Though it was lovely having them in London all those years.'

'Oh yes,' said Isabel, still rummaging. 'So generous. Hotels are horrendous in London. Thea, you didn't turf it overboard, did you? You wouldn't have done that to my BlackBerry?'

'Do you know why I never stayed for more than one night?' asked Thea. 'For all that they had a huge taxpayer-funded flat and no doubt expenses galore and she had all the time in the world and a cleaning lady.'

'Ah, here it is,' said Isobel, holding her BlackBerry aloft. 'In ten, girls? What's the name of this place again?'

'I think I know what you're going to say, Thea,' said Stevie. 'And perhaps you too, Isobel.' She looked into Isobel's glazed eyes. 'Perhaps not right now.'

'The first time,' said Thea, 'as good house guests we took them a little Kiwiana present, something wooden from memory, and put aside one night from all our theatre-going . . . well, you don't like to think you're simply treating them as a motel . . . and offered to take them for a meal.'

'As you do,' said Stevie, beginning to smile broadly.

'Oh yes, "That would be lovely," Joyce said. They lived in Hampstead, which even then was full of nice little local eateries, Italian, Jewish, Russian, all sorts. That's what we had in mind.'

'We too,' said Stevie, chuckling.

'I can't find taxi on my *Search*,' said Isobel. 'I know it's here somewhere. I've got taxi chits.'

'Thea, either Isobel's so gone she can't hear you,' said Stevie, 'or she's indulging in some displacement activity, you know, distracting . . . I think she knows this story too?'

'I don't know what you're talking about,' said Isobel. 'I am only slightly pissed and because it's 3.35 p.m. I'm trying to be responsible and stop gossiping and call a taxi.'

'But we say to Joyce in all innocence, you know the local restaurants, leave the choice to you,' said Thea. 'End result, we don't walk down the road but get in a taxi and drive for twenty minutes and have a very nice five-course meal and vintage French wines in "one of Dennis's favourites" which turned out to be one of the most expensive restaurants in Knightsbridge, the sort of snooty place where the waiters wear tails and white gloves, and Eric gets presented with a bill for 397 pounds. And that's without the tip.'

'Ours was in South Ken and nearly 500,' said Stevie. 'Don took one look at the bill and I thought he was going to have a stroke. He hid it very well, poor old thing. Lot of money then. Joyce didn't bat an eyelid, but Dennis knew exactly what he was doing. He got through two bottles of wine just by himself.'

'Over a thousand dollars, for a meal for four?' said Thea. 'Well, you only get taken for a sucker once. We'd have done better to get a B and B in central London.'

'They chose Simpson's-in-the-Strand when it was our turn,' said Isobel. 'That was bad enough. Brian said next time he'd eat underdone roast beef and greasy Yorkshire pudding with people he liked. Do you think that was why her presents were always so lavish, to the point where it was almost embarrassing? A sort of peace offering? Atonement?'

'Possibly,' said Thea. 'Or else as an expat away from base camp for years, getting paid in pounds sterling, she just genuinely forgot about inconvenient things like exchange rates.'

'I'm sure that'd be it,' said Isobel gratefully.

'For every visitor they put up, a top-notch meal,' said Thea. 'Not a bad bargain, I'd say.'

'Let's go to a film,' said Stevie. 'There's one on at the Academy I've been . . .'

'I'm ringing the taxi right now,' said Isobel.

'Not in the mood for Joyce,' said Stevie. 'I don't want to see her looking like she's ninety-five, as decrepit and pathetic as my bloody mother. Or we could go out on that America's Cup boat. They're selling tickets now, look? If we ran down we'd make it.'

'Don't be preposterous. You're not running anywhere in that skirt,' said Thea.

'Sir Peter Blake was such a hero,' said Stevie. 'I'll never forget that victory parade for the America's Cup, tickertape and such. I always wanted . . .'

'We're going to Joyce's party,' said Isobel as firmly as she felt able. 'And regrettably we're going to be late.'

'Oh dear,' said Thea. 'How reprehensible. How thoroughly naughty. Do you know it's thought that when people are late or forget, it's not that they're just late or forget, but they really don't want to do . . . whatever in the first place. Sort of deep-down insurrection going on. Rebellion. Subversiveness. I never know whether to say subversiveness or subversion.'

'All makes perfect sense to me. Aren't you a preachy old thing, Thea,' said Stevie fondly. 'Always telling us about research, and psychology and history and stuff like that. You are so clever.'

'We must leave *now*,' said Isobel.

'Oh, come on, girls,' said Stevie, 'do we really want to go and sit with all those dreadful old powdered biddies under Thai silk curtains, playing happy birthdays . . . Happy birthday to you . . .' Fortunately for her, Stevie's mezzo petered out after two lines. '. . . and blowing out seventy fucking candles. We can send her a nice card.'

'No, we can't,' said Isobel.

'You did have quite a good voice once, Stevie,' said Thea, adding happily, 'Ladies, I think I have the casting vote.'

'No you haven't, because it's not being put to the vote,' declared Isobel. 'Joyce is seventy and she'll be dead inside three months and no question, we are going to her party. Taxi immediately, *tout de suite, s'il vous plaît.*' Mademoiselle's perfect sense of timing had her standing patiently alongside the table with a black folder in her hand, smiling uncertainly as to which of this trio should be the recipient.

'I'll take it,' said Stevie, fumbling in her bag for her wallet, while Isobel reached up authoritatively to take the folder. 'I do hate old ducks who scrabble around in handbags, don't you? Mother used to say it was a recognized helpless-little-woman technique — "I fumble, you pay." Never let it be said—'

'We're thirding this,' declared Thea.

'I'll pay for the wine, I said I would,' said Stevie, finding her wallet with a little cry. 'The point is, are we going to upset Joyce more if we turn up late and let's face it, not quite as sober as we might be, or if we ring through and say we've all come down with migraines or had a puncture or something and sorry sorry, just can't make it.'

'No-one has punctures these days,' said Isobel.

'You will not pay for the wine. It's thirds,' said Thea, throwing her credit card on the table.

'Let me have the pleasure, please!' cried Stevie, applying her friendly Dior again with remarkable accuracy, all things considered. 'And Isobel and I are going to shout you a trip across the Tasman to see your darling mokopuna.'

'Are we?' said Isobel.

'No you're not, on either count,' said Thea. 'I pay my own way in life, thank you, Stevie. Isobel, it's *thirds*. There's my card. Take it.'

'Let's go to a film, do,' persisted Stevie. 'By the time we get there through the traffic, the drinkypoos and the birthday cake will be over. Though on second thoughts, it's probably only stewed Lady Grey tea tasting like monkey's piss and raspberry lamingtons.'

'We are going *now*,' said Isobel, handing over the black folder, gathering up her bag, her wits and such sense of responsibility for herself and her group as remained intact.

Mademoiselle, recognizing Isobel as the leader who would with any luck organize the signing of the credit-card chits and the payment of generous tips over at the desk, gracefully and discreetly helped her and each of them as they signalled readiness to rise and stand upright.

She took the trouble to escort them over to the musicians to shake hands and thank them for their lovely music and down the stairs to the waiting taxi, fortunately barely comprehending a continuing conversation which touched variously on the danger of falls; the daylight robbery of the parking building from whence they would eventually salvage their cars sometime in the early evening; the excellence of the restaurant, the food and the service; the inestimable value of truly honest female friendship; and how their friend in the retirement village would of course generously forgive them for being only forty minutes late. The begonia would have to remain in Isobel's car, sadly.

Joyce would, they agreed in the taxi, be so delighted to see them that their individual 'disapproval' ratings would naturally be put aside in the general joyousness and party atmosphere. They would go to the toilet to freshen up on arrival and on their dramatic late entry — 'Ladies and gentlemen, here are

Joyce's three oldest, closest, *dearest* friends,' the matron would announce — they would stay as long as it took, being exemplary and gracious guests.

They would admire the Thai-silk curtains and the wonderful view over the Waitemata harbour and the delicious lamingtons. They would tell Joyce with great diplomacy that she looked wonderful and be so interested in her new friends and her favourite caregivers. They would not, in deference to Joyce's childlessness and the memory of dear Dennis, go on about their families and/or grandchildren, nor make any rude comments about rest-homes per se. Nor would they even *think* about randy and/or grumpy-old-men inhabitants, or tell any of those awful rest-home jokes about Parkinson's or incontinence or senior moments or anything else inappropriate.

They would, all in all, make their dear dying friend's seventieth birthday party one to remember, despite the Lady Grey tea in lieu of a good strong gin.

Nonna

I always knew that my burial would be a short, dismal affair, just a dribbling fool of a priest nearly as ancient and cracked as me and a handful of family in the Wellington rain.

Look at them, following me to the Karori cemetery in their black motorcar: a balding son who sells houses and has long forgotten his mother tongue, his bossy thin-lipped wife who arranged this stingy funeral. She has bought new black kid gloves with little pearl buttons for the occasion. Three of my eight daughters without their husbands and not daring to say aloud, thank you Mary, Mother of God, for relieving us at long last of the weighty burden of our mother, our poor silly tiny toothless and useless old Nonna. The others too busy in their nice homes with their lace curtains and stiff-necked English husbands to even make the journey.

I have some grandchildren, I believe, ten or it might be even fifteen. I haven't asked for a long time and they stopped telling me. There might even be a few great-grandchildren, but no-one calling me *Bis Nonna* ever brought me a bunch of wild flowers or a cake of cheap soap, or sent me a little letter through the post.

No matter now. Oh, how I crave the sun, falling through heavy shutters. I need warmth, endless days of sunlight falling on my upturned cheeks, on a branch of ripe black olives, on the blue sea glittering beyond the Medici harbour walls. The ugly, windswept road to my final resting place threads between dull avenues of shapeless trees, unruly weeds around English gravestones, tombs of Jewish people, stained Catholic angels. My family has ordered no angel for me, not even a small tablet of stone like the one we've come to a halt beside. One daughter stands under her black umbrella and mournfully reads this tablet, which is as well for me, who never learned to read or write in any language. 'Giovanni Penco, died July 12, 1906,' says Nina, that's the one who married a Protestant. Not even, for me, the simplest engraving of a few words like those I arranged all those years ago for Giovanni. The dribbling fool of a priest will finish his fancy Latin mumbling and they'll walk away, and no-one will ever know that Maria Ida Penco née Ferrari — wife of Giovanni Penco and (counting the dead ones) mother of thirteen — once of a village on the coast near Pisa, Toscana in Italia — also lies here for all eternity, as she should, with her husband.

Ah, Giovanni, *mio caro Giovanni.* Your little headstone grows mildew and sits crookedly in the grave among foreign weeds. The spade that dug the hole for me glanced off no remaining bones of yours nor rotten wood from your coffin. Too long ago. Now we lie together as we once did behind an olive grove in a Toscana field — do you remember, I was still bleeding, about the fourth day, and you said it was no matter, when you so loved me? — but above us lying together now is that ungodly ugly thing I've heard they call a cabbage tree. I've seen better-looking cabbages from my lazy, drunken son-in-law's back garden. I'd rather lie under a bed of artichokes, which at least provide good food, and when you get to the tender heart of it, some real pleasure. They don't eat for pleasure in this stiff Protestant country; they, who've never tasted an olive or a fresh sardine, think they are superior, who cook in the putrid-smelling fat of animals and despising a dish of pasta or the lovely smell of roasted garlic.

Early mornings beneath the rose-pink walls — waiting with others for bread from the baker's oven, crisp white loaves to sop up the juices of Mama's fish stews and creamy goat's cheese and tomatoes and olive oil pressed from the fruit of her uncle's old trees. The baker's wife, who had bad feet and no daughters, sometimes gave me extra, a half-burned or misshapen loaf she couldn't sell. She had a soft eye for me.

This miserable grey place stinks, of that nasty onion weed and pee from stray dogs. The wind blows incessantly. Mercy, have mercy, sweet Jésu, is this where I shall lie?

The day we buried you, Giovanni, I don't think that scraggly cabbage tree was here above your grave. Perhaps it was and I didn't notice. Your end in the hospital was a blessing, with your jaw half eaten away with a cancer, your pain terrible to watch until dimmed by morphia, and in the end they just let you starve away to death. Face misshapen and sunken, hair gone, eyes faded, the trembling fingers of your right hand stained brown and yellow by the cigarettes you smoked all day long — that decrepit old body nearing death was not my brave red-haired soldier in Garibaldi's army, big and strong enough at fourteen to lie (you told me) about your age and go off fighting in the south, even as far south as Sicily. In that hard hospital bed, you were unable to swallow even if someone had tried to ease your last moments with a glass of red Tuscan wine or a dish of plump olives. I, your wife, held your hand at the last rattling breath and heard my eldest daughter thank the busy English nurses, but later, burying you in this same bleak place, I was too overcome with weeping to notice the trees, or the everlasting wind and rain, or take pride in our two sons in their dark suits, then so strong and handsome and earning their own money as you had, as carpenters, good and respected workers of wood. I dressed my eight nearly marriageable daughters in black and wondered, while a stooping young priest peered through a monocle at his Holy Scriptures and spoke his lies, what would become of us.

I did not deserve to be left alone with that burden, Giovanni.

You didn't talk about the lonely responsibility of marrying eight daughters that day when you came home from seeing a notice in the town, back there in Toscana. You promised me and our boy great riches on the other side of the world. There we would soon own a home, some land and some animals. We would give our children learning, meats and foods better and fresher than any we could find in Toscana. And remember you said we would soon have saved enough money to go back to Italia, to where the sun kisses the pink and yellow walls, shines on the canals and the olive trees and the fields of wheat and the black grapes? Where it sinks huge every hot summer night into a sea turned the colour of ripe apricots? Remember the boatmen in the Medici harbour, using your fine oars to ferry full loads of ships' cargoes ashore? The fishermen unloading their overflowing baskets and standing for hours beside the canals mending the holes in their nets? They knew you, Giovanni, and the good, strong reliable oars you made for them. They knew me, too, your little Maria, and sang with us and got drunk on grappa the night our son was born. So we still lived with my family, nine to a room, we had no water and the canal outside stank to high heaven. That didn't stop us singing.

But you saw a notice pasted up by a man with a fast tongue on a town wall, offering a free passage to paradise, and we went on a journey across grey heaving seas, too long and cold and terrible to remember. Waves like the Pisan mountains above the Arno river plain, too high to forget. Many children died, there was fighting among the Italians and the sailors over cards, women and food. The surgeon treated me for something he called scurvy; he said I had to eat more fruits and vegetables to stop my teeth getting loose and my joints from aching. Fruits and vegetables — on board that damned ship after three months at sea of porridge and salt biscuits and salt meat? What fruits and vegetables? What good would a few sour lemons do anyway? After 116 days at sea, we arrived at a place of cheapskate wooden houses, treeless hills, damp and rain and wind and mud, everywhere mud. The scurvy went away. And after a lifetime of mud, hammering nails into buildings, scrimping even on your beloved cigarettes and your beer, learning wog's English so you could talk to your workmates and your children, but forgetting how to sing, even how to laugh any more — you died.

My sons kept us from starving. They were good boys, Giovanni, but they married, and had English wives to put first. One son, they told me, sailed away on a ship. He never said goodbye, or wrote and told me where he went. I forgot about him. The wives were barren, it turned out — I never heard of children. I knew that you were eager for our daughters to learn to read and write, and to speak good English and become fine English ladies. I didn't want to take them young from their schools and set them to work, earning enough to pay for our shoes and extra blankets and firewood and medicines. But what else could I do? They were handsome daughters, Giovanni, with fine heads of hair and good teeth, and I hoped they would find good Italian husbands among the fishing families from Stromboli and Massa Lubrense living over in Island Bay. Those families looked after their own. So one by one, as surely as if their father were still sitting each night at the head of the table, your daughters fulfilled your dream, rather than mine. One by one, they married good solid English men. Shopkeepers, clerks, tradesmen. We scraped up money for poor weddings, a white lace dress, a veil — except for the one who married a Protestant in no church at all. Apart from the shame of her, you who kept your faith longer than I did must be pleased with me, Giovanni.

Ah, my own wedding. My oldest sister's wedding dress, used five times over, needing my nimble seamstress fingers to let it out a touch at the waist and the sleeves. I could stitch such a good straight seam, then, before my eyes failed, and as fast with my needle as any. We stood within San Sebastiano's yellow walls, on the black-and-white-check marble floor, that martyred saint stuck with arrows like a pincushion and looking down in holy anguish at us from behind the high altar. When I took my confirmation in that church, Giovanni, those arrows gave me terrible dreams, but on my wedding day under my lace veil I kept my eyes down as I said my vows and in a few furtive glances saw only you, the red-haired singing maker of oars, in stiff clothes and his thick hair combed back with oil. Your brother was there, who gave you his passport for our journey, my brothers, sisters, my parents. Gone, gone — who knows to where? All gone.

Have mercy on me, sweet Lord, as the grey earth falls on my cheap pinewood box, and my daughters smile at each other to hide their mortal shame. Giovanni, did your pitted remains of bones embrace me as I was lowered into this foreign soil?

On the ship you were Giuseppe Penco, and you told me I was Mariana. You never told me why you needed to use Giuseppe's passport, why you didn't have one of your own. If we had not had a passport, if we had missed the train and then the ship and never gone to paradise, I believe I should have been happier, no matter how poor. I cried as the train left the river plain and went climbing into tunnels through the high north mountains. I cried in that port they called Amburgo and out into the grey sea beyond sight of land and through the hot equator and the hell of the Southern oceans when I was too sick and cold to my marrow to cry from being ill with seasickness and scurvy from lack of fresh foods for so long. The German doctor forced me to eat lemons and you made me drink rank water so my milk wouldn't dry up. You didn't get into fights over food and cards, Giuseppe Penco, like the other men from Toscana, for fear of trouble and for needing to look after our son when I couldn't. He wanted to climb on everything, up everything. The rails, the masts, the ship's boats, onto the forbidden decks among the better-off passengers who spoke German and English and looked at us down their long noses. Lord, how he climbed, that child. It was a blessed miracle that he and I survived.

And did we find paradise? We found rain, mud, cabbage trees, damp, wind — sweet Jésu, how it blew! Bad times with banks and bad feelings against Italians. Oh, how I craved a glass of red country wine, the good earth naked and the colour of walnuts after the wheat harvest, walking alongside the ploughed fields in autumn to visit aunts and cousins on long warm twilights. The cries of the *ragazzi* playing in the streets, the clatter of carts and horses over cobblestones. No work *in paradisum* for you, Giovanni, and others from our ship except as labourers for dirt money, digging out tunnels for railways; no lodgings except draughty wooden rooms; no fresh meats and foods; no animals; no pity; no understanding; no little gestures of kindness. They had enough oar-makers, ones with English names and pink English skins. So you trudged miles through the mud to work six days a week hammering and sawing on houses and big government buildings, learning the work of an ordinary house carpenter, banging in nails from dawn to dusk. You had holy Sundays free. You were Giovanni Penco, carpenter for a wretched pittance, you were Italiano, an I-tie, a wog. I learned about ten English words — thank you, goodbye, please, I'm sorry — and when I learned 'dirty little wog' shouted by a neighbour at my second son with such contempt, I vowed I would never speak another word of that language until the day I died. For buying food, weddings, doctors, funerals — even to the persistent soft-voiced smiling priests who used to pay calls on me — never one word more of English did I utter.

My children spoke for me, and my eldest daughter never lost her mother tongue. The others did, as they bought their houses and their kid gloves. I don't suppose for a minute they bothered to teach it to their children, my grandchildren or the great-grandchildren I'm supposed to have.

Ah, children. Thirteen long labours, Giovanni, all hard. You went to build houses and government buildings and I laboured with babies. Two I lost before they could even sit, poor little things, with their burning fevers, no matter how warmly I wrapped their little trembling bodies, turning to convulsions and death, and no money for doctors. The third, I don't talk about.

Too many deaths. Too much loss. Brothers who went away to Garibaldi's wars or to the south, never heard of again. A grandson, they tell me, went from this country on a big ship with an engine, not sails, to Italia and now has died fighting against his own cousins, Italians? His nonna's homeland, and him being killed by his own countrymen, does that make any sense? Comes of living too long, does no good — too many deaths and sorrows. After yours, Giovanni, I dried my eyes and became Nonna, in a long black dress shiny from too much sitting, and died a different kind of death in my eldest daughter's house. None of my other daughters' husbands would have me. I listened to her weeping when her bad-tempered oaf of a husband drank away his earnings, or lost his job, or gambled away money on horses. Six children they had, and I heard her sewing their clothes after midnight and watched her out my window digging potatoes at dawn and pegging out their faded, mended clothes. Then she would tell me, 'We are moving again, pack your bags, Nonna' — to a run-down hotel where he was barman, or to another hotel by a long beach with dirty black sand where he called himself a manager, then back to the city.

Always moving, we were, always selling things to pay the bills, while that nasty man drank and smoked and gambled my eldest daughter's very spirit away.

But she did not have to look after me, Giovanni. Never! In my back room, I cooked and washed for myself. I cut my own toenails until they turned to bone. I pulled out the teeth that got loose and hurt, not that I told anyone or they even noticed. I rubbed that Vaseline she bought on my hands and into my dry, sunken cheeks. I sewed hems for her, sewed on babies' buttons, even mended his socks. I sewed my own underclothes and the seams of black dresses of some cheap shiny stuff, even after my eyes went cloudy and my fingers got bent and gnarled and the pain got too bad. I told them to take the mirrors out of my room. They gave me a cast-off wireless, but what was the use of that, crackling and squealing and gibbering away in a foreign tongue, the music of barbarians? No, I kept to myself. Perhaps that family had a birthday or two, or a dinner for a saint's day or the feast of Christmas, but I don't remember any, all those years. Or they didn't ask me. Or I said no, not wanting to listen to their foreign, unintelligible chatter making me a stranger to my own family. Probably there wasn't any money for birthdays or Christmas. I ate enough from what they gave me, often bread that was grey and stale, fatty mutton chops, green potatoes and hard yellow English cheese, fit better for pigs. Yes, I would have sold my soul to the devil for one dish of black olives, those small ones gathered from my mother's uncle's olive trees on the high terraces above the Arno river plain, or a glass of Tuscan wine.

Jésu, I once started a fire at the hotel where he was barman. I had a poky ground-floor maid's room beyond the kitchens. It was my candle, you see, I'd left it too close to a curtain while I popped outside to empty my bladder on the grass — oh, my eldest daughter used to get so cross with me! — and squatting there in my nightgown, I saw a red glow in the window. I pulled my nightgown back down over my bum and screamed for help. The men came out from the bar and put out the flames with buckets and blankets. I was penitent, of course, but my eldest daughter's husband was angry with me. I heard him shouting at his wife, about that disgusting dirty old nonna peeing in the bushes. She was a damn nuisance. She cost too much, her food, her clothes. She smelled, she took up a room, she started fires. Let her go and live with another daughter. But they wouldn't have me. So after that I did it outside all the time, even my movements covered with a handful of grass and weeds, and hoped they saw me, rather than sit on the same seat as him.

A timid little grandchild used to sleep in my room sometimes, when there weren't enough beds for everyone in the house. She was tiny, like me, a little dark bird, very shy, never smiled. Few words passed between us. This grandchild of mine spoke only that foreign tongue, so even if I had wanted to, I couldn't have told her of her Nonna's family in Toscana or about taking a walk along the canals at twilight or about her handsome grandfather, Giovanni, or the journey we once did on a ship, five months at sea.

Besides, she could have been Carola come back to life. Carola, only nine, who took ill one night with the typhoid and died five weeks later. I nursed her day and night, even though I had the others to care for and was heavy with the child that arrived two weeks after the funeral: another scrawny girl, ugly as sin and never stopped crying. I have not forgiven you, Giovanni, for delaying getting the doctor for my sweet Carola until it was too late. It wasn't you who went without sleep, who boiled her water and sponged her burning forehead and changed her clothes and sheets, but it was you who said wait until tomorrow and by dawn she was rigid and her forehead as cold as marble. The silent grandchild curled up in my bed probably senses that old Nonna does not care for her presence, does not like to be reminded of that sweet little face or that funeral or the screaming labour of that last child or your great anger, Giovanni, when I forbade you for ever from my bed. Though she is already taller than me, that grandchild is afraid of her Nonna.

My eldest daughter died too. A stroke, I think, from overwork, about sixty-five she was, whereas the tall priest is looking down into my hole under which lies the mortal remains of my husband and saying Maria Ida Penco was a good woman, a good wife and mother who came from Italy and became a valued citizen of this country and lived until her eighty-ninth year. Very nearly ninety. That's something, all my sons and daughters! Twenty-five years more than my eldest daughter, thirty-two more than you, Giovanni. In thirty-two years Italian girls would become grandmothers, sons would be born and be killed as soldiers. I wonder, would I have lived so long in Toscana?

After my eldest daughter left me, I was moved around my other daughters' houses, like some old cat no-one can quite bring themselves to have put down and gets food out of habit. The days passed in their dingy back rooms, sitting, sleeping, waiting, and talking to my mother, my sisters. I told them in my own tongue what I could never tell my own children or grandchildren: about the ship, the windy dark town and damp wooden houses we lived in, the rats, the cockroaches, the mud, never enough water or food, my children's bare feet, the sneers from the English people, my faithful Giovanni — though, yes, one time I thought he was visiting a woman in the town and set my eldest daughter to follow him, to spy on him. He spanked her as he would a son and burned my best dress, Mama, for punishment. Imagine that, the waste of a good dress, and I never got another. But I was so frightened, Mama, that even my Giovanni I couldn't trust. I had ten children, the eldest only seventeen and forgetting his mother tongue already, laughing already behind his hands with his smart friends at his mother's funny little foreign ways.

There he stands now, Mama, as the earth falls, my balding first-born son, holding the gloved hand of his wife, my three daughters in black, already stout in middle-age, none of them able to understand their mother. Have their husbands gone to fight in a war, I wonder? Did I dream that my second son came back without his wife from America, after a lifetime of neglecting his mama, to say goodbye to her? The daughter whose house I last lived in — was she the one who married a Protestant? — no, the one with the pretty singing voice, Lord how she could sing, she should have been sent to Italy for her voice to be trained, to sing in opera. In her little back bedroom with the hunting dogs on the wallpaper I spent many summers, winters — forgetting and nearly forgotten, Mama, until the day I popped out at dawn and took a nasty fall on the wet grass. I often liked to pop out, to see the people walking in the town, find myself listening to the children or standing in the rose gardens or by someone's nice well-kept garden with mown lawns and peonies and cyclamen, stocks and roses — always craving light, yearning for warmth, colour, sunshine — and some kind person, perhaps a soldier and his girl, or a woman wearing a smart hat would bring me home to my daughter's house in their motorcar, but this time, I swear it, I was only looking for a bush.

I lay there in the rain for a long time, wetting and soiling myself and crying aloud with such a pain in my hip, until the daughter coming out to breakfast thought to send her husband looking for me. I think I went to a hospital but I wasn't interested in living any more, and the doctors weren't interested in keeping a shriveled-up, foreign old Nonna alive. They sent me home as soon as they could and after that I lay on a hard bed in that singing daughter's house until one day I began to cough, and got a fever, and sometime later, my tired old heart stopped beating.

How did you die, Mama? I never heard how you died. Did you get a stomach cancer which blocked your arteries and made one leg twice as thick as the other, or take a stroke which left you like my eldest daughter, paralysed down one side and speechless? No-one answered the letters Giovanni wrote and sent to Italia, so he stopped trying. No letters ever reached us — I suppose they didn't know where to send them. Did you, Mama, or any other of your children live to nearly ninety? Did you ever wonder about your sixth daughter to wear the white dress, the one who went away on a train with your little grandson never to return and is now consumed with terror as rocky foreign soil falls on her head?

Mama, what's that? I can't hear you. Did you say something about putting down my sewing and going with my sisters for a walk at sunset along the canal, where perhaps I should meet a handsome fisherman, one perhaps mending his nets and dreaming of the children he wants, the sturdy little boys first and then two or three pretty little girls? The air is warm and silky, and we are walking down the stone stairs from our two dark sixth-floor rooms to narrow, cool lanes which take us past the baker's wife scolding her husband for his drinking to the pretty Medici bridges over the canals.

Mama, you don't know: it's not a fisherman I'm taking this twilight walk to meet, but an oar-maker with red hair and a long scar on his chest, the right side, down to the hip, from fighting in the south for Garibaldi, and he will be singing and holding out his strong brown arms for his little Maria.

And I have chosen you

From: Tabitha Preston
To: Patricia Dedieu
Subject: YOU

Dear Ms Dedieu

I hope you don't mind me emailing, but I got your email from *Properties* from that one sent around about the women in Afghanistan (my aunt's friend is a writer too and just noticed your name on that great long list and she showed me how you just click *Properties* to get the address and it's quicker than writing to your publisher who always take ages, she says). Anyway, we're doing an assignment on New Zealand authors and I chose you because I LOVE your books and my teacher who loves them too said it would be alright to ask you some questions.

- When were you born?
- Do you have any children?
- How many books have you written?
- Where do you get your ideas?
- What's your favourite book?
- Do you have any pets? Hobbies? Favourite foods?
- Are any of your novels like, well, mostly true stories?

I'm twelve next month and in Room 27 and my teacher is Mr Graham and he's into drama big-time and quite neat. Thanks for answering my email and it's actually due in next week, please try to answer by July 14.

Yours sincerely

Tabitha Preston

PS I HATE my name, so you can call me just Tabs when you reply.

PPS I have two pets — a cat called Flea and a lab-cross called Tessie. Both are old 'cause I'm the youngest in my family and they were got for my big brother who's twenty-four now and a pain. Oh, and I also share two goldfish with my sister. T.

From: Patricia Dedieu

To: Tabitha Preston

Subject: A suggestion

Dear Tabs

Thank you for your email and for choosing me for your assignment. Authors always think it a great privilege to be chosen, although I always feel my novels are perhaps more suitable for people of, say, thirteen and older. You must be a very good and mature reader. But I think you'll still have enough time to look up some websites where you should easily find the answers to your questions — the New Zealand Book Council is the best and will link you to others. There are also some good books about contemporary NZ writers — myself and lots more — which your school librarian should know about, or the children's librarian at your public library. (I love librarians — they are the most helpful people in the world, almost without exception.) After that, any more specific questions, I'd be happy to try and answer. Before July 14.

(Perhaps you could share this with Mr Graham; if he doesn't know already about these websites for being a wonderful way of doing a little basic and very helpful research, I'm sure he'd find them really interesting.)

Best wishes

Patricia Dedieu

PS Is your aunt's friend a well-known writer? Would I know her? PD

From: Tabitha Preston
  To: Patricia Dedieu
Subject: **RESEARCH**

Dear Patricia

You're right!!!! Those are really helpful websites and Mr Graham was amazed. I was able to print them out, pictures and everything, but he says I can't just cut and paste them onto refill paper and call it my assignment, no matter how different — with fonts and borders and stuff — I made it look, because the words are still the same and that makes it plagiarism which is a really ugly word. So, to make it look like I've done some REAL RESEARCH, I'd still like to know:

- Have you met lots of other authors?
- What sort of a name is Dedieu?
- Which is your favourite book? — Mr Graham says I should say, of YOURS.
- Do you like writing fiction or non-fiction best?
- Why did you say in a really serious long article about you the librarian showed me from her vertical file you don't like being known as a gay

writer? That was all you said.

- Do you write about gay relationships because you want to encourage girls of my age to think that it's actually normal and OK?
- Do you live by yourself, or have you got a partner?
- If you could have one wish to change the world, what would it be?

I wish I could agree about librarians, and I do really, but there's one at our public library who's not really old but grumpy and growls when you talk. Even when you're telling someone about a really neat book!!!! And she always takes the oldies first. And she's thinks Enid Blyton and Nancy Drew and those boring <u>boring</u> school stories are really good books for girls. So lots of my friends won't go there at all.

Love from

Tabs

PS My aunt's friend is quite well known but she said I better not tell you when she showed me how to do *Properties* because she said you mightn't want emails from strangers, but if you were that secret you wouldn't have agreed about the women of Afghanistan in the first place.

PPS Do you go surfing? Mr Graham thought you did.

From: Patricia Dedieu

To: Tabitha Preston

Subject: Your questions

Hello Tabs

Try talking to other librarians, not the grumpy one, whose

knowledge of children's books seems to be surprisingly limited. In any big library there are always quite a lot of librarians and most of them are wonderful. But I'm sad to hear of your friends being put off going there, by one unfortunate and probably sad person. To me, libraries are the most exciting and magical places in the world, offering centuries of accumulated knowledge, the heart and soul of any community.

Your questions:

- Yes, I've been lucky to meet many authors over the years, usually at writers' festivals or women's gatherings. I never dreamed when I started writing that I would do so much travelling!
- Dedieu is French. My great-grandfather came from France.
- My favourite book (of mine)? I'm proud of them all. But it's always the one that's still in my head, with characters I'm still emotionally involved with and making important choices for.
- I wrote non-fiction for many years as a result of my university women's studies teaching (many reports and research papers), but the older I get the more I want to explore the deeper truths of storytelling.
- Writing books about gay main characters doesn't make me gay, or a 'gay author', any more than Witi Ihimaera or Patricia Grace should always be known as 'Maori authors' or others as 'black authors' or 'Indian authors' or 'feminist authors'. (Not so long ago, heaven forbid, we used to be called 'lady authors' or 'authoress'.) We are all authors, writers, artists, serving whatever story we are driven to tell. And no, my books are not 'autobiographical'.

- Gay relationships *are* OK, but I'm not 'encouraging' girls towards gay relationships any more than say JK Rowling is encouraging boys to think they too could be wizards and fly through space or any number of writers for young people who write about first heterosexual love affairs are 'encouraging' teenagers to start kissing. We are simply, even in fantasy, writing of and reflecting truth as we see it.
- I enjoy living alone.
- One wish to save the world? Ah, where on earth would one start? Perhaps here: that after about 3000 years a time will again come when female values carry as much political, cultural and societal weight as do male values.

Good luck with your assignment.

Patricia Dedieu

PS Yes I do surf, nearly every day, most of the year, though admittedly I don't stand up on my board any longer and don't go out far when it's really rough. The young men — and a few young women — are quite used to me now. PD

From: Tabitha Preston
To: Patricia Dedieu
Subject: **What do you think?**

Wow. Are you the oldest 'lady surfer' in New Zealand?

This is my assignment. I think it's probably too long with the pictures of you and book covers we've got from the internet, so I had to shorten your answers, but here it is anyway.

Patricia Dedieu, author, activist, role model
Patricia Dedieu was born in 1943 and lives by herself in
Raglan, the surfing capital of New Zealand. She has written five remarkable books which have touched the hearts
and minds of many adolescents. In 1962, she got married
and moved to London and then to Baltimore, USA.
Patricia Dedieu has two sons. She returned to New
Zealand in 1971. Her first children's novel, about two
sisters, is called "Rosie and Rio" and was published in
1979. Her next novel was for young adults called "Two's
Company". It won many awards and is about the relationship between a girl and her mother who separated and
got a new partner who is female. This was read over radio
in ten parts and produced as a play in Sydney and that
must have been something Patricia Dedieu is really proud
of. Her next book "Not Violets" was about two girls
discovering their gay relationship and might be made into
a film. Patricia Dedieu has also written many non-fiction
books on feminist topics and was active in the women's
movement in the 1970s and 1980s. Patricia's hobbies are
reading novels, biographies, history, feminist works and
children's books, gardening, travelling and walking. When
her sons were growing up, she had a dog called Magnum
(it was a very small dog). I sent her an email with some
questions, and she told me that she's met lots of other
famous authors. 'I never dreamed when I started writing
that I would do so much travelling!' Her favourite book
(of hers) is 'always the one that's still in my head', and she
objects to being called a gay writer just because she sometimes writes about gay relationships. She wants to write
more fiction now she's older. She thinks gay relationships
are OK and her one wish to save the world would be

that women's values get as important as male ones.

Please tell me how I can make it better. And I want to write a story for a competition with really big fat prizes but beginnings are my worst enemy. How do YOU do BEGINNINGS?

Love

Tabs

PS One goldfish died, so Mum said we can get three more, to make two each. What would you name a goldfish if you had one?

PPS It's not a big library, so there are only five librarians, but I'll try to go when Mr Kingi is on duty, not grumpy old Mrs Brooking who I spoke about earlier. I go to an area school near Dargaville, in the wop-wops, Mum says, but lots of cheap kumaras. Dad's got a garage that's got a car-wash, and Mum teaches at the primary school. I play netball and our school netball captain is Hinewehi Patterson.

From: Patricia Dedieu
To: Tabitha Preston
Subject: Beginnings etcetera

Dear Tabs

I rather dislike that moniker 'role model', though I must admit I had few such people to look to for guidance and support when I was growing up as a teenager in the 1960s. They were very confusing and revolutionary times. Nevertheless, thank you for the flattering thought.

But (since you ask for comments on your draft assignment) I do think that it's a pity you've not used all or even most of my answers. Not because they are such splendid pearls of wisdom, but because they are 'yours', the result of your own research. No-one else has this material. So what about cutting down on the images you've taken from the websites and thus giving yourself more space for text, to quote me more fully (and in fact more accurately)? Just a thought.

(You may have heard the saying 'One picture equals a thousand words.' I don't think that's true any longer in an age where we are bombarded with images, icons, logos, graphic designers' many fancies and foibles. Many of our magazines and even once reputable mainstream newspapers have become triumphs of image and style over substance. I think what people want now from printed material is facts, background, history, analysis, commentary — words, ideas, dialogue, debate. Not so much images, any more.)

Beginnings — don't get anxious trying to write a 'memorable' first sentence. Get going on your story and come back and re-visit the first paragraph or two after you've otherwise finished. I find this helps.

Patricia D

PS The more usual style these days is to write book titles in italics, not in double inverted commas, thus *Not Violets*. You might like to check with Mr Graham. Just a thought.

From: Tabitha Preston
To: Patricia Dedieu
Subject: **THANKYOUTHANKYOUTHANKYOU**

Dear Patricia

Sorry you haven't heard from me in ages, but I wanted to tell you I did quote you all in full as you suggested and I did cut down the size of the book covers to thumbnails, and when I put it in a proper plastic file Mum bought at Paper Plus for $3.25 it all looked really good and Mr Graham gave me an A+ and it was displayed in the library when another famous author (a man, and funny, but not as famous as you) came to our school for Book Week. So thank you for your help. (I had to look up moniker!) Since then I've been really really busy with netball comps and Hinewehi Patterson — that's our netball captain — thinks I'm going to be quite good as a shooter, but not too busy to read your last book *Not Violets* again, and perhaps I didn't read it properly the first time, but this time I realized that you don't really say whether the two girls in the story are gay, or go on BEING gay for just a bit, or ARE gay for EVER AND EVER. Or do they really get to like boys later on and start dreaming of being a bride in a white dress and go on dates and have babies?

Did I miss something? I have read it two times, and I still don't know. Is that what you meant? How do you know you ARE gay? I don't mean you as in 'you' — but like in 'people'. Like, how do people — girls — well, know????

I'm still trying to decide whether I like a book that finishes without you knowing what happened to the main characters, really. I hope you don't find this insulting, for some reason. But the more I think about it, the more I want to know if Tina did grow up to be gay and stayed gay and had female partners and they bought a house together and all that stuff. Did she become the sort of gay in denim dungarees and a cowboy hat who Dad when he sees her on TV yells 'that butch bitch' or the ones I've heard Mum call a 'lipstick lesbian'? I guess that's one who wears nice smart clothes and high heels and make-up but because she just wants to look good, not to make guys think she's sexy and available. I think both those titles aren't very nice, bet you agree! I bet you don't wear dungarees, or you aren't wearing lots of make-up, foundation and eyeliner and stuff, in your pictures. I think you look KIND and WISE, and the little bit of garden behind you looks lovely.

Also, I read your email again about your one wish to save the world. What happened about 3000 years go? What was it like before that? Why were there more women's values before now?

Three of the goldfish have died, the ones we called Deep and Fried and Assault. So now there's only Battery left. Dad says that's the end of the frigging goldfish. I think Mum's quite glad 'cause she did most of the cleaning and water testing. I did help with the feeding though. So I'm sad. I liked my goldfish. I liked how they just swam around without any troubles.

Please tell me about *Not Violets*. I'm desperate to know.
Love
Tabs

From: Tabitha Preston
  To: Patricia Dedieu
Subject: **About Tina**

Before you answer, remember I told you about Hinewehi Patterson being our school netball captain. She's in Year 11 and she also helps coach the junior teams. Her dad's a sharemilker in the district and her mum (she's Maori) works in the hardware shop in Dargaville and she's got four younger brothers and sisters, so she's the eldest in her family. Apart from being terrific at netball, she's also into the kapa haka group, and has had proper classical guitar lessons, so sings and plays solo in talent quests, and she played Portia when the school did a Shakespeare scene for a big drama contest in Wellington last year. I can't remember what play it came from, but we saw it before they went to Wellington and it was in a courtroom which was quite good because she wants to go to university to be a lawyer when she leaves school. She wore a proper funny lawyer's wig. She might also be good enough to be a netball rep and play for New Zealand, 'cause she's very tall and has got long arms and man, can she jump!!! Like a kangaroo, man. As well as all this, she is really beautiful and it doesn't matter that she hasn't got nice clothes because she's one of those girls with broad shoulders and a long neck and slim hips who looks like a model in just a pair of jeans and a t-shirt and no bra and according to Dad, absolutely stunning in her short netball skirt. (I don't, look like a model I mean, I'm quite slim too, but I just don't.) Mum thinks Dad comes to my netball matches just to look at Hinewehi Patterson's legs.

Anyway, why am I telling you about Hinewehi Patterson? Because Mrs Harris who runs netball has asked me to be the new captain of my team, and that means I get to go to captains' meetings, and I don't know why I am so afraid of my feelings that I might stop netball altogether so that I don't have to sit in the same room as her or know that she is standing on the side of the field and watching me play.

All my friends in my class are starting to get really peculiar about boys, and buying make-up and bras, and giggling about periods and condoms, some are even going on what they call dates with Year 11 and 12 boys and talking about what the boys do. Like, wanting to poke their tongues in their mouths and feel around inside their knickers, and get the girls to lick their — the Education for Life lady says we should use the proper words, so I'll say it — penis. Penises. Though the girls say cocks, or pricks, or other words I don't want to write down 'cause they've got ugly sounds and people look grinning and stupid and ugly when they say them. And they all say that this is fine, it's OK, it's not real sex, just playing around and that's what Monica did for Bill and since everyone knows and laughs so it's OK really. Is it OK to have it in your mouth and swallow their well, wet dream stuff? Yuk. YUK!! And I don't know what's WRONG with me when I just don't want any boys to look at me and think about those things they might do or get me to do, but all I want to do is be in the same room as Hinewehi Patterson or on the sidelines clapping when she shoots lots of goals or be in the front row of the kapa haka group wearing black lipstick and a moko and with her eyes pulling those fierce strange expressions they do or sitting up straight with the prefects in a school assembly — just to be close enough to see the beautiful glow of her perfect smooth golden skin, and her half-Maori big brown eyes and model's mouth, except she hasn't got that dangerous collagen stuff of course, and all I want is to get back just one look, one smile at ME, silly Tabs Preston. If this is what being in love means, then I am.

Patricia, when I asked you about Tina from your book it wasn't really about Tina, it was about me. Probably you guessed that. So with all my friends mad about boys, and I'm mad, crazy, obsessed about a girl, does this mean that I'm born gay and that's the way I am and I can't do anything about it, even if I wanted to? I know that Hinewehi isn't gay, at least I don't think so, no, she's got boys around her like flies around a honeypot so she'll never take any notice of me, but one day am I going to look at a girl I <u>know</u> is gay and think I felt like that about a girl once and I must be like her and if she likes me I'm probably going to let her touch me, and stroke me, and kiss me? And we might sleep in a bed together and do more intimate, caressing, stroking things like you hint about but never quite say in *Not Violets*. But now I'm team captain, I think I'm going to go crazy to be seeing more of Hinewehi and never being able to show her or tell her what I feel. To her I'm just another little pesky Year 9. I carry round a picture I cut from the school magazine, and have another one under my pillow and I follow her home from school, and I offer to carry her netball gear and put up notices, it's truly that bad.

Do you think I should give up netball, become a library monitor and one of those nerdy people mostly boys who stare at computer screens every lunch hour and at their bedroom computers when they're not sleeping? If I'm looking at a computer screen, that keeps me looking anywhere else, and thinking about anything else. Lots of those people never talk to anyone, they're like scary aliens and zombies. Should I become a zombie? But I am really afraid that maybe soon I am going to lose the plot, Patricia, and do something really stupid and embarrassing.

Please help me. Could I come down on a bus to Raglan to talk to you?

Tabs

PS I think Mr Graham has guessed about me and H. Everyone knows he's gay and no-one cares too much. He's the best teacher I've ever had.

From: Patricia Dedieu
  To: Tabitha Preston
Subject: **Not Violets**

My dear Tabs

This must be a very honest and perhaps quite tough letter, in reply to your honest one, written from the heart, to me. Please read it carefully because it must be the last communication between us.

No, I don't think it is a good idea for you to come to Raglan. I am not a counsellor, nor a mentor, nor a granny figure, simply the author of a book of fiction that spoke to you, about one kind of that special experience we call 'first love'. Later in this reply, I am going to indicate where you can get the help you might need.

But first, about *Not Violets* — I deliberately left open the question of whether Tina and Sarah were by nature homosexual and therefore committed to a lifetime of same-sex partners — or whether their homosexual relationship was possibly one intense, memorable experience which they would always treasure but in time, as they formed partnerships with males, come to realize was part of their growing up. As to whether people are born, or become (through outside factors) homosexual, that is still the matter of intense academic and political debate, the so-called 'nature or nuture' debate. My instinct and research tells me it's a bit of both, and the proportions vary in different people.

You will have realized from my replies to your questions that I am intensely private on the subject of my own sexuality. I see this as my private concern, for me alone. I deeply dislike the current fashion for loudly declaring one's sexuality, whatever it is, to the world.

And yes, I do have a great problem with those very presumptuous people (and you, my dear, were not one of them!) who assume that because I have chosen to write fiction about gay relationships between young women, because I was at one time deeply involved in the feminist movements both in America and here, because I live alone and prefer to enjoy concert-going and other city pleasures with women friends, several of whom might be gay, that therefore (despite an early, clearly unwise marriage and two sons) I am gay. If you reduce this argument to its most absurd, then anyone who writes novels about say, vampires, is therefore a vampire. Or, turning it around, the best person to write a novel about being say, a teenage tennis champion, is a current or former teenage tennis champion. This is patently nonsense, just bollocks.

Writers of fiction should be able to research and write about whatsoever they please, without accusations of their personal, intimate involvement in the theme or topic. They may choose (and many do) to use their own experiences, but readers should never assume that they have done so, in any work. This is to challenge the very basis on which storytelling rests: the power of the writer's imagination to create — with only the tools of language, observation, research and sometimes, personal experience — profoundly believable and truthful fictional worlds.

However, that said, I do want to tell you about my own 'pash', because that is what we called our heroes, our loved ones in the early 1960s. (My *Oxford* gives the meaning as a brief infatuation, deriving from passion. These days I understand the word has a different, quite sleazy and unpleasant connotation.)

Until quite recently it was understood that young adolescents would perhaps experience very intense feelings for an older person of the same sex. To the Greeks of classical times it was perfectly normal that a boy in early puberty, round thirteen or fourteen, would be 'in love' with an older man, mentored and encouraged and schooled by him in the arts of war, love, sexual techniques, politics, debate and so on. Other cultures (like English boys' 'public' schools), though less open, practical and understanding of it, have called this developmental phenomenon 'hero worship'.

The object of my worship was a girl called Sandra. Like you, I was about twelve or thirteen and I carried round portraits and tokens, looked for her in every lunch hour, followed her home, literally worshipped the ground she walked on. Like Hinewehi, she was charismatic, a leader, a soloist in the school choir, slim, blonde and elegant, though why I chose her in preference to other equally attractive sixteen-year-olds is part of that great, little-understood mystery of why any two people of whatever sex and age are particularly attracted to each other.

Unlike you, who feels alone and different in your passion for Hinewehi, most of my classmates were also pining after senior girls with varying degrees of intensity.

The switch of our attentions to boys was very gradual, probably in our thirteenth or fourteenth years, some earlier than others. We accepted that this was a perfectly normal progression. Though you might find this hard to believe, the word 'gay' to mean homosexual had not then been coined, and 'lesbian' was in the dictionary but simply never uttered in polite or even impolite conversation. If two women chose to live together, ostensibly for reasons of economy or companionship, it might be murmured they were 'a bit mannish'. There were certainly no films or TV dramas which showed lesbian women passionately kissing with open mouths or writhing round in bed together, as you very probably have seen on a screen by now.

So no-one ever 'warned' me that the fiery intensity of my passion for Sandra might or even inevitably lead to a lifetime of lesbianism. Neither should they have. No-one thought like that, then. Around twelve or so, we had our 'pash', and in time, around our fifteenth year, we probably had our first yearnings for a boy's tender kiss.

It makes me unutterably sad to think of how Western childhood has been sexualized — which means, girls from about eight on being encouraged by the powerful advertising and music industries to put great emphasis on making themselves attractive for the opposite sex. When I see ranges of cosmetics in the chemist's, packaged and aimed at seven-year-olds, or a video of the Spice Girls or Mariah Carey or Britney Spears, I literally shudder. This cynical, exploitative and unnatural pressure, driven by nothing other than voracious, ruthless greed, is not what I want for my granddaughters.

Please, Tabs, read this letter carefully. I have written it carefully, because I believe you to be a mature, lively girl who will not embarrass herself or do something she might regret. I would just like you to know that in my opinion your passion for Hinewehi is perfectly normal and OK and not to be afraid of. It will run its course, and you'll be grateful for it, all your life. Later, guided by your instincts, and in your own good time, you will decide your sexual preference. Meantime, you should relax, and enjoy your netball and pets and music and schoolwork and friends and all the other things that twelve-year-old girls enjoy.

I said that this would be my last email to you, and so it will be. I'd rather you didn't reply, because an unknown author whom you have never met is not an appropriate substitute for a parent, or a grandparent or a counsellor — however much you have enjoyed her books and been moved or intrigued by them.

If after a few weeks you still feel powerless and unhappy and in danger of 'losing the plot', then please talk to your mother or grandmother — or, if that doesn't seem like a good idea, go and quietly see your school counsellor. But please see someone.

If you do talk to your mother or a counsellor, you can show them this or any of my emails, if you wish.

Your question about the resurgence of women's values and what happened 3000 years ago — if you wish to know more you should ask your public librarian (Mr Kingi, perhaps). The world's great religions since that time have been fundamentally and profoundly patriarchal, displacing previous matriarchal or 'goddess' cultures. Again, please talk to your parents, or Mr Graham.

With all my best wishes

Patricia Dedieu

PS That Shakespeare play was *The Merchant of Venice*.

Portia is a very smart young woman who in that famous courtroom scene impersonates a man, a learned lawyer, and prevents an unjust sentence of death. It's an unpleasant piece, though, my least favourite Shakespeare play.

From: Tabitha Preston
To: Patricia Dedieu
Subject: It's alright really

I know you said not to write, but it's ages since I did, and I'm in Year 10 now and this school is now a Hinewehi-free zone! Actually, it was really funny, after you wrote that last email, it was like it was a trigger 'cause some really weird things started happening. I hope you don't find it boring if I tell you, but when Mr Graham told me about you getting that big grant of money, and you being on TV (I missed it though, sorry), I just wanted to say congratulations, even if you must have been upset when it said 'the gay writer' PD in the paper. Did you write to the editor and complain, or did you move on?

The weird things. Well, you said that H was just a pash, probably, and I'd grow out of it. But SHE didn't. Hasn't. At least I don't think so. After I wrote that email, Leah, one of the other senior girls (another netball player) started being friendly, and wanted to lend me books, something pretty dense called *The Well of Loneliness* (I couldn't get into it) and books by Paula Boock and Patricia Dedieu! I said I'd read them thanks, but she had a few others, Aussie and American writers, mostly about gays. Then H is suggesting that I be the 'junior voice' for a 'netball focus group' with about six others, and of course H would be heading it, so off I go and it's all fine though Leah's there too and we yabber on about netball and I'm in heaven until about the third time when it's going to be at a café in town and I get there and find that Leah and one other in a denim jacket with a zillion zips and rhinestones and her cleavage showing are holding hands under the table and the waiter is grinning his head off and it's all got a bit cosy and friendly in a way that makes me feel really <u>really</u> uncomfortable. So I start thinking about why I'm there and is H just being kind to a promising junior or is there something else I should know about?

Anyway, I dropped netball and took up hockey and it's a much better game, not so bitchy, so it's alright really. But I'm still off boys. And I'd be off H if she was still at school, and this is the really weird bit: word got around that she's gone to Waikato to do law but over the holidays she got pregnant and had an abortion. Confusing, huh! Suppose she's just bi. (Looks funny written like that, but guess you know what I mean.) Dad still thinks she's got the greatest legs in the universe. She might even play for Waikato this season.

I did go to the counsellor and she was great. Thanks. Thanks for your help. I really am over it. (Didn't show our emails, they're private.)

Lots of love

Tabs

PS We're reading *Romeo and Juliet*, the Leonardo DiCaprio film was fantastic. You probably didn't like it so much, but we did.

PPS Mr Graham says there was a shot of you on the beach at Raglan, going into the water with your boogie board. In May?!

To: Sandra Player
From: Patricia Dedieu
Subject: A billet-doux

Dear Sandra

It must be a good fifteen years since we met, at that rather gruesome school reunion, and as I probably told you then, I've watched your career over the decades to the very top of the corporate tree with great interest.

I've often wondered if you ever knew the impact you made on my life, and a recent correspondence with a young reader, followed by a less happy one with her parents and school, has prompted this long overdue exploration for me of what exactly that impact was, and why. I believe the modern buzz word for what this email represents is 'closure'.

The twelve-year-old girl who emailed me was ostensibly doing an 'author study' with me as the chosen one (I get quite a few such requests for help, despite the FAQ in my website) but in reality was deeply concerned with her passionate infatuation for an older girl — her 'pash', ah, remember those? — and thus the possibility she might be inevitably, irreversibly gay.

My correspondence with her, carefully disengaging when her real agenda became clear and urging her to talk to her mother and/or school counsellor, has alas led to an unpleasant exchange with her parents and school principal and Board of Trustees, in which I was accused of encouraging lesbianism by stating that 'gay relationships were normal and OK', of sullying her with 'unsavoury details of past affairs', and of promoting goddess worship to children!

To say that these comments were distorted, truncated, taken out of context, would be an understatement. It was only with the greatest difficulty and perseverance that I persuaded the principal that if the matter was leaked to the press, the impact on the twelve-year-old girl concerned and her whole family would be profoundly, permanently damaging.

I would not, I said, even to 'defend' myself, enter into any public debate with any salivating media interrogator, and that to parade a child on TV for the sake of political correctness (I remember some years ago a hapless teenager alongside her reverend father, 'supporting' his hypocritical bleating about an 'unsuitable' YA book he hadn't read) was in reality child abuse of a particularly subtle, vicious and enduring kind.

Thankfully, the matter remained internal, though unpleasant, and no doubt in the end they thought that I had been sufficiently reprimanded and chastened. Writers, fortunately, have no watchdog, no Commission to which official complaints can be laid and inquisitions conducted, though you may argue that television and especially those who are the inquisitors, with the flimsiest of qualifications, these days fulfill that role. I believe (and hope) that the child concerned, whose emails and my replies had unknown to her been read by a teacher, remained unaware of the ruckus.

In any case, I had a chirpy and perfectly 'normal' email six months later, saying that she was 'over it' and getting on with her young life. I hope she has a sufficiently open and enquiring mind to research the fascinating topic of 'goddess worship' for herself, later, perhaps with my contribution to the literature, if she so wishes.

Why this email, then? My young reader's desperation, her eloquence on the subject of her 'pash' reminded me of mine for you.

Did you know the real extent of it? That in your Upper Sixth year there was down in the lowly Thirds a devoted admirer, suitor, lapdog who adored and idolized you? Who ran messages, carried books, put up notices, dressed like you, walked and spoke like you, wrote billets-doux (unsent), yearned to excel in those things you excelled in, yearned for one smile, one thanks, one acknowledgement that I, little Pat Dedieu, even existed — that grotty little turd with pimples, stumpy hairy legs and funny ski-jump nose, unflattering glasses and embarrassing parents, who knew that by morning break she had BO and in the days before roll-on deodorants, could do nothing about it? Did you have the slightest clue?

Of course you did. You didn't become the corporate boss of a top PR company for nothing, paid liar for all sorts of righteous causes from anti-smoking to child molestation to prisoners' rights to drunk driving to children's hospitals; you are endlessly quoted as only working for those clients whose causes you personally, morally and ethically, believed in. Of course.

But you knew exactly what you were doing when you were sixteen and remained quiet and allowed me aged twelve to take the public rap for a certain incident involving a banned book, a box of chocolates, a cynical and sinister English teacher and a giggling assembly, remember? If you remember, it must surely be with shame; if you don't, it proves my point that to you the incident, and I, meant nothing.

Would you agree, you now as a loving granny, wealthily

retired, a *grande dame* of Auckland society, a darling of Government commissions and taskforces on media and education, a columnist with a respected weekly magazine, regularly pontificating on TV, that it is not desirable a twelve-year-old should feel such degrading humiliation at the hands of a senior girl and her co-conspirator, both four years older? To be branded so publicly and permanently as someone 'un-natural?'

I gave my young reader such wise advice, as gently as possible: 'You'll get over it.' Such lies, such dissembling and evasion.

I didn't get over it, Sandra. I was shunned at school, left at the earliest possible opportunity, avoided relationships at university and in desperation consented to a hasty, defiant and dishonest marriage in a registry office (frowned on, in those days) which broke my mother's heart. I gave my intellectual and emotional life to 'women's studies' and more recently to novels about young women enjoying and exploring, though not without pain, the kind of human pleasure denied me from the moment I walked from that assembly. Any opportunity I've had for a relationship — and there have been two, one in my early thirties, the other about five years ago, menopausal no doubt — has died in the early stages for want of courage and honesty. And forty-eight years later, here I am telling another twelve-year-old only half the story and hoping that when she is sixty she will not be suffering such a feeling of loneliness and waste.

Why did I not stand my ground, and tell the teachers and that assembly the truth? Those expensive chocolates (imported from Belgium) tasted sweet, the one kiss in the empty cloakroom sweeter. You denied it, your friend testified as a 'witness', you both knew you were lying. That English teacher, with a remarkable lack of understanding, allowed it to pass unchallenged, either then or more appropriately in private later. And so, like a Sparta weakling, I was left on the bleak hillside, alone in the snow.

I am going surfing now, to join the young men already out there in rows. It is particularly wild today. I feel the need for something scouring and clean.

Patricia Dedieu

PS That banned book — how harmless Henry Miller seems now, when any child can have more or less free access to *American Psycho* or *Cleo* magazine and their ilk, to internet material and 'adult' videos dealing with war, sex and crimes of unspeakable nastiness now freely available in video stores, all of which you and I would find unwatchable, sickening, sick.

But then if you read any of my novels, you would notice a certain enduring innocence. There's a lofty school of thought that those of us who make an intellectual decision to write fiction for children are actually ('poor things') suffering from arrested development; we write best for the age at which our emotional development, for whatever reason, was arrested.

Having met a number of the literature's greatest, like the American Katherine Paterson and the Englishman Philip Pullman, not to mention our own regional community of fine writers — well-educated, mature, wise and compassionate people all — I don't go along with it myself, but it's an interesting thought.

Mrs Harold Rex

Mrs Harold Rex had learned in her life to be a patient woman. She had waited fifty-six long years for this moment. Now that it was here, finally, she almost — almost — wanted to prolong the exquisite tension.

She crossed her short legs and minutely adjusted the skirt of the Harris tweed suit bought in David Jones on that short visit twelve years ago to Melbourne. Harold had liked her in well-cut classic suits, lined of course, mid-calf-length, tailored in fine Scottish wools for daytime wear and for evening, the more subdued Thai silks. This one, his favourite tweed, a dusky pink, she had picked with great care from the wardrobe, along with the slate-grey English court shoes and classic Italian bag, also from David Jones. Harold had thought this suit particularly slimming; it was an appropriate choice for today.

'Are you alright, Mother?' Her eldest son leaned over from his seat in the row of four lined up in front of the lawyer's astonishingly untidy desk and squeezed her plump hand.

'Oh, yes, thank you, Andy — I'm fine. Just fine.' She smiled to herself; accountants never had any imagination, and Andrew was always the most literal and pedantic of creatures, a dull, anxious boy and growing duller as he got older. He didn't know his mother at all.

Nor did any of them gathered in this scruffy lawyer's office, which clearly belonged to a seriously disordered mind. The desk was chaotic; file boxes were stacked untidily against the walls, possibly awaiting shelves yet to be installed; the contents of the bursting Manila files thrust sloppily into a tall rotating stand threatened to spill themselves out onto the floor at any moment. Mr Fowler's club tie was slightly askew, his pin-striped suit not a recent addition to his wardrobe, his sparse hair uncombed. His half-glasses only partially obscured a disturbing crimson birthmark below one eye, its wart-like texture encroaching onto a prominent nose.

Trust Harold, she thought, to have a lawyer well past retirement age, one of the old school, probably working only three half-days a week and probably cheap. He did not inspire confidence. She was trying not to look at the birthmark.

Mr Fowler was, at this moment, searching through a large, over-filled box. Mrs Harold Rex, in a momentary burst of anger, heard herself take tight, disapproving breaths. She told herself sternly, Margery Rose, stay calm now, control your breathing, still the trembling in your fingers, your mounting anger and exasperation. Why wasn't the last will and testament of Harold Frederick Rex sitting significantly alone and ready on the large desk when they were all ushered in? Why, he'd even kept them waiting, perched on the arms of the green leather sofa and one armchair, for over fifteen minutes past the time of the appointment.

It was inexcusable, unforgivable, when they'd all arrived early and eager in the tiny anteroom outside, to be cooped up for a quarter of an hour with old *National Geographics* and *Newsweeks*, a dirty ashtray and a bowl of pink plastic carnations.

Andrew had announced within seconds of his arrival, 'Tim wants me to ring him, Mum — as soon as we get out of here.'

'Tonight, perhaps.'

'Why tonight?'

'Half rates, darling. Your father never rang anywhere at full rates. He considered it . . .'

David said mildly, 'For God's sake, Mum . . . he's got a cellphone.'

'He always said there was no news so important that it couldn't wait a few hours.'

'Tell that to an ambulance officer or a stockbroker,' said David. 'He did talk some absolute nonsense.'

His mother let that pass. She smoothed her skirt across her knees and admired her discreet pink nails, the colour chosen this morning to match the suit. 'I really don't know why Tim had to go flying off back to Perth quite so soon.'

'He has a job to do,' said David, excusing a younger brother who had escaped on the earliest possible flight after the funeral to avoid any part of this charade. He wished his mother's perfume was less liberally applied, and her lipstick of a less shiny, forceful pink. 'A big deal about to go through, I think he said a commercial property worth millions. Thousands in commission.'

'Let's hope this one sticks,' said Andrew. 'About time something did.'

Mrs Harold Rex sighed, feeling a little ashamed of herself. She tended to ignore snipes at Tim. And she knew her sons had cellphones, but the habits of a lifetime, even a husband's habits, die hard. Accountant Andrew, country GP David and if she was honest, struggling real-estate agent Tim in Perth — they were all good boys, good husbands and fathers with steady if unspectacular jobs; they had not, like some friends' sons and grandsons, strayed off the rails into drink or drugs or fraud or abandoning their children, legitimate or otherwise. And today, each of them — and undoubtedly their wives — quite understandably wanted to know if they would be any the richer, and if so, by how much, and how long it would be before they got their hands on the money. These days, she had been warned by her recently widowed friend Glennis, probate usually came through in under six months, but any will could, she added darkly, be challenged.

All things considered, Mrs Harold Rex believed that her comparatively dutiful, loving, respectable and responsible sons didn't deserve this treatment.

But neither, with greater justification, after fifty-six years and nine months of servitude, did she. In the silence, she examined again, as she had done frequently as his death drew ever closer, the very real and unpleasant possibility that Harold might have left a will that wholly favoured their three sons. It was not impossible that in the next few minutes she could find herself in effect utterly dependent on their charity for the rest of her life. She had never previously thought herself a jealous or resentful woman, and she found these thoughts profoundly disturbing.

'How did you sleep last night, Margery?' asked Felicity, looking up from her *Newsweek*. 'Funerals are really tiring.'

'Oh, David's sleeping pill helped me through. Quite well really.'

'That's good. Everyone thought how brave and stoic you were yesterday . . . so long married . . . and him so sick . . .'

Felicity decided it best to say nothing further. Margery's overly dutiful sons could, for once, do the small talk. The last six years had been ghastly for everyone, all the possible complications of diabetes, including failing sight and an amputation which had not gone well. David at his beck and call, and Margery, always Harold's tight-lipped, unappreciated handmaiden, required to be a night nurse and secretary on tap as well as everything else. When they had — apparently — pots of money, the woman was a martyr, a doormat, little more than a slave. It was pathetic. The very thought of her father-in-law, dead or alive, a man who never laughed, whose tantrums and put-downs were legendary, made Felicity's stomach churn.

'Nice to see the mayor,' said Andrew. 'And all those Rotary guys. I'm glad they all turned out. Dad was very respected, you know. Although who the secret Freemason blokes were is anyone's guess.'

'The mayor and the Rotarians,' said Felicity tartly. 'Secret societies, all of them.'

'I'm due back in surgery in an hour,' said David, looking at his watch. 'Unlike this fellow, I never keep patients waiting — well, hardly ever.'

Andrew picked up his cue, chanting, 'What never?'

David sang, softly, 'No, never.'

'What, *never*?'

'Hardly e-vaaaah.'

This was for their mother's benefit: a little brotherly code remembered from a school production of *Pinafore*, and long a family joke. David, though the younger, had played the Captain, with Andrew in the chorus.

'Shhhush, David!' said his wife. For a moment Margery had looked inexpressibly sad, before her face had tightened and shoulders had straightened. 'Not *here*.'

There was a long awkward pause. Apart from Margery, sitting placidly in the uncomfortable armchair, occasionally smoothing down her skirt, all flicked idly over magazine pages. After several minutes, Andrew looked up.

'You've met this Guy Fowler chap before, haven't you, Mum?'

'Of course I have,' she lied.

Andrew was looking nonchalantly at the ceiling as he asked. 'So you . . .'

She let his question hang in the air for a few seconds, then said clearly, 'Know Harold's intentions?'

Margery Rex looked at her two sons' casually expectant faces. Andrew may be dull, but he wasn't stupid, and he knew exactly what a loaded question he'd posed, one that none of them dared ask in Harold's lifetime, or even as he lay in the hospice in and out of comas, holding them all to an interminable dying.

For fifty-six years and nine months she received her weekly housekeeping allowance. She knew nothing of Harold's affairs, his investments, his income as company director of more than one financial institution, his other lives as a Freemason or city councillor, at various times chairman of a rugby club, a local Rotary and, when it became fashionable, a bird-conservation trust — so why should she, who as a married woman had spent most of her evenings in a large house quite alone, know *anything* of his intentions?

Admittedly, he had invited her to fly down to the Wellington investiture where Harold Frederick Rex had received an MBE for services to business and the community. He'd told her, on that occasion, to make sure she looked nice; the invitation stipulated women wear hats, he said, getting out his gold Parker pen and writing her a cheque for the unimaginable amount of $3000. She'd bought a new couturier-label silk suit, cream with red trim, with red shoes and bag, and enjoyed the extra treat of visiting a milliner and having a hat made, a smart boater with a half veil. He had taken her arm and patted it approvingly as they got out of the taxi outside the Government House porch. Mrs Harold Rex, dressed by El-jay, salon make-up by Elizabeth Arden and drenched with Lanvin, met with approval. He never knew that she'd chosen a cheaper bag than the one she really liked, so that a little of the $3000 had gone on a new garden hose and spade, which she had then felt obliged to keep well hidden under the house.

Andrew was prompting her for an answer. 'Mum? I asked a question?'

'Oh . . . oh dear . . . a sneeze, it's those flowers . . .'

'They're plastic,' said Felicity. 'Aren't they vile?'

Your own perfume, thought David.

'Excuse me . . .' She played for time with the tissue tucked in the sleeve of her pink Harris tweed suit — got it out, blew her nose daintily, simulated a tiny sneeze, folded the tissue over — and was rewarded by the door of the inner office opening, and a gaunt woman in an ill-fitting beige suit announcing that Mr Fowler would see them now.

'Forgive me, Mrs Rex, come in — it's been some time since — very fine funeral, m'dear, 300 at least — and a fine eulogy, Andrew, if I may say, very fine — you did your father p-p-proud — I could have sworn it was in this box — maybe she . . .'

Mr Fowler pushed the button for his secretary and sat down, flustered, mortified by his apparent lack of preparation and detesting that miserable dead skinflint Harry for the position he'd put his old friend in. They had been good friends, once, without a doubt, through university and many enjoyable games of golf. As the years went by, true to the diminishing respect in which he was held around the town, Harry had traded cold-bloodedly on their friendship. His cheques, without consultation claiming mates' rates with some jovial turn of phrase or quote from Shakespeare on embossed linen notepaper, had underpaid the invoices, already discounted; he wasn't above ringing Guy's home late at night or at seven in the morning to ask for urgent advice; he'd played his will as close to his chest as any client Fowler and Spence had ever acted for in forty-five years.

And now, here he was, good old Guy cast as the trusted

family lawyer, in a scene straight out of John Galsworthy, required to read a will to a new widow and her family the day after the funeral. Harold had trusted no-one, not even him. It was intolerable. It must be fifteen years at least since he last had to read a will in such circumstances. Even when it was not uncommon, he'd always loathed this particular ritual, indulging men who should have known better — and should be ashamed of themselves — but who wanted control even beyond the grave and so often set faithful but distraught and exhausted wives against their children and partners. Today's wives wouldn't stand for it. They had Relationship Property Agreements and discussed their husband's wills with them. Probably wrote them, he thought sourly. And these days, adult offspring were nearly always brought into the picture, they insisted on it. Some things were being dragged out of the nineteenth century, were being done better.

Mr Fowler glanced briefly across at Mrs Harold Rex as she sat serenely opposite him, flanked by two of her three sons: Andrew who gave the dreary speech; overweight doctor David; plus one unsmiling daughter-in-law, David's wife. His secretary had had to bring in another chair. He was fairly sure none of them had the slightest idea what was coming; their solemn, relaxed air of calm, the studied indifference betrayed them utterly.

It was all pretty simple. When it came to the point, Harry was nineteenth-century man personified, a Soames Forsyte. Fortunately he'd all but retired from business before the revolution of the 1980s, spending the last twenty years of his life managing his own investments and basking in the role of elder statesman. Harry Rex would never have coped with Rogernomics, the aggressive New Right, the ideology of market forces, the fixation on transparency and accountability, the rise and rise of assertive and powerful women in politics, medicine, law, corporate life — never in a million years.

The secretary appeared. 'Agnes, Mr Rex's will? Have you . . . I can't seem . . .'

'I put it on your desk. Have you looked *under* that box?'

'Ah. Yes, so it is. Thank you kindly, Agnes. Now, Mrs Rex, down to b-b-business, eh? Let me see, yes . . .'

Mr Fowler took the will from its plastic pouch, resisting the very strong urge to slide the ten-year-old document across the teak desktop and tell these four silent, frantic people he'd not do their old man's dirty work for him — they could read it for themselves instead of always remembering his own stuttering reedy voice as the voice of their husband and father's last wishes.

Instead, he flipped through the pages, refreshing his memory. 'Yes . . . mmm . . . yes . . . that's right . . .' and in an ill-judged, light-hearted, incongruous blurt, lifted his head, smiled encouragingly and firmly stated, 'Yep.'

Four pairs of eyes fixed Guy Fowler to the back of his padded chair like laser beams. He cleared his throat, adjusted his half-glasses and lifted the document into a comfortable reading position.

'Now,' he said with a sudden burst of inspiration; the Law Society's younger advocates of plain English would be proud of him. 'Shall we have the long version, with all those nasty legal words, or the short version, just the salient facts in words of one syllable?'

Four faces frowned at him, taking this in. He realized his question, though well meant, had probably sounded extremely patronizing. He blundered on.

'Traditionally, I should do the former, but I can d-d-do either, m'dears! If I were you, myself, in your shoes, just to begin with, I'd go for the latter.'

*　*　*

The question hung in the air. Now that the moment of truth had arrived, Mrs Harold Rex had a moment of utter panic. She searched the lawyer's disfigured face for clues — did she see embarrassment, sympathy, what? Perhaps he'd left it all to a cat's home, or that bird-conservation trust. How foolish would they all look then! What rights did any of them have, really? Even herself, when it came to the point?

Their wedding day, a hurried and modest affair just after war was declared, was the last time Harold told her he loved her.

Instead of endearments, she got a weekly white envelope, her housekeeping money, in cash: never enough, never negotiable, and only rarely increased to cope with inflation. Instead of enlisting as did all his friends, somehow he managed to avoid going away to active service in the Middle East or the Pacific — she never knew on what grounds — but stuck around Auckland running a business, she never knew what. Instead of enjoying a father, her boys grew up with an absentee figurehead, always away at meetings, administering occasional, regretful beatings on his return when, inevitably, he heard of misdemeanours. 'You will not treat your mother this way,' he would say, before the first stroke of the thin cane across clenched bared buttocks. His family learned to present an untroubled, united front.

Instead of going back to her job as a librarian, Mrs Rex was firmly told her husband did not believe in working wives. She became instead the long-serving secretary–treasurer of the Friends of the Library. Instead of being proud of her home, she had grown ashamed of its quite unnecessary and increasing shabbiness; Harold simply stalled any suggestions of repainting or replacing tired drapes, until she lost all enthusiasm. Instead of a shared bed, he had insisted quite early in their marriage on single beds and not too much later, on his own bedroom. And instead of companionship and love, she had experienced only its opposite: not hate, but indifference in all things, except on those rare occasions when he required a well-dressed, smiling, fragrant and silent wife on his arm.

And now, instead of sharing the confidence and trust due to a companion of fifty-six years, she sat here before this scruffy, sadly disfigured but all-knowing lawyer, feeling like a beggar, a penitent, a tramp. At the moment of truth, Mrs Harold Rex felt a great surge of pure hot anger towards Harold Frederick Rex MBE and no less to herself for a half-century of incomprehensible, shameful weakness. She was pathetic, her whole adult life had been pathetic. She had run a library department once, with respect given and received from twelve staff. They had given her an engraved crystal bowl when she resigned, and come to the church to see her married. How — *how* — had it happened?

'Just the salient facts,' she said, her voice now slightly trembling. Incongruously, she saw him as one of those tuxedoed people at the televised Oscars, standing at a desk and opening the envelope — reading it — looking up smiling — savouring that hushed, tortuous moment — an audience of expensive bejewelled people on a knife edge, unable to breathe.

She murmured, like a child, as he again picked up the document that held her future, 'Please, tell me just the facts.'

Glancing up again, Mr Fowler caught the anguish in Mrs Harold Rex's pale blue eyes. He was reminded of that reproachful look, one he would never forget as long as he lived, given him by his aged and infirm cocker spaniel as she was led slowly away by the vet to a lonely, anonymous death in the spartan clinic next door. Harry had undoubtedly given his wife a rough ride, and though there'd be some hostility from the daughters-in-law — that he knew for a monty — from all accounts the sons were reasonably successful and not badly off and their time would come.

He fixed his gaze on the dumpy grey-haired woman, neatly dressed in a sort of pink tweed but clearly bone weary and terrified for her future, sitting patiently on the other side of his untidy desk.

'The short version then.'

'Please.'

'Basically, m'dear, Mr Rex has left his entire estate, as consistent with the conservative man of t-t-tradition he was — to you. You are the sole executor. The house, contents, his investment portfolios — at current value they amount to about $5.7 million. New Zealand dollars, that is. B-b-both cars go to you, and the holiday cottage, though there is a provision that the running costs and use of the cottage shall be amicably shared by your sons and their families, with own your right of usage, of course. I'll help you with that. There is also a provision for your care, should you need it later.'

It was quite astonishing. Although there was no real physical change — he told his wife later — nor barely any perceptible movement, Mrs Harold Rex altered before his very eyes. Perhaps there was a slow intake of breath, a slight lift of the chin, an uplifting of the carriage of the bosom under the slightly tight double-breasted jacket. Perhaps it was the uncrossing and careful crossing of the plump little legs, the smoothing of the skirt. It was though she had been injected with some subtle life-giving substance, a shot of adrenalin perhaps, and the results were visible within seconds. She looked and sounded suddenly about fifteen years younger; not a small, unremarkable wife, but now a woman of property. It was quite astonishing.

The sons were clearly not pleased, of course, and rightly so, to have been passed over as executors. It was certainly unusual.

He'd tried on several occasions with Harry to indicate how they would receive it as a slight, a snub — to no avail. Today, of course, it would be quite unprofessional of him to have passed any opinion whatsoever. They got to share among them some golf clubs, his Freemason's gear, some silver bits and pieces, tennis racquets, antiquated riding tackle and fishing rods, antique horse pictures, school cups, leather-bound books won as prizes: the 'gentleman's stuff'. And eye contact was certainly lacking between the four of them as, with minimal and subdued courtesies, they left his office clutching photocopies of the will; Mr Fowler could see plain as daylight that the gimlet-eyed daughter-in-law in black was particularly displeased.

'Of course,' he added wearily to his wife, for it had been a tiring day and his birthmark was devillish itchy, 'I'll advise Mrs Rex to set up a family trust immediately and start gifting money to her sons. Harry, the mean bugger, should've done that decades ago, and so help me God, I tried, several times, but he'd have none of it. She's got plenty to live on, and by any measure, she deserves every last cent of it. As that young grandson of ours would colourfully say, what a t-t-tosser!'

Mr Fowler was retiring from the practice soon, sighed his wife. With any luck he would never have to be put through that again.

Margery Rex thanked her lawyer Mr Fowler and regally led the way from the office. All four crowded silently into a small cage that did duty as a lurching lift. Chanel No 5 overpowered its usual smell of cleaning fluid.

On the pavement outside, she stopped. Her suit jacket was feeling a little tight this afternoon, and she undid the leather buttons.

'It will be alright,' she said calmly to her two speechless, grim-faced sons who at this moment she believed deeply resented their mother's very existence. 'I'll talk to Mr Fowler next week. I read something in the *Herald* lately about setting up family trusts. No doubt your father should have done something like that a long time ago.'

'Right on,' snarled David, not trusting himself to say anything more and looking at his watch. 'Well, that's it. Over bar the shouting. We're off. I'll ring you, Mum. I'm on call this weekend.'

Dutiful, feather-light kisses were exchanged. It was obvious and not surprising, thought his mother as she watched them walk off towards the car park, that Felicity was already having her say.

'Of course, I'll need your help with the finances, Andrew,' she said. 'I think I'll sell the cars immediately, divide that money three ways, yes. Just to give you all a bit of a boost. Heavens alive, who wants a great black Jaguar, a Range Rover *and* a Mini Cooper at my stage of life? Dreadful gas guzzlers, all of them. Though I might replace my Charade. A nice little Toyota or perhaps a Renault? What do you think?'

As Andrew still seemed incapable of speech, she went on, 'We'll all have a talk about the trust and the house, very soon, I promise, and then there's the cottage. Goodness!'

For a moment, she felt quite faint. 'Just give me a few days to gather myself together, dear, that's all I ask.'

As she poured herself a stiff gin that night — and that was another thing, his infamous piss-weak drinks — Margery Rex surveyed all the florists' bouquets of flowers smelling out the silent house, maybe twenty of them, and wondered about rituals that stank of hypocrisy. Andy as eldest son at the funeral, volubly honouring the dead father he hardly knew; two fellow directors acclaiming

Harold's distinguished contribution to industry; a priest insincerely praising a community leader and uncomplaining patient who faced his death bravely, with great consideration for those around him. Such untruths! All such terrible, terrible deceits! Why had she allowed herself to be talked into such a charade, instead of insisting on a private family funeral? Three hundred people had nearly filled the cathedral for someone whose meanness and pomposity and self-interest and short fuse — she knew his reputation in the city — were legendary. Perhaps they were simply the mark of a civilized society, these gatherings for sacred rites held equally for the loved and the unloved, for who, in the end, was entitled or sufficiently qualified to judge another's ultimate worthiness? Only — and she was not at all a religious woman — that being or presence who, for want of a better word, we called God and all of us stood before, in the course of time.

But . . . he must have had some remaining feeling for her, some affection? She could not bring herself to believe that he made her his sole beneficiary simply because of mere gentlemanly tradition, or simply to spite his sons, despite plenty of evidence long denied that since they were newborn babies he had secretly resented the energy and affection and time she spent on them.

No, she was not that cynical, not quite. Gentlemen of his generation and upbringing left their widows honourably well cared for, and that Harold had amply done.

His old mates, equally dyed in the wool, would definitely approve, if they knew — and perhaps at least with them he had still laughed, listened to jokes or repeated yet again a hoary old tale himself, just sometimes?

But what fun she was going to have, with the boys' and Mr Fowler's help, managing all this money, giving it away to them and to her grandchildren and two or three charities. Struggling libraries perhaps; a fund for new books?

And she might do a little travelling, while she still had her health, to countries she had yearned all her life to visit: Italy, Japan — there were wonderful tours designed for people of her age — even (she almost giggled) do a cruise . . . yes, wonderful books she could now buy for herself and her grandchildren . . . a new sofa to replace that shabby ancient thing that had belonged to his selfish old crone of a mother . . . free at last of guilt and fear. Her capacity for tolerance, for getting out of bed in the morning, blocking her ears, turning a blind eye, minding her tongue and towards the end, swallowing her bile, had constantly amazed her.

Did you love me yet, Harold? she thought, gazing at the large portrait that he'd expensively commissioned of himself in his silly Freemason's Grand Master gear, just after his MBE in 1975. For more than two decades it had dominated the gloomy living room. She loathed it then in its heavy gilt frame and as she scrutinized it now, she loathed its flattery and dishonesty, the silly Masonic apron and gloves, even more. She'd overhead him instructing the painter summoned to the house: 'My wife wants a portrait with gravitas; my own wish, above all else, is to appear to posterity as—' (he'd had the good grace, she remembered, to feign a little cough, indicating modesty, perhaps?) '—not to put too fine a point on it: kindly? Benign.' Her *Concise Oxford*, well thumbed for the cryptic crosswords which passed the evenings, had supplied 'solemn demeanour' for gravitas; she knew what benign meant and it was not a word she'd ever heard applied to Harold. She looked at the carefully upturned but thin mouth, the 'laugh lines' around the pale blue eyes which did little to counterbalance their essential calculating coldness; the artist, though (she later heard) acquired cheaply, had not been a complete fool, and Harold was too vain to realize he'd been denied the last laugh.

When you put your signature to that will, Harold, was there some faint memory of those happy months before our wedding, your laughing pleasure when after two months a shy nineteen-year-old virgin, deeply in love, told you she would marry you? Is that what your will, if little else in fifty-six years and nine months of marriage, would have me believe? Why did you stop laughing? Why did I?

It gave her the greatest, primitive pleasure to draw back her arm and hurl a nearly full glass of nearly neat gin at the grave countenance on the wall. She should have done that, or something like it, decades ago. And at Harold himself, not this facsimile.

The fine Bavarian crystal exploded and shattered satisfactorily. She picked up and threw another from the silver tray on the sideboard, and another, and another. She threw the heavy square decanter and the engraved tray and a pair of sterling-silver candlesticks. She took off her Italian shoes and threw those, and finally, the three rings from her left hand: the showy engagement ring with its three sapphires, the diamond-heavy eternity ring and the plain white-gold wedding ring.

As the portrait was of oils, the hard objects bounced off and the liquid merely ran down the uneven texture of the paint, but Margery Rex believed she saw the face melt and collapse while she stood exhausted before it and wept.

Maria

We were wed on Boxing Day at the smallest of the four churches considered kosher, the others being, of course, the cathedral in Parnell and those two white churches in Remmers.

Toby wanted it to be asap in a registry office, or someone's nice garden with a hastily summoned celebrant, though after that disastrous office party it was hardly going to be at Olivia's Victoria Avenue mansion, was it? 'Not in a church, please,' he groaned from my rumpled bed, whisky in hand. 'I'm a heathen tosspot and no-one will come; they're all away up north on their yachts or skiing in Colorado. If you won't countenance the registry office, woman, just find a celebrant person in the Yellow Pages.'

He'd reckoned without my determination to have a proper wedding, even with both of us heathens, only two guests and the day being as soon as possible after Christmas when all his dreadful relations would be conveniently away on holiday. You don't wait this long to tie the knot in a registry office. It took me only a few phone calls to find out that the historic little chapel on the hill with the harbour view, plus vicar and organist, had a one-hour slot available midday on Boxing Day, for a fee. Some groom had cancelled four days out.

So there we were on the deep red fleur-de-lis carpet parroting our *Common Prayer Book* vows to a vicar baby-faced enough to be my grandson, with only our erstwhile colleagues Andrew and Fabian from the office to sign as witnesses. Mr and Mrs Tobias Wynde. (As in, Toby always informed people, 'three sheets in the . . .')

The bride wore a Trelise Cooper number in cream chiffon with Italian sandals, carried a single orchid from an Indian dairy, and befitting her first time up the aisle, was completely sober. The groom wore a fifty-year-old Savile Row morning suit belonging to the only uncle of similar girth still talking to him, and having been drinking with his journo mates until dawn prior to his third plunge into matrimony, was sloshed.

Our exit to Widor's 'Toccata' (the splendid choice, the organist told me, of Princess Margaret and many Remmers weddings since) saw Toby's patent leather shoes barely touching the red carpet; he's a big man and it took the three of us to keep him upright as far as shaking the vicar's soft hand on the sunlit lawn, and hearing that this was the exact place where the Constitution of the Anglican Church in New Zealand was signed in 1857, before piling him headfirst and not a moment too soon into the hired white Roller. A Silver Shadow, apparently.

It was, nevertheless, a wedding, with 1 Corinthians 13, verses 1–13 (the ringing King James version, of course), the 23rd Psalm, the traditional vows, two golden rings, a marriage certificate and photographs taken at the porch door by one of Toby's paparazzi mates to prove it. All things considered (and if you don't know that Andrew and Fabian are just outside the frame, literally propping him up), Toby looks quite distinguished and only half-cut, and my smile doesn't look too much like the cat that's swallowed the canary. Our picture did not, however, appear in the society wedding pages of Olivia's magazine, despite Toby's unimpeachable ancestry.

Well, she wouldn't, would she? Not our lovely employer, not after the previous week's office party, which will go down in local publishing history, and which already, two days later, was the subject of a salacious titbit in one paper's 'We Live in a Very Small Town' column, thus:

> Who was the gorgeous brunette magazine editor, daughter of one of Auckland's oldest families, outed as gay, and which four of her loyal senior staff (one also scion of a founding family) quit their jobs on the spot, when a practical joke turned very public and very sour at an exceptionally well-funded office Christmas party? We are told that any passing resemblance to a certain Shakespearian comedy — a love letter of dubious provenance was involved, along with a spy in drag and allegations of mental illness — is 'purely coincidental'.

Now that would mean very little to practically everybody except the major players and possibly not even to the writer, who undoubtedly cobbled together her piece from a number of gleefully incoherent sources. Olivia's outing, the bit of mischief and our resignations were not actually directly connected. To deconstruct will take a little effort. Bear with me, please.

I had risen to be Olivia's indispensable PA from humble beginnings. Business college with barely School Certificate from a country school, various office jobs through my twenties, thirties, forties, when, still unmarried, I was headhunted (*moi?*) by the offshore company which owned a number of local magazines — fashion, gardening, cars, cuisine, babies, boating and so on. My working environment improved overnight: an office with sofas, weekly flowers and even a tiny water view, *darlink*. The legendary Olivia presided over a curiously successful hybrid, a city magazine with fashion, gardening and gossip but also political and social commentary, quality and lengthy interviews, aimed at an older forty-five-plus demographic. A not-quite-so-posh, colonial version, Toby claimed, of *Vogue* in its heyday. I began in her inner sanctum as dogsbody, but applied for the position of PA when I heard a whisper that the incumbent, a prickly dame named Raewyn, was up for review and Olivia wanted someone more mature, without any 'publishing baggage'.

To my delight and Raewyn's outrage, the job was mine. I believe she went as PA to the sales manager of Ezibuy.

Olivia was a dream boss, calm, courteous and clear, though she told me straight up she was still recovering from a family death and please to forgive her occasional moods. Many and various — staff, freelancers, designers, agents, politicians, lawyers, influential people of all kinds — beat a path to her door. I knew one of a PA's principal functions was as gatekeeper. Thus, I soon became very aware of two staff known to me previously only by reputation.

Thus, Toby, pushing sixty, the office drunk, who held down his job as a staff writer (the gossip said) only by Olivia's indulgence, making infrequent but brilliant appearances in the magazine, usually a long, insightful interview with some controversial figure or foolish celebrity rueing the day they consented to talk to him. They both came from Old Auckland families, had moved in the same circles as pampered children and through their riotous teens. Toby had also been a good friend of her late lamented brother. I liked him on sight, even when he wandered unshaven into my office of a morning straight from a night's drinking, wanting to cry on Olivia's shoulder or borrow money; even when I heard that he was long divorced from two wives, alienated from all five offspring, and along the way had somehow lost his grand inherited home and any money he once had. Younger journos told me with awe of his degrees — MAs (Firsts) in history from Auckland and Duke, and his jobs over the years — senior journalist, columnist, political commentator on top papers here and in the UK, correspondent for *Time* for a decade, pieces in the *New Yorker* and you don't get much grander than that — but I sensed that the ambitious ones saw his fall from grace as a terrible warning. For all that, his was a self-deprecating, Hugh Grant natural charm; impeccable manners even when drunk. He always kissed my hand on the way in to see Olivia; in return I warned him when she was moody, or had heard the stories circulating about his latest escapade and he would be advised to lie low for a few days. He praised my efficiency and discretion, made me feel valued, sexy even, and that was something novel for a plain virgin of fifty-three. He told me discreetly which power suits and colours worked on me, and which didn't. He encouraged various younger staff to flirt with me, invited me for a glass of pinot noir in a snooty piano bar occasionally after work, and sent me dirty joke emails. I set my cap at him.

Thus also, one Marvyn, seeking almost daily meetings or phone conversations with Olivia. I disliked the man at first sight. Pushing fifty, our general manager and office bully, a time-pleaser. An accountant by training, never married but (the gossip said) considered straight, not an undeclared gay. Just a soft-spoken, over-promoted prig, a humourless bore obsessed by balance sheets and cashflows and sending out staff memos demanding compliance with this or that austerity measure, constantly advising Olivia to clamp down on departmental budgets and the outrageous demands of overpaid writers and photographers. As the money man, the self-appointed voice of prudence and sound judgement with something to say on most matters at most internal meetings, he smugly gloried in his power. But efficient! A superb grasp of policy, memory for figures, for who said what when and why, for every last detail. But like most huge egos, utterly without irony or wit.

It was inevitable that Toby would soon disclose to me his long-standing loathing of this weasel, this pompous pen-pusher, this pathetic functionary who regularly sent memos questioning his taxi chits and other necessary expenses, and failed to appreciate his bad jokes. Though Marvyn was rather more careful in his dealings with me personally, it was also inevitable that I would soon come to agree.

Thus, Maria and Toby, united in hatred after a particularly noisy Friday-night office drinks session was interrupted by Marvyn working late, complaining of the racket and warning Toby of Olivia's patience wearing thin. Old Auckland and The Functionary exchanged bitter and very personal words. When even I, stone-cold sober, was told to watch my step, I was provoked enough to tell the functionary to piss off.

'The fool thinks I fancy him — and he's half in love with Olivia,' I said after he'd withdrawn sulking, not used to people coming back at him. 'It would be quite intriguing to see how he reacted to some suggestion of interest from her, yes? Perhaps she could write some obscure epistles of love, a fond little email, suggesting a tryst?'

Toby and Andrew were captivated, and not too drunk to picture the mischief that might result. It was simple enough to send an email that night from Olivia's computer after she had left. As well as expressing admiration and romantic interest ('a nice little lunch at Antoine's, perhaps'), I added that he could please her greatly by lightening up his dress code a touch; perhaps a stylist could help him consider something a little more in tune with the office culture ('classic well-cut denim always looks good on mature men') besides his grey suits and old-boy tie.

Oh, the joy! I caught him looking at her in meetings with a sickly, conspiratorial smile, but that was nothing compared to the whole office agape the morning he turned up in a denim jacket, jeans and T-shirt straight out of Ponsonby Road. Adidas sneakers and hair gel, possibly even blonded! Oh dear. Unfortunate choice of stylist, my friend, I thought happily from behind my desk. If I'd been in cahoots with her (or him) myself, I could hardly have hoped for a better result. Olivia's face was a picture, but her amusement quickly turned to bemusement, then irritation. She gave me instructions to say, when he wanted ten minutes of her time, that she was tied up in a meeting. Toby, well, he was beside himself with glee, and if he wasn't hanging round my office to observe the fun for himself, expected text messages at regular intervals. As the days went by, I saw all the signs of an internal battle between our prey's growing discomfiture and puzzlement on the one hand, and his huge ego on the other, reassuring him that this was all to be endured for a proper purpose, his entitlement, a happy ending. Olivia's fuse got shorter by the day. Too, too delicious.

We had not reckoned, however, on her deciding that our general manager needed urgent counselling for what could only be explained as stress, a burnout, even the beginnings of some clinical mental illness, even. He was put on 'special duties' and given a quiet office away from the madding throng, and sent off to twice-weekly sessions with a very fashionable and pricey psychologist. I will not detail here how Toby, urged along by Andrew and Fabian, tormented him. I did nothing to discourage them. What can a mere woman understand of men's minds and choice of tactics, given such opportunities? Eventually (rather too soon in my opinion), they decided enough was enough, and let him gather such wits as remained in his back office in relative peace. The whole office was certainly the quieter.

And so we come to that Christmas party, which got off to a very bad start when the editor-at-large of a rival magazine company got in his cups and let slip that a beautiful young award-winning journalist who had been hired by Olivia some months previously, was in fact — shock, horror — a young (Asian) male in very high-class drag, sent undercover by him to get inside knowledge of the workings and culture of our office. More, she/he unexpectedly reported back that no less a person than Olivia had made advances — I must say I'd wondered about that young woman's ability to get frequent appointments with her editor, though *never* about Olivia's sexuality — which was not an acceptable state of affairs as the editor-at-large and he/she were now officially an item. The assembled company of nearly a hundred people was suitably agog. The legendary and exceedingly well-connected Olivia, once married, single by choice, frequently linked in the gossip columns with glamorous and/or wealthy men, *gay all along*?

Fabian told us later that both the Italian-suited young person in question and Olivia were understandably pleased for the diversion when Marvyn, dressed as a Roman patrician for the fancy-dress party he'd naughtily been told it was, now burst in on the chattering throng, waving an email print-out.

You sent this, he accused Olivia, who in turn, her mind working furiously and being no fool, looked around the now-silent room for me, her handmaiden.

But Toby and I, warned by a text message from Fabian that Marvyn was on his way, had already slipped away for the simpler pleasures of a candlelit dinner *à deux* at Toto's. Two bottles of Moët later, I'm not quite sure which of us actually popped the question. It may have been me; though I've always let Toby think the notion was his alone.

Back in the spotlight, Fabian nobly took the rap for us both — the email was his and Toby's idea, he admitted with suitable remorse and decorum to the hushed crowd, and Maria had been but the instrument. If Olivia so desired, our letters of resignation would be on her desk in the morning. (Olivia coolly beat us to it:

on arrival, a letter on our desks informed us that personal effects were to be cleared and keys handed in by 3 p.m.)

But our Marvyn had not been denied his big moment. Hearing the truth behind some of the torments visited on him of late in his back office, brushing aside Olivia's attempt at sympathy, and apoplectic with fury, he clutched his toga around him and stormed from the party vowing revenge — and into the city gossips' long memories.

After our Boxing Day wedding, I got an emergency passport at vast cost and we flew off to a Fijian island for two hot and peaceful weeks. The recent military coups and general political unrest meant less to one-time war correspondent Tobias Wynde than the cheap deals being offered by desperate resort owners with all-night beachside bars and a challenging repertoire of cocktails. He drank, slept and read; I discovered that he could do with, but didn't believe in, Viagra, learnt to snorkel and wondered at life's strange turns.

Fast forward through that summer — a testing time of weighing up Our Assets: two poky townhouses (mine owned and his rented) in drab parts of the city, two small cars, my modest savings, Toby's reputation and scrapbook of past triumphs, my CV and new-found talent for name-dropping — and Our Liabilities: no proper job between us, no likelihood of references from Olivia, little ready money, one partner's decrepit and dependant parent and one partner's expensive and set-in-concrete drinking habit.

At times, lying awake at night listening to Toby's bass bassoon snoring, I wondered about the cost of becoming a certificated Wynde, even if I had yet to meet his ancient parents or any of his siblings' or cousins' families I vaguely knew existed from pictures in society pages. Even if he was an outcast, Toby was still born and bred Old Auckland, and could never understand (if and when any contact with his family happened) that I would always feel a badly dressed gatecrasher with an unacceptable accent.

Suffice to say that by the autumn we were living in a reasonable inner-city apartment, and I'd convinced my sad little mother she'd be far happier with her peer group in a rest-home in Glen Eden.

I was again working. Hallelujah, the androgynous young person who had been Olivia's undoing apparently sang my praises to his editor-at-large, sufficiently well for me to be offered a position in their marketing department. Promotion, better pay, chance to learn at first hand about publicity campaigns, production of printed material and event management; what more could a one-time farmer's daughter want, though I don't imagine Olivia was best pleased. I thought of writing her a friendly note, but decided not even Olivia's gracious and subtle manners would prompt her to reply; nothing would be gained. So I moved on.

And I was beginning to devise a grand and secret plan, which was not so much about my own career, at least not yet, but what to do about Toby.

Make no mistake, I'd read in women's mags about the silly deluded females who despite all evidence to the contrary thought they (and they alone) could reform the men they married. Cure their alcoholism/drug habit/gambling/philandering/selfishness/bad language/whatever. Or the gold-diggers who bought into a vicious and endless family fight by marrying some randy old widower expecting to end up with all or most of his money, and the sooner the better. Of course, the most extreme examples end up in a courtroom faced with either a stepchild's wrath or a charge of murder, or both.

I had no illusions about Toby, none whatsoever. He was a basket case, an alcoholic, and had been for most of his life. Even at university he'd developed an insatiable taste for Moët, Stella

Artois and neat Glenmorangie. He wasn't above a DB Bitter or cardboard chardonnay if that was all he could get. As we all know, journalism has long encouraged heavy drinkers — as long as they get the stories and don't badmouth the bosses, who cares?

At some point his Rich List family (estimated fortune from importing/liquor/property interests, $375 million) gave up on him. He'd long been seriously offside with Father, for choosing the heady excitements of journalism ahead of the Family Firm; with Mother, for taking away grandchildren at various times to live in London and Toronto; with two dull Older Brothers, upstanding heirs to Wynde Inc., for having more fun; and with all the rest of them for his unpatriotic, early objection to the All Black tour of South Africa in 1960 and the Vietnam war and his generally traitorous left-wing, anti-American, anti-Establishment views. He voted Labour! At some further point — about five years ago and quite why, his lips were sealed — he was told by a lawyer's letter to expect nothing from either of his parents' estates, nor to have any future input of any kind into the several trusts they tightly controlled.

So, wedded to one disinherited and largely unemployable old soak, no-one could accuse me of being a gold-digger, or Florence Nightingale. To all outward appearances, since he was now sponging on me rather than Olivia, the only thing to have changed was that Toby had gone down-market. My investment in him would take a little time and effort to reap the dividend I had in mind.

The trick was, of course, to have Toby think it was his idea to cash in on the insatiable public demand for memoirs, and the more brutally frank your revelations, the more shocking your problem or treatment at the hands of others, the better. When I started looking around in bookshops and the library catalogues for such books, there seemed to be no shame any more. You could serve time for greed and fraud and come back on your own TV show, do some truly evil deed and earn untold zillions for your story. You could even go on being President of the United States while everyone knew you weren't above having oral sex in the Oval Office while discussing foreign policy on the telephone.

I totted up Toby's credentials for a best-seller. A drinking problem slowly ruining a brilliant career was nothing new or special, but Toby could add to the mix his famous and not very likeable family: father a tyrant and breeder of obscenely expensive racehorses, mother a gin-soaked retired charity queen, sister a recluse believed to spend her days doing rather fine petit point. The two ex-wives were both anorexic shopaholics and botox junkies, thick as planks, one batty old uncle was a notorious womanizer with a very large professionally crewed vintage yacht, yet another's addiction was nubile young men and gambling, poker and backgammon on a majestic scale.

Then there was his own rebellious upbringing, those riotous university years, three decades as a controversial journalist in five countries — and he could write, when reasonably sober, like a dream. In his heyday he'd interviewed politicians, royalty, corporate bosses, generals, judges, celebrities, victims and crooks, covered scandals, wars and conflict of every kind, written about everything except himself. He'd appeared as witness in high-profile trials, been threatened with more than a few defamation suits and death threats and lived fearlessly on the edge of violence, wars, social upheavals — but in the end had fallen victim to a deadly twentieth-century malady. Yet I knew the thought of a decent life without the pleasures of drinking was simply unimaginable; he was long past the reach of counsellors or any well-meant suggestions of rehab. He was a (mostly) loveable drunk. 'I'd rather be pissed-poor than a fucking miserable old teetotaller,' was one of the few comments he made to me on the subject. 'Not ready to go out to grass just yet, m'dear.' There were, he chuckled, a good few stories in him yet, a few scandals and scoops, a few more bastards, silly cows and general lowlifes to be called to account.

'So it's time to write your book,' I whispered.

Such a crying shame we're having this launch today without him. It was his naughty idea to combine the book's launch and the funeral. 'They'll all turn up, you see,' he croaked from his hospital bed, 'the journo and media crowd to farewell another old fallen warrior, and the Wyndies in force to make damn sure I'm safely dead and boxed up. They can be titillated about the book at the same time. Bloody marvellous!'

And here they all are, on a beautiful but cold June morning, pouring into the wooden St Mary's church next to the cathedral in Parnell for the funeral of Tobias Wynde, unsuspecting that they will also be treated to the launch of his memoir *Breaking Wynde: a journalist's tale*. The silver-bearded archdeacon in his white linen frock has just told me the historic building, one of Auckland's architectural treasures, seats around 1100.

'You definitely made the right decision to have it here, Mrs Wynde,' he purrs. 'A great tribute. Your husband made a wonderful contribution to public debate in this country. I used to read him in *The Times*, wasn't it?' No doubt his family would have agreed that this was the appropriate choice, if I'd asked them; Wynde family funerals are probably always held in the cathedral, or small private ones in the little chapel where the Constitution of the Anglican Church in New Zealand was signed in 1857.

I wondered, as I stood a trifle nervously at the porch door an hour ago in my cream Trelise Cooper under a tent-like black pashmina, whether they would acknowledge me or pretend I didn't exist and walk right past. But Old Auckland will not be less than gracious in its inspection of the black sheep's down-market widow. I imagine they take their cue from HRH, shaking a frosty hand over the years with Wallis Simpson, various Spencers or Camilla. So too would they offer a kid-gloved hand or a double air-kiss, with condoling murmurs: My dear Maria, so sad . . . Dear Toby, such a rascal . . . but what a wordsmith he was. At least it was quick . . . He didn't linger, did he, poor lamb, ghastly when they linger . . . Aren't you coping well! And a trifle cuttingly: I don't suppose he would have been very easy, and Don't we all love Trelise, bless her.

Well, yes, I think, he wasn't and we do, while they greet the archdeacon as the dear old friend he no doubt is and troop inside. I eyeball grim-faced Father, waxwork Mother, upstanding Older Brothers, homespun Sister. In the group that musters in the courtyard are various geriatrics who must be Father's generation and the slightly less decrepit who must be the many cousins and their wives, along with a few of the third generation. Glad of sunglasses, well aware that I am being openly looked up and down, I am limply clasped by the two stick-insect ex-wives, their partners and four of Toby's five adult children, two of whom look unnervingly like him and another two who have the good grace to be nearly crying. All of the whanau are exceedingly well-dressed in unrelieved black — finest linen, Scots tweed, Italian wool and leather — with many gold chains, rings and costly stones hung about their persons, giving off that fragrant air of privilege that comes from never having to give a toss in their whole lives what anything costs.

Coping well, you think? I am, I am, thank you for asking. So would you, if you knew what I know, learned in two years of marriage and a month of saying goodbye, and what I further found out only yesterday.

Besides my own editor-at-large and his Asian Ken doll —

sorry, partner — plus a gratifyingly large contingent from the office, I have no idea who are the many others who have crossed the courtyard and after a few words disappeared inside. Quite a few introduce themselves as old mates from this or that paper, this or that assignment overseas in the sixties/seventies/eighties; others as CEOs or senior staff of various media and publishing houses. A bunch of lawyers, his doctors, other survivors from King's Prep in the 1940s and Christ's College in the 1950s. There are some city councillors, a mayor or two, a few MPs, two Cabinet Ministers (Culture and the Arts, Communications). I am surprised, though thinking about it perhaps I shouldn't be, at the younger generation represented, from not only print but all branches of the media. I recognize a few names from radio and faces from television. It seems that to them he was some sort of a legend. This perhaps explains the *Herald* photographer with the digital camera of arresting size and (a touch alarmingly) a crew from TV3. I had been asked by *Breaking Wynde*'s publisher if I'd agree to their publicity people approaching the media.

The lovely Marvyn, of whom nothing has been heard for over two years? Unlikely, I think, though his social-climbing instincts or vow of revenge might urge him towards the direction of Parnell on this day, lugubrious in a black suit. I keep a weather eye.

Olivia arrives, fashionably furred and booted and not quite late, just as Fabian and Andrew are suggesting we should go and take our seats in the front pew. 'Nice to see you again, Maria,' she says kindly, 'though not in the happiest of circumstances. I gather his suffering wasn't too protracted. He was a great writer.' She exchanges pleasantries with Fabian about the beauty of the white church and its panelled interior which will be like a fridge; for this particular public appearance, she is on the arm of an infamous male TV executive who has just been dumped noisily and simultaneously by both his board and his wife. 'As Toby's last employer,' Olivia says looking me coolly in the eye, 'I would happily have contributed a eulogy.'

'Yes, he was always sad you had to "let him go",' I say sweetly. 'I decided to ask only Fabian.'

The choice of speakers, pallbearers and music was actually all Toby's. The archdeacon visiting his hospital bed warmly welcomed a stated preference for the traditional service, dust to dust, ashes to ashes etcetera, none of this modern write-your-own nonsense. Just one speaker — certainly none of the whanau, please, nor embarrassing obsequies contributed from the pews — and as one of the more presentable journos, Fabian fitted the bill as well as any. Andrew would read an extract from *The Prophet*, and the Anglican faithful and heathens alike could let fly with 'Crimond' and 'Praise My Soul'. Pallbearers were trickier, but he asked for Fabian, Andrew, his long-time lawyer, my editor-at-large, myself, and if he could find one drop of charitable blood in his veins, his eldest son. As for the music, Toby made it easy: there'll be a competent organist up in the loft, tell him just anything by J.S. Bach. The great D-minor toccata, perhaps, 'for when I'm finally trundling out feet first — let it rip, baby.'

I manage my composure through that testing moment of first seeing the coffin sitting there draped with the White Ensign (he did his CMT in the late 50s in the Navy and was a Navy correspondent in Malaya for a year or so), the welcomes and prayers, the hymns, readings and solemn words. The church is about two-thirds full; about 700. Fabian rises nobly to the occasion, although taking twice the agreed ten minutes to read his chronological tribute to Toby's full and rich sixty-one years. Of his three wives, only Maria is acknowledged for the happiness she brought Toby in his final two years, along with her unstinting support in the completion of his last work, the memoir which will shortly be launched. I hear a rustle of surprise behind me as Fabian invites the publisher, Mr Jordan Bellamy, to come forward. The archdeacon, seated in front of the choir stalls, encourages him benignly.

It's now, as Jordan takes the lectern and two eager publicity girls wheel a large display stand into the centre of the aisle, just below the highly polished coffin on its trolley, that I feel, if I'm not careful, I might lose it. The girls are handing Jordan two specially flown-in advance copies of *Breaking Wynde* and behind it, the display stand boasts enticing A1-size posters of the cover and a rather solemn portrait of the deceased author. The title and the name, prominent features of the design, are partly obscured by a sealed band of heavy brown paper wrapped round the book.

Unsurprisingly, a titter or two reaches me. I steal a glance at the thirty or so whanau seated across the aisle — at four pews of profiles set in stone. I can almost hear the gurgle of their stomachs sinking. Is there no end to it, they are wondering, even as our infamous son/brother/father/cousin lies there in a coffin, laughing his head off? More importantly, just what is in the book?

I nearly do lose it, listening to Jordan's soft voice detailing how Toby first approached him with an explosive sample chapter of a promised memoir, and how Toby and myself long-lunched with him to put together a contract. We were tough negotiators. But louder still in my head is Toby's croaking bitter laughter — the day he first thought that the publication date of the book and his own departure for the great daily newspaper in the sky might conveniently coincide.

He'd been in hospital for two dreadful alcohol-free weeks, first rushed in after a blackout and collapse, then a few days of inconclusive tests, then more blackouts, scans for brain damage and a liver problem. The prognosis, while not crystal clear, was not good either. His blood pressure and heart rate were haywire.

He appeared increasingly exhausted by the struggle, unable to remember simple things, weaker by the day. It seemed there was a serious problem with the liver. 'I am dying, Egypt,' he muttered darkly that day when I arrived with the usual clean pyjamas and bunches of black Californian grapes, but perked up at the thought of the possibilities provided by a posthumous launch which his whanau would find themselves dutifully attending.

'There's no index!' he cried suddenly, exultantly. I said, 'I thought you were very upset and critical about that.' 'Yes, I was,' he said, 'because it was for reasons of saving money. No index drives reviewers mad. But here — it's fucking terrific!' He slapped the coarse hospital sheets in glee, sending sections of the weekend newspapers scattering to the polished floor.

'Why so?' I asked. 'Because, my mettle of India, they will come to the launch and afterwards they will do what guests at a launch of an autobiography always do.' He nodded me on. I suggested, 'Look straight at the index to see how they've fared?

Toby said, 'No index? *Pas possible*, no *index*? *Mon dieu!*' Together, we chorused happily, 'Then they'll *have* to buy the book!' Toby's coughing fit lasted a few minutes, then he spluttered, 'Even better . . . if we put some sort of plain brown wrapper around it, they can't window-shop.'

The emerging marketeer in me said, 'Brilliant.' The devoted wife in me thought 'Right on!' when in the very next breath, he declared, 'Christ, I've got a literary estate now! Got a pen and paper there, my sweet? I need to re-write my will. Call the lawyer in. Can't have the dreadful children thinking . . .' He broke off for more coughing. I tenderly offered him water.

Jordan has hit his straps. This, he declares, waving *Breaking Wynde: a journalist's tale* aloft, is one of the most savage, penetrating commentaries yet written on twentieth-century New Zealand society, political life and world affairs. It is not only

Toby Wynde's amazing life story, here and abroad, told with all the brilliance, energy, passion and yes, painful self-knowledge that characterized his writing, but also his last testament, his plea — using the tragedy of his own life as a metaphor — for a better understanding of how Western society, led by the self-interest of the baby-boomers and the insatiable greed of rich and powerful industrial barons and multi-nationals, has taken false, dark paths which can only lead to ever greater polarization between rich and poor and financial, ecological and social disaster. Cor.

Fabian and Andrew and the people behind me might now be thinking I'm overcome with tears of grief for Toby and the human race. My sunglasses and two of Toby's best linen handkerchiefs are obscuring the reality: tears of laughter.

Laughter for and with Toby, his irrepressible, irreverent spirit for which I truly honestly came to have great affection. With Toby, for the thought of all his family members hastening into the nearest bookshop straight after the funeral, finding they had to wait a week for the book to arrive, paying their $49.95 and back in the car park sitting in the Merc thumbing through the pages to see if and how and why a black sheep with nothing to lose finally deals to the authoritarian, conservative and powerful family that threw him into boarding school aged seven, pressured him to perform and conform without any questioning of his ambitions and values, and threw him to the dogs. Naturally they were fearful. Likewise would other old foes be making a beeline for bookshops with the very same qualms. And laughing with Toby, because I know exactly what was in his early drafts, and what the lawyers said could conceivably be retained if he was prepared for the very real possibility of being sued — 'Fuck it, Paul, you know I fucking am,' was his response to that — and what hair-raising passages or comments, assuredly, without *question*, Toby, *must* be taken out. He'd got reckless, braver and crueller, as he got into it. And believe me, what finally was approved by the legal team for the 600-page hardback was still pretty incendiary stuff. Many people had good reason to be alarmed.

And tears of amusement for myself, who everyone thought was a fool to saddle myself with a tragic old lush like Toby, long past his use-by date. Because they'd seen nothing of late under his byline in Olivia's rag or anywhere else, they assumed he was merely pottering around at home or killing time propping up bars with equally pathetic mates, bloody lucky to find a woman silly enough to support the sad last drink-sodden act of a once-admired life.

I'd known all along he had a terrific, important book in him. Those two years were the busiest but happiest time of my life. (Mama died in her sleep four months after our marriage, and left me her very modest savings.) My own working hours were mostly predictable. At 6.30 a.m. I'd leave Toby in bed, fairly confident that during the day he might go out for coffee and get through a bottle or two of pinot noir but probably would also put in several hours at his laptop, either writing or researching via the vast e-library online. We got heavy-duty broadband as soon as it was available for the very purpose. After dinner, tucked up together in bed with a bottle of Glenmorangie, he'd read me the results; I would be suitably amused, touched, scandalized, even shocked to the core at what I learned of the skullduggery, cruelty and greed he'd confronted or stumbled across and put himself at risk to expose. In the first month or so, he needed industrial-strength encouragement and flattery to get down even 2000 or 3000 words, but it soon grew to 5000, up to even 8000 words a day with only light psychological maintenance. My confidence in my ability as editor, to spot occasional repetitions, anomalies and inconsistencies, grew with what I was also absorbing at work. I'm a quick study.

The title was mine. Brilliant, eh! Not just scatological, but embedding the notion of the breaking-down of a free spirit — but importantly, an action not fully complete, not broken. Those who read his book will find out that his spirit was firing on all cylinders right to the end. He got to 170,000 words inside nine months. Enough! said excited publisher Jordan Bellamy, dollar signs in his eyes, enough already! But he couldn't stop, and I encouraged him all the way, at some cost to my sleeping hours and general equanimity.

So, back to the compulsive youthful joy of writing, at the top of his game: a novel next. A political thriller, set in the Europe of the 1980s he remembered. Rome, Venice, Paris and a village in the Cotswolds. It's terrific, believe me — move over, John le Carré. The villain is an appalling creation, an accountant he admitted was a combination of Marvyn and his father. He finished it at white heat the week before his collapse. (Never let it be said that I in any way hounded him; I simply provided the environment for his creativity to flourish, and the expectation of nocturnal pleasures as a reward.) No-one knows about this manuscript yet, not even Jordan. It's possible that sheer exhaustion contributed to the blackouts and the final collapse, but I think he knew, better than anyone, just how little time he had. Jordan had fast-tracked the editing and production side of *Breaking Wynde* in under four months, good timing, as it turned out. I'm glad my dear Toby had that profound pleasure of holding the advance copy in his hand. 'Thank you, Maria, my little muse,' he said.

For the novel, I'm looking for an overseas literary agent, an international publisher. The advance alone could be worth millions, plus film rights, serial rights, radio rights, translations into seventeen or more languages; the possibilities are considerable. I daresay Jordan won't be best pleased, but I have to put Toby's name and rekindled reputation first. And you might be thinking, it's my superannuation, and you'd be right. We wrote his will together.

Andrew is digging me in the ribs, to stand for the solemn last prayers, the blessing and the carrying out. The rimu casket is heavy; as I said, he was a big man. The funeral director insists that the surly eldest son goes in front, with me between him and my editor-at-large, probably for reasons of the distribution of weight among the stronger bearers. Some battles are not worth fighting. We pass the whanau and the Cabinet Ministers, the many suits, the women's winter pale faces.

The D-minor toccata thunders around the high wooden rafters, magnificent.

As we slowly make our way down the aisle, I lift my eyes towards the entrance, for a glimpse of the waiting black hearse. I notice a black-suited figure standing slightly out from the end of the pew like the Angel of Death. I will pass within less than an arm's length. It occurs to me he could put out a leg to trip either the eldest son, or me, or all of us. He could slip a blade between my ribs. But Marvyn just raises a cocked hand to waist height, and the gesture of the forefinger and the gun-shooter's glint in the eye add up to a clear message. 'Haven't forgotten,' they warn. He's sallow as ever, and has put on weight. I don't see him again as people mill around the courtyard, the hearse departs and we head for the cup of tea and club sandwiches in the adjoining cloisters. I'll lose no sleep over Marvyn.

But there is a happy coda to this story of Maria and her sadly departed Toby. The next day, while I am sorting out his clothes, Olivia rings. Other than the funeral, it's over two years since we had any contact.

She says, 'How are you, Maria?'

I say warily, 'I'm fine.'

She continues, 'I have to say, Toby's book is a triumph.' There's almost a chuckle in her voice. 'I think I've personally come off rather lightly. Compared to some.'

I reply, 'He admired and liked you, Olivia. And he well understood why you had to fire him, and me.'

A slight pause, then she says, 'How's the job? Enjoying marketing?'

I reply, 'Very much, thank you. I think it suits me.' But this is not why she's ringing. What is? To offer me a position? Unlikely.

'The reason I'm ringing — ah, this is rather irregular, and off the record . . .'

I assure her, sincerely, 'Of course.'

'. . . but I thought you might be interested to know. I have an old friend who works in A and E at Auckland Hospital.'

Olivia's network of old friends, old lovers, spies and informers at every level of society is reputedly unsurpassed, but what's to the purpose?

'He has just signed the death certificate of another former employee of mine, brought in close to death after a cardiac arrest. He said the ambos had been so busy trying to keep him alive they didn't take much notice of a letter he'd just started writing, still clutched in his fist. They couldn't revive him. It took a bit of effort to divest him of the letter. It's probably stretching a point to suppose a book sitting open on the desk, a recently published and controversial memoir, the letter and the cardiac arrest were in any way related.'

'Yes, it probably is.'

'So sad. Not all that old. He was a loyal servant of the company for many years. I believe he'd been hiring himself out as a financial consultant since he left us. Anyway, I thought I'd let you know before you read the death notices or saw it in a gossip column somewhere. I'll courier the letter to you.'

'Thank you, Olivia.' There didn't seem anything more to say. So I waited.

'You're a cool customer, Maria, I'll say that.' Takes one to know one — high praise from Her. 'If you ever think of needing a change of workplace, give me a call. My marketing department is struggling a little at the moment.'

'Thank you. I'll keep it in mind.'

'*Ciao* — and good luck.'

The desperately creased letter, smoothed out flat inside a clear plastic file, arrives by urgent one-hour courier. I don't doubt she's kept a copy, for her records, though I don't think she'll stoop as low as dropping a hint to her own mag's gossip columnist. Not the classy Olivia, with far bigger fish to fry. We live in a small town.

Poor Marvyn had got only as far as his opening salvo. I can imagine him hunched over his desk bristling with indignation and outrage, blood pressure and heart-rate rising with every passing second, that black-and-gold Parker fountain pen scratching at the linen paper. *To the former Miss Maria Handisides: You take me for a fool, but I can see your evil hand in this publication, madam, your venom stamped on every page. Not content with losing me my position — God forgive that.*

Goodness, that he should credit humble me with even one momentary flash of Toby's literary brilliance. I should be so lucky. Thus the whirligig of time will see me secure in the knowledge that I will never again have to give a toss what anything costs. A true Wynde, at last.

Did I mention? The day before the funeral, an English bank emailed Toby's lawyer about a forgotten account in his name, with Pounds Sterling 24,072.16 in it, some employer-insurance scheme, apparently overlooked and not drawn on since 1993. Any more like it, I wonder?

Vanessa

Poor Vanessa once informed me it was a well-known fact around the town — behind him, in every classroom, staff room, shop or library he visits, Hugo Markham leaves a trail of broken hearts.

Work it out — this was not, I think, just a fifty-one-year-old girl's embarrassing and ill-judged flattery, displaying a regrettable lapse of taste. I'm a working scriptwriter, I understand subtext — what Robert McKee defines as 'the life under the surface, the thoughts and feelings concealed by behaviour', something like that. So, I gave Vanessa the wry, conspiratorial smile she was hoping for, and muttered hasty and dismissive self-deprecations, but actually, to be honest, putting aside the subtext, the lady wasn't totally wrong. You could add to her list the cast of every play I've ever been in. I happily admit it — I make the ladies laugh, feel good and a little risqué, because they've only ever been respectable small-town citizens, their lives unfolding to a totally predicable script, but I'm a survivor from the naughty seventies. I'm a Gen-u-ine Ageing Hippie with seriously slim hips and tight jeans, a propensity to bare feet and longish hair (sometimes fetchingly ponytailed), an anarchic wit and a surprisingly tony British accent; I'm not noticeably degenerate from a decade or more of magic mushrooms (among much else), aromatherapy, yoga and advanced Zen Buddhism, along with significant time spent as a roadie working on lighting rigs for the Bee Gees, but even with a docile little wife and two kids living the simple, rural Good Life in beautiful New Zealand,

I'm not completely reconstructed either. I entertain and intrigue both the ladies and the men, and I listen with unwavering eye contact, utterly focused, oozing empathy — there's no-one else but you in the room — isn't it so easily done? Like a latter-day Bill Clinton. They eat out of my hand.

I haven't thought of Vanessa in nearly ten years now. When a show is over, it's over. Though I have to admit, I've always kept that file not quite closed, for the irresistible film script I might one day write on crazed, obsessive-compulsive love, or infatuation, or caprice, or erotomania or whatever you like to call this particular and peculiar self-indulgent perversity. Death makes it rather specially compelling and appealing, know what I mean? Normally, I never read the local rag. Maybe my wife left it open on the kitchen table yesterday for me to see, maybe she didn't and it's just one of life's odder coincidences. I won't bother to check one way or the other; unsurprisingly, Jane came to loathe Vanessa with every bone in her body.

But my eye catches the name, along with the words 'inquest' and 'alcohol poisoning'. My first reaction is one of surprise (she didn't drink) and annoyance (I don't want this particular knowledge) in about equal measure. Momentarily, as I scrunch up the paper into tight balls for the bin, I hear an echo of that slightly over-loud laugh; I feel those following, wanting eyes, the body language of yearning and desire, the excuses for contact that she naively thought so well concealed. Then I hear Kerry and Anna yelling from the garden, reminding me I'd promised to play cricket with them. Jane has ridden off over the hills to give one of the ponies a whirl. I'll work on my latest script idea tonight, after cricket and supper and *The Simpsons*. When an autumn Saturday is this still and bright — when the view from the patio down to the willow-lined creek and across the distant paddocks is that golden and glorious — when I congratulate myself, as I very frequently do, that for fourteen whole mostly marvellous years I've been fully 12,000 miles away from London sleet and my unspeakable parents — who needs to be reminded of the very bad dream that is Mistress Ford?

I'm intrigued that the great Harold Bloom clearly detests the *Merry Wives*. According to Gary Taylor's marvellous book on reinventing Shakespeare — do you know it? Fascinating! — the *Wives* was for two or three centuries the Bard's most popular comedy, by far the most frequently performed of any of his plays in Restoration England. Bloom gives it four grudging pages in his book, out of something like 700, from memory. I wouldn't give it the time of day now, either. To be honest with you, I wish never to hear a line from the play again.

Taking it from the top: about twelve years ago, this newly arrived teacher of English at this coastal township's area school greatly pleased the local am-dram scene by writing a comedy for them. Full-length, local setting, a cast of identifiable archetypes, plenty of in-jokes and great one-liners; it went down a treat. Admittedly, since I had this opportunity handed to me on a plate, I wrote a good big part for myself: bumbling but good-hearted husband, a sort of Richard Briers *Good Life* character, an Australian immigrant at loggerheads with the council and local iwi over Maori middens and priceless greenstone artefacts discovered on his property. In blissful ignorance as a recent immigrant myself, I could be very politically incorrect, very daring, as rude as I liked. I have to say it was a bloody good example of what's now come to be rather grandly known as 'community theatre'. Yes, I was also director. And I don't mind admitting I just love doing accents. My Ocker is bloody spot on, matey, and my Welsh not bad, look you.

Then, following this success, some fuckwits on the drama club board decided, God knows why, to do a Shakespeare and homed in on *Merry Wives*, that well-known farce about middle-aged love. Actually I know exactly why they chose it. The chairman of the school's Board of Trustees is a bulky amateur thespian with more self-confidence and hair than talent, and possessed of a lifelong yearning for Falstaff — or what Bloom calls the pseudo-Falstaff. In this hick little town, one of the serious *Henrys* was out of the question, but the *Wives* — the inimitable Sir John in love — would do. All that farcical stuff involving the laundry basket and cross-dressing would bring in the punters.

Hugo would, of course, direct? They didn't need to know that for me this was actually virgin territory; I'd not done a Shakespeare before, as either actor or director. I learned of a BBC video, duly acquired on a trip to Auckland. The lovely Prunella as Mistress Page — who will ever forget her Sybil in *Fawlty Towers*? Judy Davis and Ben Kingsley terrific as the Fords. A Mistress Quickly who was not at all funny, merely tedious, didn't work for me and a lacklustre Falstaff, confirming incidentally that Bloom was right — there's something unpleasant, meretricious, about Sir John's bumbling attempts at courtship and the humiliation it brings. I watched the video a number of times. It certainly would be a challenge, but with the inevitable shortage of competent men, I suggested to the Board, perhaps I could have a bit of fun myself, as the ranting, jealous Master Ford? (He's the jealous husband who gets to beat up Falstaff, who is disguised as an old woman and trying to escape from a pathetic attempt to seduce Ford's luscious and scheming wife in her own home.) Over to you, they said. It's not every lowly teacher of English and one-time flower child who gets a chance to publicly beat up his school Board of Trustees chairman.

But alcohol poisoning? I'm quite sure Vanessa didn't drink. Or not at the time she heard me at a staff meeting before school, announcing auditions for my home-grown piece of 'community theatre' and appealing for production crew. I'd seen her name on the drama-club list, so wasn't surprised when she came straight over and introduced herself as one of the two part-time school librarians, and a bit of a writer too — just short stories, she said, nothing serious, though she did enter competitions from time to time. She'd been shortlisted twice, she added in response to my query.

The lady was diffident, nervous, without charm. 'I'd like to audition . . . if you think there's something suitable . . . nothing too big,' she stammered. Her voice was not encouraging, slight, girlish, and I was still finding Kiwi accents hard to take. To be honest, I still do. In appearance, she was your standard-issue archetypal librarian: dumpy, greying, glasses hanging off a chain, eager to please, dull of dress and demeanour, a chin whisker or six. Of menopausal age, but pleasant enough. I said, 'It's set in the local council offices.' She said, 'I've always wanted to wear a power suit.' I said, 'There's a forty-something communications manager who's smart but stone deaf. Only a few lines, but she's on stage a fair bit of the time.' She said, 'Sounds right up my alley.' 'You'll have to audition, of course, to be fair,' I said, smiling kindly. She said, too hastily, 'Oh, of course, of course.'

I didn't cast her. I cast Lillian — yes, yes, I plead guilty, she was the local newspaper proprietor's wife who turned up out of the blue. She had a slight lisp, and though no actor, she looked right enough. I know which side my publicity bread is buttered, matey. Vanessa, who'd arrived at her audition visibly trembling, now sidled up in the staff room before school, apologizing for wasting my time and offering to be the prompt. Since I had no other takers for this thankless job, and she had free access to the library photocopier, I accepted gracefully. No alarm bells were ringing; actually, we'd shared some pleasant lunch hours discovering similar literary tastes: John Donne's sonnets, Wilde, Causley, Larkin. Dickens and Philip Pullman, Marina Warner, some contemporary Americans and post-colonial Indians. The Bard, naturally; she'd surprisingly read Aphra Benn and Wycherley, too, even Pinter and Beckett and Sam Shepherd. We agreed wholeheartedly that C.S. Lewis and Tolkien and Eoin Colfer were all in varying degrees over-praised but disagreed about Rowling. I'd only to think of the pleasure that lady had given my kids. Vanessa's had left home, of course. She had a husband, an electrician I think, an extremely forgettable person. She thought Rowling clever enough but for all her reputation and impact, lightweight.

In rehearsals, she soon became much, much more than prompt. She became a virtual AD *and* ASM. No cast member was too formidable to scold for failure to learn lines (which was often) or being late (equally often); nothing was too taxing or time-consuming to make my job easier; no joke of mine, either on-stage or off, too feeble for a smile or a full-on laugh; no rewrite or memo to the cast or draft for publicity handouts was too long or messy to type and print out, multiple copies if necessary. She was first to arrive, always cheerful, always a starter for after-rehearsal coffees, last to leave. She had Stamina. She had Commitment. She had Enthusiasm and Energy. In spades.

It would be fair to say that without Vanessa the play would probably have gone on even more under-rehearsed than it did. (Thank God for audiences both indulgent and ignorant.) And it would be true to say that from about week two I well knew why.

Week three, the newspaper proprietor's wife, a veritable fruitcake, threw a tantie and pulled out. From not only the play, as it turned out, but also from her marriage, the town and the country. Lisping Lillian did a runner to the Gold Coast with the freelance photographer who was supposed to be doing our publicity stills. Day-yam! So, admittedly with a few misgivings on my part, Vanessa got to wear her op-shop power suit. By that time she'd got down virtually the whole play, word-perfect without book, so she simply became an on-stage prompt. Useful insurance, I have to say, against poorly prepared actors missing cues even at the tech rehearsals, or blaming me loudly for unsayable lines and wanting to be frightfully post-modern and rewrite the script off the cuff. She was a stickler, I'll give her that; you might even go further and say, something of a blessed anchor, for the whole cast, and for me wearing my triple writer/actor/director hats, at some cost, I have to say, to my sanity. As Barbara, the deaf communications manager, she quite pleasantly surprised me with some nice touches of business compensating for the few lines, stealing a few laughs; and in make-up and power suit at the dress rehearsal, eyes sparkling, flirtatious, more than a few kilos lighter, hair a few shades blonder, spectacles ditched for contact lenses — well, she looked fifteen years younger and quite unrecognisable, light years away from the dumpy librarian with the dangling glasses and chin hairs I'd first sighted in the school library. Her chain-smoking, ordinary Kiwi bloke of a husband couldn't take his eyes off her.

Somehow word about the upcoming *Merry Wives* got around. She came to my dressing room one night, blushing and biting her nails like a schoolgirl. Finally she got the words out: 'Hugo, I'd like to audition for one of the wives, if you think it's worth it, if I've got even a snowflake of a chance?'

You've probably gathered that by this time alarm bells were definitely ringing, loud and fucking clear. I demurred, as usual, ttered the usual twaddle about the protocols of auditions and a bit of a rush on because there weren't ever many fun parts for mature ladies, and in this play there were no less than three, but I guess I decided there and then to have a bit of fun, know what I mean, and risk it — incurring the wrath of the two netball teams of thespian equivalents of Falstaff eyeing the three juicy female roles. I would give her Mistress Ford, the younger, sexier one, the ditzy, daft Judy Davis character. I'd realized that Vanessa, surprisingly, had stage charm in buckets; she'd know her lines; she was ready and willing to party. Though she wasn't the only one who wanted a hand into my trousers, she was the only one with a brain, an evident and unshakeable faith in my abilities as actor or director and a free photocopier. She introduced me to Frame, Ashton-Warner and Curnow; I to her, Hardy, Ford Madox Ford and H.G. Wells; she ploughed through the whole of *Riddley Walker* — remember Hoban's literally unreadable cult novel from the early eighties? — just so we could discuss it over our Marmite-and-lettuce sandwiches. And it's not every ambitious scriptwriter and sometime guidance counsellor who gets the chance to watch what happens to an on-stage wife who's suffering a bad off-stage case of the unrequiteds.

Don't tell me, please, I should've been more upfront with her, not accepted her little gifts, lattes and the use of her Xerox machine, nor allowed her to babysit my kids, bringing the wife geranium cuttings for our patio's many terracotta pots. That I should not have offered her lifts home after late rehearsals when her husband had the car for night classes on making undrinkable feijoa wine; nor encouraged what became regular little rituals of touch, bear hugs with playful kisses — both cheeks, *à la francaise* — acceptable as *de rigueur* between actors and good friends. I definitely should not have agreed to critique her very ho-hum short stories, nor shared with her the film script that I was working on, nor sat in a sunny corner of the staff room many lunchtimes discussing Henry James' European novels or Harold Bloom's passion for the wit and wisdom of the real Falstaff? And in hindsight, without a doubt, I should not have consented to extra one-on-one rehearsals for her scenes, nor used her as the principal outlet for my considerable frustrations with a Falstaff who couldn't remember lines, an flaky and unpunctual Mistress Page, a sadly miscast Mistress Quickly, a Doctor Caius with an ego the size of Russia, a Sir Hugh Evans with an immutable Glaswegian accent, a Shallow and Slender given to improvised bouts of seriously unfunny slapstick and a fifteen-year-old Anne Page — admittedly gorgeous, red haired with a skin of finest alabaster — who announced at the first rehearsal she was three months' pregnant but hey, that's OK!

So you think I shouldn't have been grateful for the sake of the production and my directorial reputation that Vanessa blossomed into a marvellously sexy, witty Mistress Ford? Her Elizabethan tight bodice and farthingale revealed a waist that I suspect hadn't been sighted in twenty years. With coaching from the dialogue specialist I imported (I have to say, in some despair) for a weekend workshop, she learned how to breathe properly and her voice dropped about two octaves, suddenly and permanently. Now, she could be heard clearly with no particular effort at the back of the elderly and acoustically challenging war memorial hall we had to use in the absence of a better venue. And I plead guilty to actually enjoying the acting exercises we were put through — quite intimate and physical and playful some of them; well, we were playing husband and wife — by another imported specialist. I had good contacts in Auckland, some interest there even, in an amateur Shakespeare being done in the sticks, and by about week four I was getting desperate; my cast was not coming satisfactorily up to speed and at the end of the day, it's the director wot carries the can.

Alright, there is a confession I need to make here: one episode in those classes I do remember with a smidgeon of guilt. We were instructed to lie on the floor, any old how, like Pick Up Sticks. On a wicked impulse, disdaining any one of the twenty-six other cast members I could have chosen, I promptly laid my six foot three-and-a-half inches face down about sixty degrees across Vanessa's supine form, and observed with interest that for five or six full minutes she didn't move a muscle. Not a twitch. Hardly breathed. Catatonic, possibly. But against my groin I could feel her pulse throbbing in a vein, about 190 at a guess, and I believe I can imagine her thoughts: his weight, a thrust of hips, a coming together of lips, ach, in your *dreams*, Vanessa, and — well, in her shoes I'd have been thinking, Hugo, you absolute shit, you cynical ruthless game-playing tosser. Upright again, she was pale, possibly — forgive my flippancy — from lack of oxygen. She saw out the class, but took herself conspicuously to the other side of the room to get partnered for the rest of the evening by the Welshman with the Scots accent. I took her for a conciliatory coffee afterwards and lunch at an organic food café a few days later; by this time she had a passable familiarity with some of my little eccentricities, that I am vegetarian with the added complication of not being able to eat anything with tomatoes in it, which always guarantees me my fellow diners' sympathy and a waiter's full attention — though I swear it's a genuine allergy — and I prefer a good cup of tea to a Heineken or chardonnay anytime. These days, tea — that's ideally Twining's best English Breakfast, good and strong, with three sugars — is my only remaining addiction. I'm quite sure she didn't drink.

The fact is, over these months, until things started turning to custard six days out from the opening, I'd grown to rather like the woman, even if my interest in a fifty-something librarian going through The Change was, to be honest with you, somewhat forensic. And I couldn't discuss Sam Beckett with Jane, for sure. On stage Mistress Ford positively sparkled. Never was a wife more playful, but at heart, more dependable. *Pardon me, wife* (this is Act IV, Scene 4, the crazed, exhausted Ford tenderly and bashfully apologizing to his wronged wife), *Henceforth do what thou wilt; I rather will suspect the sun with cold than thee with wantonness: now doth thy honour stand, in him that was of late an heretic, as firm as faith.* Disentangle, if you wilt, the 'subtext', the overtones, the resonances throbbing in that little gem between the parallel harmonies of real and fantasy life!

Paradoxically, I felt less threatened than you might imagine. Behind the spectacular make-over, the general willingness and playfulness and brittle laughter, Vanessa remained a staunchly reliable member of the cast, and I had come to believe she was a woman of principle. Although in her head she was almost certainly enjoying all the delightful euphoria and attendant angst of a full-on, romantic affair, a cerebral *affaire de coeur*, if you like, nevertheless she would not go the next step and betray her family, nor mine, and attempt actual seduction — of that I was fairly sure. Too proud, too fearful of being rebuffed, too sexually timorous and fundamentally bourgeois, know what I mean?

Perhaps I didn't mention that she was thirteen years older than me. She was not quite, in police or counsellors' terms, a 'stalker', though I was certainly conscious of almost daily 'chance' meetings in the library, staff room, corridors, along with spontaneous offers of books, magazines, presents for the kids, phone calls on matters of trivia, anything that would result in opportunities for verbal or personal contact in and outside school hours. She sat in on rehearsals she was not called for, made endless cups of tea for us all, soothed the SM when she was near exploding and massaged Falstaff's monumental ego after he'd accused me of never giving him positive feedback — which I didn't, and to be honest, couldn't — and of being an immature and self-satisfied prat. I occasionally caught her off-guard, sitting in a corner of the rehearsal hall thinking herself unobserved. With the mask momentarily dropped, she had Viola's *green and yellow melancholy, ne'er told her love but sat like Patience on a monument, smiling at grief.* Wonderful lines, what? I must do *Twelfth Night* sometime. A crack at the deliciously self-important Malvolio, perhaps.

From this point on, the beginning of production week, when the tension gets suddenly cranked up and actors — and their ever-loving families — bend and sometimes crack under the strain, I can only relay the facts as I know them, or those rumours I remember.

Scene: at school, my office, which I'd made clear to all kids and staff, Vanessa included, that this was my private space, as much a no-go area as a bedroom. She understood that, yet an hour before I'm due to leave for the tech rehearsal, she rings from the library and tells me she's coming over, now. I stand guard at the door, but am unable to withstand the forcefulness of her need. You better come in, I say. I shut the door. She slumps into the one easy chair, tucking her legs up under her like a teenager. I can't do this, she witters, avoiding eye contact. Do what? Forget my lines, miss cues, let you and everyone down, she says. Most of all, make a complete fool of myself.

I sit quietly (my leaning-attentively-forward, fingertips-together Clinton pose) believing that she needs to spill it out, and doesn't want immediate, easy platitudes. She has, it seems, been dreaming of Mistress Ford, all dressed up in her fancy Elizabethan gear with the high collar and wig and all but paralysed with fear and unable to deliver the goods, and people are whispering behind their hands, openly jeering and laughing. She doesn't know why she ever thought she could do it, be flirtatious and sexy and desirable, at her age. She is going to look ridiculous, just as her mother said she would. Mother is not coming to the opening; the brainwashing of mother's early childhood in a closed Plymouth Brethren family has resurfaced; industrial-strength disapproval. Electrician husband is bewildered and threatened; he has been waking her up at five in the morning for his conjugal rites; has been aggressively and constantly demanding reassurances that their marriage is rock-solid, intact. He can't understand why her being in a frigging stupid play should so change her, change everything, so much.

And daughter. Daughter, aged thirty-one, who lives twenty ks away on a lifestyle block, has just been diagnosed with breast cancer. The medium- to long-term prognosis is yet undetermined. As a mother, Vanessa weeps; she should not be prancing around on a stage when her daughter has possibly terminal breast cancer.

So all this is as much about guilt and fear as nerves, and about drawing me into her private, emotional life, securely binding me, and obligating me, and making herself special in my eyes. Though my mind is running through the rejected female thespians who could conceivably learn the lines in two days, or do the part adequately with the book, I've swiftly concluded that a primary reason for this surprising visit, her fear of foolishness and failure, is a passing self-indulgence easily treated with my taking the directorial high ground. I trust my judgement implicitly, I tell her gently, and she must trust it too. With every rehearsal, I'd seen improvement in control, confidence and daring. She could say her lines in her sleep; she was the most 'giving' of anyone on the stage; she was a real pleasure to work with, blah blah blah. I'd understood from the start that Mistress Ford was a big challenge for her, a huge risk; as her director making judgements and watching progress throughout the whole process, *I would not have let her fail*. She would not fail. There was no question of it! My confidence in her was absolute! Blah blah blah.

To the other reason, her family troubles, I reacted warily, determined not to take her personal life on board. There were dangers here in familiarity, complicity. I said I was very sorry to hear of her daughter's cancer, and fell sincerely silent. Recovering composure, swiftly realizing boundaries were being maintained, she reassured me that the prognosis could be worse, that treatment was under way; in such circumstances her part-time job had its advantages. She wanted it kept quiet. She did not foresee any problem with turning up each night to all the tech and dress rehearsals and then the seven scheduled performances. She promised, she would be there. Already she was a trooper.

That promise Vanessa kept. From the dress rehearsal on, to the final-night curtain, the cast and audiences believed she was having the time of her life. Only I knew the cost, the strain in her eyes. From the small titbits of information she couldn't resist giving me, daughter's cancer wasn't looking so good; husband was demanding; she was, literally, barely sleeping at all. Two or three times I made it clear, but gently and tactfully, you understand, that I didn't have the time nor inclination to listen to her personal woes. I said, and it was not a question, you do understand the boundaries here, Vanessa. She put my reluctance down, I believe, to an over-stretched director balancing ongoing teaching during the day with keeping Master Ford's appointment by night with the *Merry Wives of Windsor* in the clapped-out war memorial hall, all the while keeping the actors happy, the lighting guys happy, the SM and backstage crew happy, front-of-house happy, the anticipated reviewer from the local rag (a pompous fuckwit) very happy. She remained discreetly solicitous for my needs, my burdens, my well-being.

Scene: the final-night party. Even there I don't believe she was drinking. I'd allowed myself to accept from Falstaff a flute of *méthode Champenoise*, my only occasional tipple. Overall, with the seven houses on the thin side and not too many laughs, there wasn't that much to celebrate, to be honest. The *congratulations, darling, you were wonderful* for Mistress Ford were among the more sincere. My ranting OTT Master Ford had been judged a success; Mistress Page's lack of focus and unreliability came home to roost and twice she'd missed entrances and had to be fetched from her dressing room while the folk on stage stood and lamely admired the colours and perfumes of the Windsor roses; by closing night daughter Anne was about a stone heavier and clearly no virgin, despite her costume being let out as far as it would go, adding a certain piquancy never intended by the playwright to the final courting scenes in the forest. Falstaff, against all my increasingly alarmed injunctions, had taken to writing his lines on cards concealed about his immensely padded person and among the crêpe-paper roses. He was frankly an embarrassment, though Harold Bloom would say that was largely Shakespeare's fault.

Somewhere in the memory of that noisy night I have a recollection, admittedly blurred by *méthode Champenoise*, of a weeping Vanessa buttonholing me late in the proceedings in a corner backstage, and more or less telling me that she was a serious mess. I wasn't so pixillated that I was blind to the very real possibility, nay danger, that we just might be about to cross the bridge between Hugo as friend and confidant and Hugo as amorous target, forever compromised. After that, there would be no going back, so I briskly dusted off a stratagem used successfully at least once before. I said, disingenuously implying innocence and ignorance, before she actually articulated or tried to embrace the target of this hopeless secret love, 'My dear Vanessa, if it's unrequited feelings for someone engulfing you, I do so feel for you, being in exactly the same position myself.'

Before her eyes could widen in amazed hopefulness any further, I revealed with all the sincerity at my disposal that the object of my desire was an actress in faraway Auckland. At a scriptwriters' seminar four months ago, I'd seen her across a crowded room and been helplessly, hopelessly smitten by Cupid's arrow. She was gorgeous, she was twenty-three and she had a partner, the same one for eight years. I was thirty-seven and happily married. I had two children I adored. Hopeless on all counts, no future in it now or ever. I saw her nightly on *Shortland Street* and irregularly for lunch when I went to Auckland, but I had never told my love. But I did understand, believe me, Vanessa, I did understand the anguish, the pain, the desolation. I understood where she was at. All things pass. This, believe me, my dear friend, will pass.

She had no option but to believe me; in two minutes we had become fellow sufferers and penitents at the high altar of Unrequited Love. I gave her a particularly long and understanding bear hug and believe she was within a whisker of blowing her cover and tilting her head up for a shot at a full-on-the-mouth kiss. Being so much taller, I was able to gaze in an Olympian and stoic way into the folds of the black curtains around us, pretending to be unaware of the potential inherent in this moment when no doubt for her, making bodily contact from head to knee, the earth was standing still.

Scene, and is it any wonder: the following day, a beautiful winter Sunday, the distant paddocks glistening with a light frost, thoughtful Jane in her blue candlewick dressing gown waking me with a cup of tea. The kids are watching cartoons, their Sunday-morning treat. She shuts the door, an unusual gesture for her, and sits on the edge of the bed warming her hands around the mug of tea. She asks, 'How was the play last night? Good house?' 'Passable,' I say, doubly thankful that my no-nonsense Jane likens herself to a vicar's wife not being required, just because she's the vicar's wife, to attend every Sunday service or run the ghastly women's fellowship, and makes the point very loud and clear that she doesn't do openings or last nights. I go on, sensing trouble, 'A bit ragged, but last nights usually are. Party was pretty dire, but you know, director, all that, I had to be there.' She says, 'I had a ring from Debra this morning.' (Debra was the new props person, and a friend of Jane's from kindy days.) 'And Debra says, "Sorry Jane, this really pains me, but I think you should know — Master and Mistress Ford, those two are bonking."'

Red alert, Hugo. Though it's a complete slander, totally untrue, and my conscience is utterly clear, some damage control is needed here.

'Debra is a silly bitch,' I say, relaxed and smiling, 'who doesn't know the first thing about theatre, the sort of closeness and trust that every member of every cast needs to develop to make a play work. Just to *survive*, as actors!'

'Debra says—'

'Vanessa? Give me a break! She's fifty-five if she's a day. And probably menopausal.'

'She's fifty-one if she's a day,' says Jane implacably. 'And she's dyed her hair blonde and got contacts and lost about thirty kilos and menopausal or not, Debra says, and all the cast were saying, she's got the hots for you, big time.'

I say lightly, 'Alright, she's fifty-one, whatever. Who cares? So she's got a passing crush, big deal. Middle-aged female wannabe actor given permission to be sexy on stage by person-able younger male director: trust me, it's the oldest theatrical cliché in the book. Give me *some* credit, Jane.'

Laughing to show the ridiculousness, the incongruity, the sheer ludicrousness of it, I pull her down towards me. My tenderness is heartfelt, soft and exquisite. 'Sweetheart, you know ever since that day I tripped over you in a corridor on a train to Exeter, we've never had any secrets. Believe me. Trust me. Yes, I've enjoyed having Vanessa in two casts; she's been staunch and fun to work with. Yes, as colleagues and local literati we sit in the staff room over lunch occasionally and talk about books. Yes, I have occasionally given her a lift home at night, or taken her, among others, for a coffee. Please trust me, Jane, there has *never once* been a sexual moment, nothing which has stepped over the boundary of just good friendship. Pu-leeze! She's just about old enough to be my *mother*, for fuck's sake.'

There is a long silence. Jane sighs deeply, and says, 'I hear on the grapevine her husband's been threatening to walk out and she's got a daughter with breast cancer. Did you know that? Did she tell you any of that stuff?'

I reply briskly in the negative, expressing my complete surprise, lying like a flatfish to demonstrate that our friendship had quite narrow and well-understood limits, that Vanessa had told me nothing of her daughter or of her personal life. I was truly surprised, I go on, how well she had kept her troubles hidden, how utterly professional she'd been. I knew that tackling such a major part had caused her some strain, understandably, but as to coping with family miseries of this sort, I hadn't suspected a thing.

I was learning, though, with people who've got the acting bug, one thing tends to lead to another.

A few weeks later, having declined an invitation to direct the next play, a dreadful bedroom farce, mostly for the sake of restoring peace and tranquillity at home, I take a call from Falstaff. In another life he is a lawyer and leading light of the local Rotary. A glittering dinner and charity auction is being planned, fundraising for child-abuse victims; he wants an Original Entertainment involving the stars of the recent Shakespeare: himself, myself and Vanessa. I don't think so. But his persistence includes the enticing prospect of a bunch of stuffy dyed-in-the-wool Rotarians newly interested in the arts. They might be amenable to sponsoring a further Shakespeare to the tune of a few bob. I'd have his support for director, despite, he chuckles, my being a conceited Pommie prat.

So I silently, swiftly, assess the further future payoff: when the time comes, he will of course want Sir Toby Belch, but the role is a notably long and subtle one, way beyond him, and he's too old for much else — he'll get Fabian, the servant, which won't overly please him, or if I'm feeling generous and there's no other candidate, Feste. But for now, he desires fifteen minutes of sparkling entertainment for his glittering black-tie dinner. Vanessa has been sounded out and predictably is game. We have five weeks to conceive, write and rehearse a script. The scriptwriter and the comedian in me cannot resist.

It is a mistake. A bad, bad call. We meet one night at Falstaff's large and gracious home with a panoramic view of the beach and throw around various ideas with humorous potential, including setting our piece in an old folks' home, or disinterring something from Noël Coward, one of his revues, but that means singing, and I, frankly, can't hold a tune. In the end we decide our characters will be teenagers, the worst sort, commenting on the usual ghastly

Is She Still Alive?

teenage preoccupations: parents, pimples, sex, drugs, drinking, teachers, younger siblings, global warming, the ruination of the planet, the meaning of life, the end of the universe. My character will be smart-mouthed, stoned and in drag; Vanessa's drunk and ditzy and straight out of St Trinian's; Falstaff's porky and priggish, a Billy Bunter prototype in a school cap too small for him and voluminous shorts. We craft a storyline of which McKee would have approved, I draft a script which we brainstorm and workshop. Vanessa's contributions are surprisingly funny, cruel and successful. The fear of making a fool of herself has completely vanished; on the contrary, some of the more risqué, even filthy, suggestions are hers. She is even prepared to sing. We will involve the audience, targeting the oldest, most doddering and most pompous men, the most mutton-dressed-as-lamb women, and at a Rotary function there'll be plenty of choice either way, know what I mean? It will either be hilarious, the comedy hit of the year, or an embarrassing disaster.

In the event, as far as the audience was concerned, we scored a bull's-eye. It was the talk of the town for weeks afterwards. I couldn't walk through the main street without some jolly smiling Rotarian coming over with jolly congratulations. Didn't know the town had such talent, what? Should be on the telly, old chap, marvellous. But right from the early script conferences, for me it had been a complete nightmare. Behind the apparent fun of the workshopping and rehearsals, the dressing up, I was feeling increasingly trapped, even suffocated. Jane was not pleased with me. My children resented the closed study door, or nights driving away at homework or *Simpsons'* time. From England came news of my father's stroke and very possible demise, raising the possibility that I might have to cancel the Rotarians outright and fly over suddenly, or leave the day after the dinner to be in time for a bedside reconciliation or a funeral.

Vanessa remained her dependable and solicitous self — as well as typing scripts, she acquired our costumes, wigs and props and virtually stage-managed the event single-handed — but was increasingly brittle, intense and truth to tell, crazy, just barely in control. I heard whispers around the staff room of neighbours in her street hearing volcanic midnight rows. Backstage at the dinner, as the guests out front got drunker and one-upped each other bidding for Pacific cruises, Bavarian crystal decanters and overpriced Italian handbags for charity, as the make-up girl from the local pharmacy, fortified by a couple of mega-glasses of Gisborne oaked chardonnay, transformed me with wig and paint into Britney Spears, I looked in the mirror at Vanessa's laughing, freckled, geriatric St Trinian's face and my own rosy-pink cupid's lips and thought, I could do with a good slug of Dutch courage myself and what the fuck am I doing here?

When a show is over, it's over. The old Dad, whom they thought recovering slowly, died suddenly of cardiac arrest two days later. I went to the UK for a brisk week of family business and a small measure of reconciliation with my mother and brothers. I came back with a few resolutions.

You'd be surprised how easy it is to avoid someone working on the same school grounds. She was only part-time in the library, so I made sure I went there only on her off-days. I went late to the staff room for lunch; if I saw her there already — and I have to say she looked shocking — I made a point of joining another group. If she joined my group, I was polite but almost immediately excused myself, on grounds of a student waiting or a pile of marking. Her mediocre short stories, firmly fitting into short fiction's menstrual school, I put without explanation or comment into her cubbyhole.

There was a strange episode one holidays when I discovered my office, and only my office, completely ransacked — nothing taken but books tipped out of shelves, files emptied, students' essays waiting for marking ripped apart, pictures pulled off the walls, a cup of cold tea poured into my computer keyboard, the charming word 'arsehole' scrawled in red permanent marker across the monitor. The caretaker had heard or seen nothing; the police put it down to student thugs, questioned me and the senior staff fruitlessly for known hostile elements; charged nobody, but I always wondered. Erotomania is known to stretch to revengeful acts of vandalism, or worse. She would have worn gloves, and been careful, under cover of darkness. Of far greater concern, the police had a local rape on their books, as well as four aggravated robberies, several violent domestics and ongoing drug inquiries among the resident gang. Unwilling to ask Jane for any gossip, and avoiding the staff room, I remained unaware for many weeks that Vanessa's marriage had finally fallen apart. The family home apparently was on the market. Then it seemed she'd gone to some hall in the South Island for a month, for time out and treatment for serious depression; she came back to a daughter needing yet another debilitating round of chemo. About fifteen months later, when *Twelfth Night* was in early rehearsal, it got around the staff room that her daughter's cancer was terminal.

I didn't go to the funeral. I don't do funerals, especially of the younger deceased, always particularly miserable and snivelling affairs. I read somewhere, grief is largely self-pity, in the end — a self-indulgence best avoided oneself and not to be encouraged in others. It was a Tuesday in the holidays and I did a runner that day to Wellington, on the off-chance of an appointment with an elusive producer there, whose backing might yet eventuate and bring with it Film Commission development money. I convinced myself that Vanessa was well over me by then, she had bigger things to worry about, but to be honest with you I really didn't want to see Patience sitting on her monument. To be completely frank, I didn't want to be so forcibly and powerfully reminded that my own children, any children, were vulnerable and mortal. There can be nothing worse, more lonely, more desolate, than to bury a child.

And I didn't want to feel a wee prickle of guilt that I never fronted up to her after the Rotary dinner was over, which might just conceivably have helped her get closure, get through it, see her infatuation for the treatable psychological disturbance it was, with its roots (if I remember from the books correctly) in a childhood which featured rejection, loneliness, pain and abandonment. If, one-on-one, she had accused me for my sudden unilateral 'cold turkey' cessation of our friendship as being ruthless and shitty, I would readily have agreed. (My late unlamented father told me bitterly at least twice in my adult life that 'under all that apparent warmth, that façade of charm, you, dear Hugo, are a remarkably cold fish'; my bloody mother never forgave me for siring and raising her only grandchildren in an uncivilized country 12,000 miles away.) I concede the lack of closure was probably ruthless and shitty, but frankly, you know, flat to the boards with marking, teaching and family life, and learning lines for the next play — I decided to audition for, and got the lead role in a ho-hum Alan Aykbourne comedy (on condition Vanessa, in the unlikely event she auditioned, didn't get cast) and I subsequently cast myself in that great Shakespearian role all comics want to play, Malvolio — well, any sort of closure with the pathetic part-time fruitloop over in the school library just didn't seem that pressing a matter. The days and weeks and months went by and frankly with more important things to do I just never got round to it.

If we're being completely honest here, I didn't consider myself so very responsible and really couldn't be bothered. I didn't owe her anything. I knew Jane's concerns were needless; I had done nothing wrong. Vanessa would survive, she'd get over it. Menopause doesn't go on for ever and speaking as a one-time acidhead, time heals pretty much everything. Though I admit, the last night of *Twelfth Night* I went on for the MOAI letter scene, and got the shock of my life to see her sitting near the front, over by the side aisle. She was stony-faced, unlike those I could see in the front rows with that half-smile of enjoyment and engagement actors work hard to achieve. I don't mind admitting, I was momentarily thrown right off my stride. I got out 'Tis but fortune; all is fortune well enough,' but I did the rest of the scene and the play on autopilot. It wasn't one of my greatest performances. When we got to the curtain calls, she'd gone. I'm interested now, a little puzzled, that her presence affected me as much as it did.

And in the end, when push comes to shove, when the chips are really down: not my problem, not my pain, not my responsibility. I can hardly be blamed for being six foot three, of passable Guardsman good looks and known as charming, talented and witty with it. Nor for ending up pushing forty, teaching English in a small town in the Colonies when my parents had, let's say, somewhat higher hopes: a Cambridge First just like the old Dad, not wasted years of wandering around the North American continent penniless, stoned to the eyeballs, fucking my bloody brains out, getting work and money and food whatever legal or illegal way I could in the great University of Life. It's genes, don't you know, just the naturally adventurous and questing spirit I showed from an early age. One day, the Oscar-winning film of my utterly original and brilliant script, set in Mexico starring Brad or Jude or possibly even Johnny D as a beautiful seventies' flower child — that will show them all.

I suppose, though — alcohol poisoning? — you might conclude that on the face of it Vanessa didn't survive. Husband gone, son in the UK or somewhere, only daughter dead and buried.

Over the years I've heard occasional mentions of her in the staff room and seen her once or twice from a distance in town. Grown porky and grey, sloppy in her dressing, vague of expression, forgetful; she apparently became a local eccentric of some curiosity and pity. I heard she bought a charmless and cheap little brick-and-tile unit close to the industrial area, gave up all library work, helped out at a run-down playgroup with mostly Maori kids, and went regularly to sit in the back of the congregation at the Anglican church looking like some medieval, self-flagellating, pasta-indulging Italian nun. Was otherwise reclusive. Never acted again, of course; the briefly quite glamorous thespian Vanessa was never sighted again. God knows what she lived on: the dole, sickness benefit, some invested monies, I guess. Husband remarried, the widowed son-in-law likewise, and they formed a very cosy and weird little foursome on a lifestyle block hereabouts, growing red table grapes for export. That didn't work. They dabbled for a year in raising ostriches and last I heard were planting the Next Big Thing, olives and lavender.

But alcohol poisoning? I don't mind admitting, that disturbs me somewhat. No-one ever mentioned that she'd taken to drink. I imagine the grief and desolation and loneliness and probably plain boredom just got to her. Perhaps that final night she was trying to drown her sorrows in one desperate binge — went out and bought a bottle of cheap brandy or gin, and drank the neat spirit steadily to dull the self-imposed pain until she threw up, and drank again until she passed out, and coming to, feeling like shit, drank again until she lapsed into a coma, never to wake.

Hah — now I come to think of it, one night recently I did have an odd late phone call — some heavy breathing, snuffling, perhaps sobbing before my pearls of wisdom were cut off. I'd asked who was calling, and because I was once a counsellor, worked for suicide and youth helplines and so on, asked gently in my most empathetic voice was she in trouble, to *please* say who she was, help was always available and no-one need deal with their troubles alone, no problem was so bad that it could not be shared and resolved. You know, the usual smooth spiel, non-threatening, non-judgemental, soothing, defusing, healing. As you do.

Who's to predict how different it might have been, had she identified herself, or had I articulated the thought that did pass through my mind: is that you, Vanessa? Would I have leapt in my car at one in the morning and gone around? Aye, there's the rub. Would she have wanted me to? They didn't find her body for six days. I didn't go to that funeral either, even when the ex-husband wanted me to be a pallbearer. Ye Gods, no! No way. I told him I didn't do funerals, end of story. He was quite nonplussed, but I had nothing more to say. Never apologise, never explain.

A letter arrived about two months later, from a local law firm — not Falstaff's mob, thank God, not even lawyers can be trusted with secrets in this town — and marked strictly confidential. Among her papers had been found a sealed and quite bulky envelope. In accordance with her instructions, it was hereby enclosed. The outside bore the legend: 'In the event of my death, I would like this envelope forwarded to Hugo Markham. I want him to know how he broke my heart.'

Not interested, Vanessa.

I didn't toss it in the bin, however. The letter is still unopened in a bottom drawer in my office at school; it might be useful background reading one day, on the general topic of erotomania in menopausal women. McKee always says that the metre-high pile of research papers on your desk and in files should always be ten times greater than the lean eighty or so pages positively throbbing with subtext you finally pitch to a producer.

I took an unsatisfactory phone call from Wellington yesterday. The producer just *loves* the script — they all say that, know what I mean? — but she wants a few changes, nothing too drastic. They all say that too, knowing full well that they're about to kick the writer in the guts. She also hints at problems with her cashflow, confirming rumours I'd heard about receivership and my suspicions that with that particular lady I've been wasting my valuable time. Clearly now, hell will freeze over before any Film Commission money comes her way.

But sitting here in the sun, listening to my kids down by the creek and being momentarily reminded of Vanessa has made me wonder if there isn't the beginnings of a script hiding in this story somewhere. Don't we keep reading that all the ageing female stars in Hollywood, the Streeps and the Fondas and the Mirrens, are absolutely desperate for good roles? Any roles? Say, older woman, repressed all her life, obeyed all the rules, boring as hell, develops all-consuming love for much younger and unavailable man and goes completely off the rails? I'd have to have my Vanessa character horribly murder the target of her passion, of course, or at the very least, seriously attempt it before she comes to her senses. Swelling violins as she boards a plane for Alaska to see her long-lost estranged daughter. Menopausal, out of control, yet never directly tells her love. Set in small-town, outback Aussie, for a crack at Australian Film Commission money? Or the American Midwest, or better, Texas, which I know quite well, and aim for a Hollywood producer, and Harvey Weinstein onside? As the lead: Meryl Streep, or Judy Davis. Geraldine James. Pity Judi Dench is a touch too long in the tooth, Maggie Smith, the older Redgrave likewise. Julia the Mouth Roberts is always Julia Roberts. I like the idea of Geraldine best. Or you forget the star system altogether and film it on a shoestring with myself as director and a cast of amateurs, complete unknowns to the industry; this always raises eyebrows and interest, and come to that, if it works, the director's profile. Perhaps it's time to dig out that letter. I must dip into my McKee again. Marvellous book, *Story*. Hear it from The Master, Hugo.

Look at the light on those hills! It's good to be alive with such transcendent beauty, as tomorrow the old millennium makes way for the new. There's a horse and rider returning — my Jane, to whom I have been and will be totally faithful, at least until the kids are gone and it's time to reassess and perhaps move on to another life stage in the Great Journey, as my guru in London once predicted I would. I was dismayed at the time, naturally, thinking that I had found my soul mate, but now I appreciate and understand the need for openness to possibilities.

Down by the creek, my beautiful kids, their tanned limbs dappled gold under the fresh green of the willows, their voices full of sweet energy. I'm prone to melancholy today, tearful for those poor children in Ethiopia, homeless, abandoned, so permanently damaged in body and soul, so betrayed — such distressing news footage last night that I watched it sobbing. Such a softie Dad at heart, basically, I am.

I'm so glad Jane never let me do cast parties. Vanessa never came here and thank Christ for that. I do love this country.

Flying the nest

When Leo and I got married in St Barnabas Anglican Church, I think it was in 1975, I had my natural blonde hair in a weirdo Marge Simpson beehive, but plaited and glazed like a loaf of bread they have at church for harvest festivals. Leo wore a midnight-blue cummerbund and his collar outside his jacket, and had those hairy Cliff Richard sideboards. He worked as an accountant then. We had Hayley six months after the wedding, and Luke two years after that, and little Hamish was a mistake really.

So by 1980 there we were with three children and a do-up property in Devonport. It was of those old derelict wooden villas with no garage in those scruffy streets behind the naval base, before they got tarted up all fashionable and cute and cost a bomb. It had finials and a return veranda and square, dark rooms off a dark hallway; a grubby kitchen beyond looking over ancient grapefruit trees dropping loads of fruit in the back garden. The agent said it had great do-up potential, but after ten years of do-it-yourself, three children to educate, grandparents who were worse than useless and his job, Leo had a sort of nervous breakdown. We call it burnout these days, but call it what you like, it was still a breakdown, big time. He didn't talk to me for seven months. Not a single solitary word.

After that he drove a taxi, my poor Leo, and loved it. Without saying more than OK and thanks, he could get passengers across Auckland like nobody's business, knew all the short cuts, the lights and spaghetti junctions and motorway tails in the rush hours and which one-way systems to avoid. Drunkards vomiting in the back, and all sorts of tantrums and the occasional drawn knife weren't much fun, but those didn't happen too often.

When the kids went to the grammar, and my mother was taking her own good time to die from breast cancer, I began to study for my real-estate exams. Devonport, up the peninsula as far as Hauraki Corner, was a good area for real estate. There were the old wealthy homes, and those with Rangitoto channel views, of course, but there were also lots of shabby California bungalows and run-down turn-of-the-century villas like ours. Oh sure, fiendishly expensive compared with a similar sort of house in Point Chev or Mt Roskill, but still worth putting money into.

These days, Devonport is a very desirable place to live in Auckland. I specialize in the lower-priced properties, the family homes, or the final resting pads for better-off senior citizens, farmers and stock agents and such coming in from the country. I leave the two-million-dollar-plus properties to the suits with the Beemers, smarmy slimy creatures to a man; they give me the shudders. Our own villa is pretty gorgeous, really, it is. The Peace rose creepers I planted are huge and mature now, and the mauve wisteria and the kowhai trees. I love that house to bits, but I don't live there any more.

Leo and I have just moved to the back end of Glenfield. He's the house-husband, mostly. I have to drive down to Devonport to the office most days. The boys and a few others now live in the villa. I don't know how many, exactly.

They were good kids. Hayley was a Spock baby, but that's fine. I like the way he started off his book — 'You know more than you think you do' — though I don't think any terrified new mum reading that ever really believed it. How could you 'know'? You have to learn to be a mum, like anything else, really. I taught her those Glenn Doman words, you know, teaching your baby to be a genius with big cards, before she went to school, but she still ended up with a reading problem. Dyslexic, they said: eight with a reading age of six. So we went private for her. It was hard. I think the boys never quite understood why they couldn't go to Kings or Kristin or somewhere posh, and just had to go to the local primary and grammar like everybody else.

But those boys went to a good school. The headmaster was a former All Black, and they both got into the Second Fifteen. They weren't dyslexic like their big sister, at least no-one ever said anything, but they did mess around a bit as boys do, you know, thinking it was clever to fail exams and get into trouble for smoking or not turning up to class and their uniform grey socks being in folds around their grubby ankles. These days it's their pants half-mast and underpants and bare torso showing, have you noticed? Girls too, showing all sorts of skin and flab? Hard to think of what they can drop off next, really.

It helped being stars of the Second Fifteen, in subtle little ways, and not so little ways. One set of rules for the First and Second Fifteens, another set for all the rest, that's how it seemed to me. There were a few drugs in the school, everyone knew that, but nothing that involved our boys, at least that we heard of. Well, except one little fright, a warning when Luke did a bit of shoplifting. Just Mars bars and crisps and such from the dairy, you know. Just a little warning. But Leo had got really upset seeing that burly policeman at our door wanting a little chat. He always got a bit stressed when we were summoned along to parent evenings.

But we were doing OK. Leo was back on an even keel, driving his Holden taxi. I was proud of the nice house we'd created, with flowery wallpapers and picture rails and stripping all the kauri doorframes and floors back from tacky green paint to bare wood. I became quite a dab hand with the varnish brush. We got a nice new kitchen with a dishwasher and an add-on rumpus room with a bar and a pool table and a second telly. I was quite a good land agent, though we had good and bad years. 1988 was really bad, and the four years after that worse, just terrible. No one was buying after the crash, no one had any money, the whole country was depressed. But they still took taxis, thank God, though poor Leo was working a seventy-hour week to make enough.

Hayley finished school and went off to Waikato to do a marketing degree, and then Luke to Auckland Uni to study law. I think Luke quite liked being in that big scruffy flat in Mt Eden. Dirty flat, if I'm really telling the truth. Actually, it was truly disgusting and vile. Hayley's in Hamilton was a bit better, but no-one ever bought or cooked for anyone else, let alone did any cleaning. I think they lived on takeaway left-overs, and every now and again one of the girls would buy a few things to put in the fridge. I don't think they even owned a vacuum cleaner. Or an iron. Or knew what dusting was, or picking up rubbish from the floor. They both had quite big student loans, which I'm pretty damn sure they've never paid off and don't intend to. I'm not supposed to know, and I never told Leo, but I think Luke did that wedding-scam thing in the early nineties, you know, got married in a registry office to some girl so they both qualified for a bigger allowance? I was a little bit shocked at that, I must admit. It didn't seem right; we'd had them christened by a proper vicar and taken them regularly to Sunday school when they were younger. But I wasn't sure enough to risk asking him about it. If I'm being really honest with myself I'd say I was a bit frightened to.

Don't you hate it when your friends go on about their children, them doing so well? Promotions, steady jobs, bigger houses, trips overseas, boats, ever more grandchildren on the way? Eyes shining, pictures of littlies out of handbags? Jesus, they never stop! Darling, they twitter, our lovely family Christmas is being spent on the Gold Coast this year! (Or Rarotonga, or Tahiti.) There'll be sixteen of us, all together, coming from all over, isn't that *amazing*? Last year we were all walking in Tuscany, don't you know, and the year before was cycling in Provence, and the year before puttering through the French canals. Eastern Europe is the coming thing, a nice little chalet in the forests outside Moscow would you believe, as if there'd never been Khrushchev and a cold war not so long ago. They never seem to notice that I don't volunteer a single word about our boomerang babies. Well, what would I say?

Anyway, Luke dropped out of law after eighteen months. He went on the dole and came home because he couldn't afford to stay flatting. Hayley came home too, when she finished her degree. She got a job at some advertising agency as a creative director, whatever that means. She looked after clients and marketed those dog biscuits you see on the telly and travel agencies and such. I thought she might have wanted to get a flat, but she didn't because she was saving for her OE. It really helped, thanks Mum, you're neat, you're a star, she used to say, saving her shelling out $150 a week for a cold, poky little flat and food and telephone rental and power which was all so expensive. Leo asked her for money for board but I don't know, she just never got round to it. He was too tired working his seventy-hour weeks to follow it up.

By that time Hamish was doing his sport and recreation degree at Waikato, that's when he wasn't out at Raglan surfing. Raglan is the surfing capital of New Zealand, apparently. The surfies' Mecca. He said he needed to get a bigger, better car to get out there. I gave him a little cheque, just a secret between him and me, for his twenty-first. I never saw any of his flats in Hamilton. He only took two-and-a-half years extra to finish his degree.

It was really important to me and Leo that they all go to university. I didn't and he didn't; he just got his accountancy qualifications through that accountants society. I learned being a real-estate agent on the job, though I did the exams, of course. So we wanted all our kids to have good qualifications, to be able to stand on their own feet, so much.

Let me get this list I have. It's the one the counsellor asked me to compile, of all the comings and goings of the kids during the nineties. I started doing it with Leo, but then he said he didn't want any more questions about the kids' comings and goings because the kids' comings and goings were nothing much to write home about from our point of view and they upset him. So it's just from my own memory really. The counsellor thought we might discern some sort of helpful pattern here, you know?

Well, there was the crash in '87, and some hard years, but student loans and the dole are wonderful things. I used to think I'd be so ashamed of any child of mine being on the dole, but not any more. We've always paid our taxes before July the seventh, always. I just think of it as money being recycled, and our kids as entitled to it, if they're having a rough patch, just as much as any Maori kid from Otara or a tumbledown shack up the Hokianga. It doesn't pay to be proud.

Where was I? Oh yes, it says on here Luke came home when he was nineteen and we built him a room out the back because he wanted to practise his electric bass guitar and Leo couldn't stand the noise right in the house. Thunk thunk thunk thunk all day, and Leo works shifts so sometimes has to sleep during the afternoons. We had to cut down the old grapefruit that was there. I squeezed gallons and gallons of fruit so it wouldn't waste, but no-one would drink it so it all went fizzy in the end and I never thought to make ice-blocks of it. Leo did most of the work on the room himself to save money, even the electrics, though I think it was actually illegal to do your own wiring in those days. He just got a plumber because Luke wanted a washbasin and sink and a baby stove, so he could cook if he wanted. I never saw him cook there or anywhere.

Then just when the room was finished, and my bloody mother had finally passed away from her breast cancer, Luke went off to Sydney for two years. I think he worked there as a waiter, or I think he said, something in tourism, which could have meant anything really. Guide, ticket collector, driver like his dad, I don't know. I hope he did, but even so, he used to ring us collect occasionally and ask for a bit of money to tide him over. 'Dad, I'm really desperate, it'll be the last time, I swear,' he'd say. Leo would huff and puff, but he'd cave in, in the end. I have to admit, Leo was right when he said he'd never see it again, not a cent.

So Hayley had the room. Then she went flatting with this boy. That was in 1994, about then. He was a musician in a band and she was now earning megabucks compared to her parents. She could have afforded a nice flat, but she went into his place in Grey Lynn. I thought it was a mistake at the time, but she had stardust in her eyes. I suppose she just didn't see the mess, the horrible squalor. She told me he had skull tattoos on his upper arms and smoked a bit of pot, you know, just to calm him. From what I could gather, he worked at night and slept all day. He did gigs and then smoked his pot and discussed philosophy and art and God and politics and the meaning of life until about five o'clock with other similarly inclined musos and then drifted off to sleep until rising like Lazarus about the middle of the afternoon. I suppose in a bed with Hayley, but I don't want to think about that. She was trying to hold down her job. She'd got five silver rings put in each ear, one in her eyebrow and one or two in hidden places. She said, you don't want to know, Mum. That's right, I don't.

So for a while Hamish had the room, and it became like a sort of headquarters for all the surfers in the district. When the surf was up at Takapuna, they'd meet at our place and talk surfboards and breaks and stuff and drive out to Piha or for a real thrill, to Maori Bay at Muriwai or Anawhata when the surf was really running big. I went to watch him in a competition there once, and couldn't bear it, him paddling miles out beyond the break line and getting swamped by those enormous, evil waves, and me with my heart in my mouth wondering if he'd ever come up. Hamish told me guys did crack their skulls open occasionally, being thrown down and hitting the bottom head first. One died, once. They did mouth-to-mouth on the shore, and those electric paddle things on his chest: no use. But I quite liked all his friends coming and going through the house. The wetsuits all over the place were a bit trying, and Leo's moaning ditto, but they were good kids really.

Hamish did work for a while. He had a good job at the North Shore City Council for nine months, until he took one day off too many to go surfing. They didn't know that of course. He had a big annual report due for the printers and it didn't get done in time to be presented to a council meeting. His boss was furious and said it was the last straw, and the deputy mayor was even more furious and got him fired, which means that he won't get another job in any other local body in the greater Auckland area. Or the whole of New Zealand, probably. It was a bit harsh, in my opinion, though Leo didn't think so.

So Hamish went on the dole for a bit and is talking about

taking out a personal grievance case for wrongful dismissal. He's talked to Leo about a loan to pay a lawyer who specializes in these things. But it turned out he'd had some warnings, it was all above board and legal. His boss had done all the right things, so Hamish taking a case probably would lose. We didn't know he'd had official warnings. It was very upsetting. Leo would have talked to him earlier, before it all got out of control. He said if Hamish wanted a lawyer this time he could pay for one himself.

Now Hamish is working as a waiter at a Turkish café in Devonport, between surfing times. So he's never really left home, and when Hayley came home depressed with the baby and Luke came back from Sydney penniless and two stone lighter because of the hepatitis B, he still refused to budge from the back room. Squatter's rights, he told them. They were furious, especially Luke who said that Dad built the room for him. But Hamish kept the door locked and Leo said if Luke, or Hayley for that matter, tried to break in and throw Hamish's things out, he'd call the police. He said they should be grateful to have a fucking roof over their heads, and a mother as slave and servant girl. If he really had his way, he said, he'd tell them all to fucking leave. Leo never swears.

Now I must say at the time that hurt a bit, 'servant girl'. The Bible talks about good servants and Jesus himself spoke of being a servant of God. Yes, it's true that I went on asking them to give me their dirty washing. It was easy enough to throw it in the machine. Sometimes, yes, I'd pick it up off the floor. It was gathering dust, otherwise. And I'd bring it in off the line and iron it. They'd just put it on all crinkled if I didn't.

It's true that the person who vacuumed the floor was me, or sometimes Leo if I had a house sale about to go unconditional and buyers ringing my cellphone every half-hour for another look at the property in question. OK, it's true that none of them ever came to the supermarket food shopping with me or helped me in with the bags or the rubbish or even brought the mail in. Hamish sometimes cooked a meal for his friends, with a lot of noise and fanfare, I must say, and a day for me to get the kitchen straight again. Otherwise, I cooked. Leo and I cleaned up. Sometimes I'd ask for a bit of help, you know, with little chores. Take a rubbish bin out, go up to the dairy when we ran out of milk, sweep the front steps. They'd say yeah yeah, in ten, Mum, but it didn't happen. So I'd do it. It was just, you know, daily family life, everyone coming and going, always on the phone, people yelling for car keys, you know, somehow easier all round to do things yourself? I wouldn't like them to think of me as a nag.

And yes, when the counsellor asked me straight, I had to admit that none of them ever got around to paying board. Oh, I suppose that was our fault. Poor lambs, they were always in debt, you see. Not just the student loans. I don't think the Government will see their money back from our children. No, hush my mouth, I think Hayley did pay back her student loan. That was when she was still working as a creative director, whatever that means. I never quite knew what she earned, but she used to joke to her friends on her cellphone that it was megabucks. When she wasn't earning megabucks and had the baby, she needed money for baby clothes and a car seat. The musician father had done a runner, to New York, I think. Luke was paying off his new electric guitar — have you any idea how much those things cost, it's criminal? — and his Valencia orange sportscar. And Hamish lost his council job and the dole wouldn't cover a new surfboard. Never mind his petrol out to Piha and his Les Mills gym subscription. I think those braids and tattoos cost quite a lot of money, too. He had quite a lot of CDs, about 2000? Though DVDs are all the rage now, I believe, and of course there's the cellphones they're always texting people on, the ones that send pictures and can even get email and stuff like that.

I'm not going to tell you very much about the cot death, because it upsets me too much. Hayley had gone back to work, and Leo had cut back his taxi hours so that we could cope with the baby between us. She was such a dear little soul, even — I suppose I shouldn't say this — even if she was half black. Her father was a black American from Florida, I gather. I never met him.

The worst thing was it happened while Hayley was away for three days. Not even working. She was with a new boy-friend up in the Bay of Islands. Well, I suppose she's entitled to a life. Anyway, she was away and Leo woke in the night with a bad feeling and went in and found the baby not breathing, sort of blue-grey and dead as a post. Hayley had turned her cellphone off; we couldn't get her even though they put her name over the radio stations, so it was three days before she knew. The police got involved. Leo has a psychiatric history. Depression, you know, what they used to call manic-depressive which sounds pretty depressing, doesn't it, and now they call bipolar. Much nicer. He's so honest; when they were just chatting one policewoman with a nice open face said casually, 'Were you the sort of parent that sometimes smacked their kids?' He admitted he'd once hit Hayley, and the boys perhaps more than once. But only when they were younger and being little shits. I thought he was a fool to say this, myself. There was an autopsy and those questions asked, of all of us, over and over, until they were satisfied that there was 'nothing suspicious'. Plain English, that means we hadn't killed the baby. Leo as a baby killer, or even a regular hitter, that's the silliest thing I ever heard — absurd, even when depressed. He's the gentlest man on the planet. There was a coroner's report and an inquest. I was glad when it was all over, though it's never all over, really. Not many of those books in the library talk about grandparents when a baby dies, how they feel.

After that Hayley resigned her job. She was too depressed to work. She blames us, she blames Leo especially, which is hardly fair. He was just the one who found her. It could have been me. The child was rolling around; she said we should have tucked her up firmer, we should have checked more often than we did. The mattress was giving off deadly fumes, that's one theory. She'd only had enough money for a cheaper mattress. She should have bought the best. She didn't have enough money. Why didn't we lend her some? Why didn't we effing check earlier? What happened to our sixth sense?

Leo got over his depression, eventually. He needed quite strong medication and heavy-duty psychological counselling, and I was glad when the suggestion of shock treatment didn't go any further — 'get traction', that's what you say now, isn't it? He took out a loan to help Hayley go to Melbourne and start over. Well, she couldn't on her own, no bank would touch her with a barge pole, she had no equity. No bank would lend her a bean. But she's bright. She'll get a good job. She'll survive. I suppose Leo and I will. He has lost his taxi licence because of the publicity. My heart is pretty much broken.

The boys are still in the house, with their BlackBerries and iPods and such, all the gear and enough CDs and DVDs to fill a warehouse. Leo put the hard word on them, for the rent at least, but it's always the same. They've got all these debts. It'll only be for a few months more. They'll pay back the money.

They're victims of the nineties, they say, of the deliberately high unemployment, Rogernomics, Ruthenomics, economic rationalism, new right, work for the dole, WINZ and whatever else they called all that shit. They trot out all these words. I don't know about that. I think my lot might be registered as sickness beneficiaries.

Now they've got a new tack. Don't laugh: advances on their inheritance. You want to get rid of us, they ask? Luke wants $25,000 to set up his own recording studio with a partner, in Ponsonby, where else? Hamish wants $10,000 to travel to England and tide him over until he gets a job. He wants to work in Bristol or Plymouth. They're near to the only decent surf beaches in the UK, down in Cornwall and Devon. He'll get a work permit, no sweat. Wasn't one of his grandmothers a Pom? I'm letting him find out the hard way. Only grandfathers count when it comes to work permits. I think Leo should only give him $5000.

Hear this. Dad, they say, take it out of our inheritance. What inheritance, I say. What makes them think we've got that sort of money? We've got the house, and some money invested for if one of us might need a rest-home, and a bit of extra income from those investments and that's about it. We're a while off from super, that's for sure, as long as the government doesn't shift the goalposts in the meantime. So Leo caves in, and comes back to me like a whipped dog. He says he's going to talk to the lawyer about the rest-home money. I really don't know how it's happened: three children, good degrees, good health — but not a proper job between them, no decent partners let alone a legal spouse, one dead half-caste baby, no money. Once I hoped for grandchildren, but I am not holding my breath, not now.

I won't let Leo go back to the house. Not until they go. It's become poisoned, for him, the very air. It makes him sick to his stomach even to think about it. He doesn't know about the complaints from the neighbours about the thunk thunk boom boom of the stereo systems with floor-to-ceiling speakers. The friends' cars that lack mufflers roaring up and down the street at four in the morning. Girls and gays who come and go. The lawns are unmowed, the hedges falling over, weeds everywhere. I have a friend in the street who's warned me she's on the verge of reporting them to the police for suspected drugs, failure to put out rubbish bins, noise pollution despite repeated warnings after midnight, barking dogs and yelling girls, and screaming brakes and tyres every now and then. I hope she does. I told her she'd be doing me a favour. And sooner rather than later. It's out of my hands now. They won't fly the nest. We are apparently incapable of pushing them. So they will be plucked out by something bigger, say a big local council cat with strong sharp claws. I quite like that metaphor.

The funny thing is they seem to have no conscience at all. They see nothing strange about being boomerangs and their parents quitting the ancestral home. Poor Dad, they say. Good for him to have a change of scene, take the pressure off. And your job, Mum, you always said you liked driving. Lake Road's not so bad outside of rush hours. We'll look after the garden. My arse.

Sometimes Leo weeps. He asks, how? A possibly gay son with a bald skull, one with dreads, a daughter with a brass ring through her navel. Let's face it, all of them no-hopers. Where did those good little innocent kids go? The ones he used to carry on his shoulders to the park and help with their homework. The ones we took camping and he made trolleys and dolls' prams for. I don't have an answer. I don't want even to think about it.

Glenfield is not so bad. Leo is working as a forecourt attendant in a BP station. He can walk there, which is good because I have to have the car for my job. It's my fiftieth birthday next week and he's taking me out to dinner. Somewhere in the Viaduct Basin. It will cost a bomb, but he says he doesn't care, I'm worth it. I sound like those pink hair-colour ads, those American models always saying, rolling their rrrs, 'Because you're worth it.' He will put on his 1980s suit, and I'll get dolled up in mother's best string of pearls, the only thing she left to me, and we'll get a bottle of local bubbly.

I'm not reminding the boys about my birthday. I doubt they'll remember. I'm not expecting any presents, of course. Hayley is in London. I suppose she is. It's about two months since she rang to ask for money, so she must be alright. I don't expect a toll call on my birthday either, even collect. None of them ever rings just to say 'How-de-do, Mum?'

Houses are selling round here again, rather better than Devonport. It's quite convenient for me at this time. I work hard, seven days a week; my clients can always get me any time of day or night. And they do; phone calls at two in the morning are not so unusual — you'd be surprised how demanding and ruthless and tense people become when purchasing or selling a property. My work means I don't have to think about my children, or that little dead half-caste moppet sleeping in her tiny white coffin, or our beloved villa. Leo has his bad times, but he's doing OK. I had to choose between them and him, in the end, and I chose him. It was what you might call a lose–lose situation.

One day before we peg out, we might be able to afford a little trip to the Islands, or Queensland. I used to think Europe, a riverboat down through France, the sunflowers in Tuscany, Big Ben and the Tower of London, but not any more.

I'd be quite pleased actually just to take a trip down to my house in Devonport, to find it empty and not burned down or anything. I have to believe the mauve wisteria I planted is still there.

Post mortem

'Jacqueline Le Gros, without a word of a lie,' Alan declared firmly, bristling at the blunt Australian challenge. 'I'm telling you, her name was Jacqueline Le Gros.'

'But that's hardly credible, from what you've told us.' Alan's initial dislike of the plain, academic lady from Sydney was strengthening as she continued, 'That name was deliberately chosen, surely, self-referential, even self-mocking. I can't believe it was an accident of birth.'

'All the documents said Le Gros,' said Alan. 'All of them: birth certificate, passport, driver's licence, credit cards, everything. I saw them. I had no reason to believe otherwise.'

'Fat people are very often their own cruellest critics. They can put themselves down quite mercilessly.'

'And heavily. Remember that woman who broke the chair, Nance,' chuckled her husband, eyeing the table for any tardy recognition of his laboured pun. 'It was at a conference, the informal late night for delegates in a restaurant. She actually broke it, the chair I mean. And she was truly *enormous*. The look on her face as she sank slowly down. The noises of buckling, cracking plastic giving way under the load. I've never laughed so much in a long, long time. Though to give her credit, no-one laughed longer or harder than she.'

Alan, suddenly weary of their nasal accents and ivory-tower air of authority, listened to the lunch party, now arrived at coffee, throw around names of amusing or weird inappropriateness. They all had at least one: a PR consultant named Fudge, the

Happy Family monikers of Cleavers, Carpenters, Drivers and the rest, none of any real wit. Although convivial by nature, after twenty-five years of passenger ships Alan had had his fill of dinner chitchat. He could answer any question about his current ship or the professional life at sea in his sleep; he had told every seafarer's story in his repertoire a thousand times; his rapt audiences always knew that many more dramatic, bizarre and heart-wrenching tales tucked inside his head were subject to patient confidentiality and could never be divulged. Ship's doctors, dealing with passengers and crew, saw Life In The Raw; they faced life-threatening dramas and dealt with life-ending emergencies. But here, today, he could not send his apologies via the Head Steward, nor get up after the main course and smilingly plead pressure of work, patients waiting.

Larry, at the head of the heavy glass-topped table set for lunch beside the pool, was an old university friend and his host; Mrs Larry, dear Paula, had kindly put together this party especially for him. She would have told her guests about the English doctor, only just retired from the sea and hating it, taking a trip by car around Europe to visit friends and galleries before he went back to settle down in Plymouth. She might have mentioned he'd long been a widower; he'd be less pleased if she'd mentioned why. She probably had. Alan rallied a little as his glass was refilled with an excellent Côtes de Provence rosé, crisp and full-bodied. He could be gracious with the best of them.

They were seven around the table, and they had enjoyed a splendid lunch. Larry and Paula had lived overlooking the famous deep-water bay at Villefranche-sur-Mer for forty years. Both were slim, deeply tanned and sleek as seals. With that fortunate combination of energy and money, both could pass for twenty-five years younger than in fact they were. Alan knew Paula to be sixty-nine. The combination of gold jewellery and designer bikini with a deep, even tan — and almost certainly artificial — along with blonde streaks on her head and permanent removal of hair from anywhere else, added up to a radiant image that was more Latin than English. He'd seen enough female bodies stripped of clothes to know that for Anglo-Saxons, which she was, such smoothed bronzed sleekness at her age took work. At nearly seventy, in her scarlet bikini, her buttocks shining like polished russet apples, her back straight, skin unlined, eyes twinkling, she was admirable!

While Larry, a boyish chap whose solid income came from a lifetime working in a Monaco-based family medical-publishing business, played at going native in a red-and-yellow sarong and large straw hat, though his chest sported a hedge of honest white hair. Apparently he drew the line at chest-waxing. They spent the summers watering the oleanders, plumbagos, lavenders, begonias and delphiniums around their pink Côte d'Azur villa and, since Larry semi-retired, skied away the winters from a second home in Austria, in a village close to Innsbruck. Alan had no doubt that both were splendid skiers, always immaculately turned out and never less than upright. There were three successful children dotted about Europe, and enough money to visit regularly, with whole families flown in for Christmas and special birthdays, the grandchildren for Easter breaks and other holidays.

The other English couple, with the house in Antibes and the chalet in Kitzbühel, had less natural charm about them. Anthony (his wife insisted, with the 'th' voiced, please) was a retired airline pilot, jumbos of course, stockily handsome and 'some years' retired from flying; he'd fudged his reply to that question. No doubt he was also ten or fifteen years more than his bronzed appearance; it was a mystery, this deeply embedded western equation of sun-kissed skin with youth, vigour and good health. Anthony would dominate the conversation for at least the first hour, and so he did, through sheer habit, helped along by cues from enraptured women and everyone else's oft-told airlines stories inevitably thrown in. With a few notable exceptions, thought Alan, pilots always held the floor, especially jumbo captains and even more so, those who had flown Concordes. In social situations like these, pilots certainly outranked ship's doctors, and even most ship's captains. Masters of the new generation of cruise ships carrying 2000 or 3000 people generally did alright.

Sipping his excellent rosé, Alan had relaxed and let the flow of near-disasters, comedies, irritations, SARS, terrorism and other post-9/11 worries, snippets of in-house airline gossip and technical matters flow past him. The patio was shaded by the leaves of large, flourishing banana palms; it was unusually hot this year for June and he was rather sorry he'd not taken the offer on arrival of a dip before lunch in the turquoise pool along with the flute of a very good champagne. His own body was neither sleek nor bronze — skin, chin, nipples and belly had irretrievably sagged, legs had gone blotchy and scabby and a little bowed — in this company, he was not altogether proud of the figure he cut. Shipboard life had been a little too comfortable, the gin a little too cheap and the buttery hour-old breakfast croissants always too tempting. He'd played a regular game of deck quoits with the middle-ranking officers, and walked the decks occasionally. He'd not sunk into a deck chair squarely facing the sun, as Europeans did, with their eyes blissfully closed, for many years. Nevertheless, without any conscious 'work' at all, he could boast being not much over the weight he'd been at eighteen. A gradual shrinking, of height, muscle tone and spirit, awaited him.

The food was excellent: vegetable crudités with a heavy, handmade mayonnaise, then a rabbit pâté, a pork-based pâté *en croûte*, and Paula's always-popular Coronation Chicken, a famous English recipe (involving apricots, red wine, cream and a pinch of curry powder) unknown to the Australians, served with four or five imaginative salads, mustards from Dijon, Breton butter and baguettes. By the cheeses (a Camembert, Port Salut and Roquefort with origins and pedigrees carefully described by Larry to his guests), Alan had decided that Anthony was a Grade-A airline bore and his blonde Yorkshire wife, Penelope, while as bronzed, firm, adorned with gold and almost as remarkable as her hostess, was actually one of those persistently genteel English-women programmed with a shrill, disparaging remark on every subject, no matter how arcane, political or personal.

The comparatively unadorned Australian couple, more confidently estimated to be in their mid-fifties, were devoid of charm of any sort. Apparently the lanky, gingery Graeme, a noted writer on European art and related topics, was here for six months to research a book on Gauguin, with Nancy concurrently taking a sabbatical from her Sydney institution. She was a social scientist of some colour and in the pool her unshaven legs seemed less like a political statement, than laziness, or even bad manners. She was plump, dark-haired, sloppily dressed, one of the plainer women Alan had seen in a long while. While used to patients' English spoken with every possible level of competence, accent and grammatical eccentricity, Alan was struck afresh by how flat and dull the Antipodean speaker of English could sound. Only Americans could make English sound more monotonal, lacking any of the light and shade, the musicality and precision of French or Italian. Such flatness contrasted oddly with the natural high energy and good humour that he always associated with Australia. He was sorry he wouldn't see Sydney, that stupendous harbour, again.

Below in the bay, he'd noted boats coming and going to two of the smaller cruise ships anchored there. Web addresses and garish slashes of paint did nothing to improve their box-like lines, their lack of any traditional grace. Thank Christ, thought Alan, he'd got out in time.

He contributed occasionally to the conversation, so as not to be thought ungenerous or uninterested. Anthony had become passionate about Chirac's insufferably high-handed attitude to the Americans and everyone else, producing a riposte from Nancy that she wished her own country's PM had similar guts and not played second poodle to Tony Blair's first poodle over the justification and legality of the Iraq war. Anthony countered that Tony Blair was absolutely right in his stance, history would vindicate him, and all power to his arm. Nancy said they'd have to agree to differ, but it was the one time in her life she wished she'd been born a New Zealander. That otherwise forgettable country was not one of the Bush's 'coalition of the willing'. Graeme quoted *Newsweek*, or it may have been *Time*, on the mess the Americans had made in post-war Iraq, the sinister incompetence of the neo-cons Rumsfeld, Wolfowitz, Cheney and their ilk. They all noted the comparative lack of Americans on the Côte d'Azur and reportedly, in Paris, this summer.

'If they're staying at home, I'm not sorry, not one teeny bit,' said Penelope, sniffing her Rocquefort cautiously. She was a small and fastidious eater; so, Alan noted, was the splendid Paula. 'Those loud, twanging voices! So nasal. The gay couples from California with the careful little moustaches and tight T-shirts, you can pick them a mile off. The roly-poly women in their check Bermuda shorts, white sneakers and baseball caps. Truly dire! Those huge college girls, waddling around with their fat white arms and stumpy kitchen-table legs! I simply shudder.'

'That's something you don't see much on the beaches here,' said Nancy. 'Overweight kids.'

'Wouldn't they rather tend to stay away from beaches?' asked Alan mildly. Being slightly detached from the conversation since the crudités, his wine glass seemingly always full, he was now feeling a little light-headed.

'Maybe, but you don't see them in the streets either. There must be something about the French diet.'

'Or a civilized attitude to living, generally speaking,' said Alan, expecting that Penelope at least would rise to the bait. She was clearly not one of the more contented expatriates in the south of France.

'Civilized?' cried Penelope, her Knightsbridge voice rising predictably. 'It's all absolute tommyrot, a myth they've created for themselves. I don't consider strikes *civilized*, all those long-haired people in jeans and berets on silly marches and no trains. Their frightful little dogs, the dog poo around the place? The post office is hopeless, letters take *weeks* to get anywhere, and the telephones aren't much better. Taxes, well, don't get me started, it's simply daylight robbery, not to mention all their ghastly bureaucrats! What do they *do* with all that money besides give it away to the farmers?'

'It's a socialist state, Penelope,' Larry reminded her. 'They have thirty-five-hour working weeks. People are generally happy, the health system works, which is more than you can say of the NHS these days. The babies are well cared for, the mothers paid generously to be mothers. The arts flourish, the water is good, electricity happens.'

'That's only because it's nuclear,' began Graeme.

'I'm not complaining,' said Larry calmly. 'The dog shit gets cleaned up. The streets are free of rubbish and full of flowers, the buses are wonderful and trains ditto when they run which is most of the time.'

'When they run,' muttered Penelope. 'Not that we use them much.'

'A hundred and sixty million tourists like it enough to visit every year, with or without the Americans. It's the most visited country in the world. They are clever, proud people in a well-balanced society.'

'Anyone would think it was nirvana, Larry, listening to you,' said Penelope.

Larry opened his arms wide to embrace his guests, the view, the salmon-pink house with its terracotta patio, the luminous pool, the bananas, scarlet and white oleanders, orange cannas, the balmy air, the light that inspired painters to works of genius. His shrug and quizzical expression said it all: what more do you want? There sits a supremely happy man, thought Alan, a touch enviously.

Paula said, 'Just think of all the music on during the summer, up and down the Côte. Every little chateau. Opera in Nice, and Monte Carlo, concerts . . .'

'Tell me . . .' began Nancy.

But Penelope, her dander up, husband nodding mournfully in agreement, was not to be deflected.

'We're not opera-goers, Paula, and chamber music is certainly not my cup of tea.'

'Don't you go to the jazz festival in Nice?' asked Paula, mischievously. 'We go every year.'

'We're not "into jazz" either,' Penelope snarled. 'You know I can't stand it. But you can't deny, these co-called civilized and charming French, they are so cold, so unfriendly. Have we ever been invited out to dinner in a French house in eleven years, Anthony?'

Anthony shook his head. 'Nope.'

'The way they won't speak anything but French,' Penelope

went on. 'And speaking for myself, I think French *cuisine*—' Her lips shaped the satisfactorily plosive word with deep scorn '—is totally, totally overrated.'

'Perhaps that's why the kids don't get fat,' quipped Anthony, by way of support. 'Uneatable food. You can eat only so many baguettes. If I was a kid I'd refuse to touch a plate with rabbit on it.'

'Overrated and overpriced.'

'Penelope, that's just silly and well you know it,' laughed Paula fondly. Alan admired her skill in gently reproving her friend before strangers did, and only just in time.

'If you don't much like France or the French, tell me, why do you live here?' The blunt Australian question hung in the air before Nancy added, 'It's a better standard of living than you'll get on a fixed income in England, surely. And no-one ever got a suntan like yours in England by the sun's rays alone.'

The men all smiled slightly. Penelope opened her mouth to speak, but Nancy, capitalizing on her advantage with timing born of long practice chairing departmental meetings, had turned to Alan.

'Going back to this question of food, if it's true that European kids aren't getting obese like the rest of the Western world, America particularly, why do you think that is? Any theories?'

'Oh, we all know why Americans are fat,' said Penelope, undaunted.

'Tell me,' invited Alan innocently.

'Chips, hamburgers, junk food generally, fizzy drinks, candies, cookies, too much television, bad parenting, not enough exercise or vegetables,' intoned Penelope, counting the items off on long fingers with perfect crimson nails and seven heavy rings, diamonds aplenty. 'A culture of instant gratification and no self-discipline. Simple.'

'If only it were,' he said. 'Of all the difficult problems I saw in my clinical days, obesity was about the most intractable.'

'The least successfully treated,' said Nancy.

'Putting aside the cancers, the strokes — yes, true obesity has little long-term hope of success. So many factors involved. As with any addiction, the change can only come from the patient's intent and inner will to change. Nothing one says has the . . .'

'With respect, doctor, anything you said . . .' Nancy had made this point before to skinny male doctors and knew it always succeeded in making them prickly and defensive. 'What I mean is, women fundamentally, *deeply* resent being told to do this and that about food by genetically slim and patriarchal men who have never in their entire lives had the ongoing responsibility of feeding a family month in month out, or had to make a choice about eating or not eating something because of what it might do to their body shape.'

'That may be true,' Alan murmured thoughtfully. He was becoming a little embarrassed at the seriousness and personal nature of this post-prandial discussion around a Riviera pool, the men's lack of interest evident. Penelope's body language, slumped back in the chair examining her crimson nails, indicated much the same.

Anthony, though, had also read in *Time*, or was it *Newsweek*, of ridiculous lawsuits currently being taken out in America against burger, cookie and fizzy-drink makers for tricking consumers by 'misleading advertising'. Why, only yesterday he'd read in the *International Herald Tribune* that the big food-makers spent fifteen billion dollars a year — that's US billion — on advertising. Fifteen billion, mind, up three from 1998. The group was united in its scorn of Big Macs and Happy Meals, of self-indulgent, lazy and foolish little fat people trying to place the blame elsewhere, and the smarmy well-fed litigation lawyers who would be the only winners in the long run. 'You might equally well sue your mother for giving you the Big Mac or the cookie in the first place,' said Anthony.

'Or your father,' said Nancy. 'There's research showing that nagging fathers are the most potent and destructive influences of all. And I have this theory, though it'd be one hell of a research project to set up.'

Alan looked at Nancy with renewed interest, as she went on, 'I reckon if you took say 200 family men of normal weight and fitness, from families of normal slim people, genetically slim people and completely reversed the roles so that they did all the family shopping, the planning, the cooking, the clearing up — and this is the crucial bit — for no less than a year, even better two years — then, ipso facto, they would put on weight. Their attitude to food would be more complex, less controlled, and it would show around their waists.'

Alan chuckled. 'Well, you may be right.'

'It's all that thinking about food, all day long. For most women it never stops. We had three sprogs, so I do know. What's for dinner tonight? Breakfast tomorrow. What to put in the dreaded lunchboxes?'

'Thank God for our school dinners,' interrupted Penelope.

'Hubby says "Let's have a dinner party or a barbie," but who does the planning, the shopping, the . . . yes, Anthony, I know men, even Englishmen, just love standing over barbies, and a few do occasionally stoop to clogging up supermarket aisles, but my point remains — who usually does the cooking?'

'Anthony helps,' began Penelope stoutly. 'He draws the line at shopping, but he's been known to set a table in his time.'

'Only the person who has to feed a family seven days a week for fifteen or twenty years knows about the pressure of providing,' Nancy went on. 'All those weight-loss programmes — every diet under the sun — for women anyway, they're doomed to failure before they even start. Obese males have a better chance, if they can just restrain themselves enough to eat what's put in front of them and stay out of the kitchen.'

'There's certainly evidence that most programmes don't work for most people, in the long term,' mused Alan. 'I had one patient . . .'

He looked around at the group. Damn the rosé. He needed to stop this conversation. He was beginning to suspect that Nancy was more professionally involved in this topic in some Sydney institution than first appeared. And the very thought of Jacqueline Le Gros had been followed almost instantaneously and mysteriously by another: the memory of a promise made a year ago, and not kept. Good Lord, the *tape* . . . he had completely forgotten the tape. He felt himself go pale, unable to immediately recall exactly where it was. Most of the stuff from his final ship, the electrical equipment, CDs, papers, books and clothes that for decades he'd carted from one cabin to another, had already been packed up and sent off to Plymouth. Perhaps it was still in the briefcase he tossed on his bed. He had never been cavalier with his patients, even dead ones.

'Yes, one patient? Man or woman?' prompted Paula. But he looked distracted. 'Are you alright, Alan? Too much sun?' She got up to adjust the square umbrella of cream canvas that partially shaded the table.

'No, it's fine.' He took a glass of water. 'Thank you. A loose end to tie up when I get home, that's all. A little circuit in my tired old brain just got reconnected. Funny how that happens.'

'I don't get the impression it was a happy one, old boy,' said Larry. At university in London, reading history, he'd shared digs with Alan, lean and lanky, a bit dour, conscientious to a fault. Forty years of doctoring hadn't changed him. A Christmas card came every year, no matter which of the high seas he was on at the time; he always rang them whenever his ship was off Monaco or Marseilles. 'Tell you what, I'll send you a postcard as a reminder. What shall I put on it?'

'Just . . . Jacqueline.'

'Jacqueline? Sounds interesting.'

'Was she a patient on board?' asked Paula, cutting off any further teasing assumption that Alan might have had a love life or quips about cruise ships known to be full of rapacious single women, old, rich and easy meat. As far as she knew he hadn't had a serious relationship since Beatrice drank herself into an early grave, twenty-five years ago. At least, he'd never mentioned a friendship with a woman heralding his return to normal life ashore. Ship's doctoring, for a childless widower then in his early forties, had seemed a reasonable solution to having to resign a good hospital job, see Beatrice protractedly and painfully off and sort out a few personal issues. Larry had assured Paula at the time that Alan wasn't an undeclared gay, just anguished and hurt. He had become, understandably, very wary and very private.

'Or you can't talk about her,' Paula said. 'Patient confidentiality and all that.'

'It's not that . . . she died. Rather a gloomy story, I'm afraid. Wouldn't you rather we talked of something else?' he said, a touch desperately, kicking himself for having raised the daunting spectre of Jacqueline in the first place. 'I'm going to Nice tomorrow. I need advice. What's on? Where should I start?'

'A notably big woman with a weight problem on board a cruise ship?' said Nancy. 'Where the temptations are so obvious? Sounds a tad weird. Asking for trouble.'

'She wasn't quite so big when we started.'

Graeme asked, 'Was she one of those rich American widows who go round and round the world, same cabin, same ship, gorging on the food and bonking the stewards and anyone else game?'

'She was on my last ship for four years, except of course when the ship was in refit. Came for one round-the-world voyage, then a second round the Med, and just stayed on. In effect I became her trusted physician, and did my professional best, but essentially, yes, food killed her.'

'How, when it came to the point?' asked Anthony, who'd had his share of cabin service directors phoning through four hours out from some airport to say there was a major problem with a passenger.

'Choked on a French fry in a Biscay storm, two days out of Southampton. The steward found her the next morning.' His sunglasses would be shielding his distaste at the general smiles, especially Penelope's unrestrained, tinkling laughter. 'But the writing was on the wall. I'd warned her, this would very likely be her last voyage. She was starting to need more care than we could or should provide.'

'Do you do post mortems at sea?' asked Anthony. 'We always had unmarked ambulances take our stiffs off.'

'Not now. In the old days, yes, when ships were ships, and not floating blocks of apartments and theme parks . . . like those.' One of the cruise ships looked like it might be preparing for departure.

'So they go in a morgue? In those awful sliding drawers?' asked Penelope.

Alan looked at her coldly. 'Yes.' He would prefer not to be reminded of twenty-one inert stone of Jacqueline in the freezer, reduced by a French fry to one of the 'friendly four', as the morgue accommodations were known. The two orderlies and several of the brawnier stewards had been required to lift the cadaver from her cabin double bed onto the trolley.

'Standard scene in costume dramas, what?' said Anthony. 'Captain reading service, body tipped unceremoniously into the sea. Something about "committing thee to the deep". They still say that?'

'Commend thee to the deep, to be turned into corruption, looking for the resurrection of the body when the sea shall give up its dead,' said Alan. When younger, he'd heard those sonorous phrases a few times. His own ashes were to be scattered at sea.

There was a moment's pause; the notion of bodily corruption was an unwelcome one in this company. Anthony helped himself to the Côte de Provence. 'And didn't they have a tradition on the old windjammers of taking a turn with the needle through the nose to make sure the person was dead?'

'Anthony!' Penelope protested. 'How grisly is that?'

'Or gristly!' said Graeme.

'I believe it to be true,' said Alan. 'We used to do burials at six in the morning, so as not to upset the passengers. No more. Nowadays bodies get landed ashore at the first suitable port and flown wherever.'

'What did you tell the other passengers?'

'In Jacqueline's case, nothing. It was early on, third day out. Passengers on big cruise ships are very focused on their own good time. They simply don't notice, or if they do, talk about it briefly and quickly forget.'

The wine was starting to make him sleepy. But Nancy hadn't finished with him or Jacqueline yet.

'So in four years at sea she went from big to very big, gargantuan. Don't you regard that as a personal failure?'

'Not at all. She'd inherited a great deal of money and believed that she was a lost cause, beyond the reach of any treatment. Surgery, by the way, for her, was not an option. She had an absolute passion for ethnic food: Chinese, Italian, Spanish,

Thai, Turkish, high French, Mexican, Russian, you name it, and that particular ship had eight different restaurants. It was her version of going out in style, a first-class gourmet's passage to heaven.'

'To that great global Michelin five-star restaurant in the sky,' scoffed Graeme. 'Sounds utterly self-indulgent and disgusting to me.'

The asphyxiation from the rogue French fry would have been harrowing but relatively quick. Alan wanted more than ever to shut this conversation down.

He said flatly, 'Any patient you look after for four years . . . well, now tell me about Nice, what I should—?'

'Was she thick as two planks as well as big?' asked Penelope.

Alan sighed: did these women never let up? 'She was intelligent, sensual, funny, generous and larger than life. Between meals she relished everything the ship had to offer: the library, every show, every film, gambling nights, fancy dress, many of the lectures, on science or anything else, shore excursions when in port . . . she was there.'

'An interesting past, I bet,' prodded Nancy.

'She spoke three languages, and knew her way around Europe's cities. She wasn't always wealthy, but she married well, twice, and had her own business in Paris as an interior decorator to the very rich. Like many apparently successful people, she was given to depression. She was surprisingly short on self-esteem . . .'

'Ah! I knew you'd say that sometime,' said Penelope triumphantly. 'So boring. Don't you get tired of dotty and inadequate people banging on about their self-esteem?'

Alan ignored this. '. . . and pathologically addicted to the rich and sensual food which eventually killed her.' He looked at the gleaming faces fixed intently on him, wanting more; Jacqueline in a nutshell. But case closed. 'Now, won't someone please tell me where to go in Nice or Monaco tomorrow? Exhibitions worth seeing?'

'I bet a hundred pounds she never used the pool,' said Penelope, admiring her own racehorse-slim ankle, the perfectly crimson toenails. 'If you were that size, honestly, would you?' She smiled smugly around the table.

'You would lose your bet, ma'am,' said Alan coldly. 'Even in the last year, when she had to get a steward to help her, I believe she was quite often in the pool at midnight or later. Her energy was quite extraordinary. I grew to like her very much.'

Paula, he registered during the silence, had not been party to the inquisition, but was gazing, apparently listening and relaxed, across the Villefranche bay. He leaned forward to empty the rosé bottle into her glass and the clinician in him observed with surprise the tension around the neck, the tremble in the fingers. Were those outsize sunglasses perhaps concealing tears? Is our hostess Mrs Larry, he wondered, a less happy woman than she, or her husband, would have us believe?

'How old was she, when she carked?' demanded Nancy.

'A mere fifty-one.' As he anticipated, at that the lunch party fell silent.

The case of Jacqueline Le Gros was not quite closed, however. There was the mislaid tape. It had not been lurking in his briefcase, as he hoped, but eventually turned up towards the end of unpacking his gear, nearly lost among his beloved tapes of Mahler and the Russian late Romantics. He had little enough to show for twenty-five years at sea, barely enough to make the apartment, with a small sea view over Plymouth Hoe, anything like as homely as his various-sized cabins.

Larry's postcard from Villefranche-sur-mer had duly turned up: 'Remember Jacqueline — and give yourself some decent treats, old man of the sea — advise take up golf and/or bridge. Brush up your French — or Shakespeare?' In other words, old chap, 'get a life'; the *cliché du jour*. They were shortly off to Austria for the winter, which he hoped would perk Paula up a bit. (Perk her up? From what? The ageless golden woman living in Mediterranean paradise?) The picture showed rosy villas nestled in cypress and tamarisk trees above the bay, superyachts dominated by one of P&O's behemoths. He put the card on the bare mantelpiece.

Jacqueline had made him promise to observe one strict, non-negotiable condition: she would make this tape, and Alan would listen to it only after he fulfilled his intention on his return to England to get immediately in touch with a classmate from medical school days, now an emeritus professor and worldwide authority on obesity. He would listen only if he had kept his word to offer himself to the professor's research programme as a field researcher, paid or unpaid.

'Anything I put on here, darling,' she had said, turning the blank cassette over in her stubby fingers after making him sign and date it, 'is for your professional interest only. It's not for a cheap laugh, or to be played at parties or read on the radio.' He had protested forcibly; how could she even think he was capable of such a thing, but she was serious. 'It is to be treated as bona fide research. Promise! And you, my friend, are desperately going to need something to do when you get off here.'

A day after her fatal encounter with a French fry, while he and the female baby doc were clearing out her cabin, he had found the cassette, ominously tied up with a red ribbon, and a note that said, 'I have really no idea what's on here, I think I got drunk, and perhaps made a decision, but what the hell, love and kisses all the same. Listen soonest as per promise.' And, after hurriedly checking the first ten seconds or so — yes, that was her throaty voice — he'd put the cassette into his pocket and later into a drawer with a jumble of other tapes. He had meant to play it as soon as he could but had then been run off his feet by seasick and injured passengers — they ploughed through the edges of an interminable Atlantic gale — and himself off colour from some bug or other he'd picked up. In the end, he'd just forgotten about it. How could he forget? Inexcusable!

At a Plymouth store, he bought himself enough plain furniture to get by and was engaged by the grateful, underfunded emeritus professor as a twenty-hours-a-week field researcher into the causes of childhood obesity, helping set up a desperately needed long-term study. America, and increasingly Australia, the UK and others, emailed the professor, were in the grip of a growing pandemic of childhood obesity. Much research was needed, so that politicians, educators and health professionals could formulate proper programmes to halt the alarming spread of fat.

One spring Sunday morning, rain pelting down outside, Alan decided the tape had sat with Larry's postcard on the mantelpiece looking at him accusingly for long enough. And now that the moment had arrived, he found himself nervous of what he might hear. It might be embarrassing rubbish, the ravings of a disturbed and, despite all evidence to the contrary, desperately lonely woman. He brewed a pot of coffee, got out a pad and paper for notes, and turned on his answerphone to take incoming calls, such as they were. He checked the counter was at zero. Ninety minutes, possibly, of Jacqueline Le Gros waited patiently for an audience.

She had walked into the French restaurant, that first cruise, the first night away from Southampton. Alan remembered already being seated with several other passengers, and his eye catching a short square woman waddling towards his table, asking confidently if she could join them. Although undoubtedly grossly obese, she was also an arresting image, dressed in yellow paisley silk, a long tunic over a floating skirt teamed with an outsize scarlet pashmina and a great deal of jewellery. She was skilled with cosmetics, her long hair was black and piled up with gold pins into elaborate coils, her nails were manicured orange. Her perfume was heady and no doubt costly. He expected that inevitably, sometime quite early in the voyage, he would see her in his surgery; that same afternoon, a discreet request for details from an assistant purser informed him she lived in Paris and was travelling unaccompanied in First Class. She gave her age as forty-seven, her nationality as British, her marital status as widowed, her job as interior designer.

At the table that first night, she demonstrated several things: a generous wit, a capacity for listening to and enjoying others, fluency in French and Italian besides English and passable German, a broad cultural knowledge, well-informed opinions on world affairs, a raucous cackle and a gargantuan appetite. She ate her way through five good-sized courses, each without embarrassment or restraint. She asked the waiter for more rolls in the common basket, more butter, and ran bread around her plate to sop up the juices left by a moistly pink, specially underdone piece of New Zealand fillet of lamb. 'Take a tip from the earthy Europeans, darling,' she chuckled at a pair of disapproving female English eyes sitting opposite. 'One day our Liz will be doing it too. Or Charles, bless him. He probably does already.' She chose a tiramisù for dessert, downed two limoncello along with the petits fours, and three cubes of sugar went into her espresso. Alan found himself watching this intake, fascinated if also somewhat repelled.

His finger poised on the *Start* button, Alan felt his eyes misting over and told himself to get a grip. On that first and subsequent voyages, he'd seen her regularly in his surgery with a series of minor worries, and always vague promises to watch her diet and go for walks around the deck; occasionally he came across her in the saloons, at one of the various shows or films. She was easy to spot, always colourfully dressed, always with a noisy, laughing group of people, always radiating good humour, and always with food and drink on the table in front of her. An apéritif did not pass without generous handfuls of the finer nuts or plump anchovy-stuffed olives; morning coffee was accompanied by several of the chef's excellent pastries, baked overnight; lunch was a feast; tea was taken with club sandwiches and butterfly cakes and after-dinner coffee with petits fours or little sweet Dutch biscuits or the Belgian truffles she bought on board to share around. He saw her only occasionally at actual meals, but came to realize that she was methodically doing the rounds of the various restaurants, and according to the stewards, setting records for consumption in each one of them. Serving her, one told him, was both fun — she was so appreciative, ate with such gusto, flirted outrageously with them all, even the poofs — and verging on the disgusting. If you laid out on a bench all the stuff she put down her throat at one meal . . . three times a day . . . never mind all the snacks . . . it just didn't bear thinking about.

Ah Jacqueline! Could you not have enjoyed those years of voyaging round the world — you were only in your late forties, for heaven's sake, you had money, you were personable and confident and generous — without the baffling need to inflate yourself from seventeen stone to nearly twenty-one and counting? You could have become one of P&O's best regular first-class passengers, one of its most beloved eccentrics, a legend among the crews, without eating yourself into a circus freak and finally, the ship's morgue. Where were the digestive hormones that kick in and tell most of us when our stomachs are full? In your case, what terrible compulsion overrode nature's own brakes?

He had warned her, scolded her and later, as he got to know

her better, pleaded with her and finally tried to seriously frighten her.

'Yes, doctor,' she would say, self-mocking, even to comments that within five years she was a sitter for type-two diabetes resulting eventually in daily injections of insulin, probable amputations and blindness, that her cholesterol would lead to bypass operations and cardiac arrest, her blood pressure to strokes; the sheer body tonnage itself to multiple knee or hip replacements, gradual skeletal collapse. Assuredly, if she continued to gain, she would not see her fifty-fifth birthday. Sometime during the first year, her eyes gleaming with mischief and defiance, joking about taking horses to water, she refused point blank to get on his scales. At some point, probably in the third year, although still intellectually intrigued, he silently washed his hands of her. He wrote out her scripts, and treated the weight-related but still minor complaints that she presented at regular intervals. Until the last voyage when she increasingly took to her cabin, he quite frequently enjoyed her company in the public rooms and on deck. And that, he'd come to realize, was exactly what she wanted from her doctor, no more and no less.

What was he going to learn from this tape — anything he didn't know already? By way of explanation or corroboration, a litany of childhood deprivation, bullying, beatings and abuse, parental separation, rape, incest, pregnancies, tragedies, rationalizations, excuses? In that first year aboard, he'd soon realized she was noticeably unforthcoming about the background that gave her the money to keep an apartment in Paris and float round the world first class for years on end. Any questions about her family or childhood, prompted by genuinely trying to understand her addiction, how best he might help her control it, were skilfully deflected and went unanswered. She would not be drawn into anything resembling counselling sessions. He spent many of his free hours on a ship's computer, searching new papers on morbid obesity, clicking on subscriptions to university research findings; he ordered books from amazon.com to await him in the next port. For all the huge variety of ailments, injuries and personalities parading before him daily, even though sometimes he didn't see her for several days, he found himself intrigued by the weighty mystery of Jacqueline Le Gros.

Alan got up and made himself another cup of coffee. The rain had stopped, the sea beyond his balcony was grey, featureless. Just one ship on the horizon, the passengers queasy on the first day. Most vessels setting out into the Atlantic were too far out to sea to be visible, even with binoculars. The English Channel had nothing to recommend it at the best of times.

How in God's name had he washed up here, apart from some vague notion of returning to his home town, his family roots — if a couple of tedious cousins and their dreadful offspring can be considered roots. He could expect no support from that quarter. A ship's doctor socialized with his patients to an extent an ordinary GP, even in a small town, never did. Was what he had come to feel for Jacqueline a hopeless, despairing kind of love? Hopeless because of the horrible comedy of it (tall reedy chap with huge wife, the stuff of music-hall jokes) or the shame of it (Jacqueline on his arm, the incredulity and pity and repugnance in people's eyes). Constant embarrassment about her and for her; it could never work. The phoney intimacy of shipboard life often led to disappointment and failure ashore; then there was the impossibility in that environment of disentangling the professional and personal. Doctor–patient relationships were forbidden, and neither had time on their side. He had seen an addiction take one wife to her grave, lived through hell for eight years before it was all over — was he being so unreasonable or selfish to believe there was no possible, imaginable future? I'm sorry, he would probably have said had a conversation ever taken this turn, I'm just too old, too tired, it would be a huge mistake.

Had she ever entertained hopes that she might meet someone in her four years of cruising the world? Didn't they all, those melancholy armies of single, questing women? Was that someone actually him, despite their age difference (nothing of consequence), and if so, was she slowly, painfully, disappointed and finally, disillusioned?

A background hum, the ship's engines and air-conditioning, announced that she had begun recording.

'Jacqueline Le Gros — one, two, three testing — here we go, Jacqueline Le Gros, recording this in her lovely first-class cabin on board the *Pacific Princess*, June 24, 2003. Research subject for Dr Alan Baines working with Bristol University, ongoing research into obesity in children. This tape is made according to certain conditions agreed with Dr Baines, and will remain his property and copyright. His signature is to be found on the case. Any information contained in it will remain confidential to him, and will be used for research purposes only, at his sole and absolute discretion.'

He smiled at the quasi-legal language, but there was also an edge of self-mockery. Two days later they were sliding her body into the cooler.

'*Alors*. The question before the court is: how does a sensible, intelligent, talented slip of a girl at twenty-one end up a disgusting mountain of flesh at fifty-one, the extreme embodiment of Miss Piggy? Is there *anything* I can contribute which will help a female child avoid this path?

'For starters, take the most powerful and sinister propaganda tool the world has ever known. Don't you think that it's weird, simply bizarre, that in the name of free-market ideology, governments let their television stations promote unhealthy foods that will as surely as night follows day make people fat, and then spend millions of dollars on health programmes everywhere *except* on television—because isn't it ironic, they can't afford to buy airtime to tell them how bad those same foods are? None of the worthy programmes on good health and sensible eating work! Will ever work! It's pure hokum. Madness, duplicity, monumental stupidity . . . words fail me how stupid it is. And a complete waste of money. If I were the Minister of Fat People I would stop all television advertising of food, and drink and cigarettes immediately, this stance permanent and not negotiable. Then the poor kids would start to have some chance. They and their parents would not be brainwashed daily into thinking that a limp squitty sodden hamburger with about half an ounce of fatty protein, a flap of lettuce and one piece of gherkin sliced so thin it's transparent, plus a great pile of French fries cooked in dangerously saturated oils, is a decent meal. Ah but . . . we must have our "free" media, and to pay for the free media we need advertisers, and the darling noble advertisers fill up airtime and bring lots of lovely spondoolicks into the government coffers.'

She paused, to steady her voice, thought Alan. She had been almost crying with rage.

'There are some sacrificial lambs involved here, folks, in maintaining this ideological corporate and political madness, this merry-go-round of very, very large sums of money. Witness beautiful, normal but vulnerable children, millions of them in the Western world dominated by the ideologies of commerce and advertising, being set up for a lifetime of failure by ignorant, struggling parents indoctrinated and betrayed by an international army of callous, avaricious madmen and murderers.

'You didn't know I could get this passionately political, this cynical, did you, Alan? And I must get off my soapbox *tout de suite* before I start berating myself yet again for missing the one splendid chance I had to get into politics. Politics? *Moi*, the party girl? At age twenty-seven, having made an impression as a feature writer on a national newspaper, I was asked to run for parliament. I declined. I made sure you didn't know very much about me, all said and done. It drove you mad! I could see the frustration on your face as you slipped — you thought discreetly — into counsellor mode, prodding me for background information. Did I have a family history of . . . ahem . . . large people? Did I have . . . puppy fat? My two pregnancies, how long before I put my ordinary clothes back on afterwards? Was I, perhaps . . . ahem . . . bullied at school? And you never got much in return, did you, before my time was up and the next patient had to be shown in? I said "Yes doctor, no doctor," and trotted serenely out the door.'

There was a short pause. Alan thought he heard a clink of ice against glass, a swallow. What was she drinking . . . her usual cognac?

'Why the privacy? Some years ago I vowed I would never pin any blame on my parents. I was a responsible adult, and if I really wanted to shed a few stone, reveal the thin goil inside that fat goil longing to get out, I would. Yes, I would. I could! I could.

'Couldn't I?

'Well, no, I couldn't. I couldn't at twenty-five after my first baby, and I couldn't at thirty. Not at thirty-five, or forty, or forty-five. By the time forty-seven came along, I had tried every diet known to woman. The silly dangerous Atkins, the grapefruit, the cabbage soup, the all-the-vegetables-you-can-physically-eat diet, the South Beach, the Scarsdale, the Suzanne Somers Get-Skinny-on-Fabulous-Food diet — hah, pure chicanery, that one! — the bran diet, the Zone. Literally ad nauseam. Weight Watchers and Jenny Craigs and all the similarly duplicitous variations thereof; treacherous because they know from countless studies that for most of their customers, in the long term, what they offer simply doesn't work. Overeaters Anonymous and their twelve steps thingy works for a few, but not for me, in the long run. For a while the GI Revolution, the "only low GI foods" regime worked, but frankly, I was a hopeless recidivist. High-protein, low-protein, high-carb, low-carb, high-roughage, water, with or without alcohol, miracle diets, believe me, I've done them *all*.

'Other strategies? Become a vegetarian and eat nuts, but y'know something, I can eat a lot of nuts. I took up smoking, worked in food shops hoping I'd simply get bored with food. Dear oh dear. I have been to spas and dieticians and health farms, done hypnotherapy, yoga, been to the gym and what a dreadful humiliation that was. In the eighties, even though by then doctors knew better, a Canadian quack put me on amphetamines. Wow-wee, for a while. Then it was Chinese herbs, which taste uniformly like monkey's pee. Five years ago it was that miracle pill which stopped your fat absorbtion, and I tell you "faecal incontinence" is not pleasant, knowing you are leaking crap, sorry faecal matter, in bed at night and farting uncontrollably like a dray, specially when it proves futile eventually. I bet the makers don't tell you medicos in their glossy brochures about all those orange fat globules coating the sides of the toilet bowl: not nice. I've been wrapped in clingfilm, and wired up to electrodes, and sprayed and coated with creams which disingenuously claim to reduce your cellulite.'

He heard a deep breath. 'But not surgery. No way. The very thought of liposuction, sucking it out into a bucket with a vacuum pump, or wiring up my jaw or stapling the stomach were never options for me, *never*. My fright factor is simply greater than my fat factor. I'm as squeamish as hell, the very sight of blood sends me into a spin. Don't tell me this is inconsistent; I know that, well enough.

'And I know every women's mag dieter's trick in the book: don't weigh yourself every day, don't shop for food when you're hungry, don't eat standing up, use smaller plates, never take seconds, chew slowly, leave something on your plate, eat no more butter, not even a scraping, as long as ye may live. Don't miss breakfast, drink eight glasses of water a day, set realistic goals, walk, exercise, get a life blah, blah, blah . . . God, it's so boring.

'Why? Because nothing works. Nothing. I went up and down like a yo-yo, two stone off here, two-and-a-half stone on there, over and over and over again. Hopeless. Nothing works. So I'm a lost cause, darling, simple as that. At forty-seven, I inherit a pile from an uncle I never knew I had. My ungrateful male offspring are long gone, and the dreadful husbands; and one day, in a classy London restaurant celebrating with friends that I have just acquired rather a lot of money, over caviar and truffles, a melt-in-the-mouth Scottish salmon, white asparagus, a chocolate mousse to die for and a very good French champagne, I bow to the inevitable. I am trapped to the end of my days within this irretrievably inflated, nay bloated, body, so I may as well enjoy it and everything life has to offer. I walk out of there into a travel agent in Bond Street and the rest is history.

'Selfish, self-indulgent? The woman has a good brain, a good business in Paris, no less. If she doesn't have to work anymore, she should do good works, run for parliament, become a patron of the arts, write a book. Well, it won't be for ever. I'm officially menopausal and terminally addicted to food. I'll get bored with this life, or peg out, whichever comes first. Maybe you would judge me less harshly, Alan, if you knew that between meals on board I have been studying. Quite seriously in fact, through Bristol University. Distance learning, they call it now. Stage three Classical Philosophy towards the BA I should have done as a filly.'

A noise on the tape indicated it had been paused. This happened twice.

'Aaaah.' Alan heard a long, satisfied sigh of deep melancholy.

After a moment, more clinks of ice, then she started again.

'I just tried a little experiment. The steward brought me some tea, with five club sandwiches oozing good things like smoked chicken and avocado slices and delicate pink shrimps, plus two of those gorgeous flat Florentines, all hazelnuts, honey and dark chocolate. Mmmmmmm. Of course it was all beautifully presented, the fine china, the silver teapot, the ship's white monogrammed Irish linen that the steward said even the wealthiest first-class passengers are not above stealing. And I thought, can I wait until I've finished this tape, or at least the first side of it? So I got the steward to put it out of sight. You know, out of sight, out of mind? Show a little discipline, Jacqueline! A little self-restraint here, please!

'And you know what? Right on! You'll be thinking I set myself up for failure, and so I did. I couldn't. I simply *couldn't*. My mouth literally watered. Those goodies sang their siren song to me from behind the cupboard door. I could smell them. I could feel their succulent, subtle flavours on my tongue, the textures pleasuring my taste buds, my teeth sinking into the salty white meat of the chicken and tarragon tang of the mayonnaise, the honeyed chocolate sweetness and crunchy texture of the Florentines. Irresistible, literally. I was completely incapable of knowing they were there and not eating them. So I failed and what the hell. And now I've had my fill, and poured myself another cognac, and perhaps it's time to ask myself *why* I was incapable. Why couldn't I just wait for half an hour? Is this pathological or what?

'My parents — now they were kind, good, caring people, both perfectly normal size. My father was a company accountant, my mother was of that generation frogmarched back into the kitchen after the war. Until I was eighteen, I was the normal weight for someone who admittedly didn't do much exercise. A size twelve or thereabouts, pushing fourteen? Now, I once read that one of the tasks of childhood is to achieve "physiological stability", something about getting through puberty and settling into your regular adult shape. Fine, if you happen to be male, which no doubt this "expert" researcher was. The worst that can happen to you is a beer belly at forty and your hair falling out. And perhaps you can't get it up any more. All your life, ninety-eight percent of the time, someone else will put food in front of you and that person will almost certainly be female. I've not much sympathy with the Billy Bunters and pot-bellied drunks. Actually, I can't stand fat men. I despise fat men.

'But a girl — she has periods, babies, hormones running wild, menopause — her life has built-in change at regular intervals. Often the changes are negative and not of her making. Stability? "Physiological stability?" Hah! The female condition has never been compatible with stability and never will be. And she's most likely to be the domestic provider of food, so she has to think about food for other people every day, all her life. Why are all the great chefs men? 'Cause to them it's a creative, exciting well-paid job that gives people pleasure and them lovely warm fuzzies and fawning adulation from people who are paying well. Apart from the lovely Jamie Oliver, they don't expect to get kicks out of the routine stuff at home; they don't have to shop and cook day in and day out, on a tight budget, for picky kids and neurotic teenagers, and husbands who demand roasts and sausages and daily puddings and think salad is food for rabbits.

'Perhaps I should tell you about my mother after all. Goodness, that rather large cognac slipped down a treat, didn't touch the sides. Mother was a good British cook, and that's not always an oxymoron. She did fine traditional roasts, chops and stews with mashed spuds; luscious steak and kidney puddings, the proper sort with suet. Not so hot on serving the veges *al dente*, as I remember. Great on fruit crumbles, fruit pies, bread'n'butter pudding, summer puddings bulging with berries, apple pies, all smothered with double cream. Baked a damn fine fruitcake for Christmas, and you should have tasted her melt-in-the-mouth mince pies and brandy snaps! Yum!

'As the years went on she got a little more adventurous, a spag bog, a pizza even (on a thick supermarket base), but not greatly so, simply because at heart she *loathed* and *detested* cooking. Hated it with a passion, always had and always would, and — this is the interesting bit — she made no effort to disguise the fact. In fact sometimes she even boasted about it. So every single meal was an effort of will, enduring evidence of her love for us, and every forkful I put in my mouth was absolute proof of my love for her and gratitude. At every meal I was served a plateful of love, and like a dutiful daughter I ate, as I was told to do, every scrap . . . and this is the even more interesting bit . . . *I asked for more*. Now you're the psychologist, Alan, the researcher: ponder on that!

'And why did she loathe cooking? Because she was a bright woman with a good degree, and domestic drudgery used about eight percent of her talents. And why didn't she get herself back into the workplace? Because my father wouldn't "allow" it, that's why. He didn't want a working wife, he wanted one who would have his whisky ready poured and his pork chop sizzling under the grill when he came home at night, and a civilized, cooked British breakfast every morning. And since I'm talking about fathers, I read some research that indicates that behind many fat women stands a caring, proud but super-critical papa who nagged and criticized his daughter about her appearance from early childhood on. Makes sense? Do you get fat to spite the father figure? And did mine nag and criticise? Oh yes, in spades! On and on and on, ever since I can remember, about my eleven-year-old's flares and fifteen-year-old's short skirts — this was the sixties, for Christ's sake — and my platform shoes and fat arms and Mary Quant hair and too much eyeliner, and later, after each baby, "Time you trimmed yourself down, girl" like a cracked record. Did I need him to tell me that? I think I married Dr Andre Bertrand, five years younger, largely to get away from it. Universities in Paris, London, Dublin and then Milan where my handsome but feckless thirty-four-year-old husband was killed on the *autostrada* to Genoa. That was 1989. A lorry jackknifed at 125 ks in front of his Citroën, very final, very nasty. They needed dental records . . . and yes, you guessed correctly, it appeared he was on his way to see his bit of Italian fluff. She turned up at the funeral, all seven stone of her.

'I did my best with the boys, but essentially they left home at eight, away to boarding school because I thought — mistakenly — they needed male role models, and then their gap years in Canada, university, good jobs in IT. Of course I'm a proud mum; they achieved their "physiological stability", but are they proud of me, their mum who ran a successful and fashionable business in Paris? Oh, I made money, that business did OK, it did better than OK, but they didn't get on with my second husband — neither did I after a couple of years — and essentially, I disgust them and their wispy boring self-centred little "partners" in their little black dresses and skyscraper-high Italian pumps costing 300 pounds a pair. I hate the pity I see in their Mac-polished faces, and the resentment that I'm literally eating away the family fortune. Well, bugger them . . . together they're earning more in their twenties than I ever did, or their father, come to that, and we did well enough.

'Aha, I can hear you saying. Oops . . . ah . . . shit . . . that's better . . . classic disapproving father, negative maternal attitude to food, violently dead and unfaithful hubby, cold sons, colder daughters-in-law, unsuccessful second marriage, single woman with low self-esteem, self-disgust, unresolved grief and anger, seeking affirmation and love . . . aha . . . "Comfort Eating Syndrome". And where more comfortable than the eating to be had on a twenty-first-century cruise ship, the ultimate in hedonism: limitless gorgeous food, an audience, no demands, no distractions, a glorious suspension of reality.

'I was a damn fine cook myself, and I made sure my little boys knew that I enjoyed cooking for them. The opposite to my mama. "Finish what's on your plate, dear," she used to say, smiling lovingly, and if I hesitated, because my little tummy was actually full, "Remember there are little children starving in Indo-China." She had been in her gingham pinny cooking this simple modest meal since four in the afternoon, hating every single second of it. It was my Christian and filial duty to eat up! Eat up large, Jacqueline, and make your poor little mother and the little children in Indo-China so happy. Eat up, dearest. Eat up. Eat up!

'Oh m'gawd, I'm sorry, I think I'm getting a little drunk.

'But I never made my boys finish anything at all, never. I loaded up my own plate, but I gave them modest portions and let them ask for more. In the kitchen I surrept . . . surreptish . . . oh shit, sur-rep-tit-ious-ly gobbled anything they'd left. I hated leftovers in the fridge. After a dinner party, I wanted to throw them away, but Andre wouldn't let me. Do for tomorrow's meals, he would say. But I was incapable of not eating them sooner or later, and usually sooner: the anchovy-stuffed olives and the roasted cashews . . . the dregs of the creamy oyster soup in a cup . . . the cold but golden roast spuds coated in congealed butter . . . browned, salty ends of the lamb roast . . . pink flakes of smoked salmon . . . cold ratatouille . . . four uneaten pieces of tiramisù . . . the raspberry sorbet in the freezer . . . the half-empty box of Belgian truffles . . . this rapacious seagull would go scavenging within twelve hours. Lying in bed, rigid, eyes wide open looking at the ceiling, reading with a torch to distract myself, but the food reaching out to me like a fucking magnet, I tell you. Eventually sliding out of bed for a sortie to the fridge, stealthy as any commando . . .

'Andre knew I did it. We had volcanic rows; he told me, all these midnight feasts, I was killing myself. Afterwards he would bury his face in my flesh and murmur that he loved me this way. Talk about mixed messages! Why didn't I just defy him and throw the stuff away? Beats me, looking back. I'd stay with friends and raid their fridge at night, rearranging the food so they'd never know about the visiting gannet. I was bloody clever. I couldn't buy a litre of petrol without adding a gourmet lamb-and-mint pie to the bill. Too tired to cook after work? A Chinese takeaway, perhaps pork and black-bean sauce, or lemon chicken; meant for three, but I'd scoff the lot. They didn't do half portions. Luscious butter chicken from the Indian; green chicken curry from the Thai. Greasy but succulent five-piece packs, the nice'n'spicy, please, from jolly old KFC. A pizza the size of a lorry wheel, meant for four. Even a Big Mac or two has been known to pass my lips . . . God, I'm making myself hungry again, and it's only five o'clock.

'But, since this is confessional time: Jacqueline Le Gros also couldn't pass a coffee shop without sitting down to a latte with three cubes of sugar and two citron tarts. A kebab shop was dynamite. In France, the nougat, the cheeses, the artichokes, the crêpes and truffles. On buying trips to Italy it was the pizza, the figs, the gelati. In England, the pork pies and summer puddings made with raspberries covered with clotted cream, Yorkshire puds. In America, the bean salads, sweet pumpkin pie and Midwest T-bone steaks the size of dinner plates. In Germany, the brawn and the wurst, even a good sauerkraut can please the soul. In Spain, the paella and the seafood; in Australia, the king prawns; in Singapore, the crispy salty skin on a Peking duck. A good home-cooked Irish stew is a thing of surprising beauty, likewise haggis I once tasted in Glasgow.

'At home I used to get out my sharpest knives, or the mandoline, put on nice music — opera, bit of Oscar Peterson, Ella, Sting — and spend hours preparing salads. Chop and slice, tasting here and there as I go, a sublime way to spend an afternoon. You want mayonnaise to dress the salmon? Sit for twenty minutes with a bowl, a wooden spoon and Placido Domingo . . . two egg yolks, fresh black pepper, the best extra virgin drop by drop, a touch of salt and fresh lemon juice . . . OK, your arm gets tired but my mayonnaise was lovingly made to Placido singing *Don Carlos* and it never curdled.

'I get so sad . . . really sad to think my mother never knew the pleasure of creating a mayonnaise, thick and glistening, that everything she did in the kitchen was impregnated with deep boredom and deeper resentment. Isn't that just awful, darling? My aïoli, my tiramisù, my lamb shanks, minestrone, risotto, roast legs of pork, rack of lamb, filets of beef and white veal, bouillabaisse, grilled river trout, *coq au vin*, cassoulet, mousses, tortes, soufflés, blueberry crêpes, panforte, home-made limoncello . . . all were legendary. Forgive me, but I was a very advanced cook. I was "at home" to my Parisien friends on Tuesday nights, and for visitors and sometimes clients, I gave fantastic dinner parties. I have 472 cookbooks.

'Gluttony is not a nice word. Sloth is . . . onomatopoeic. Two of the seven deadly sins. I'll admit to the first, but not to the second. I am a glutton, but I am not a sloth. I have an eating disorder. I am clinically, morbidly obese, which is not a nice word either. Obese, beast, beastly, bestial — all horrid, horrid words. More than fifty percent of the Western world is overweight. Several fortunes are being spent on research to find an answer. First off, as I said, I'd throw all the fucking advertisers off the airwaves, every last one of them pushing their plastic pizzas and fatty fries and hideous piled-up platefuls of food because they know that ordinary people can't resist a pile of chips and their cooped-up, force-fed, over-salted, greasy chickens. All of them, banished, for ever! Begone!

'Some old geezer got it right: appetite comes with eating. My oath, it does. It might have been Shakespeare? Rabelais, perhaps? Succulent, fragrant well-prepared food invites you to put out your hand and taste. Somewhere between that moment of choice and the tasting comes a moment of intense guilt — *you shouldn't be eating this, Jacqueline, you are a pig, Jacqueline, you are breaking your diet, Jacqueline, you are already pre-diabetic, you are going to die painfully and young, Jacqueline* — but the primitive, sensual pleasure of taste, of eating, of falling to the temptation, is greater. Simple, really. Addiction is all about the insistent little voice in your head that whispers, just one more. Just one, promise? And never learning to say, well, actually, that food is really nice but I'm not hungry any more — or, I've got better things to do with my time than play another game (just one more game, promise?) of Solitaire — or, I've actually had enough liquid refreshment or sausage rolls for the time being — so piss off. That's the guts of it.

'This self-loathing thing. I am supposed to be full of self-disgust. True, when I'm having a shower . . . or in a department-store changing room lined with a zillion mirrors trying to find something to swim in, self-disgust stares back at me, you bet. A nice little size twenty-six bikini, madame? I don't think so. I hate the rashes I get under my folds and flaps, my dangling wattles of upper arms, like giant half-filled saveloys. Sideways is worst: I look like a sixty-year-old who's in the family way. Didn't one actually . . . in Italy, impregnated by some mad doctor-scientist chappie looking for everlasting glory? I think she was fully sixty-two when she pushed her unfortunate *bambino* out into the world. Sixty-two! Mamma mia!

'Yes, I truly hate my widow's stoop and three chins and puffy ankles and dimpled thighs and four rolls of fat around my torso. I can't go for a walk in skirts because my inner thighs rub together and in ten minutes the skin is rubbed raw. I hate the airplane aisles

I can only go down sideways, and those diddlysquat seats three abreast and the contempt on the painted faces of the trolley dollies. Even in business class, I hate the expression on the face of the person who finds he's next to me, who watches me spilling out of even a business-class seat and unable to do up the seat belt without assistance. I especially hate supercilious size-two stick insects in frock shops, their sneers and titters the reason I use a dressmaker. Having my photograph taken is sheer living hell. Yes, I'd sell my soul to the devil, like Dr Faustus, to look at a photograph or in a mirror and see a slimmer, elegant me, the one that's trying to get out.

'There are frequent times when I wish I were just simply dead, just to be liberated from this mortal coil. Just for the relief of it, the finish of the struggle, the eternal peace. In the same way that they say the chronically seasick had to be tied down to stop them jumping overboard. Or people with intractable, terrible pain, or some ghastly skin infection so compulsively itchy that they tear themselves to shreds, all the while just longing to finish it. Some fatties do come to this, Alan — top themselves, I guarantee; and you would probably find it in the medical literature. Every night, drying after showering, I look at myself in the bathroom mirror, and swear on my mother's grave that tomorrow will be the first day of the rest of my life. I will resist temptation; *finally*, I will do something about those majestic, overhanging terraces of pink blubber around my torso, the obscenely fat and pendulous upper arms, the elephant thighs, the full-moon, triple-chinned face, the hateful Humpty-Dumpty profile — knowing full well, deep down, that tomorrow I will fail at the first hurdle: the third tempting warm croissant dripping with Lurpak butter and French raspberry *confit*.'

She burped, inelegantly and richly.

'Yes, I do have those dark moments, occasionally: that yearning just to be done with it, be released from my struggle, my absolute preoccupation with my fat self. But life goes on, the weeks come round, efforts have to go on being made and when I'm all ready to sally forth, I look terrific, a clipper ship in full sail. Elegant in my own inimitable way. "Eee by gum, she's a character, that Jacqueline," the stewards say in various Scottish and Indian accents. I love my flowing Indian and Thai silks, arranging my coiffeur, sitting in front of a mirror putting on make-up, deciding which jewellery to wear, the careful choice of perfume. Skinny women get wrinkles and their neck tendons look like rope. Not me. I'm a handsome woman. My face is unlined. It provides a smooth base for the finest and costliest French cosmetics. People remember me. Men want to get their arms around me. They don't slobber around little chic Parisiennes in their sexless little Coco Chanel suits and pointy lethal shoes. They want something warm and cuddly, like Mama. Ponder on that, Alan.

'So do I loathe myself, with deep-down industrial-strength loathing? No. Listen, I'll say it again, I do not loathe myself. I just love food more. I adore food and eating the way some people adore music, or doing up their bathrooms, or buying shoes or playing bridge, or listening to opera or playing with trains. As I said earlier, no matter what I did, there always has been and there always will be about eighteen to twenty stone of me. So if that's the metabolic me, from childhood, set in concrete, as it were, what's the point? If the price of being a size eight Parisienne in a Chanel suit is nibbling 300 calories of lettuce leaves a day . . . never tasting another chocolate, another lightly battered Malaysian-style prawn, another lemon tart, another fine pinot noir, just subsisting on rocket, two flakes of white fish and sticks of raw carrot . . . you can forget it, buddy.

'So it's a twenty-first century pandemic, yes? Why little fat girls? All doomed to die in later middle age of diabetes and heart disease.

How do we get the message across? No telly ads, ban Gameboys and PlayStations, more playing outside, make the cooking and selling of French fries a criminal offence.

'But I do wonder: most people walking around this ship have got it right. What's the difference between people who can eat anything and still be like fishing rods, and *moi*, who eats anything and has a rear end like a hippo? Is it only genes, in the end? I suppose one day there'll be a fat pill that won't turn your poos to chocolate custard or some blissful injection that does it in one, resets your metabolic rate. In heaven I will eat anything at all and be size ten . . .

'No, let me rephrase that. In heaven I will be a normal size twelve or fourteen, and my brain will be in firm, unyielding and total control of the naughty little hand that just creeps out of its own accord and takes another Belgian truffle until the box is empty. So I will not pig out and stay size twelve, I will eat just like other people who don't actually ever need to pig out and I will stay size twelve or more realistically fourteen. Marilyn Monroe was a fourteen.

'Christ, I've been happy on this ship. I would still be, but . . . confidentially, Alan, I had a bit of a shock just before I joined. Bad enough that for medical reasons I'm now borderline as a passenger. This is my last voyage, you said, as kindly as you could. But I had to go to my doc in London for something and she insisted on a frigging blood test. A fasting one. She was a locum, and nerdish with it. Wore enormous black-rimmed glasses and trackpants and sneakers under her white coat and looked as though she ran a marathon every day before breakfast.'

There was such a lengthy pause that Alan wondered if that was the end of the tape.

'Oh God, out with it, Jacqueline . . . drunk or not . . . I'm advanced type-two diabetes on a bucketload of drugs, and unless

I lose six stone and lose it for good, I'm doing insulin jabs within six months. I haven't told you yet, and wasn't going to unless I absolutely had to. And you're not surprised, not one iota. Of course I didn't tell her in the trackpants I was about to sail away on one of the world's biggest cruise ships . . . fatties' paradise.

'And am I being a good girl and reading the latest research on the glycemic index versus glycemic load and cutting out all pastries and cakes and gelati and pannacotta and truffles, and monitoring every mouthful of food for its antioxidants or GI value? Pricking my finger for glucose levels every three hours? No, I am not. And do you know why I am not?

'Because it's too late, Alan. It's *finito*, old bean. It's too late for me and it's too late for you. I don't want to get old and have to plunge a syringe into my belly three times a day and in the course of time get literally cut off at the knees. Or go blind, or bedridden in some overheated geriatric hospital that smells of old people's farts from being force-fed too much boiled cabbage. I don't want my face to get lined like an ancient potato and my enormous boobs to hang pendulously all the way down to my crotch. I don't want hot flushes, I don't want a menopause. Hell, a hundred years ago most women didn't have one at all. By fifty, forty or thirty-five even . . . most them were all worn out with childrearing and demanding husbands and dead.

'And you. I can hear you say, but this is the twenty-first century and you're only fifty-one, Jacqueline, there is time! Time! With proper motivation and management, You Can Do It, you could have another twenty or thirty years, Jacqueline!

'But I don't want another twenty years, if I couldn't spend it with . . . oh for crying out loud, Alan, I don't know what you call it, love or something, but a few trips ago I began to realize . . . didn't you suspect, some of my visits to your surgery were for pretty paltry reasons? I worked out where you tended to go off duty, and was pathetically pleased when you'd join my table. I'd have got that weight off if I thought . . . yes, I could, I could, with enough motivation and going regularly to Overeaters Anonymous, who look to root causes and do seem to have more success than anyone — but what's the use . . . when you . . . look, I know he shouldn't have, but he did . . . my steward is a sweet boy, and he adores me, and somehow, Christ knows how, well, you know how the lower decks talk, he found out that you're not going to make old bones either, some progressive family disease whose name I'm too drunk to remember, but which, sure as a tide coming in or going out, is going to get you, sooner rather than later.

'So the one and only reason I can think of for wanting to live another twenty years or even another five . . . or even two . . . is third time lucky.'

Another long pause, gathering up courage, perhaps?

'I used to fantasize about us together in Paris, you not under a death sentence and me slim and gorgeous in a dinky pinky Chanel suit . . . suddenly . . . this morning . . . I'm so sorry, don't suppose you want a nurse, do you, clean, kind, reliable, cheerful disposition? No, of course you don't, oh, what's the point . . .'

Alan slunk into his chair, trying to absorb what he had heard: a proposition? He had no doubt Jacqueline's Paris apartment was as interesting, warm and cultured as its owner. He had a quick vision of shutters opening onto a park, a fireplace, silk drapes and Persian carpets, Venetian glass, a comfortable leather chair, with an antique reading light, a good book . . .

The future reality was a stale-smelling, cheaply furnished flat and distant Plymouth Hoe. Trying to make himself useful to an old mate who'd done no better at medical school forty years ago but ended up an emeritus professor and a knight of the realm. Who probably saw Dr Alan Baines as a charity case.

Jacqueline's husky voice startled him again.

'When you hear this, you'll be in Plymouth . . . being a good boy now, researching away for the good professor, volunteering for this and that. Remember me . . . Jesus, I sound like Hamlet's ghost . . . remember me!

'Perhaps I will tell you anyway, sometime soon — tis better to have loved and lost, than never to have loved at all. Who said that hoary old cliché? Perhaps I am grossly underestimating you. Perhaps there *is* a life growing old in Plymouth. Of a sort. Rotary and other good works, trips up to London? Writing your memoirs. Stuff like that.'

Another pause, and then she hiccupped and said, 'Oh, fuck it. This, my friend, is what I want to say. I should rehearse it. Yes. Pull yourself together, girl!' (Some whispering, while she rehearsed.)

'Would you consider my Paris apartment, my dear friend, as a place of abode? I have tenants in there at present, but I can throw them out tomorrow. The French health system is the best in Europe. Or if you don't fancy Paris, somewhere in the south, where you can look out over the azure sea and watch the cruise ships go by and sincerely thank the Good Lord the lower back pains and the ingrown toenails and the phantom pregnancies and unspeakable acts down in the crew quarters are all someone else's problem. I always liked Nice. We can go to the Hotel Negresco together — take a dainty Sunday tea among those plumed and painted wooden horses in the carousel — and prop each other up for gentle walkies together along the Promenade des Anglais singing "Oh, I do like to be beside the . . ."'

The second side of the tape, Alan found, was empty.

Larry's phone call came out of the blue, a few unsatisfactory months later. Calls to Alan's number, from France or anywhere else, were a rarity, especially at ten on a winter's night. Larry was apparently in London and perhaps, not entirely sober.

'Rather need to see you, Alan. Train up to London tomorrow?' Before Alan had a chance to decline on grounds of two scheduled research interviews, he continued, 'One every hour or so, I believe. Can you do one o'clock, lunch? Royal Over-Seas League good as anywhere?'

After some unnecessarily detailed instructions as to how to get to the Royal Over-Seas League off St James, he added: 'Sorry, old man, bit pissed. Had a bloody hard few days, family dramas. See you at one. And bring your toothbrush. They say it's going to snow.'

Alerted enough not to ask any leading questions ('How's Paula?'), Alan was left holding the phone, pondering the calls necessary to cancel the interviews. He spent the next thirty minutes on the net booking a train to Paddington at 07.47. There were few people he'd travel four hours to lunch with, especially with snow threatening, but he knew a measure of desperation when he heard it; he packed for three days.

Larry's shockingly gaunt appearance contrasted with the prosperous air of Over-Seas House, the lobby's tasteful décor of national flags, gilt-framed pictures of bejewelled royalty and very large bowls of (probably) artificial flowers. His shirt and striped suit both looked crumpled and a size too big, his white hair in need of a barber's attention. An unhealthy pallor had replaced the Riviera tan. A five-kilo weight loss, at least, thought Alan, remembering Larry nicely trim in a floral sarong on his patio six months ago. Now, as he rose unsteadily from the deep armchair, he looked like an ageing and demoralised businessman fronting up for yet another job interview.

'Larry, I can't say you look well,' exclaimed Alan. 'What troubles bring you to London?'

'Paula. I buried her yesterday. As she wanted, beside our son.' He looked close to collapse. 'I thought I could do this by myself.'

Judging that the normality of food would be safer than whiskies in the lounge, Alan forewent the formalities and steered him discreetly into the dining room and to a quiet table. He'd swiftly recognized symptoms of shock, the early phases of what counsellors now liked to called the 'five stages of grief'. He was in a slight state of shock himself: he had never seen a fitter sixty-nine-year-old than Paula, and he'd not known there was a son who died.

'I've sold up, Alan,' said Larry after Alan had ordered the vichyssoise, fillet of beef, a good burgundy and sticky-date pudding. 'Everything: business, house in Villefranche, house in Austria, the lot. Washed up right now at Paula's sister in Fulham. She was insanely jealous of Paula's life on the Med and never much liked me, but she's rising nobly to the occasion while I sort myself out. I've pots of money, a shitload of guilt and absolutely no idea what to do next. I need some advice.'

The easiest thing in the world to give, my friend. Alan was not in the advice-giving business these days, medical or otherwise. Gradually, he pieced together a story going back nearly forty-five years. Larry and Paula's eldest son Marcus would now be forty-four, but at thirty-two, had been picked up virtually dead by Sydney police in the back streets of King's Cross, drugged out, homeless and penniless. The ten years between him dropping out of university at eighteen and their disowning him at twenty-eight had been an ongoing nightmare: twice into rehab for months on end, an exhausting pattern of crises around money, sickness, women, the police. At twenty-eight, avoiding prison on drugs charges on a technicality, he conned his parents once too often. Enough, they had said, returning shattered from a week in London, he was on his own. They grieved for their lost son, unaware that he ended up in Australia, and, it appeared from his passport, three years before that spent in Athens, Lahore, Sri Lanka and Bali. How he survived, got money for food, rooms and travel let alone his drug habit, they dared not imagine. He had no employable skills, other than a bright charm and a fast tongue in three languages. His journey ended in a King's Cross gutter, another statistic.

Paula grieved afresh, became a chronic insomniac and silently blamed Larry for sending Marcus to prep school and then Winchester, pressuring him to Cambridge, high-handedly assuming that in time, with a good degree and a gap year under his belt, Marcus would return to continue the family tradition, and make his life in or near Monaco. She had pleaded with Larry to *listen* to his son. He didn't want to be a businessman in a suit, he wanted to be a writer. In the end, Larry complained at dinner parties, none of the children showed any interest in the business opportunity being handed to them on a plate. They went into computers and law and fashion, and did well. Friends learned not to enquire about the one-time golden boy.

His tragic self-destruction they relayed to no-one, not his siblings nor their families, their wider family on both sides, their circle of friends. To any queries, they explained that Marcus had chosen to cut all his ties, and had gone his own way in the world. Sad, but there it is. They had his body brought back from Sydney for quiet internment in a Hampstead cemetery, sang no hymns, shed no tears, never talked of him; numbly followed instructions from their lawyer; and at home, obliterated all evidence of Marcus, clothes, photographs, postcards, childhood toys, toiletries in bathroom cupboards, files of childish artwork and poetry, any small thing that carried even a ghost of a memory.

Easy enough, said Larry, pushing aside the uneaten beef fillet, to remove the physical evidence. A young mother's memories of her first-born — no rubbish skip or delete button for those.

Gradually, inevitably perhaps, storing up all that anger, resentment and loss, Paula had slipped into a clinical depression so deep that she didn't talk to Larry or leave her bedroom for eight months, nor the house at Villefranche for well over a year. Larry hired a day nurse costing plenty. Specialists speaking French and English — psychiatrists, psychologists, grief counsellors — came to the house. Slowly, a regime of drugs and many hours of counselling took effect, and in the second year — this would be about ten years ago, Larry mused — her self-neglect was gradually replaced by a regime of exercise, diet and regular visits to every type of beauty specialist and spa that infested Monaco, Nice and the other Riviera resorts. Regularly, Paula's hair was cut and coloured, nails shaped and painted, bodily hair waxed, face peeled and patted, eyebrows and eyelashes darkened, the rest of her massaged and creamed and oiled. For that splendid tan, she spent hours under sunlamps as well as spending a fortune on those new self-tanning lotions.

There were also surgical procedures — she was a bit coy about these — for frown lines and laugh lines around the eyes, smoker's lines around the mouth, for a nose which suddenly became too big, for lips she wanted fuller, for the slackening pouches of flesh around the jaw line and the now unacceptable rolls around the waist. She had regular medical check-ups, blood tests, bone scans and chest x-rays. The end result of about eight years' pursuit of bodily perfection was the recreated mature goddess Alan had seen last summer. She had cost a king's ransom, but when they dressed up and went out, Larry admitted he took pleasure in the respect and admiration she commanded. Now there was a woman who hadn't let herself go! On more than one occasion he'd been mistaken for her father.

Alan gave him time to pick at the date pudding. He'd barely eaten a thing and his hands were trembling no less than when they sat down at the table nearly two hours ago. 'The strain on your marriage . . .' mused Alan.

'Was immense. But I'd made up my mind that I was not going

to let that little shit Marcus succeed in destroying us. I simply absorbed everything she threw at me, all the sly hints of blame and guilt, until we stopped sparring. A kind of exhausted peace broke out. We coexisted, for want of energy to do anything different. And all that time spent in beauty parlours and the gym — at least there she was safe, meeting people, doing what made her happy. It was better than lying alone in a darkened room, or having affairs. But about two years ago I could see that it wasn't enough any more. She became more and more brittle. She lost interest in the grandchildren, cancelled a few of their visits at the last moment. Our sex life had gone long ago. We called back the psychiatrists, reviewed the drugs, agreed to try new, fashionable psychologists. The body was still rigorously maintained, but the mind was under siege.'

'Brittle describes what I saw last summer,' said Alan. The dining room had emptied and the girls were setting tables for dinner. 'Behind the façade, there was a lot of tension. But hardly enough to ring warning bells.'

Larry smiled for the first time in two hours. 'Our Paula could put on a show. Last summer wasn't good.'

In the autumn, when they normally followed well-established procedures for their winter relocation to the lodge near Innsbruck, Paula started to talk about breaking with tradition and spending four weeks in Australia. After Christmas with family at the lodge, they should head to Sydney. Larry loved his uninterrupted winter of skiing and had no great desire to go to Australia, but he saw it as evidence of improvement. Better than apathy. He'd agreed readily enough. They made business-class bookings. They would have been there now.

Falling silent, fighting back tears with limited success, Larry allowed himself to be relocated to the deserted lounge with coffee and port. Alan noted that outside the tall windows, snow was falling; he'd not be getting back to Plymouth tonight. In the deep floral armchair opposite, Larry appeared spent and shrunken.

Stirring his coffee, Alan said quietly, 'Larry, I'm puzzled. Where are your family in all this? You're staying with your sister-in-law, but aren't your children . . . ?'

'We had the funeral a week ago in the local church. They all flew in, with the older grandchildren.' He hoisted himself rather more upright. 'It was horrendous. Mothers of nearly seventy are not expected to kill themselves skiing over a bluff. They were shocked to the core and angry as hell. They forgot the loving Christmas matriarch, the fun granny crawling around on the floor only weeks before — now she was selfish, vain and stupid.'

'That's harsh.' Also, he thought, predictable.

'I was worse than a fool. I should not have taken her skiing in dodgy conditions. At her age it was ridiculous, she was an accident waiting to happen. And then they dragged Marcus into it, how I'd pressured him, then left him in the wilderness.'

'Did you . . .'

Larry guessed his question. 'No. Somehow, in the turmoil, I managed to keep my counsel. You can imagine the reaction, if I'd let that slip. Paula's note said she wanted to be taken to Hampstead to join Marcus and there was only to be me at the graveside. It was a hard ask, Paula.'

Her note? This was suddenly as far as Alan wanted to go on Larry's journey. From medical journals he knew something about the burden of guilt parents carried round after an adult child's death, suicide or not; and he'd seen at close hand the blame game played around cases which had ended in suicide. It was a wonder that poor Larry was still standing. He also knew about notes, or recorded tapes, voices from dark places, and he didn't want to go there. But Larry had got his second wind.

In hindsight, he thought the Sydney exercise began as a weird attempt to get closer to Marcus, to see where he'd lived and died. For the first month at the lodge, Paula was morose, apathetic, barely sleeping. Her days passed playing endless Solitaire, reading trash like Jackie Collins, hours in the kitchen, cooking eccentric meals in a desultory sort of way. Mostly, she sent Larry skiing by himself. But sometime before Christmas, she perked up; he put it down to the children coming, the village decorations, the shopping, checking all the usual Christmas arrangements. She was a natural manager, quick, clear, thought things through. She'd been only twenty when they married, already an unusually competent PA; born thirty years later she'd have been a CEO.

This Christmas had been their happiest ever. Everyone had treated Paula with kid gloves, and each other with unaccustomed consideration and tolerance. She glowed in the warmth of their kindness and appreciation of her fantastic organization, the loving little touches, the grander-than-usual gifts. The youngsters had behaved. They'd all gone skiing and skating together, taken several sleigh rides along the valleys. Paula, nightly reading the *Lonely Planet* guide on Sydney, had talked with enthusiasm of the forthcoming trip. Christmas Eve after fresh snow — the village choirboys singing 'Silent Night' by torchlight outside the little onion-domed church — going home to their own laden tree, opening gifts — it had been pure magic.

All three families had left by January 3 and high up on the *piste* the next day Paula strayed into known dangerous territory and over a bluff.

Unusually, at her request, Larry had gone ahead, totally confident, 110 percent sure that she was following him the usual trail down through the firs. It was a well-marked run they'd enjoyed together many times before, not at all testing and well within her capabilities. Her skis, bindings and boots were the best, new from last winter. The snow was fresh powder, ideal, and the sun hazy; they were keeping a weather eye for conditions forecast to deteriorate later in the day.

Larry dutifully stopped at a resting place halfway down, but turning, was surprised to see no sign of a bright gold anorak approaching. Plenty in pink, navy, lime, scarlet, everything but the colour of sunflowers. There was no alternative route.

At that point, the nightmare that would have no end began: his anxious few minutes' wait scanning the slopes above before deciding to ski on down, either to take the lift back up himself to check — probably a simple explanation, like a twisted ankle, broken goggles — or raise the alarm. He skied fast, recklessly, and sought urgent help. The ski patrol discovered tracks near the top leading through an area of virgin snow marked off as dangerous, and 200 feet below the overhang, they found her nearly lifeless body brought up against an outcrop of rocks.

Distraught children flew in to comfort Larry; Paula remained in a coma until two days later when they agreed to life support being discontinued. Interminable police inquiries over the next four weeks found no evidence of failed gear or even the skier losing control, the autopsy no support for theories of cardiac arrest or a stroke, and not enough to be certain about a sudden blackout at high altitude. The authorities concluded it was an accident, cause unknown.

Of course Larry had told them about the depression, the drugs, the names of her specialists, why should he not? The last twelve months hadn't been brilliant but nothing like past episodes, not even close. Lately there'd been signs of real improvement. Plain sailing, until one of them, a right little prick, put the question to him: 'Sir, I have to ask, any possible motives for suicide?' Dear God!

While Larry struggled with tears, Alan considered his options. Paula's tragic story had been heading inexorably towards the probability of suicide. There was a note. He was done with doctoring the living, and had no wish to hear any further voices from the dead. As soon as tactful, he would suggest a taxi back to the sister's in Fulham. He had a train to catch, with or without snow.

Larry hadn't found the note until two days before the funeral, tucked inside the book he'd been reading. It was John le Carré. How had Paula imagined he could ever read *The Tailor of Panama*, under the circumstances? He'd knocked the book off the bedside table, and out fell an envelope. Before dawn that long night he'd decided no one else needed to know, not family, the police, his lawyer, not a living soul. What was the point? Officially it had been declared an accident, cause unknown. What was to be gained? Nothing, only more misery for the family. He told them he'd decided she should be buried close to her birthplace, in Hampstead. A bit weird, they thought, at that late stage, but they respected his wishes. He declined offers of support on the day — the grandchildren needed their parents more, at such times. It would just be a formality with the necessary officials, an undertaker, over in fifteen minutes.

So, yesterday, it was done. A hard ask, Paula, a fucking hard ask.

Recognizing Larry's rising anger, and indeed his own, Alan searched for a way out. He'd always loathed writing a death certificate for a suicide, establishing the cause of an often messy death; it enraged him, this ultimate act of grandstanding and selfishness; it denied all his training, his whole life's work. But Larry was taking an envelope from his breast pocket and thrusting it at him.

'I'm not sure I should read that,' he murmured, playing for time. 'Larry, my friend, you're exhausted. I'm a mite weary myself. Let's have another coffee, or a tea, and talk about general plans, then I'll take you home.'

'You're the one person who can read it,' Larry insisted. 'The one person who can tell me how that letter and deliberately skiing off a precipice in any way match up with the woman I spent Christmas with.' He shifted forward, holding out the letter. 'Take it, please! Alan, I am utterly baffled.'

Trapped, reluctant, but despite himself, curious, Alan unfolded the two pages. Another ghostly voice, another time bomb. Whether a lengthy chat or a short note, the impact would be the same. The original, Larry muttered on remorselessly, was on cream linen writing paper, best quality. Paula was classy, give her that. Even her dramatic departure, going flying off a mountain in a bright yellow anorak had a certain *je ne sais quoi* . . . gas ovens, slit wrists, overdoses or car exhausts didn't have quite the same ring, did they? He'd sent the original by secure courier to his lawyer in Monaco, with instructions it remained sealed and unopened. He wasn't quite sure why he'd bothered — why not just put it in the fireplace then and there? Should he have destroyed it, Alan? That was the only copy he'd made. Could he read it aloud? Please.

The note was handwritten but easily read, that small precise hand typical of the perfectionist:

> My dearest husband
> I just can't, any more. I'm so sorry. We should
> have talked about Marcus, but we never did. A day
> has never gone past without me feeling <u>so</u> guilty
> since the morning we finally abandoned him, that
> appalling row in the street, remember? Him and his
> lawyer cocky at having got off, the police and defence
> furious, and you sick to your stomach, blood pressure
> through the roof with rage and shame. You really
> wanted him in jail, I think, to teach him a lesson once
> and for all, but all I wanted was to save him from

himself, from anything <u>more</u> that might hurt him, as I'd always done. Isn't that what parents do, and go on doing? I fantasize he's still alive somewhere. But the strongest memory are those last words, accusing, bitter.

I'm so tired, Larry. I've needed to look in a mirror and see the young(ish) mother the innocent child Marcus saw and ran to, before he got into difficulties. Wasn't he such a beautiful little boy, such a darling? And a handsome youth, though we knew even then about his fatal charm, his laziness. Yes, he could be manipulative and selfish, but he still didn't deserve to die a pauper's death alone on the other side of the world. He was only thirty-two. He might have made it as an author, writing about his journey through life. Plenty of others have, and we know he could write well when he chose. To abandon him was not my decision, and it ill-became you, normally the most genial and understanding of fathers, no old-fashioned 'disciplinarian'. You had different rules and expectations for him. At the time I despised you for it, and wondered how I could sleep nights in the same bed. But I learned, and in time I gained a little understanding of your disappointment, the blow to your pride. But understanding something doesn't make it right, or forgiveness any easier.

I can only assume you've learned to live with the guilt, but I haven't. Despite what I've just written, guilt and the blame I still place on you keep coming back at me and dragging me into the void and make me think that I <u>have</u> to stay in my two beautiful houses, going skiing and swimming and giving

parties, because I'm too weak and pathetic a person
to leave and this wonderful privileged life is my right
and proper punishment, the worst for someone like
me. A daily reminder that I'm not worthy, don't
deserve it. Because, when all's said and done, <u>we</u> are
alive and Marcus <u>isn't</u>.

But I'm tired of the pretence, the lie that looks
back at me every day from the mirror. It's all got
too hard. I don't ever want to look old, all wrinkled
up and joints stiff, just pathetic and helpless, having
to be eternally grateful to everyone, apologetic for
just going on breathing. I don't want to look in the
mirror and see my own great-grandmother staring
back at me. Every morning I wake, wishing I hadn't.
The light of day is too bright, the nights too long.

Despite everything, I have always loved you,
Larry. You are a good and generous man and rightly
respected as such. Nothing seemed to faze you
— business worries, staff, new technologies, family
life, children, even me. A <u>good</u> man, through and
through, and Marcus your cross to bear. I know
you've tried so hard to get the best possible help, see
me get 'better'. I'm sorry. It wasn't to be.

Take care of your good kind self and our kids. Life
will be easier for you now.

With all my love
Paula

Alan was aware his voice had slowed, the last sentences barely
audible. He'd been chilled by Larry's bizarre request, but they
went back a long way, to those basement digs in Hammersmith.
Two batty old codgers, he thought absurdly during a lengthy

silence when a uniformed staff member walked through, greeting them with a brisk smile. Slumped into his armchair, his head sunk onto one hand. Larry looked to be sleeping, a little aged gnome. But he was sobbing silently, and he repeated the question. 'Why, when she was so much better?'

Alan fell back on lack of up-to-date knowledge, and his own limited training in mental health compared to today's students — but it seemed that suicides often seemed improved to family and friends for a few days or weeks before they . . . took action. At some deep, little-understood level, the internal struggle was over.

Above them, HRH The Duke of Edinburgh in his admiral's uniform stared out sternly across the room.

'Would it have been quick?' asked Larry.

'She almost certainly blacked out before impact.'

'She broke practically everything, never woke up. But her face . . . untouched . . . just looked asleep. At peace.'

Alan folded the two sheets of paper, almost reverently, but filled with a sudden sense of desolation. His last sight of Jacqueline had been overflowing off a morgue trolley, her plump face contorted in death. He had to remember the musical voice, slightly tiddly, offering him a life, which also wasn't to be.

Larry would mend his relationships with his children, rebuild his life. It'd take a year or two. He'd get an expensive apartment with a view somewhere in Europe, near one of them, share the pleasures of the grandchildren as they grew up. He'd probably drink too much, or write a book. He might take up gambling, or bridge, or even find himself prey to all those questing women on a cruise ship. And he'd get some counselling from time to time when the grief and guilt and the self-imposed burden of his twin secrets got too much.

In counsellor-speak, he'd 'integrate' Paula's death into his life as he — apparently — had his eldest son's. Eventually, he might even unburden himself of his terrible secrets to his children, a challenging but ultimately very wise move for whatever time he had left. But he was in no shape to hear that sort of advice now.

It felt unsatisfactory, close to betrayal, to accept Larry's thanks in the lobby, wishing him good luck under the Union Jacks, but Alan couldn't do otherwise. Too bruised, too tired, too old. He despised himself for the clichés of farewell, the insincere invitation to come down to Plymouth for a few days, sometime in the spring. Alan waved as Larry's taxi pulled away, bound for Fulham.

Larry would get through it, as he had, twice — as everyone did.

Alan caught his own cab to Paddington through the snowstorm and on the last train knew he'd find some excuse not to invite Larry to Plymouth. It then occurred that they'd not thought to exchange addresses, so he had no way of contacting him anyway. The sister would be listed in the phonebook under a different name, and he had no idea where the offspring lived. One distant day, a sprightly Larry might call.

His tears in the crowded train, he knew full well, were less for Larry and the tragic Paula than for himself. Counsellors warned against self-pity, but wasn't a little pity for the self allowable in testing times?

He also knew long paralysed days filled out by playing computer Solitaire for hours on end, reading trashy whodunnits in the warmth of the local library, watching rubbish on television, going for long solitary walks, worrying unnecessarily about paying his bills and ignoring the unmistakable early signs of the Parkinson's that would get him sooner rather than later.

He would do what work was required of him on the obesity study, as long as he was able. If nothing else, he would keep his promise to Jacqueline.

Fair stood the wind for France

How do you know I'm doing the ironing? What asthmatic sound — oh, you mean the steam coming out in fits and farts? Well, it's a crappy old iron, it don't owe me much. The lovely Kevin was supposed to get me a new one two Christmases ago, but he bought me a shiny brass winch instead.

So I hear you say, I'm giving him a steam iron, the absolute Rolls Royce of steam irons, for his fifty-fifth birthday? I don't think so.

Ma petite soeur, I always do the ironing when you ring. I think to myself, now this is Beryl on one of those Kiwi five-dollars-for-as-long-as-you-can-still-draw-breath calls from the other side of the world — and I go straight to switch the iron on. I wasn't ever going to tell you that, petal, but now I have — really, aren't these cordless phone thingies amazing, what you can do while you're yabbering away? So liberating. I sometimes take it into the garden and pull out weeds in the path until it starts to shriek at me, you know, when you go too far away from the battery whatsit? Or I peel the spuds, do the washing-up, file my nails, clean the bath, sew on his lordship's buttons, mend his blazer pockets. All those detestable little jobs I keep putting off? I love my cordless with a passion.

Guess what you're doing? You're not! Get off there when you talk to your big sister, or at least put your finger over that little hole — I mean the hole on the phone, idiot, the little slots where you talk into. Then I won't have to listen to the sound effects, you pissing and plopping away. Honestly! It's bad enough having to pull Kevin's chain occasionally — yes, he does — well, he just forgets. Too busy thinking about the boat, and before you say what boat and why did he buy me a brass winch, let me just go and get a nice stool and some hangers, cause I think there might be about forty-seven shirts here . . . just hang on a tick . . .

That's better. Now, how long is it since we've had a good old yak? Really? That's the whole summer, so you don't know anything about the boat, do you? Are you sitting down? It's what, ten at night down there, nine with summer time? No, first pour yourself a stiff nightcap, darling. That's something else you can do with a cordless, get yourself a quick one when it's the lovely Kevin on the phone banging on about the kitchenhand who's not back from a tea break and never there when he wants him — whose fault is that, at the end of the day? — or the vicar's hopeless little wife reading out lists of people who still have to be chased for the jumble sale — yes, Beryl, we do still have them over here and I do not live in an episode of *Miss Marple*, and even you have admitted that cosy English village life *à la Midsomer Murders* has its attractions. Yes, of course I miss home, you ask me that every time, even after twenty-four years — and yes, we will come back to Godzone for a visit soon — I *know* the exchange rate makes it a bloody cheap holiday for whingeing Poms — look, I'm *trying* to tell you about this boat and why I got a parcel last Christmas, a mighty peculiar shape wrapped up in pink tissue paper with a silver bow which turned out to be a lovely brass winch.

His mother died. Just bear with me? You know the old girl died, I told you last year, and good riddance. We all thought she didn't have two sous to rub together, but it turned out that she owned an island in the West Indies. Truly nobody but nobody knew, it was probably acquired by a dreadful old

ancestor with filthy lucre from slavery — I always thought there
was something weird about that family. So when Kevin gets his
third-share after the probate he says Val, dearest, now listen up,
you — in the twilight of my life, I'm going to fulfil my dream of
a lifetime and buy myself a boat.

But Kevin, says I, fifty-five is hardly twilight and you don't
know how to sail. You don't know anything about engines and
knots and tides, let alone about how to put a sail up or what to
do in a force-nine gale. Where would we put it? And weren't we
saving up for a trip home to see the family?

We will keep it in the marina in Plymouth, says he, and I do
so know something about sailing — having once raced, he goes
on, against Russell Coutts in a P-class — he was a competitive
little bastard even then — and just missed out as gun crew in a
crack eighteen-footer training to go to Sydney, not forgetting
stints on a Pied Piper and the occasional mullet boat round the
Waitemata. And the grandkids will still be there next year.

But — it turns out that he's been quite a busy boy for months,
the sly old fox, and the boat is virtually bought with a partner and
all, another Kiwi expat and P-class Grant Dalton buddy-buddy
called Bob Stirling-Jackson, now living in Plymouth and doing
something frightfully important in the Works Department at
the Plymouth City Council.

They met at the yacht club, which Kevin, unbeknownst to me,
had joined, and got talking over a Steinie, and surprise surprise,
this Bob, he's between boats, and looking for a partner with a
bit of spare dosh — and so after a few more Steinies down the
hatch, Bob's your uncle, or rather Bob's your partner, and we,
Val and Kevin Fenton, of Fenton's Devonshire Teas, that famous
West Country landmark on the A38 just outside Plymouth, are
the proud half-owners of a thirty-two-foot ketch-rigged plastic
fantastic called — I kid you not — *Have a Nice Day*.

It — no, hush my mouth it's a she, Kevin insists — she sleeps six, has a nice silent engine and clean terylene sails. She's only nine years old and berthed in Plymouth Yacht Haven, which plus the insurance cost about as much as the boat, and it's — she's — just waiting to whisk us off across the Channel to lovely sailing holidays in France and into the Med and all those lovely Aegean islands, you know, with ruins of Greek temples and tavernas beside the sea and donkeys and such.

So he got the boat, a last Chrissie pressie from Mumsie darling — God, she was a cow, I can't tell you — and I got the winch. Well, the port one broke the first time they took it out — I don't know *why*, it just fell to pieces, literally. Don't be like that, Beryl, it was a very nice port-side birthday winch. It has a nice long brass handle which goes in its own special hand-stitched leather pouch on the cabin top, and has only had to be replaced once when I dropped it — the handle, that is, not the winch — tacking up the river to Morlaix.

Where's Morlaix? Hold your horses! I haven't told you about Grace yet, who's Bob's half-black second wife, skinny as a fishing-rod — and don't you say a single, solitary word about a female Laurel and Hardy — and only thirty-two and a charge nurse at the hospital in Plymouth. She's a high-tensile, steel, bronzey-coloured fishing rod, gorgeous but actually tough as old boots. And she's never done any sailing either, but when the chaps tell us of their plans to take us lucky but very useless wives across to the coast of Brittany in August, they've thought it all through, oh yes, they have. They've asked a third man to come as extra crew. Percy's a pommie friend of Bob's, a chemistry teacher at one of the Plymouth high schools, and a terrific sailor, they say. He knows this part of the world like the back of his hand, does our Perce.

What they don't say is that he's been on Prozac since his wife walked out on him five months ago, and even with Prozac, he's frankly a bit of a mess.

Hold it, both me and the iron need a drink of water . . .

So here we are, nice summer's day at Plymouth Yacht Haven, Kevin and Bob showing me over their pride and joy, puffed up like mating pigeons, Kevin spouting Masefield, though he gets it wrong and fades out after two lines. You know the one: *I must go down to the seas again, to the lonely sea and the sky* — that one. *And all I ask is a tall ship and a star to steer her by* — anyway, Nurse Grace works shifts and has already had a look at her new boat, and one of the first things Bob says to me is that of course I'll want to get together with Grace pronto and have a wee girly chat about the catering.

Bob? They'd sailed P-classes together as kids, at the Murrays Bay Club on the Shore, though I must admit first look and I wondered — the sheepskin coat over the reefer jacket, boat shoes, comb-over hairstyle, natty little moustache, tony accent — and gloves and a monocle, would you believe! I mean, Kevin and I — most people still pick up our accents quite early, and usually think we're Aussies, but not this one. He's a quantity surveyor, something to do with building materials. Smooth-talking, very BBC. Late forties, perhaps?

Yes, yes, it's all legally tied down, trust me. Kevin made sure of that — look, he's a businessman — I don't know how many businesses, about six, but he always broke even, and the teashop's doing just fine — yes, I'm still working there, day and night as you put it — Beryl, *listen* will you, we've got seven other staff and he knows what's what! I'm sure! I know you've never got on, you and Kevin, but will you get off my back? And it's his mother's money, at the end of the day. And no, I'm not telling you how much our share cost.

Where was I when you so rudely interrupted? Oh yes, Grace

is just lovely. We had a coffee one day and talked about the food and she's really lovely. Half-Jamaican, and of course fascinated by Kevin's mum once owning an island round there. Gorgeous-looking — coffee-coloured, cheekbones to die for, and so *capable* — you'd expect her to be, charge nurse and all, and young enough to be my daughter, but I really liked her, so much more than BBC Bob. We had the food sorted in no time, and then she told me what wet-weather gear I'd need to go out and buy, and wasn't that a mission! Needs must if you're going to go boating in this part of the world, and get rained a blizzard on and frozen to your marrow even in summer. Kevin got himself all kitted out, skipper's hat too, with Mama's lovely money — no, sis, I paid for my own. Quite the part in our yellows, we looked.

Come the great day, and it's pouring with rain, and there's little Prozac Percy waiting on the dock with his plastic sextant in a little box — and would you believe, before we've even got on the boat, my great clumsy oaf of a husband in his brand-new boat shoes slips over walking down those marina thingies. Ramps, you know, jetties with boats tied up on either side. Whatever, they were bloody slippery and he slipped.

So Charge Sister Grace insists on whisking him off for an x-ray — his arm, primarily — while the rest of us load up. Now you'd think with two men in the prime of life that I'd be able to leave the really heavy boxes to them. That's what you'd think, right? And I do enough humping round of stuff, boxes of bread and milk and whatever at the teashop?

Turns out Bob has got to be careful of his back — it goes 'quite unpredictably into spasm, m'dear' from time to time — and Percy has recently had an operation for carpal tunnel. That's the thing that makes your hand go all claw-like and you need an op to straighten it out. Yes, bit strange for a sailor, not to be able to grab a rope, but they make him navigator and I'm standing there thinking, well, three of them: Percy can do most things but pull a rope with his right hand, and Kevin can do most things except anything that involves his left arm — no, it wasn't broken, as we thought, just muscular — and Bob can do most things except anything that'll give him a spasm in the lower back.

So, with Capable Grace and me fat and fifty but actually quite strong from going to the gym and humping boxes and standing all day and always willing to give it a go, we've got most things covered.

All the food and gear are stowed away — Bob's the sort that stands there with the clipboard, supervising, don't you know — and the tanks are full of fuel and water, and we're wearing every last bit of the wet-weather gear, so that's easy — and it's Bob calling 'Cast off the springs, chaps,' though with his right hand and Kevin's left arm out of commission, I'm the chap who actually throws off the ropes — and Bob's standing at the wheel as we motor bumpily out of the harbour in the pouring rain yelling 'Fair stands the wind for France.'

That's not Shakespeare, by the way, even though everyone thinks it's Henry the Fifth going off to win the battle of Agincourt. I looked it up. It's 'The Ballad of Agincourt' by a contemporary of Shakespeare's called Michael Drayton, if you really want to know. And it's really 'Fair stood the wind for France, when we our sails advance . . .'

Gosh, this old iron chews up the water . . . I'm up and down like a bride's nightie — anyway . . .

Did I say it was August? The worst August since 1973? It's all a bit hazy now, but it rained every day for the first of our precious weeks. We saw the Channel in the murk, and Roscoff — that was our first port in Brittany — hardly at all, also Morlaix — that's where I dropped the handle of my Christmas winch in the river — and we had to use Bob's cellphone to order a new one to be picked up from a chandlery in Guernsey.

Bob was not pleased with me, Beryl. No. Not at all. His monocle got fogged up with displeasure. We had to improvise a handle from another bit of pipe and use a different lead for the rope on the deck and put up smaller sails, all because I couldn't quite reach to put the thing in the hand-stitched leather pocket right at the exact moment when the boat hit a gigantic wave and nearly turned turtle.

Never mind that I nearly fell out of the boat myself, and landed in a heap on top of little Grace. She was sweet about it, even though I could see in her eyes that it was quite painful, but Her Husband was not pleased. He didn't quite say it, but it was written all over His Lordship's face — we've got a right fat menopausal one here.

Mind you, I wasn't pleased with fat and menopausal little old me, either. Not with the hot flushes and being seasick three times in the middle of the Channel — being unable do anything below except to lie on the downhill bunk until we got to port — being cast by all three of the guys as fat and hopeless — she can't even keep the sailor chaps going with the cups of tea or instant chicken-noodle soup and cabin biscuits.

And hot flushes are not pleasant in a six-berth boat, believe me.

But it's funny, Beryl, here's me who's had three children and worked in various kitchens all my life — and if anything's teamwork, kitchen work is — and after about five days I'm thinking, if Prozac Percy tells us one more story about navigating round the Greek isles or gives a forty-minute lecture about the cheeses of northern France — if Bob tells me when I'm on the wheel one more time that I'm 'pinching her' — if my darling husband moans once more about his sore arm, or asks me to rub it with Deep Heat — I'll scream.

I don't *want* Percy to enlighten me about characteristic Breton rabbit pâtés or teach me how to use a sextant or take a running fix — we've got a GPS, for God's sake, but he says he likes the old ways best, it keeps his tiny mind alert. I don't want Bob's sensitive smile when he goes and puts on the radio quite loudly after breakfast, which is the sure sign that he's going to do big jobs in the loo and doesn't want us to hear the accompanying farts and eventual plops. We do hear, though — he's that close, unless you're up on deck and even then if the hatches are open and the radio's going full bore, how can you not? And I don't want Kevin treating me like an hard-core idiot even though with both arms functioning I can actually work both the Christmas and the non-Christmas winch and take my turn at the wheel and read the tide tables a whole lot better than he can.

So why haven't I joined the club and filed for divorce like lots of other sailing wives? How many? In Auckland? Golly. Here, I wouldn't know. One night in a café in Tréguier — that's another pretty little fishing village in a river a bit further up the coast — Percy produced a book of sailing cartoons by someone called Mike Peyton, and we all fell about laughing, hysterical.

But if you think about it — and I did, that night, when they were all asleep, I took a torch up into the cockpit and had a good long quiet look — all these cartoons were really all about pathetic male creatures, husbands, amateur sailors getting their longed-for boat and getting it wrong. Disasters about to happen, relationships about to fall apart: one clever, cruel drawing after another. Well, like boats just about to fall off cradles or crash into half-submerged rocks or be run over by oil tankers; anchors not holding or getting tangled; people about to fall into the water; navigators about to land them on hidden rocks or bump into buoys; crew about to pull on ropes which you, the reader, just know are going to bring something crashing down on top of their heads or land them in the drink.

And here's Prozac Percy giggling into his pastis — which, by the way because of his medication he very definitely should *not* be drinking — Percy having that very day nearly navigated us, I kid you not, despite the GPS, into the wrong little fishing harbour with hidden rocks. And Bob, who forgot about the tide going out when we came back from a sublime seven-course meal in a little local café — what? Oh, chicken-liver *terrine*, artichokes to die for, *quiche, poisson, salade verte, crème brûlée*, fruits, *fromages, café au lait* — where was I? We come back to find the tide has gone out and the dinghy hanging by its string off the wharf and all the local French fishermen having a good laugh at these pathetic Brits dressed the part in their shore-going reefer-jackets and boat shoes, but forgetting about the thirty-foot tides. And Kev, insisting that we try out the smaller spinnaker and getting such an hourglass in it, which then wrapped the whole of itself around a forestay, so we had to hoist Grace, being the smallest by a country mile, aloft on a halyard with a seaman's knife and get her to cut it down. Pound signs flashing before our very eyes.

But no matter, over dinner the blokes all think Mike Peyton is absolutely *hilarious*, old son. Have another round, whose turn is it this time, who's got any of these froggy francs left? — until they were legless, totally plastered and Grace and I had to lead them back to the boat by the hand. Like toddlers on a little outing, you know?

But you know what was the worst of it? It actually wasn't the storm. Yes, we did have one storm and it was pretty hideous. We should never have left Guernsey, but we had to be back in Plymouth by Sunday because Percy *had* to be back at school first thing Monday, start of school term and that, and Bob had a

Very Important Report to deliver to the Mayor and Council by the following Wednesday, and we'd had a cellphone call from our manager to say that the teashop had been burgled. No, no guns involved, nobody hurt, and not much money in the till, but . . . what it meant was, we left Guernsey with a dodgy sort of forecast and that night got caught in a gale in the middle of the shipping lanes and there we were, all up all night keeping watch.

It was just hideous, Beryl, and we broke a few bits of gear, and a window got stove in by the sea — and at the time I thought, if and when I get to dry land that's it, I'll never set foot on this or any boat ever again, so help me God.

And next day I was on the wheel and Grace was lookout and we just sailed and sailed and sailed and the coast of England just never seemed to get any closer. The tides, silly, that's why, and light ten-knot winds and Percy just out of it until we simply had to drag him on deck to find out what course we were supposed to be sailing. It was Sunday morning, three nights at sea, and when we finally tied up at the marina, all absolutely shattered, I'm thinking to myself now that's supposed to be fun? *Pleasure?*

But even that wasn't the worst of it. You know what was? It was seeing my Kevin all puffed up with owning — part-owning — his own boat, and telling me what a good chap Bob was, and his face when we first left the marina, even if the rain was pouring down. It was a picture, a kid with a new longed-for toy beyond his wildest dreams. And naive old me thinking, poor Kevin, nearly fifty-five long years of not quite making any business work and now thanks to his bloody mother owning an island in Jamaica he's got a chance to have a bit of fun.

But owning a boat isn't mostly fun, Beryl, it's bloody hard work, and you pay a pretty big price for the fun when you have it. And Kevin, he's such a fool — no judgement at all when it comes to people, which is why I've always done the hiring and firing. Thinks too well of people, he does. So he gets chatted up in the yacht-club bar by this smooth Kiwi ex-pat Bob from his P-class days and they go out on a trial sail together round Plymouth harbour to see how they get on — and because both are on their best behave, of course it's OK old chap and so they sign a two-year agreement with the lawyers and now we're stuck with him and Grace for two years minimum.

Oh yes, Bob paid his share. That's one thing he did do. And give him his due, he didn't interfere with all the food bills and catering orders and stuff. I hear you thinking that I've done the ordering and the accounts for Kevin all my life so why should he? Grace and I did the galley together without the men getting involved and we worked out everybody's shares, no sweat. And Bob spoke enough French to deal with the waiters and know which wine to have and whether *service* is included so he did have his uses.

No, what was really hard was two weeks of seeing Kevin just subtly put down all the time, you know? And I couldn't say anything? Bob's done no more sailing than him, really, and they'd agreed that rather than one of them be skipper all the time they'd do it in a 'collegial' way. Hah! Give me a break! Collegial? You can't do collegial on a boat, Beryl, any rate someone like Bob can't. Always got to be top dog, have the last word. And I hear you say Kev's pretty much like that too, but when two top dogs get together one of them has got to be the Most Top Dog, and that one was Bob, at the end of the day. I daresay he gets bossed around at work, and the boat becomes his big chance to be boss, tame the elements, strut his stuff.

Heaven knows what a nice girl like Grace saw in him, though she did drop a hint that she'd grown up in a pretty poor part of Kidderminster and probably saw marrying a smooth-talking forty-something white quantity surveyor not long separated as a step up the old social ladder. There are a lot of spare girls around. Perhaps they have really good sex. Any rate, we all had to listen to one flaming row between Bob and Kevin over whether we should put a reef in the main — prissy Bob said yes, and gung-ho Kevin said no. Percy sided with Bob and we did, and what a mission that was and we had to shake it out half an hour later when the squall went through and the wind died down again just as Kevin said it would. After that, Kevin just got quieter and quieter and didn't say much towards the end, and it was Bob and Percy who were making the decisions.

And when we came home he had another x-ray and found out that his arm really was broken, but someone at the hospital had misread the x-rays or something. So he'd been in a lot of pain, poor old fellow. Yep, a cast up to the elbow for six weeks. Grace is on the case, oh yes.

It was twenty-four shirts, not forty-seven, Beryl. I do the teashop uniforms, saves laundry bills.

Hey — *hey* — hold your horses, little sis. Who said anything about divorce or at the very least saying either that boat goes or I do? I don't want to *sell* it! Of course I don't. It's a lovely boat, and it's paid for, and we're going to make it work for us, Beryl, you bet.

Look, all my childhood I saw those boats on the Auckland harbour and envied people out there going sailing, and what you have to understand is — that day I had helming the boat after the storm, while they were all sleeping, and just Grace sitting quietly on the foredeck looking out for oil tankers — that was one of the *best* things I've ever done in my whole life. Watching the clouds, and the light on the waves, and the sun go across the heavens and sink into the sea. Made up for all the seasickness and hot flushes, the smelly feet and the lectures on rabbit pâté. God, aren't foodies the *most* boring people — Bob turned out to be one as well as Percy — and especially if you put two of them in a quaint village market in quaint old Brittany? Going on and on about how to tell whether an artichoke is fresh and how the French love their mouldy old *saucissons* and how that pale Breton *beurre* is so sublime and delicate in flavour and knocks the spots off over-salted over-yellow common old Kiwi butter? If they worked in a Devonshire teashop like me, making the corned-beef sandwiches with home-made tomato pickles and buttering the scones and whipping up the clotted cream every day, that'd cure them. Yes, Beryl darling, it's *always* New Zealand butter. Anchor it is. What else?

So yes, this boating lark, Grace and me have got it all worked out. We're both going off to day-skipper courses to learn about knots and GPS and stuff — I'll *find* the time, Beryl — and next time we sail together, Bob will be told by both of us to pull his head in, and the blokes will take it in turn to be skipper, and we'll be watching.

Percy, poor chap, won't be asked again, though. He got up Grace's nose even more than mine, because there'd been one night — actually it was alongside at Morlaix — when he'd shaken her awake in her sleeping bag and said he couldn't help it but he was having a hideous low patch in the slough of despond and felt like cutting his wrists —— so Grace took him for a long walk ashore and dealt with it all by her capable self, without telling me or alarming the two blokes who would both have reacted quite badly to having a depressed suicidal loony on board and spun off the planet. Funny, but he was quite good in the storm, when we really were in peril on the sea. Rose nobly to the occasion with cabin bread and mugs of chicken-noodle soup. Navigated as though his life depended on it, which actually it did, and ours too, because in the English Channel shipping lanes you've got quite a good chance of being run over by an oil tanker a mile long on autopilot. In fact one yacht went missing, presumed sunk, that night. Actually I quite liked Percy. Perhaps when he's better and agrees not to bring his little sextant.

The only thing is, I said to Kevin, I will not, under any circumstances, put one foot, not even a toenail, on a boat called *Have a Nice Day*. If he wants me to come as crew, he's got to change it, period.

That caused a bit of huffing and puffing about bad luck if you change a ship's name, but he worked through it. Had to, didn't he? I suggested we call it the *Doris* after his mother, since it was her money, or the *Grant Dalton* after their 'Boy's Own' hero but that was too much even for him.

We're working on it. It will be a collegial decision.

And I hear you ask, how long will it be before I suggest having my turn as skipper? Shorter than the lovely Kevin or you think, *ma petite soeur*.

Aunt Eleanor

Eleanor doesn't particularly want a visit from her middle-aged nephew Brian. She remembers him as a young, newly qualified teacher visiting England, left-wing and scruffy, with an uncouth New Zealand accent. He is now forty-one — she knows that because of Christopher — and very probably no more likeable than he was twenty years ago.

But he has some photographs for her, apparently, sent by her sister-in-law from 12,000 miles away. He has promised his mother to deliver them personally to her in Oxford. Eleanor hears the bell and sighs as she slots the bookmark into her library paperback; just another period romance, pioneer women bravely fighting off Red Indians, but it was getting quite exciting.

In the hall mirror she checks her hair, washed and set this Friday morning as usual despite the appalling weather, and straightens an inscrutable Malayan mask of dark, oiled teak on the wall. Again she reminds herself to urge Jonathon to have the door latch fixed; he can't expect her worsening arthritic fingers to cope with it.

'Well, you'd better come in.'

Her nephew stands before her, dripping water from his coat and shaking his large black umbrella.

'And you'd better give me that.'

'I'll leave it outside.'

'Oh no, someone is bound to take it. Here.' She reaches out and takes the umbrella. 'Come in,' she adds with impatience. The raincoat is one of those long brown Australian things and he has certainly lost much of his hair and his youth. She despises the sentimentality that has brought this man here to his cousin Jonathon's door.

'And your coat. Here.'

She is holding out her thin hand to take it, and Brian, glancing round the narrow, uninviting hallway — carpeted, ice-cold, a telephone table, one straight chair, two masks on the walls and a gold-framed hunting scene — feels helpless to suggest any alternative. 'I'll put them both in the bathroom,' she says firmly.

'Ah . . . well . . . thanks. It's pretty miserable out there.'

'It's November, so naturally it's miserable. It's always miserable in November.'

'Yeah, guess it is.' The ritual family hug is permitted, but with no warmth or response. He follows her into a small living room, also sparsely furnished, and gravitates to the two-bar electric heater in the fireplace to wait for her to come back from the bathroom. The room is dimly lit and stuffy, and carries a faintly unpleasant smell. 'This is Jonathon's place?'

Eleanor looks at her nephew carefully and wonders what else he's been told about her situation . . . that less than two years' widowed, she allowed her eldest son Simon to persuade her to sell her house in Stratford and put the equity towards some business venture which failed just over a year later? That her second son Jonathon, who hasn't spoken to his brother in two decades, has installed her in this poky Oxford flat he bought merely as an investment? That she suspects — knows — Simon to be homosexual and that Jonathon, while earning a small fortune as a high-level bureaucrat in Whitehall, has fathered five children by three different 'partners', none of whom he now lives with, and none of whom — partners or grandchildren — she is allowed to see? That, bankrupted by one son and grace-and-favoured by the other, she now lives on her pension and spends her days reading Penny Vincenzi and Catherine Cookson and her nights watching the relatively trouble-free lives of the Discovery Channel's animal kingdom?

'I'll get the tea,' she says, and brusquely declining his help, leaves him sitting in a brown armchair and rummaging in his jacket pockets for the photographs. He has rarely seen a living space so little marked by its occupier; on a table next to the other armchair lies a thick romance novel, luridly jacketed, a bookmark near the end. Beside it sits an unopened *Daily Telegraph*, a pair of reading glasses, a TV remote. The room is gloomily lit by one reading lamp and one central hanging light in an unappealing, white china shade, vaguely Art Deco and obviously cradling several decades of dust and dead flies. Something large and green in a pot stands besides a heavily curtained window. There's a small television; there are no flowers at all. Apart from a batik hanging, and over the fireplace some wooden elephants trunk-to-tail and a few pieces of brass and ivory from her days as a *memsahib* in Singapore, this could be an old-fashioned lawyer's waiting room.

And Eleanor herself: the ultimate Englishwoman, pale, genteel, formal, complaining. Tweedy skirt, court shoes, twinset and the single string of pearls. As he waits for her return, he has difficulty remembering what colour her clothes actually were, except bleakly neutral . . . was it light blues or beige? Her hair — blonde or grey? — is a stiff Queen-style ridged helmet straight from a salon. His aunt at seventy-one is not merely skinny; she has the look of a one-time anorexic. He remembers his mother saying on his first visit all those years ago, if she asks you to stay (which she hadn't) watch out for the boiled egg — always brown, always three-and-a-half minutes — and one piece of white toast, cut with surgical precision into five fingers. Every morning, no more, no less, that's breakfast. Poor Eleanor, a hard life. When she was seventeen they opened her up, hardly knowing in 1929 what anorexia nervosa was. Nothing wrong, of course, except in her head. Looks brittle, and acts helpless, but she's a brilliant and ruthless organizer, as tough as old boots. Likes a spot of gin; the ritual begins with getting out a large bottle from a locked sideboard at four-thirty daily. You could set Greenwich Mean Time by it. Her daily life is governed by ritual.

'Can't I take that?' he asks, half-rising as the slight figure appears at the door tottering slightly under the weight of a large floral-painted tin tray.

'No, it's alright, thank you.' She makes her way unsteadily across the beige carpet on heels that Isabel would have considered unsuitably high for day wear. 'I can manage. I hope you don't smoke.'

'No,' he lies.

The tea tray is deposited on the other table, and tea is poured from a pale-green china teapot and dispensed in silence.

'I've got the photographs,' says Brian, offering the small envelope of black and whites, with their negatives, taken during 1952, Christopher's year in New Zealand. If she takes it quickly, she might not notice the tears welling in his eyes.

'Yes, I imagine you have, as the delivery boy. Thank you.' She takes the envelope without any evident enthusiasm and puts it unopened on top of the paperback beside her. 'How's your mother?'

'She's doing fine. It was a big funeral, half of Hamilton. Dad knew lots of people.' He doesn't feel, talking about her newly dead younger brother, that he is so far making much of an impression. 'People from racing, and business, his local-body work, they all showed up. Quite a few came down from Auckland.'

She can't bear his accent, slovenly and nasal. 'I don't suppose your mother let you speak.'

'Sorry?'

'Too left-wing and radical for all his business friends, I would have thought.'

'I gave one of the eulogies,' he says evenly, his dislike for her deepening. That stiff hair, the insipid tweeds — the girlish, high-pitched, fake BBC accent — that stiff tan handbag standing on guard beside the chair, the way she sits with knees glued together, legs on an angle and the child-sized ankles demurely crossed; the Queen and her ilk had a lot to answer for. 'There were three eulogies. And mine seemed to go down OK. And yes, I'm left-wing enough to hope David Lange will be elected next year, but I'm no card-carrying member of the Labour Party. Never have been.'

'So you don't support Mr Muldoon.'

'No, never have.'

'Your father did, I'm sure.'

'Even he had lost faith in the National Party and that took some doing, believe me. Personally, I can't bear the man. Dangerous and overbearing, a hard-core bully. Worse than that, he's bringing the country close to bankruptcy.'

Eleanor's thin lips tighten to a line. 'That's not what the *Daily Telegraph* thinks.' Lipstick, unflatteringly pink in tone, has leaked into the downward creases at the edges of her mouth, intensifying the sneer. She hands him a small pewter dish with two thin chocolate biscuits on it.

'Those are for you. Your mother tells me you want to be a writer, now . . . she says you've had something published?'

'A couple of short stories in the *Listener*. I've won a competition or two. Just regional ones, mostly, but I've been shortlisted for one of the national biggies.' He takes both the chocolate thins at once and is pleased to see her lips tighten further. The lack, so far, of at least minimal condolences is quite curious. 'By the way, Dad said to ask you about Gran's novel, the one she wrote in the 1930s. He read it once and thought I'd be interested. Which I am, of course.'

Momentarily, Eleanor's back loses its ramrod straightness. She looks down at her pale-green Poole teacup, and knows she must keep her voice bright. It was only a novel, she tells herself, a heap of brittle paper gathering an unacceptable and unhealthy amount of dust. 'Mother's silly book, you mean?'

'Yes. Her novel.'

'Oh, it got burnt.'

'What do you mean, got burnt?'

'Just that. I burnt it.'

He is, as she anticipated, clearly aghast. He repeats, staring at her accusingly, 'You *burnt* it?'

'I was going through James's papers . . . afterwards, as you have to . . . it was sitting there, on a shelf. It all went into the incinerator at Stratford. I just thought . . . well, no-one will ever read all that stuff.'

'It was the only copy.'

'She was quite mad, you know. It was nonsense. Silly, romantic nonsense. Quite trashy actually. A whole dusty pile of nonsense, hundreds of pages . . . you'd have got very tired of it.'

Brian takes refuge in drinking his tea, not the usual gumboot but that bitter, pretentious Earl Grey. If she sees the anger, the disappointment, the outrage in his eyes, that's her problem. His father had whispered, on his last visit to the hospice, Eleanor holds the one copy in existence: get it back from her, Brian. Don't trust her or the mail. It's valuable social commentary — Frank's voice had grown fainter with every word — she wrote it during the Great War, and after . . . took her years, all about kauri gum, and coastal shipping . . . Dargaville was a big port then . . . besides lady novelists being so rare . . . I read it, you know . . . so she wasn't Katherine Mansfield but . . . you might be surprised . . . quite racy . . . a damn good read, actually . . . poor old Mum . . .

He'd closed his eyes and those turned out to be his last words to Brian or anyone. And now here was this aunt, faux-English, one who as a child was supposed to have run wild on West Coast beaches and wasn't too proud to drive ambulances in Egypt in the war, telling him with all the self-appointed, unassailable authority of the British upper classes that her own mother's novel was worthless trash and she'd burnt it. The lack of imagination and courtesy for the rest of the family, her own sons included, he finds simply astounding. And he doesn't buy grieving as an excuse. He has the right not to buy it.

Loss and emptiness, great vacuums opening up — was there to be no end to it? Now another, yet another; this time it was his dead grandmother's unique voice, thoughtlessly stilled — irresponsibly silenced — murdered, as real as if Eleanor had taken a knife to her mother's throat, by careless flames in a backyard incinerator. What stories, what insight would that dusty manuscript have provided! It might even, with some careful editing, have been publishable, adding a rare female voice to the country's early literature. How proud he would have been, as the instrument of its success, with or without any writing career of his own. Now he is deprived even of that.

'What's done is done,' she pipes. 'I couldn't be bothered with it, really. More tea?'

'No.' Swallowing hard, he can barely bring himself to be polite. 'I'm not usually an Earl Grey drinker.'

'It's Lady Grey, which I myself prefer. Twinings.' The pouring of weak Lady Grey into the green Poole cup is being done with infinite care; even so he can discern a slight tremble in her arms. 'Perhaps you don't have it out in New Zealand yet.'

Politics he can cope with.

'Until we get rid of Muldoon, we don't have a lot of things. Like a government in the real world. Lange and his crowd will be like a breath of fresh air, and as far as I'm concerned, the change can't come soon enough.'

'You're quite passionate about politics.'

'I'm a history teacher. Plus some economics. It's my job to be interested. Until I left, I wrote a weekly column for the Hamilton paper. The last one, last week, gave Muldoon a hard time, but I was leaving, what the hell.'

She puts down the teapot heavily, clumsily, nearly sending the whole unbalanced tray toppling into the tiled fireplace. 'Oh well, what would I know? It's so many years since I was out there. I don't suppose I shall go again.'

'We thought you might have come out for Dad's funeral.'

'Did you? All that way? Sitting cooped up in a noisy plane for days? Oh, no. I couldn't afford it, Brian, and besides I do dislike funerals. I *never* go to funerals. I'm sure I wasn't missed.' An anxious hand flutters insincerely up to her pearls. 'Oh dear, I do hope my flowers arrived. I spent quite a lot of money on them.'

'I can't remember,' Brian says brutally. 'The old boy got lots of flowers. Bucketloads. As I said, it was a big funeral. Eight hundred in the cathedral, and the wake at the racing-club lounge. You can't go much higher up the social scale than that.'

'I'm sure. In Hamilton.'

Again she sips tea and again he feels her rudeness stoking his dislike. Her only brother's funeral; and funds for her travel had been available. He knew that his father had left instructions with his mother and the lawyer for money to cover Eleanor's long trip, if she wished to come. Business class, if that is what she wished. But it was just something else she couldn't be bothered with.

'And how's Jonathon?' he asks jovially, breaking the silence and deciding to play the colonial bumpkin and give as good as he got. 'I think he's had a few sprogs since I was last here. Three, is it now, or four? Or even five! Mum says she's lost count.'

He sees Eleanor's pale blue eyes suddenly narrow, as though in pain.

'Just five. Sprogs is an uncouth, detestable word. I do wish you wouldn't use it.'

'Children then. Five!'

He waits for her to elaborate, as grandmothers usually do, with names, ages, their copious talents, and their latest pictures taken from nearby handbags.

'And living where?' he prompts, knowing that the answer will be revealing, whatever she chooses to say.

'Oh, all in Gloucestershire,' she says airily, declining to say at three different addresses in the county and registering an unpleasant smirk around her nephew's mouth. 'Jonathon's still in the Foreign Office, of course. He got a big promotion recently. He spends quite a lot of time these days in Brussels. Back and forth, across the Channel. He's very busy.'

'Good on him,' says Brian with a heartiness which is patently false. 'Always was a real hard goer.' She winces satisfactorily. 'And Simon? What's he up to? His marriage fell over, didn't it?'

'Rosemary left him, yes.' She picks up the envelope of pictures from the table beside her and looks at it. 'A foolish and selfish gal. Fortunately for everyone there were no children. He's in Bristol. In personnel management for a big company there. I don't really know what that means.'

'Hiring and firing. That business venture of his . . . Dad was pretty upset about that.' Or, more honestly, Dad was furious. Eleanor's two-page letter on cheap lined paper had told the story as though it was perfectly normal for a son to lose £260,000 of his newly widowed mother's money, representing her house, her superannuation and her security, and apparently — incredibly — feel not one shred of remorse nor responsibility nor shame. And now, she wrote in a postscript, it's quite sad but Jonathon won't let her talk to Simon. His father had thrown down the letter in disgust. That Simon's a no-hoper, always was, he said, banging the dining-room table so hard that the Bavarian crystal candlesticks bounced. The woman's pathetic, *pathetic*, a complete *fool*.

The little white envelope gets turned, over and over, but not opened. Diversionary tactic, thinks Brian, because she's worked out that I'm quite well informed about her dreadful sons, and she needs a prop.

It could be also an emotional land mine they are both about to tread on. The pictures are of Christopher, aged eleven, taken when he went to New Zealand to spend a year living with his Hamilton cousins. Christopher, bright, talented and generous, a good mate to Brian and according to Brian's parents, worth both his older brothers put together.

'Mum thought you should have those.'

There she sits, silent and quite still, showing no signs of opening the envelope, however curious she might be, and — he realizes again — still no sign of bringing up the events of his own life in the past fourteen months. It's not possible, he thinks — surely — that she actually doesn't know; he understood his mother had written at the time. Surely she knows.

'They're of Chris, mostly. Dad took them, in his serious photography phase. He always meant to do some enlargements. Never got round to it.'

'Oh. I see.'

'The negs are in there too, if you want to get some enlarge-ments done.'

'Thank you.'

Still she shows no sign of investigating, but leans down and slips it into her handbag. In the silence of the room, the clasp gives an austere clack, like a pistol being readied.

Brian looks away and stares at the glowing two-bar heater. Such an inefficient way to heat a room. He hopes his Foreign Office boffin cousin Jonathon doesn't stoop so low as to make her pay the electricity bill; but he wouldn't bet on it. Jonathon with the five children, none of whom he lives with, none of whom she, their grandmother, sees. Simon who took and lost all her money, and Chris killed on his motorbike at sixteen. It's inhuman.

Liddy, dead. Isabel and little Bruce, gone. This was inhuman too.

If there has been any moment since he arrived when his aunt, his blood relation, this sad, gaunt, stoic facsimile of a human being might recognize a fellow traveller, it is now.

'That was a great year, for Chris, and for me too,' he hears himself prattle, desperate to deflect the wave roaring in his ears, about to pass over and swamp him. 'He wanted to go to all the places he'd heard about — the old house in Dargaville, that's Granny's old house of course. The black beaches you went to for holidays. I suppose he told you about all that. We went camping at Muriwai.'

'Yes, he told me. He was happy enough there.'

'Once we went digging for toheroas at Muriwai. Dad took the car along the beach at low tide because Chris wanted to be so alone on a beach that you couldn't see a single person, or car or house — just like it was, like God made it, he said, absolutely empty, before everyone arrived. You couldn't do that in England any more. Just no-one. Just you and the surf, the sky above, the windswept sand, the salty mist. There was a fierce offshore wind, whipping off the tops of the waves. So we left him there on the beach and drove up one of those access roads, out of sight, and for twenty minutes he stood on the beach and had his experience of aloneness. And bugger me, on the way back we got stuck in the sand and just as well, two motorbikes came roaring along and we waved them down. They went on and got help.'

'I see. Wasn't that rather foolish?'

'What was?'

'To leave an eleven-year-old boy alone on that dangerous beach.'

'Dad was OK with it. Chris wasn't going swimming. Just standing on the sand, being alone, exulting in that solitude. He couldn't come to much harm. Perhaps he knew.'

The wave has loomed, has towered unspeakably high, and is about to break.

'We got towed out of there just in time to beat the tide. Another twenty minutes and the motorbike guys reckoned we'd have lost the car to the sea. It happens quite regularly, on that beach. Mum wasn't pleased, even with an absolute feast of toheroa fritters for tea that night, a limit bag, the sweetest and best we ever had, but Chris thought it all a great lark.'

'He didn't tell me about that. I remember toheroa fritters always had sand in them. A complete waste of time, in my opinion. I didn't like them.'

'He did. Loved 'em.'

She is holding out her hand for the teacup, which he recognizes as a signal for his departure.

'Eleanor, Mum told you about Liddy? You got her letter?'

She pauses, withdraws her empty arthritic hand. 'I did.'

'So how do you think that feels, that you've not said one single word about her? About Isabel leaving me? In thirty minutes I've been here, not one. Of all people.'

She gets up unsteadily and collects his cup, stacking it noisily on the tray with her own.

'People used to walk across the road to avoid me,' she says coolly. 'Do the most astonishing things to avoid me. I learnt to appear not to notice, not to put myself in awkward and embarrassing positions. You will too, in time.'

The smell, Brian now registers, is coming from her and it is the smell of grief, of unbearable loss.

'I was very sorry about Liddy,' she says, articulating her words with great clarity. 'And now your father's passing too, on top of everything.'

As she bends to pick up the tea tray, he notices — ludicrously — the absolute straightness of the black stocking seams up calves slimmer than his forearms.

She says, 'It must have been very hard, with Liddy, but at least you knew it was coming. We . . . a violent, sudden, stupid death . . . all his life before him. No-one can possibly . . . I didn't ask you to come.'

She is taking the tea tray from the room and she will come back with his damp Driza-Bone and black umbrella from the bathroom.

Brian gets as far as the hallway. Under the Malayan mask — Chris, he suddenly remembers, was born in Singapore — he stops and savagely wipes away the tears that herald the thunder of the breaking wave.

'I thought you might . . . the counsellor said . . .'

'Counsellor!' she snorts. 'You haven't been wasting money seeing *counsellors*, have you? They're all charlatans, every one. Foolish boy.'

'He said, in time, talking with . . .'

'He was wrong. Time alters nothing. Talk means nothing. Now take these, and you'd better go.'

Neither moves to make any sort of physical contact; the brief moment passes when Eleanor might have moved to offer a fleeting solace, one momentary touch of understanding. She can take no responsibility for his lack of self-control, his self-indulgent tears, those emotions that are called grief. To learn to live with them is the loneliest and most bitter of journeys. She closes the door.

Despite herself, she pulls aside the heavy maroon curtain to see if the weeping man in his long brown raincoat appears in the road below. The November rain is pelting down onto the road and the traffic, driving against the red brick houses lining the Oxford street, bending the bare branches of the plane trees. There is a bus shelter opposite and there her nephew stands. Even at this distance, in the lights of the passing cars, she can see that he is weeping freely, regardless of three others in the shelter. She watches them move slightly away, as if he is infectious.

He will learn. We all do. Of course she feels sorry for him, who wouldn't? His daughter — fourteen or so — taking a year to die from some nasty incurable sort of leukaemia, and then Isabel walking out on him six months later, taking the boy of nine with her to Australia. A separation following a child's death, as so often is the case. While she had made sure in her own case that didn't happen, neither she nor James, grown bewildered, short-tempered and morose while she herself had gone bitter and silent, took any great pleasure in sticking it out together.

A recent letter from her sister-in-law had told her Brian was coming to England to work for a while, get a teaching job. He had some photographs she'd found in Frank's study, nice ones of Christopher as an eleven-year-old that Frank had taken, years ago. Brian, she added, was not in a very good space; she was desperately worried about him. Perhaps, since they had both had experienced the ultimate . . .

Eleanor watches her nephew weeping in the bus shelter. She watches him take out a packet of cigarettes and, with some difficulty, light one in the driving rain. In time, Brian, you will become as deadened, as immune, as numb and as hard and tough as I am. It is inevitable that this is so, and if your 'counsellor' has not told you that, then he is failing you utterly with lies.

Nothing and nobody — not even her two wretched, altogether unattractive sons and a few lost grandchildren — not even her brother's only son in the early stages of his own grief, Christopher's favourite cousin, the one born the same year and who, he once told her, he liked and loved better than either of his brothers — nothing will ever reach her again.

So Chris had stood on Muriwai beach, savouring twenty minutes of aloneness. Her son had remembered. She closes her eyes and just for a few moments, hears that surf, pounding in, a fresh westerly it was, onshore, and the sea an eerie, luminous apple-green. She sees a slim girl in shorts running through the shallows, her feet kicking aside the drifts of white salt froth; she is doing *grands jetés* suspended above the earth like Nijinksy; she is twirling giddily, laughing, and her arms are raised to the endless possibilities of the blue heavens. She was maybe twelve, thirteen.

A bus comes and Brian, throwing his cigarette into the gutter, rubbing a no doubt grimy handkerchief across his eyes, exits from her life. She closes the curtains and straightens the satin cushion where he had been sitting. There are dishes in the sink to be done, the tea things and a small pewter dish. There is a little water to be wiped up in the bathroom. Her book is reaching its predictable climax. She might open the envelope in her handbag in the morning.

She has never cried for her son. Not one tear.

Control is everything. Neither beauty nor ugliness have any meaning and love is a tragic delusion; only control has meaning and the contemptible lack of discipline is everywhere to be seen: sons who cannot control their filthy, wandering hands; a nephew full of dangerously radical ideas and self-pity; a husband who drank himself into the grave. The separated, the divorced, the untidy, the smoker and the drinker and worst of all, the fat and gluttonous she despises utterly.

At four-thirty she will unlock the cupboard and pour the first of her three gins, measured, with one chunk of ice and a thin slice of the sourest lemon.

Madeleine and Irma

Laura had first noticed the two women as she walked across the dusty gravel, mixed with cigarette stubs, that passed for sand in the Baie de Garavan. She'd grimaced briefly at the grotesque spectacle, then lain down a towel and collapsed with a grateful sigh, determined to obliterate all memory of the twenty-seven hour journey — Wellington where it was hailing, congested Changi, worse again Heathrow, finally Nice and a long wait for a jolting airport bus.

Then, from Gare Nice Ville, the first reward: a clean, silent train speeding towards the Italian border past the glittering sea, beaches, tall palms beside rose-tinted villas, glimpses of superyachts and cruise ships, the elegant arches of Monaco's new underground station. She'd remembered to sit on the right-hand side. Five minutes later, looking back, a fabulous view of flesh-coloured skyscrapers against crags of grey and white limestone rising precipitously from a turquoise sea. A miniature Hong Kong, thought Laura, its sickly colour reminding her of those repellant ads for foundation, a glob of viscous liquid, promising the radiance of youth, spilling out of a sleek over-designed bottle.

Finally, one stop short of the Italian border, a deserted station and a short walk trailing her suitcase to a friend's tiny apartment in the *vieux ville*. Panting, she'd thrown open the shutters, unlocked her bag and pulled out swimming gear, her one thought to lie on the white beach directly below. Even gone four o'clock there was still power in the late May sun to burnish fair skin and thaw the soul.

Aaah! Despite the hardness of the gravel, the heat on her back began to release the tensions of the past two miserable weeks. Bosses, betrayers, dissemblers all, get ye hence, out of my life! Bugger you all. Laura pulled on her togs without embarrassment, as you do when surrounded by topless women, many older than her — witness those two ancient gold-plated crones yonder. She knew from two previous visits that the city fathers provided plentiful showers on their beaches but no changing facilities nor immediately visible toilets. Being still in watchful-traveller mode, not quite ready to surrender herself completely to the sun, she leaned back on her elbows to drink in the surroundings.

The beach was crowded, only a few heads bobbing out there between the embracing arms of rock that defined the public *plage* as clearly as a swimming pool. OK for now, she thought, but come August, with a glistening layer of sun oil and worse trapped within the breakwaters, more or less unswimable. No daily sluice of tides here, no long Pacific swell, no empty dunes. The Med was merely an oversized lake, a different concept of seaside altogether. Behind her rose the toy-town jumble of the *vieux ville*, in variations of orange, cinnamon, ochre and lemon, with sky-blue shutters and terracotta roofing, crammed onto the hillside and crowned by its three famous spires. Further up the ridge, even from here, she could see a marble angel, one of hundreds in the most princely cemetery in all Europe. They looked over Napoleon's military road built around the original foreshore to move troops swiftly across the border but now softened by palms and bougainvillea and the hum of constant traffic.

Laura felt herself relaxing, and wondered whether this was, even for a Kiwi, despite the traffic, perhaps one of the most stunning beach settings anywhere in the world. Above, the vapour trails of aircraft bound for Rome, Pisa, Nice, Marseilles and beyond crosshatched the bluest sky. Across the bay lay a steep and spectacular amphitheatre, its precipitous topmost crags defining the border with the terraces below cradling lemon and olive tress, terracotta villas, magnolia, cypress and date palms. Trucks Italy-bound on the A8 vanished halfway up the cliff-face into the middle of three French tunnels; tourists wanting Mediterranean waves crashing on rocks took the coastal road and also found themselves in lengthy tunnels; the well-advised tourist took the middle corniche past the *douane* and the iron gates of the Hanbury Gardens, and enjoyed the gleaming Ligurian Sea all the way to Ventimiglia. She reminded herself to set aside a morning for the Hanbury Gardens.

The *vieux ville*'s church bells rang out across the bay, chiming four-thirty. Unaccountably, Laura shivered; beaches were surely an antidote to clocks and time-keeping, and medieval bells were used as much for warning a populace of impending danger as for summoning it to prayer. After the tensions of the journey — those new fears of gunmen, bombs, innocent planes being used as paper darts and infectious diseases lately added to traditional qualms of overshot landings and pickpockets — danger and death seemed quite incompatible with this extraordinarily beautiful scene and its beautiful people. She told herself firmly, as the bells died away, that this invulnerability must be real: beaches were not places for the predatory, the infirm, the sickly or the disabled. Beaches were guileless open spaces that turned sun worshippers into gods, quite separate personae from the pale office workers who fled south from a Baltic spring, the teachers who'd survived another year in a Manchester school, or Midwest college students shrugging off parental concerns about Americans abroad, just wanting to improve their French.

Or a Kiwi escaping Wellington hail and a hard-core bastard

who'd just — two weeks ago, without warning — gone back to his wife.

They had planned to do the Hanbury Gardens together, next time. The Cinque Terre and the lesser-known palaces of Genoa. They'd lived together for three years, travelled twice to Australia and once to a Tuscan autumn, bought a house and planned a future, a companionable, comfortable, supportive old age together. She'd given up her job, knowing full well that at sixty-one this was curtains; in the rigid hierarchy of the public sector, her skills not prized by or easily transferable to the private; she'd not ever again be employable.

She was not personally ready to finish work, but she had bowed to his subtle pressure. They would have more time for doing things together, for travel, for visiting the many friends he had around the world from a lifetime of international conferences. She loved this man, as she'd not allowed herself to love anyone in decades. Handing in her resignation was her ultimate commitment to him.

And then — murmuring apologetically that, though he and Jenny had been apart fully eight years, he realized he still loved her, and always would — Guy had gone back to his bloody wife.

Well, the Hanbury Gardens are just around that headland, thought Laura, blinking back tears which still arrived uninvited from time to time, and the cruel agaves and mauve wisteria and butter-yellow Banksia roses will still be there, and that glorious villa Sir what's-his-face and his lady wife stayed in, and I'll damn well enjoy it by myself. She had a week here, solo, in the tiny *vieux ville* apartment spontaneously offered by an English friend for time to think, walk, read, be herself, be healed — time to recuperate from nights of weeping and him being so damn sorry and sympathetic and lawyers yabbering on about Property Relationship Agreements. They hadn't even had a good fight about it; out of the blue, late at night, he'd just calmly announced his dilemma and his decision. So civilized, so male, so final. Three years and a happy future cancelled out, just like that. Laura rang up the next day and booked a ticket to London. She'd sold her car. Although he wanted to stay in the house, and even expected that she would leave her furniture there and feel perfectly happy about this, she refused even to discuss either of these preposterous suggestions and arranged to put the furniture into storage and the sale of the house into the hands of a land agent. Past crying, focusing on the business matters in hand, she had visited her lawyer. She would not (could not) get another job. She was washed up, 'retired' at last and she was gone.

After the Riviera, she would do a week's cycling in the hills of Provence, then go by train to some friends in the Loire. Fly to Edinburgh to see her son, go camping in the isles with him and his Scottish partner, both in IT. Then, across the Atlantic to a daughter unhappily married to a diplomat in Ottawa, and cycling through Virginia in the fall. Five months of pleasing herself. Though undesirably single, she would join all those smugly retired, determinedly active baby-boomer couples — declaring to bemused and envious adult children that *this, darlings, is not the dress rehearsal* before departing — off biking, walking or cruising their way around the remoter places on the planet.

She'd get home poor as a church mouse, and move into the tiny Epsom flat she'd kept as equity. Sell what furniture didn't fit, buy a car, gape in horror at the Visa account and decide what to do next. If she sold the flat, really burned her bridges, next year she could go up the Mekong in a canoe, do the opera houses of Eastern Europe or go trekking in Tibet. There might be a grandchild in Edinburgh to see; one lived in hope. Or she might climb Everest. In this year of Hillary's fiftieth anniversary, a seventy-year-old Japanese had just done so. Kilimanjaro might be easier.

And because counsellors in her menopausal days had warned her against the dangers of self-pity, even while mourning the loss from a heart attack of her first and so far only husband, Laura stirred herself on the Riviera gravel and bought a large piece of fresh coconut from an Italian vendor, dressed in pantaloons as Harlequin. '*Grazie, bella,*' he murmured huskily from beneath his feathered hat before moving off with his basket, his bucket of rinsing water and his toot-toot toy horn. She loved the way Italians, even coconut-sellers in amusing suits, made a woman feel beautiful and young; even those who were quite clearly neither.

Crunching her coconut, she turned her attention to the people around, each little group — and yes, most were groups — about two metres apart. That seemed to be the protocol; any closer and space was being invaded, though she knew that the distance diminished as summer progressed and the crowds increased.

That little family, prudently stopping at two girls: the mother kneeling at the feet of the older one (and perfectly capable, thought Laura nastily, of doing it herself), anointing both methodically with oil. At five o'clock? Then, ever-so-carefully folding their clothes into a neat pile (I bet her cupboards are tidy) while the little girls poked a white toe into the water. They must be English, or northern European, but they spoke so little and so timidly that she couldn't pick up any single revealing word. Everything about them was prim and anaemic, the pale lime and dull pink T-shirts, the transparently white skin, the lank hair, the gestures, the enjoyment, such as there was. Contrast the boisterous Italian family next to them, bronzed and brightly dressed children; the mother's long and enthusiastically blonded tresses, her plump upper arm tattooed with butterflies and her full breasts bared to the sun; the coppered, ponytailed father and presumably uncles glinting gold teeth and chains, all shouting, splashing, about to burst into song. Stereotypes exist, thought Laura. On this border beach, crossroads of two countries and playground of several more, despite tutors at the writing courses she'd done in recent years telling students *please, avoid stereotypes*, they exist nonetheless.

The coconut was surprisingly juicy and cooling. Someone could profitably sell this on an Auckland beach, she thought, appreciating its crisp white texture, except they'd never get a licence from politically correct councils, terrified someone would sue them for allowing food vendors to give them food poisoning, or the local iwi demanding a licence of their own to sell watercress or lay down hangi. Nor would they countenance those robed Somalian beach hawkers of sunglasses, watches and cheap leather belts. Who bought those things — someone must? Not that French group next door for sure, five women and two men — these ubiquitous sixty-year-olds again, come from cold northern France or Belgium to sun themselves on the Riviera, bedecked with gold, as brown as berries and it's not even June. Whether courtesy of a self-tanning lotion or sunlamps, or both, in May they were, thought Laura, for us Caucasians, almost indecently tanned.

Two particularly intrigued her, for both had the brownest breasts she had ever seen on any Caucasian over thirty: one was delightfully slim for sixty-plus, but leathery; the other, a rotund French chatterbox, scratched constantly beneath the hang of a generous saddle of stomach which all but obscured the electric-blue bikini presumably covering her crotch. The convex curve of stomach, when she went to swim, still topless, was not unlike that of a woman seven months gone. Laura was both repulsed (one-piece togs look better at our age, lady) and secretly admiring (atta girl, even with the long operation scar, who cares!). And elderly, stooping males in this part of the world could apparently develop such sagging breasts they could be taken for topless women; the old markers of gender, in these days of male ponytails and female shaved heads, were no longer reliable.

After some time, watching the body language, she decided they were two couples and three widows, the women possibly old school friends or colleagues. On Kiwi beaches such groups of unclothed senior citizens were an rare sight. There, women of sixty were more likely to be in granny mode with their families, or with only female friends, or by themselves, if on a beach at all. They wouldn't be wearing gold jewellery, or topless, or smoking. She caught a whiff of smoke from a handsome couple who'd just arrived close by and without preamble were now interestingly intertwined. Italian, thirties, lovers, smokers both.

Guy smoked. Had all his life. He had tried to give it up, several times, nicotine patches and all that palaver, he but couldn't. The dangers were overplayed by wimps, he announced at practically every dinner party, and what was that PC nonsense of 'passive smoking' anyway? It was a measure of her love for him, her simple pleasure in his company, her new and wondrous sense of security, that she'd trained herself not to mind his self-serving pronouncements, the smoke on his clothes or in the living room, to tolerate the strong taste of tobacco in his mouth, even on his skin. She'd used lemon- and pine-scented air fresheners liberally, and stronger perfumes, thinking herself a throwback to the centuries when pomades, scents and snuff were used for good reason. Guy liked her Chanel No 5 best. He was generous, stocking her up with duty free in the early days of their relationship when he came back from some conference, with Chanel, Dior and Yves Saint Laurent and some of the newer, sharper American smells sold to him by canny little Chinese women. She had quite a collection. She'd left them all at home, in a box, unopened, in storage. Guy, at least a pack-a-day man, was a really good candidate for lung cancer. His wife could deal with it.

Perhaps Europeans simply don't get melanoma nor lung cancer, she pondered. Baring face and breasts, no matter how tiny or pendulous, to the full sun while puffing away at a Gauloise seemed the norm in this beautiful, if noisy, setting. And the overall age group was definitely older — according to her guidebook, this *ville* was the Fort Lauderdale of France, the Gold Coast, the Tauranga. Fifty metres offshore a swimmer was doing a double-arm backstroke, another a genteel sidestroke — both styles Laura thought long extinct. And why shouldn't a huge *grandmère* of advanced age bob around serenely in a ship's life ring, an image from a kids' picture book, surely?

As she turned to lie on her side, Laura smelled perfume, strong and sweet, not one she recognized. Her eye fell again on the two ancient biddies who evidently had rejected their earlier choice of gravel patch and moved into a space closer to her, nearer the water's edge. The Italian lovers thought their intentions just a little too close, and in one fluid movement, barely missing a puff, rolled themselves away to a more comfortable distance. That earned a gracious nod and a singsong '*Merci*' from the — possibly — younger. Good God, thought Laura, a sixty-something in bright-orange bum floss . . . she got out her second pair of sunglasses, the darker ones, and settled down behind them, pretending to sleep, for a good, long, impolite and entertaining stare.

The younger — by name Madeleine, Laura decided — was clearly the caregiver, the barrel-shaped kid sister who'd tottered over the gravel with the rush mats and the beach bags and umbrella in its shoulder holster, and was now establishing base camp for a possible assault on the blue waters, a metre-and-a-half away, of the Baie de Garavan. An estimate of her age varied between Madeleine stationary and Madeleine moving. Stationary, upright, remembering to tighten a few muscles, she might have passed for sixty-five, from a distance. Hair and *maquillage* were smooth pale apricot offset by the kohl and gold jewellery more usually associated with a Hindu bride; her swimming costume — mercifully not a bikini, but nevertheless cut high and baring most of her buttocks — was dazzling orange, nails to match. The sunlamp all-over tan and a complete top coat of oil completed the luscious image. A stout sixty-two, thought Laura, without envy, thinking of the money, not to mention the effort involved. But Madeleine moving betrayed everything; the arm flaps swung, the rolls around the waist and chins shifted and wobbled, the knees wouldn't bend, the back was sore, the old joints as she manoeuvered herself carefully down onto the mat were stiff. Eighty if she's a day, Laura decided charitably, and such care for one's appearance, such defiance and courage, such chutzpah were not to be sneezed at. Madeleine had not let herself go, *mais non*, Madeleine did not bob around in a ship's life ring. Madeleine was a battler.

Above her, Irma now stood. She'd followed, slow and unsteady on her feet. Irma was probably eighty-nine, and nearly as heavily loaded up with a dowry of gold. Her large square handbag was plaited gold, matched by dainty flat golden shoes. Irma was taking off a linen wrap-around knee-length skirt to reveal a nice little cornflower-blue number, ruched and skirted, which, thought Laura, was a relief. She was slimmer, her hair a less exuberant blonde, and her make-up less startling then her sister, for that is what Laura had now by one or two small interactions decided they were; at once familiar, impatient, critical, indulgent. They communicated in the sometimes silent, sometimes noisy code of sisters, or decades-old friends. And no help whatsoever was being offered by the younger to the older.

So Irma stood. She stood on the rush mat, legs apart, head down in concentration and folded her wrap-around skirt. Over a period of the next twenty-five minutes, Irma gathered up any two of the three sections (back, front and the front extension) together. She never quite achieved gathering in the third. One would always escape, to drop and droop, and the process of clamping the waistband together, gathering up the recalcitrant piece of fabric, would begin all over again. Irma stood in the Garavan sun and oblivious to all else, folded her skirt very slowly, her arms and fingers moving as ponderously as those 'living statues' Laura remembered seeing on last year's trip with Guy to Florence. Muttering about funny ways to make a living, he'd wanted a coffee, but Laura was mesmerized by their astonishing self-control, and had sent him to the café across the *piazza* while she stayed for nearly half an hour. With heavy draperies, wigs and faces of bronze, silver or dead-white marble, those Greek athletes or medieval German pages had moved from pose to pose, slyly acknowledging a tourist's camera or a coin dropped into their hats on the pavement.

Thus Irma, painstakingly folding her skirt, a living statue in ruched and skirted cornflower blue — and Madeleine, oblivious to the Everest being tackled by her sister, going on one of her own — into the sea to knee-level. There she remained, to engage in what sounded to Laura like fluent Italian with the male Italian lover resurfacing beside her from a cooling dip. And as far as she could see, looking around, no-one else, other than the amused female lover with the number-two haircut, was the slightest bit interested in what to Laura remained a bizarre and extraordinary sight. Thus the Riviera, thus Europe. Perhaps she would come and live here; she too could spend her diminishing euros on a dazzling array of fine Lancôme and Dior products, and make an appearance, four o'clock daily at Garavan beach, an absolute triumph of artifice over age.

Ah — a miracle, success! As the bells pealed five-thirty, and her little sister flirted in the shallows, Irma achieved the summit. The linen skirt now hung evenly down from her trembling fingers, three sections of skirt tamed. Half an hour had — incredibly — gone, and the sun had lost its bite. Laura again shivered. She'd passed through the stage of being fascinated by how long this could go on, to intense irritation: she wanted to scream out, just put the fucking thing away, woman, and sit *down*! But now, with exquisite ponderousness, Irma was folding the skirt, smoothing it carefully and — somewhat easier than Madeleine would have done — bending over to place it just so across the gold plaited bag.

There. Mission accomplished. Then she sat herself heavily down, though not bad for ninety and all that gold. The old girl sat on the rush mat like a child, or an old nursery doll, legs poked out in front, gold flatties pointing upwards to the heavens. With her face gone slack, eyes staring blankly, she looked done in. Laura decided that her first suspicions were correct: at some time, Irma had had a stroke.

Madeleine in the shallows flirted noisily on, inviting attention, accepting a cigarette from the Italian lover. The bay had become her stage, the sunbathers on the beach her audience. You outrageous old broad, thought Laura, with increasing admiration. Most antipodean crones had long since retired into their up-market rest-homes or down-market granny flats, spending long days creeping round in Crimplene dresses and knee highs making cups of tea and washing their smalls, waiting patiently for the week's highlights of *Coronation Street* and, less likely, a letter from a son. Go Madeleine!

Wishing she had enough French or Italian to strike up a conversation, Laura told herself it was swim time and levered herself to her feet. God almighty, all that geriatric stiffness was catching. Sixty is the new forty, Laura. Noting that Irma still seemed dissatisfied with the placement of the skirt across the gold bag, she walked past the fragrant Madeleine and her Italian gigolo and was soon out beyond the shallows into deeper water surprisingly clear, the seabed below of rippling sand. Bliss — both the water and the sheer pleasure of looking back at the backdrop of the *vieux ville*. Bit different from Oputere Beach, she thought, where the backdrop to miles of empty white sand and Pacific surf was unrelieved pine forest. Guy (and wife) had a bach there. A bach she'd come in the last three wasted years to love dearly and to have plans for.

When she came out of the water, it was to find the Italian lovers gone and Madeleine and Irma now sitting on the rush mat together.

Something was different; something in the body language now re-engaged Laura's attention.

Madeleine, having lost her gigolo and re-anointed her legs, was looking sullen and bored. Irma, unbelievably, was still hoisting herself off her flabby arms at about one-minute intervals to fidget with the linen skirt: it wasn't straight enough across the bag, it was touching the mat, there was, *quelle horreur*, an incipient crease. She was clearly one of those people who go round straightening other people's pictures, who line up cutlery in drawers and lipsticks on dressing tables by height like soldiers. People so obsessively well-ordered that anyone living with them will find the newspaper or book they've put aside to answer the telephone has been pounced on, tidied away; or (a Guy story) a friend's grim old aunt living by herself in a bleak Scottish manse, where a visiting nephew, going for an urgent pee in a distant bathroom at four in the morning, came back ten minutes later to the freezing cold bedroom to find his bed made.

So here, possibly, was pathologically tidy Irma and there was Madeleine, fossicking in her own bag, shakily lighting up another cigarette, who kept knocking Irma's gold bag and disturbing the desired symmetry.

Through her heavy-duty sunglasses, Laura watched this for five minutes and decided it was accidental. After ten, she concluded that some secret, subtle, deadly game was going on. They were definitely sisters. Only an older sister would be looking with such venom at a younger as she leaned over yet again, to straighten up the skirt. Only a mischievous younger sister, with decades of duelling history between them, would be appearing so apparently unconcerned at the elder's increasing distress. Was Irma *la douce* many years a capable widow, but after a stroke had become the dependent and unwelcome responsibility of a younger, unpartnered sister? Laura noted that Madeleine, for all the gold, had no ring on her fourth finger. Had a dreadful old father left them sufficient money but only on condition they cared for each other into their old age? Or were they both widows, both trapped by a classical co-dependency as real as any couple grappling with one partner's addiction?

Laura was disturbingly reminded of two-year-olds at play, the one completely engaged on its task, being closely watched and occasionally provoked by the bored and aggrieved other. It would end in tears.

The shadows on the Garavan bluffs were fading, the beach population thinning out. The vapour trails had dissipated to create a film of high white cloud. The French group with the roly-poly chatterbox and the androgynous males had packed up their camping chairs and left, as had the pallid English family with the two worshipped little girls.

But Laura, though she was receiving signals from her inner being of requiring a gin and something to eat, sat on her small towel, ostensibly staring at the sea. Irma was now directing a steady stream of low-pitched French invective at the apparently oblivious Madeleine. Whatever she was saying, Irma wasn't paying Madeleine any compliments. In her ruched cornflower-blue togs, a ton of make-up and a bank's worth of gold, she could still give her little sister a rocket.

Is the unhearing Madeleine merely dreaming of the time when she is rid of this tedious responsibility? When she is liberated, like her, Ms Laura Halliday, newly dumped, newly free and unutterably alone in the south of France.

Six o'clock's bells rang out. With the strokes, Irma's tirade ceased; she straightened her damned skirt on that damned bag for the last time. Looking defeated and under the paintwork every one of her advanced years, she lay down heavily on one elbow and then, with a little cough or two, sagged slowly onto the mat. Laura noted trembling, some twitches, before stillness. Madeleine regarded her sister calmly for several minutes, and then, carelessly tossing aside the folded skirt, leaned over and took out from the gold bag a phial of perfume that Laura recognized as an extra-large bottle of Joy. Even in France, its cost would be mind-blowing. Madeleine sprayed herself with a generous fine mist. Wrists, throat, thighs, long and lavishly, a slight smile around those glistening outlined lips. She aimed one derisory spray at Irma's supine form. Then, before lying back to aim her lacquered face at the now hazy sun, she looked around. At the end of a careful survey of the beach, she caught Laura's eye for the first time.

'*Bonsoir*,' she chimed. '*Quelle belle journée*! And lovely beach, yes? May is good. In August the crowds are too much.'

'*Oui*,' said Laura, sniffing at the Joy and deciding it was time to leave. This clever and subtle old European bird spoke quite good English, but now she had no desire to get into conversation. She got up in the manner that even fit sixty-somethings have learned to do, put on her shirt and shorts over the top of still-damp togs, and folded her towel. '*Bonsoir*,' she said firmly, and then adding, because she simply couldn't resist, 'Are you sisters?'

'*Mais oui*,' said Madeleine, smiling, patting the motionless Irma's upper arm. 'Sisters. I am four years the younger.'

On the Quai Bonaparte Laura paused and looked down at the beach. Irma was still lying there, and Madeleine hadn't moved either, from her sitting position. There was something coiled, cat-like, about her. The plaited gold bag sat upright between them like a little icon, the skirt crumpled beside it. Laura climbed wearily up the narrow streets towards the apartment and let herself in. Stripping herself naked, feeling grubby, she began to unpack her bag. Ten minutes later, from the shuttered window with its panoramic view of the whole of the Baie de Garavan, she could still see Irma and Madeleine among the thinning numbers on the white gravel.

Laura turned away, sickened. She needed a shower, to clean herself of salt water and the memory of what she believed she had seen. Because there was nothing in the fridge or cupboards, she would have to eat out, take herself down to the cafés in the Rue Saint Michel. There, said the apologetic note left in the kitchen, she could buy a piece of pizza.

It was while she was putting on some make-up, wondering why she was bothering, who this subterfuge of reddened lips and widened eyes was for, exactly, that she heard the ambulance.

She could imagine what had happened, the official version: Madeleine suddenly realizing Irma had stopped breathing, calling round wildly for help. '*Au secours! Ma soeur! Ma soeur . . . ma soeur!*' Wailing, screaming, a sound rarely heard on a beach.

Someone ringing the ambulance on a cellphone. The red ambulance now threading its way, siren blazing, through the rush-hour traffic. Irma being examined by two uniformed young men, pronounced dead, being flopped and rolled onto a stretcher in her cornflower-blue togs and carted away — Laura hoped they'd covered the old girl properly, or perhaps they used a body bag with those cruelly terminal zips. Madeleine in shock, distraught; a compassionate bystander looking after her, calling her doctor, ringing any relatives. Police, probably, would arrive soon — any witnesses . . . ?

Laura shivered as the bells rang six-thirty, much louder now, from the church just above. Previous bells had tolled for thee, old lady in cornflower blue. She looked out through the shutters, despite herself using the binoculars left on a bookshelf.

Irma had gone, and two young women, probably backpackers, were helping Madeleine dress and pack up her belongings. One folded the linen skirt easily, neatly, and put it into Madeleine's bag with other clothes, the two towels. Together they very slowly crossed the beach, the young women supporting Madeleine between them and carrying everything except the gold plaited bag, which Madeleine was clutching under her armpit, close to her heart; accessory, thought Laura, for what that old biddy knows in her heart was, if not an actual murder, then at the very least an exquisitely subtle assisted death. Never underestimate the ability of one human being to get on another human being's nerves.

And Madeleine will probably say to friends in three languages, 'It was so peaceful — though a great and terrible shock to me, of course, when I realized that she was not just sleeping, as I thought, but actually dead. *É bien*, I suppose that leaving this world on a beautiful beach, in the afternoon sun, with your loving sister at your side, the peals of bells . . . that is not such a bad way to go, *n'est-ce pas?*'

And later: 'Of course, I'll stay on in the Paris apartment. It will be nice to have a little . . . solitude? My darling Irma was quite a stickler for things.'

At the top of the steps to the Quai Bonaparte a taxi was waiting. The last Laura saw of Madeleine was a racehorse-slim ankle, a gold sandal, the orange toenails. She finished dressing and went down the cobbled lanes to buy a piece of pizza marinara and found herself sitting in a café in a small square dominated by a gaudy carousel. The carousel man chain-smoked while he waited beside the Alice teacup and the unicorn and the hot-air balloon for small passengers.

She knew it would happen sometime — but it was here, when a perfectly normal granny brings forth two little girls — aged maybe three and five, similarly and beautifully dressed, undoubtedly sisters — who clamber with shining eyes into the Cinderella coach — as the accordion music begins to play and the carousel to turn — the lovely children to laugh and their grandmother to clap with delight — that the full force of Laura's despair, loneliness and fear finally catches up with her.

It is the older of the two girls who, of her own accord, when the carousel stops turning, climbs down and runs over, shy but determined, to take this perfect stranger's hand.

Laura wipes her eyes and agrees that a ride in the Alice teacup will be just the ticket.

Just a housewife

When the boys were little and I was home a lot, I used to listen out for the postie's whistle and meet him at the gate.

Rain or shine, you could just about set your clock by that whistle. They had cloth caps then, and bike clips round their trousers. Such nice men, always stopped for a chat. One was a writer, he told me, doing a mail round before going home to write his novel. Students, too, good kids, saving up to buy textbooks.

Now posties wear tight clothes and red crash helmets, and it could be any time between eleven and two, one never knows, since they don't whistle any more. A shame, really. It was a cheery sound for us stay-at-homes. But since the family down south bought me that fax machine, I hardly get any mail these days. Just bits of paper telling me that the bills for this and that are being paid, you know, automatic payments from my bank account. I get lovely regular faxes though, the boys are very good at keeping in touch.

Today, I don't know why, I am shivering in my frilly gingham pinny by the letter box, speeding the shy young postie on his way. He has handed me a plain envelope — nice paper, official looking, no stamp. And I'm asking myself why on earth I am getting a letter from the Government.

Panic is setting in: they are reducing the Super? Or raising the age? Oh, they've done it before. I know, it's a speeding ticket, that day I was running late for the hospital and forgot about the speed camera? But I was only doing just over sixty, like everyone else. Another jury summons? Yes, I'll go on a jury if summoned, though I know people say it's pretty easy these days to get out of it. Even after that earlier experience — it was a sexual-abuse case, involving children young as six. We found the horrible man guilty, but after that I cried for a month.

To the best of my knowledge, I don't owe anyone any money. I paid off the last of the mortgage when Ronnie died. I pay my taxes, such as they are, before July 7.

There's some water lying on the concrete path, so I tread warily — no-one wants a broken leg at my time of life, such a jolly nuisance for everybody — stopping a little longer than usual to calm my beating heart and say thank you to my flowers.

You camellias have been just wonderful this winter; this lovely pure white, like a ballerina's tutu, I think you're called Primavera. I stop by the pink-and-white striped blooms — you, my friend, are rather a shameless hussy — and behind you, the scarlet Blaze of Glory, and so you are, your flowers are the size of a dinner plate.

All things bright and beautiful . . . camellias have no scent, of course, just masses of blooms, many perfection itself. Dozens of them without a single blemish. I never cut camellias for inside. Look, the first new roses. I pruned you right back in July, being cruel to be kind. *Each little flower that opens* . . . next month, there'll be plenty of scarlet Fragrant Cloud and creamy Peace for the rose bowl, and that Iceberg climber all along the veranda railing will have your snowy clusters bursting with the scent of lemons. And very soon now, sweet-smelling freesias telling me and the whole garden to wake up, everyone, it's spring!

. . . *The Lord God made them all.* I've never really understood why people think that's only a children's hymn. True, it's not like so many hymns: pompous and boring, if you ask me. It may be simple but it's quite deep too, when you think about it . . . *He gave us eyes to see them, and lips that we might tell, how great is*

. . . Though as I remember, they had it at poor Flora's funeral last month, and everyone sang lustily because it was so very familiar and took them back to the innocent days. You know, when your kids played outside in vacant sections or by a creek and no-one thought twice about it. Or you left your windows open and house unlocked; perhaps even your keys in your car and it was still there when you came back.

Speaking of funerals, the family have been at me to jot down some thoughts. Well, I'd like 'All things bright and beautiful' as the first hymn, please.

And 'Crimond', which is always lovely, but *please*, nothing tedious and gloomy like 'Abide with me'. And I don't much like 'Praise My Soul the King of Heaven' either. Too hearty for funerals, though I know everyone has it these days. And especially not that reading that starts 'Death is nothing at all' and the person in the wooden box has 'just slipped away into the next room'. It's supposed to be consoling, but all it gives me is the shudders. When Ronnie left this world, nine years ago now, he was dead and he was *gone*, and not just to the next room. I envy those whose faith is stronger than mine.

Please, donations instead of flowers; they'll want to know which of my organizations I prefer. I need to think about that, not that there'll be much money anyway. One by one, we've all been dropping off the twig.

You sit down quietly now in the lounge, Ruth, with a cup of tea, that nice Mr Dilmah's Earl Grey. Take your time. This envelope in your hot hand could be, as they say these days, life-changing.

Oh, you silly goose! It's probably nothing, perhaps your MP wanting your vote or some such. A survey, a questionnaire; someone wants your opinion on something.

Well, that'll be the frosty Friday! There's no earthly reason why anyone and especially the Government should want my opinion on anything; I'm just a housewife. I remember when Selwyn Toogood said that to a woman on *It's in the Bag*, remember? In the seventies, I think it was. '*Just* a housewife?' he asked her. Such an outcry, the feminists all upset, calling him a patronizing MCP. You don't hear that expression so often these days, do you? It's not very nice to call someone a pig, whatever they've done. Well, Mussolini, perhaps, and I was never a fan of that Mr Piggy Muldoon.

It was heresy at the time, not something you said aloud, but I always thought those feminists rather wanted to have their cake and eat it too. Now they just take it all for granted, these younger women like my daughter-in-law. They know what they want, and they get it, bless them. They say, they have to work, they can't manage on one income, but I know they want to work as well. It was so much simpler, once. The sixties and even the seventies; the men were breadwinners and most of us were just housewives and mothers. 'Homemakers'. I don't mind being just a homemaker, never have — with Ronnie's blessing, of course.

Perhaps I'll leave the letter from the Government until after tea, with a port so it doesn't ruin my digestion . . . it can't be for any *good* reason . . . it's probably nothing.

Now Ruth, you are sitting in your favourite granny chair (it's a proper La-z-boy actually, dear Francis bought it for me) with your cuppa and a nice-looking Anzac biscuit from the school fair. You used to do a good line in Anzac biscuits, but with the family gone, you don't bake much now, except your trusty boiled fruitcake for cake stalls.

Today you must plant out that sad-looking cyclamen, but goodness, you're due at the school in half an hour. They wanted some help during the lunch hour, and then there's your usual Tuesday reading sessions with the littlies after that, and you need to get to Mascos before it shuts, for that blue four-ply baby wool. Long time since you've run out of wool, my girl.

For heaven's sake, Ruth — I can hear Ronnie's booming voice now — without dithering round one single moment longer, take off your pinny, do yourself a big favour and open the jolly thing.

I allow myself one last delaying tactic, getting up to take Dad's wartime paper knife — bought in Cairo, inlaid brass — from the desk. As I slit open the envelope, I notice my heart is going thud thud thud . . .

Oh Ruth, you silly donkey, stop it! It's just a letter, probably just my MP . . . some survey or other . . .

But it isn't that, or any of my foolish wild guesses. Nothing to do with super or MPs or surveys or juries or speeding tickets.

Nothing I would have guessed in a million years.

It's a letter — beautifully typed, such lovely thick paper, almost like parchment. It's from Government House — silly me — and it's informing Mrs Ruth Malfroy that her name is being recommended to the Queen for the honour of a Queen's Service Medal for services to the community.

That much is all my eyes and brain take in at first, and these are my reactions.

First, my cup of Mr Dilmah's Earl Grey goes flying. My hand has clapped itself to my mouth — to suppress a scream, perhaps, that might set the neighbours to worrying there's an intruder.

Second, it's a fraud, a sham, a forgery. God alone knows why they'd bother, but someone is playing a very cruel, silly joke on me.

Then, they've got the wrong person, the wrong address . . . it's all a dreadful mistake. There's a Mrs Ruth Malfroy somewhere else, the pillar of a small community somewhere like — well, like my birthplace of Feilding in the Manawatu. Some farmer's wife who's been on every committee going, the PTA, local council, Country Women's Institute or whatever it's called these days, Maori Women's Welfare League, local church — probably Anglican, maybe Catholic. This Ruth coaches netball or perhaps even rugby, runs Brownies or Guides, visits hospitals, organises camps, is a school trustee, helps her husband on the farm and does his accounts, has raised her own five children and takes in foster children as well. The usual heroic stuff.

That Mrs Ruth Malfroy. Not this Mrs Ruth Malfroy.

But I know it won't do. There are only two Malfroys in the country. Francis showed me on his computer, my last visit south: the 'White Pages' on the internet. Miraculous, what it can do. Any country you want, all their millions of names, just by clicking on *Search*. He thought I should get myself a laptop and enjoy the internet, and even offered to pay for it. Not a lot, Mum, he said, they're getting cheaper by the day, but honest to goodness, what would I do with it? Whenever would I look at it? I'm too busy. Apparently the internet can tell me anything, anything, but what would I want to know?

As for the joke idea, who'd be so silly? Not my family; both my sons' partners are just lovely. I've no other relatives still alive, no people I call real friends, except my old school pal Emily who for reasons unknown went to live on Stewart Island and I haven't seen in thirteen years. We're down to Christmas cards, and she's given up asking me to get on a plane and visit her. Such a long way, and expensive too, but actually, I'm too much of a sook to say: sorry, Emily, it's the *cold*, I'm no good in the cold.

And I never had any enemies — at any rate, not that I know of. All the good folk I meet on a daily and weekly basis are more acquaintances, or I suppose you might say colleagues, and the people whose lives we touch one way or another we count as friends. What we do together is too full of joy and happiness to even think of having enemies or wasting precious time and energy on silly quarrels.

So, it must be some crazy warped person, who thinks it funny to fool a silly old duffer like me in such a way. He or she forges a letter on nice paper, to make it look really official. He then chooses some old body at random, spies on them from the street, with binoculars, chuckling no doubt. He'll ring later pretending to be a reporter wanting to . . .

Oh for heaven's sake, Ruth! Feet on ground! Use your common sense. One quick toll call will fix it.

And so it does; within minutes I have rung the Wellington number at the top of the page and a pleasant voice, a man, has responded that yes, a person of that name does work at that Government address. He's at his desk. Do I wish to speak to him? 'Oh no,' I stammer, 'I just . . .' And then I'm ashamed to say, for the very first time in my life, I put the phone down.

I am not the wrong Ruth, and it's not a joke. It's a bona fide letter that trembles in my hand as I stand here stupidly by the phone wondering what to do next.

Sopping up the spilled tea with paper towels would be a good start. You really should have attended to it immediately, before it had time to soak into the carpet. Cold water and a little white vinegar should do the trick; some of that new-fangled spray carpet cleaner if it doesn't.

Then get ready to go to school; you always try to be on time. Those poor teachers' lives are governed by bells, so it's the least you can do.

But this letter . . . why? What services to the community? I've never been a Councillor this or Madam Chairwoman that.

And what am I going to write back?

I get through my day, but my mind is on other things. Enough for Whaea Nancy at school to ask if I'm OK: 'You seem a bit down, Ruth?' 'No, I'm just fine and dandy, truly.' When I stall at the traffic lights on the way to Mascos, I get toots and nasty language from the car behind. I may look like an old biddie, young man, but I am a perfectly safe driver, and stalling the car is just not like me at all. Oblivious to toots and jeers, I restart the car and whizz off.

Mascos have the blue wool I want, so I can finish that wee matinee jacket tonight for some little scrap born weeks before his time, and his poor mother caught short.

I love my cosy evenings, putting on the gas heater and the standard lamp, settling into my La-z-boy, deciding from the *Listener* whether it'll be the television or the radio, then picking up my knitting. Tonight it's all those awful reality shows, one after another on every channel, so I try the radio, but I'm not in the mood for people talking about relationships, or the Irish Rovers, or even a concert from the Auckland Town Hall.

This coolish spring night will be several hours of silence (though maybe two or three St John's phone calls) before I hold up a little garment, nicely finished with edgings and spaceship buttons sewn on. I'll add it to the pile nearly ready to be posted off and switch out the lights and turn in. But I don't imagine I'll sleep much, tonight.

For services to the community? Well, I've never been idle, and I've never frittered away my days playing bridge and golf and bingo and such like. But what's so special about that, that I get a letter from Government House and thousands of others like me don't? Did some foolish person put my name forward, is that how it's done?

I have to advise whether I wish to accept the proposed honour . . . complete the enclosed form and return by . . . treated as strictly confidential . . . information at www.honours.govt.nz.

They have investitures, don't they? Oh dear, would I have to wear a hat?

And how could Ruth Malfroy, widow, of no career or achievement at all, possibly go to Government House and hold her head high among all those smart achieving people: the mayors, the opera singers, civil servants, politicians, businessmen, actors, sportsmen and women, writers, community leaders, television people. The sort I read about twice a year when the lists come out, famous names, getting honours for services to this and that.

Well, I can only think, if it's just volunteer work you're think-ing of and you put it all down on one bit of paper, I suppose . . .

My mother started teaching me to knit when I was eleven and I've never stopped — Aran cables, lace patterns, circular knitting — you might say I was a bit of an expert. I just like having something useful to do with my hands at night. First it was dolls' clothes for me and various little cousins, then jumpers and scarves for boyfriends, then of course for Ronnie, then garments for two babies who grew into lively boys. Something for myself, very occasionally; I knit fast. And then the boys got fussy and hand-knits went out of fashion, except for babies. Plunket, my local church and the City Mission were happy to find good homes for what I knitted. I didn't mind buying the wool; always wool, though acrylics are better now, for sure. But I love the soft feel of merino four-ply, the intense satisfaction of a garment growing steadily from row to row under my fingers.

As this little one is growing — in an hour I'll have the back and one sleeve done. It's a familiar, easy pattern I could do in my sleep. I suppose I've done dozens, even hundreds like it.

What a lovely colour this is, the blue of a summer sky.

The knitting for preemies came later, when our own wee Shirley arrived six weeks too soon. An unusual blood condition, we were told. They thought she was strong enough to come home, but then she was dead and gone, poor wee mite. She'd been making progress after those transfusions, but suddenly, just twenty-four days old, not even baptized . . .

I had a bag full of newborn clothes ready, but useless, as it turned out. The preemie clothes from the hospital were not very nice: the hand-knits well-washed, faded, some matted and slightly stained. I think even if she hadn't died, I'd still have gone on making doll-sized jackets and leggings and hats for when they come out of their incubators and the mothers are still looking dazed and all the machines and monitoring are making them feel helpless. A nice little matinee jacket, a cheerful beanie, brand new, they must help a bit. I gave Shirley's away to the maternity home.

From hand-knits it was a short hop to helping mend passable kids' jumpers and then ordinary clothes like jeans and jackets for disadvantaged kids. Someone just rang and asked one day if I could help out, they were desperate for people. Mostly it was with a local group called the Cinderella Society. We sorted, washed and repaired old clothes to make them wearable for poor families. Not nice work, sometimes. I still do it, once a month. They're good people no-one ever hears about. A Cancer Society group must do similar stuff, you know, dealing with those pink plastic bags and what people put in their recycling bins. I imagine that's not a nice job, either, as volunteer work goes. Good on them.

The local Playcentre with the two boys was where I swiftly learned that you could make time for other things, as long as you were prepared for your own house to be comfortably 'lived-in', rather than very tidy and very spotless (unlike your late mother's). You know, eat-your-dinner-off-the-kitchen-floor spotless. My dear Mama would put it as 'lowering my standards'.

They were such wonderful women, some with older children and so deeply into their PTA committees, guides and scouts, school camps, netball coaching and so on. Today people talk about 'role models': well, I suppose they were mine.

It was nothing special but, with my business-college training, I was soon seen as someone who could write passable minutes and keep simple accounts. I think I did about five years with Playcentre, eight with the PTA; six or seven with the athletics club and scout troop the boys belonged to their early teen years; I forget how many with the little trust that provides the baby clothes for preemies. Maybe thirty? Having been a PA for the manager of a big construction company, before I met Ronnie, being secretary-treasurer was easy-peasy.

The Playcentre mums regularly reminded me about why we were there in the first place — for the children — and not to forget the husbands. Several times I saw the relief on Ronnie's face when I told him I'd declined to let my name go forward for Playcentre chairperson, and later, for the new school Board of Trustees. The local community board. Sorry, I told the people who rang and asked me. Sometimes they were quite persistent; but my Playcentre friends had said be careful, Ruth, don't run yourself and your family ragged. If I'm really honest, I wasn't bright enough for local-body politics and the like. I'd been a good PA, once, and I could do minutes and monthly accounts, but district plans and roading contracts and such like . . . oh, I knew my limits.

My darling Ronnie, you constantly reassured me that being careful, we could manage on the one income, and so we did. You understood my lack of ambition to be a 'middle manager' or some such; why going back to office work didn't hold much attraction compared with the pleasure I got being useful with different volunteer groups.

I tried, I really did try to keep a proper balance between you and the boys and home and everything else. You rarely complained about my comings and goings, only when things got a bit hectic, and always with some justification. The only time you got *really* grumpy was years ago when I said I'd help out an adult literacy group in danger of closing down. 'Please, Florence Nightingale,' you said, your brown eyes a bit angry and desperate, 'you're already over-committed, just give it a rest?'

They didn't close down, actually. It was a good reminder that no-one is indispensable.

There, the second sleeve done! I turn up the heater a touch; these spring evenings are still cool. But I do want to finish this blue jacket tonight. There are enough garments now to post off a package to the trust tomorrow and there's this lovely hand-dyed wool, many shades of red and the pink of watermelons, waiting to make a birthday cardie for the granddaughter down south. Hand-knits and cardies are back in fashion, hurrah!

What would you say about this QSM, Ronnie?

Oh, no use asking you, you'd only say, 'Go on girl, take a proper bow. Put yourself first for once. Don't hesitate, lass, lap it up!'

But as the night ticks away, I am hesitating, because I'm thinking, when is service not really 'service' but actually just something you love doing anyway? Doing service, aren't you supposed to grit your teeth a bit and be a little . . . well, martyrish and heroic? A wee touch of the hairshirt?

Nothing could be further than the truth.

Really now, why should I get a medal from the Queen for my

knitting which, let's face it, is just using my small talent and free time in a productive way?

Or for spending a couple of pleasurable hours daily at local primaries to help out the teachers? I coach some of the lowly netball teams and work with the six-year-olds struggling with their reading, and I just love every minute of it. Especially when I see that glow on their little faces as they realize that the black marks on the paper are starting to make sense, that reading is not always going to be such an effort, that it can actually be easy and fun. What a momentous breakthrough that is!

Or for playing the piano for various ballet schools over the years, for a long time twice weekly, but now I have more time, three hours four times a week? It's been the nearest I ever had, as a married woman, to a proper job; an ageless fixture at the out-of-tune church hall upright, endlessly thumping out in strict tempo the Royal Academy syllabus pieces for the littlies and the more demanding ballet scores — *Nutcracker* and *Swan Lake* — for the senior students preparing for advanced exams en pointe. Ballet pianists should be invisible: dependably heard, but not seen. But no matter how many repetitions, no matter how terrible the piano, or tired the students or occasionally harsh the teacher, no matter how poor the pay (cleaning ladies get more), it never feels like 'work'. I just love it — I love the chubby (or skinny) six-year-olds frowning, pointing their clumsy wee toes, watching them slowly but surely transformed over time into slim, graceful swans.

Likewise, all those wonderful school productions, called in when a primary school didn't have a musically capable teacher. *Joseph and the Amazing Technicolour Dreamcoat* how many times over the years — five, six? *The Wizard of Oz* three times, that local show *Cats of Ponsonby* twice. Six months' rehearsing: lunch hours, after school, at weekends. Rewarded again by watching the children blossom, from hesitant little scraps into real troopers. Usually, among the thank yous at the end of the last show, I'm presented with a bunch of flowers and sometimes, a stack of handwritten letters. But that's not service, it's pure pleasure. I wonder the children can't tell that, me sitting there at the piano and the only one in the hall smiling when the musical director demands yet another run-through of 'If I only had a heart' or 'We're off to see the Wizard'.

And in a different way, my hospital work other than knitting for preemies has been another simple pleasure. After Shirley, I took an advanced first-aid course (so that never again would I have a child in my arms and not know what to do) and that led to becoming a Womble for St John's. We were rostered on in our black uniforms at weekends for people fainting (and sometimes worse) at rugby games and rock concerts. How many years did that go on, Ronnie? Fifteen, twenty? I lose count.

And that led to what I've been doing now for some years as a Fed. No-one's heard of them much either — Friends of the Emergency Department at the local hospital. We volunteers are brought in to help the patients and generally free up the medicos and nurses to do whatever they must.

Yes, Ronnie, it's often tough. I'm not and never will be immune to blood, suffering and fear; but I'm always glad to be there, to do some basic, time-saving job or hold a desperate hand.

As I held your frail hand eight years ago when you slipped into sleep and beyond, the malignant thing on your back having done its terrible work in only two short months. You were a year off getting your Super, and we'd just started making plans for our big tour of the South Island and then, our first-ever trip to Europe.

So even though I know you are probably yelling at me, 'Ruth, for God's sake say YES, write your letter tomorrow,' and even though I would be the first person to say it was your honour too, I still have a real dilemma: how can I in all conscience accept a medal for only doing what I love doing?

And what thousands of others are also doing in the same or similar organizations and in identical ways? Besides, what else would I have done all day long, as the boys grew up and became more independent?

And it's not only the work itself, or the time or money it takes. Just think of the fantastic people I've been lucky enough to meet.

The Playcentre mums for a start — one went on to become a cabinet minister, another a mayor, another a famous writer (now they all quite rightly got gongs!). Others became proper seventies and eighties feminist women, being still young enough as their children grew up to return to their original jobs like dental nursing or radiography or PA work. Some retrained at university or polytech for new careers. One got a PhD in her forties and a big job in the Ministry of Education; I often see her quoted in the papers. Several became very committed teachers, or managers, or local-body councillors and trustees of this and that. And some of us stayed at home, fitting good works in around our families.

Then the fabulous ballet teachers! One had trained at the Royal Ballet School in London, and quite looked the part: slim, dark and erect like Margot Fonteyn, strong on discipline, a perfectionist. Pupils and parents were more than a little scared of her, but her stern methods got great results. I considered it a great privilege to play for such a true professional all those years. My present teacher is less qualified and her exam results aren't so good, but she's more fun, much better bringing on wayward or sullen kids. I give her a bit of help with her accounts and GST occasionally. She doesn't have much business sense, but she's only young, and learning.

Then, the ordinary classroom teachers, dozens of them, wonderful people doing their very best for their kids, whether teaching them to read or play sports or sing and dance in a production. I see what they do all day, what planning and skills and patience are required, and it's humbling, believe me. They don't deserve all the ignorant and horrid criticism they get, for sure, in the media and other places like on talkback.

Neither do the hospitals. If people could see what I see in the A and E department, the efforts made to help injured, sick people, even when they're drunk or stoned or grouchy or critical or just plain ungrateful, they'd quickly change their tune.

But great as all these folk are, the people I just love meeting most of all are not the professionals but . . . well, I'll always call them the patients, rather than 'clients'.

Apart from all the gorgeous eager-to-please children, there are the adults. The hurt ones from teens to old bodies who, after the medicos have finished, I'm asked to see settled into their wards or sometimes, the hospice. My job is to provide a helping hand, ears to listen, a shoulder to cry on — the things the nurses don't have time for — until their families and friends arrive. Sometimes they don't arrive, so I just continue doing whatever until the patient leaves hospital. Or doesn't. Sometimes it's really hard, being available, watching people suffer, knowing there's not much else you can do. You'd be made of stone if the sadness of it all didn't get you down occasionally.

Then, the oldies who ring me as a St John's Caring Caller, mostly during the day but occasionally at night or in the early hours. Lonely old people, mostly, with no family around or friends left, who just want a bit of human contact, someone to talk to. I know I would go mad if the days and weeks and years crawled past, just me and myself alone.

Mostly I have contact with these 'clients' for a few months, until I get a call from St John's to say they've died or they're through their bad patch or gone into care, and they stop ringing. Quite often, we've become good pals on the telephone, and occasionally in real life. One such was a retired English concert pianist abandoned in a granny flat, with her family gone on a year's sabbatical and the house rented out to complete strangers, would you believe? Peggy played me her recording of Schumann's 'Carnaval' made in the late sixties and the two of us sat there a bit weepy listening to her marvellous, once-shining talent. She died suddenly that night, in her sleep, and I like to think she was happy. Well, with her family away, happier than she might have been. I treasure that old twelve-inch record. It was found on her kitchen table with a note saying it was for me.

Yes, Ronnie, I know the good telephone pals are all very well, and I would be lying if I said that sometimes, when the phone goes and it's one or two particular persons, my heart doesn't sink a bit. With the most talkative of them, or the deafest who need things repeated, or the ones who just can't find the right words, I know it's going to be half an hour at least. So, I fetch my knitting and count off a few more rows while I'm listening. Multi-tasking, they call it nowadays.

Tell me honestly now Ronnie, is a blessedly fit and modestly well-off widow in her late sixties, just sitting knitting and listening for hours to some deaf or senile old biddy on the phone, really the sort of person they give national honours to? Even one of the more modest gongs, not a damehood or anything like that?

Yes, you say promptly. Because, Ruth, without compromising your duty towards your family (and I know that better than anyone), you've given a lifetime of voluntary service without pay or recognition, to help children and adults in times of hardship and need.

Oh come on now, Ronnie, you're getting pompous and you make me sound like some sort of . . . well, sainted aunt. I've only done what thousands of others do.

Yes, and if they all downed tools tomorrow, this country, more than most in the Western world, would grind to a halt within one or two days . . . the volunteer ethic is necessarily alive and well in Godzone. Without fanfares, volunteers contribute untold millions to the national economy and to society's well-being. Without them, our schools, hospitals and social services, sports and the arts would barely function. (Goodness — my Ronnie could be an eloquent man when he chose, more than most master builders I met who ran their own small business. He didn't read the *Guardian Weekly* for nothing, my Ronnie.)

So, dear Ruth, when your name appears in the QSM list on New Year's Eve, all the other volunteers who read about you will feel their work is officially recognised too.

That's what they all say on the telly, Ronnie, the famous ones: oooh, they say, it's such a surprise and it's not really for me personally, but I accepted it for everyone I work with. Words to that effect, it's quite sweet.

I suppose someone might come around from the local paper . . . they sometimes have pictures . . . and there's the question of the hat . . . whoa now, just you hold your horses, Ruth Malfroy! And Ronnie, you go back to sleep now, you're making me embarrassed and flustered. I haven't decided anything yet.

Goodnight my dearest Ruth, QSM, you sleep tight.

The lounge has grown colder around me, and I find I have, without thinking, stitched together the little jacket, done the edgings and sewn on the first of the three spaceship buttons. Another five minutes and I can go to bed, to wrestle with my dilemma through the night. Ronnie always did say that if you just 'live with them' for a while, big decisions often make themselves. Sleep on it.

This isn't — oh yes it is — it's a big decision for me. It means telling my boys, a trip to Wellington (are families included? Will Francis and Sally come; will Gordon come back from London, with or without his partner?) Going to Government House, what on earth to wear? A hat. Some congratulatory phone calls, letters, possibly some from my young reading friends who've kept in touch or the road accident or stroke victims who might remember me sitting with them through long dark nights.

And yes, for a week or so, some slightly increased mana at my schools, at the ballet studio, at the A and E and the wards where they know me, among the Cinderella Society folk, my local shops, the lovely public library. Enough to be totally embarrassing, because I can't help thinking of all the other people who are without a doubt every bit as worthy.

I take refuge in bedtime rituals: checking the doors, the gas, turning out lights, my bath, the nightly scripture reading, setting the alarm, prayers. Even after nine years, and clutching a hottie, my bed still feels cold, empty, unutterably lonely.

Surprisingly, I do sleep quite well — until about six, when I wake up suddenly, but knowing with absolute certainty that at some time in the wee small hours I've made a decision.

I think — and it's only the opinion of a foolish old woman, mind — that people say publicly they've accepted an award as much for all their colleagues and supporters as themselves because in our culture we're not allowed to say, well yes, I am jolly good at whatever I do, I know my contribution has been huge, and I think the Government chose jolly well and not before time!

But, needing to be humble, we escape into spreading the credit around, we suddenly become the world's best team player.

It's the team being honoured, silly, not little old me. I'm just the one actually getting the gong, but it's really only on behalf of all those other wonderful people without whom . . .

But when I've looked at the QSM lists in the past, and I read about all these people giving decades of voluntary service to this and that, do I take any credit from *their* successes? Did I even once in more than forty years look longingly at the Queen's Birthday and New Year honours lists and think oooh, if I keep at it long and hard enough, one day my name might be up there in lights too? Frosty Friday!

So will my award make a single scrap of difference to all the volunteers out there who toil away at whatever they do? Of course it won't.

The volunteers I know don't do what they do for any hope of totting up enough points for future recognition from the government or anyone else. They wouldn't last two minutes if that was why they were involved. You need a stronger motivation than some distant gong to sit up half the night in a hospital with a teenager far from home and struggling for life, or endure umpteen committee meetings, or pound out 'If I only had a heart' for the hundredth time.

The good folk (yes, mostly women) I meet do what they do for a mixture of very good reasons: they simply enjoy it, they feel useful, they learn new things, they get out of the house, they meet people, they fill up time, they know there are more important things to do than earning money. And for some, it's also a genuine way of putting their beliefs into practice: they really do try, for the Lord's sake, to be kind and considerate to their fellow citizens on this earth in the sure and certain hope of a better life and meeting their beloved ones in the world to come. God loveth a cheerful giver, says Corinthians. And yes, in my experience anyway, it really is more blessed to give than to receive.

And though you always hear people scoffing at rich businessmen and yes-men politicians and bureaucrats and the like getting
in sweet with the Government and reaping their rewards —
knighthoods in the old days — I still warrant that few if any of
the real stayers down in the lowly ranks of community volunteers
ever think about an eventual QSM for their pains. Women just
don't think like that.

I stay in bed a little longer than usual, feeling the nip in the air,
hugging my decision to myself. The right decision, Ronnie. I'll
write the letter today.

And yes, if I'm honest, it was very nice to be asked. But all
that attention, having to be gracious, even if only for a week or
so. 'Thank you so much,' and 'Well, I don't really do any more
than lots of other people', over and over and over again, quickly
getting sick of the sound of my own insincerity. I get my thanks
and my rewards in other quieter and better ways.

I wonder, though, who put me up for it. One kindly person,
or a group? Now listen here, Ruth, you will not wonder about
this any more, ever again; it's of no consequence.

Ronnie's disappointed on the surface, and a mite impatient,
but underneath, he understands. The family will never know, and
what they don't know won't harm them. But I might just leave
the letter with my will. When they find it, for a moment or two,
they can be a little bit proud of their funny old mum.

I am, though, in a bit of a tremble. It's a long time since I've
been faced with such a dilemma, making me really stop and think
what I'm doing with the life God gave me, and why. Surprisingly
hard work. I feel quite drained.

It seems like a good morning to get 'Carnaval' out of its sleeve
and put it on the old-fashioned turntable I never quite got round
to getting rid of. They say vinyl is coming back! Amazing. If you

keep anything long enough, it'll come back into fashion, like ponchos and flared trousers. Gordon, who's 'in IT' in London, tells me on every visit that my house is 'irredeemably retro'. Well, Gordon, my clever modern son, I'm a sentimental old thing, I love my bits and bobs, and I can live with that.

While I'm listening to Schumann, I shall have my toasted muesli and then start on that jumper for the granddaughter. And meditate a little and thank the Good Lord for my life being enriched by such music and by wonderful people like Peggy, smiling at me in close-up from the front of the record cover. What a handsome young woman she was forty years ago; at eighty-seven she was truly beautiful.

We've only got as far as the fourth piece, the 'Valse Noble', when the phone rings. At this hour of the morning it's bound to be for Ruth the Caring Caller.

Well, I'm sorry, Harry or Violet or Jenny or Frank or the ten or so others I chat with regularly.

For an hour or two this particular spring morning, the answer-phone will cut in because Ruth's halo has slipped a touch and she is not available. Her cellphone is switched off too, so that's no use either.

Just for once in a blue moon, she's having a little time to herself.

Mother Earth

~ ONE ~

Beside a lake, facing the sunsets.

In land agents' parlance, this premium lakeside section has location-plus and limitless potential. In reality it is a flat square of earth beside a large and inhospitable lake, lashed by constant westerly winds. The square has been crudely defined with wire fencing, the meagre topsoil ripped out by machines along with the ancient blackberries and several sizeable trees that could have been saved had the developer, 200 miles away in Auckland, thought to give instructions to leave any trees hardy enough to survive the westerlies. Firewood and anything resembling topsoil has been bagged up and profitably sold. A few tall weeds with broad ugly leaves, clumps of gorse and thistles have since managed to take root here and there. Mostly, though, the surface is bare white pumice, with shallow pitted craters and outbreaks of rock.

'It's a lot of money for a pad of broken pumice and a pipe dream,' murmurs Jim doubtfully. It's also beyond him, the capacity for such dreaming. He is reminded, unhappily, of war damage he saw up close in Crete; what are they doing, even contemplating at their age committing a small inheritance and a sizeable mortgage to a windswept patch of dirt tantamount to a bomb site?

They have asked the land agent, already sensing the waste of his time, for ten minutes' private chat. He is sitting in his solid Austin Cambridge, a handsome man in his early thirties staring straight ahead, alert for any signal. It's the trim little wife, pleasant enough in a headscarf, short-sleeved white blouse and neat brown slacks, who's the keen one. She's the dangerous dreamer, she holds the balance of power.

'And this wind,' Jim adds, 'straight in from the west. Drive you barmy.'

'So you build the house to the north,' says Ellie. 'A north-facing courtyard. Or you have glass screens.'

'Earthquakes!'

His wife snorts. This is a volcanic plateau: a quake or two every few hundred years and more likely, steam appearing occasionally from small crevices in the ground, are to be expected; people living in certain Californian towns, or Wellington, or Napier also accept that the ground beneath their feet is unreliable and gives itself a good shake occasionally. Danger, with very little conscious effort, can become commonplace. There hasn't been a serious quake in this area within living memory, nothing to worry property values. The thousand-year quake could be centuries off.

'Hot sand that burns your feet,' he adds, looking towards the previously inaccessible area of shoreline being slowly opened up by the new subdivision.

'He said the hot pools don't come this far round the foreshore, remember?'

'Need a grader. And that's before a ruddy mountain of topsoil.'

'I'll grant you that.' She looks thoughtful, bends down and pursing her sensible mouth delicately as a child, blows away the dandelion clock. 'We'll need a bit of topsoil, true.'

'A lot of topsoil.'

'It shouldn't be allowed, what they've done here.'

'The cost of the house. Driveways. Plumbing. Electricity. Rates. Insurance. The cost of trees. We'd need hundreds of plants to make anything of this.'

'I take cuttings, Jim, or hadn't you noticed? I can learn to grow trees from seed. The children will give us shrubs for birthdays and Christmas. We can say to friends who come, forget the boxes of Cadbury chocolates and the bunches of flowers, just a little shrub from the garden centre would be nice. It will always remind us of you, we'll say. Something in a pot. A hebe, a pittosporum, a little native flax.'

'You say the garden at home is starting to get you down. This bombsite . . . are you . . . ?' He flaps a tired hand at the square of scorched earth, then fumbles in his pockets for the comfort of pipe and tobacco. The enormity of the challenge she's contemplating leaves him quite speechless.

Indeed, the thought of their regular two-bedroom rented holiday cottage up the back of the lakeside town, too far to walk to shops or water, is growing more attractive to Jim by the minute. There they can have their cake and eat it, so to speak.

So there's no view at all, and the cottage is built of rough creosoted brown planks, the bumpy grass around it is coarse paspalum, the only trees are leggy pink oleanders and in a far corner stands an ancient, half-toppled macrocarpa. So the kitchen is poky, the crockery is plastic, the beds have tired old spring mattresses and the bathroom is sub-standard. It's true, they had to pitch their khaki army-surplus tent on the grass outside for the growing family and their young friends, and in a hot summer following a dry spring the tanks have been known to run out of water. As a simple holiday house six minutes' drive from a lake, a reasonable rent each summer and long weekends, with no ongoing rates, insurance or maintenance to worry about between times, the arrangement has so far worked well enough for both parties.

In recent years, though, on their visits into the town, Ellie and Jim have lingered by real-estate agents' windows, and looked at the houses being offered and the prices being asked. The last couple of years, they talked to an agent, but didn't follow up his suggestion of viewing one or two properties on the spot. Back safely at home, settling into the new school year, Jim preoccupied at work with perennial staffing problems, and the garden needing attention, it had seemed a romantic, daft idea — and grown cold.

'The agent says the water you pump up is grade A,' she is saying. 'The purest lake water in the world. Something to do with the pumice acting as a filter. You like a glass of nice chilled water, Jim. No chlorine. Or fluoride. You're always saying the city water is poisoned. We might have to take fluoride tablets.'

She glances at him sideways, anxious she might be pushing him too hard. But she knows her Jim, who has now got his pipe working satisfactorily and set off to do a tour of inspection around the wired perimeter. She follows, knowing that the land agent will interpret this as wifely meekness.

'We'd have to retire here,' he says, stumbling over a rock. 'To capitalise on it properly and leave something decent for the kids. Have you thought of that?'

'Yes.'

'Long way from a decent hospital. Specialists and the like.'

'We're fit. There's a small hospital here.'

'Not so many concerts. We'll be down here, battling the westerlies, freezing in winter — this is a thousand feet up, Ellie, do you *know* how cold it gets? Bitter, they say. Month after month, right through until November. Short summer, endless winter. And we'll be poor.'

'We've got our LPs. There's the radio, good old 1YC. And we'll be rich for ever with that view. Look at it!'

The view is indeed spectacular, an unimpeded sweep of azure lake straight across fifteen or more miles to the deep cliff-lined rim of the western bays; south, forty miles to three active volcanoes, the highest streaked with its everlasting snow, the steepest puffing gently. It's an austere seascape, with few softening trees, none of the graceful gardens or public parks, villas, walls or staircases that enhance the built-up shores of lakes elsewhere; the little lakeside township is in the northernmost bay, hidden behind a low headland. Five, perhaps eight hundred years of human settlement haven't left much mark at all. And the wind is indeed blowing in twenty knots from the west, kicking up a short chop and creating an insistent, rhythmic drum roll of breaking waves on the shingle and pumice shoreline.

'That noise might get me down,' he says. 'Tiring, day and night.'

'Ear plugs,' she says. 'Or Mahler.'

'I can't listen to Mahler all night. Or the rest of your old boys.'

'Hoagy Carmichael, then,' she says patiently.

'You don't like Hoagy Carmichael.'

'So you have Hoagy Carmichael and I'll sleep in the spare bedroom.'

'So the price of this escapade will be separate bedrooms?'

'Oh Jim,' she sighs. 'Don't twist things.'

She's not sure if he's teasing her.

The land agent is guessing correctly that the wife is doing his job for him, but he has grown bored listening to the ads on Radio Lakeland and in twenty minutes has another, far more promising appointment for this same over-priced patch of dirt. He runs a tortoiseshell comb through his oiled hair, slams the car door and watches where he places his shiny brown English shoes on the white pumice surface.

'Never be built out. You'd pay zillions for that overseas.

Megabucks!' he says, cheerfully stating the obvious, but deciding, correctly, that this particular female client would be unmoved by any turned-on male charm. 'As an investment, ma'am, cast-iron. Couldn't go wrong. In twenty years this burg will be humming.'

The husband says they will let him know — and gets the usual warnings about other buyers ready to pounce; indeed one already is talking to his bank manager, as we speak. They should seriously, urgently, consider making an offer, tonight, however silly, for this rarest of opportunities. He talks only to the husband; holding hands now, this unlikely couple listens in apparent calm, even indifference, staring out over the lake, nodding thoughtfully. Fifty–fifty they will move on it, the agent predicts. But it won't be swiftly, and sadly they might be too late. He's been in this game long enough to prefer selling a premium property to ordinary people who will love and nurture it, rather than a greasy city developer who'll swear honest to God he wants it for his wife but who will, quick as a flash, throw up a monstrosity he never had any intention of living in, and flick it on for a fast buck.

'Just out,' says Ellie, wiping down the sink in the rented cottage's modest kitchen and quite enjoying the daughterly feathers she is ruffling.

'Excuse me, Mum.' Ellie steps aside and Anna clatters the nest of cheap aluminium saucepans into the cupboard. She is feeling frazzled at the end of Andrew's day on the beach, and longing for a smoke and a moment to herself. She and Roger might drive down to the lake for a twilight walk. She straightens up and says, 'But you never go just out.'

'Well tonight, Anna, just this once, you can tell Andrew his grandma is not available. You can read him his bedtime story. Or Roger can, a nice change from his everlasting cricket. Your father and I are going out.'

'Are you going to the pictures? Friends, perhaps?' This is a new, secretive mother, not the one who back at home gardens most of the day, every day, and goes out only to shop for food and occasional concerts. They entertain, or go to restaurants, once in a blue moon. Her mother does not go 'out', especially when she's at the lake with the family.

'Don't wait up,' Ellie is saying.

Anna stares after the departing grey Oxford, resigning herself to viewing the brief twilight from a deck chair and, after Andrew has settled down and the damn cricket from Eden Park turned off, the dubious pleasure of a two-handed game of Scrabble with Roger.

Or perhaps, with Andrew finally asleep, the house to themselves for once and no interruptions for possibly an hour or more, she has a better idea.

Jim pulls up beside the section, facing the lake and a ball of crimson fire about to disappear behind the hills of the western bays. They're just in time to see it touch, become halved and subside beneath the low black rim of land. The wind has dropped completely. Between the fiery afterglow and the incandescent blue directly above lie bands of apricot and a delicate lime cradling the first star. Across the lake's now calm surface of glistening molten bronze, five or six small boats drift peacefully past, parallel with the shore, ever hopeful for the tug of a trout. To the south, the trio of mountain peaks rises black along the skyline, the central one with its faint vertical wisp of steam.

'Look at that,' she says, simply grateful to be alive. She always thinks of Sibelius when she sees vistas like this that move her to tears; somehow he caught that spaciousness, the vast sense of timeless mystery better than anyone. 'Ngaruahoe, no wind on it at all. Not a cloud anywhere.'

'You're a cunning old body,' Jim says, glancing at his wife's burnished profile. He's always liked her nose, classic and sensible; he's reminded of the Queen's head on a bright new penny. His wife is neither fat nor thin, plain nor pretty, smart nor dowdy. She talks only when she's got something to say. She is comforting, discreet and reliable and he could not bear life without her. He has learned not to underestimate her stamina, her capacity for maintaining an unpopular stance come what may. And she is usually right, when the dust has settled. She has never once raised her voice to him; she would allow no major disagreements in front of the children. But he wishes daily that she played her Broadwood grand more, and he'll have to humour her out of this one.

'Don't think I don't know what you're up to,' he says.

'Well, since you know so much, you'll know why I want you to leave me here for half an hour.'

'To do what?'

'Just sit.'

'What for? There's nothing to sit on except rocks.' Since that doesn't appear to warrant an answer, and she is already nearly out the car door, he goes on. 'What am I supposed to do for half an hour?'

'Go back and read Andrew his story.'

'It's eight miles of petrol there and back.'

'Find a hotel bar that's open, then. Bound to be one, this neck of the woods. Just one pint, mind.'

How did we get to this, he wonders, helpless in the face of her will. This morning she chats to the land agent from previous years and hears about this hush-hush premium section in a new subdivision about to go on the market and now, apparently swallowing the implausibility of the story, she wants half an hour to sit in the dark on a bomb site and contemplate shackling the rest of their lives to it. The next thing will be a call to the land agent making an offer. But the thought of a pint of Dutch courage at that pub near the Napier turn-off appeals.

For she's a clever enough old body to know he is equally — or nearly equally — as keen about this section as she is. It's just possible — if they go slowly. Cut their cloth etcetera, and buy a beat-up caravan and a second wheelbarrow, and he works through at the Department until it's time for the gold watch or whatever they give out these days. Yes, it's possible. Someone, though, has to keep their feet on the ground.

'I'll come back at nine-thirty,' he calls out the car window. 'Did you realize there were no birds when we came before? No birds at all.'

'Yes, I realized.'

'Not even a squitty little sparrow.'

'They'll come back, the tuis and fantails as well as sparrows, when the trees do,' she sings, already a shadow.

Ellie is used to southern twilights, the light sucked swiftly down by the departing sun, the appearance of the single evening star, and more following until the sky is ablaze with diamonds. Sitting under the vault of stars without too many streetlights has always been one of her quiet holiday pleasures, hours stolen on the front steps before dawn while Jim and the rest of the family slept. Her early training has given her the capacity and pleasure, if she so chooses, to play through a whole sonata movement in her head, her fingers on her lap twitching but slightly, hearing nothing else. It is no substitute for the real thing, of course, but some comfort besides keeping her brain ticking over. When there are no pressing problems, she can take herself through a complete sonata, or a movement of one of the favourite concerti she studied but never played to an audience, the lovely Schumann,

Beethoven three, the Saint-Saëns, Ravel, several Mozart, the Franck Symphonic Variations, or better still, because the soloist rarely has time to draw breath, one of the two Chopin. Tonight, however, she can listen only to the sound of the water, and any messages the lake has for her.

In an ideal world, she and Jim would be sitting here together, making this decision together. But (although this is not strictly true: waiting and doing nothing still constitute some sort of response) Ellie believes that essentially she has made too few of the decisions that so far have shaped her life. A war crushed her musical hopes, irreparably altered her man and thus changed the course of their ordinary, personal histories; commitment and security, she has come to believe, are best expressed not by buildings but by working the earth, creating gardens and most of all, planting trees. She's read somewhere that there is a species of pine that has lived on this earth for more than 4000 years.

Her trees will last for centuries too.

This decision, because she knows that Jim will trust her without question, and will agree with only token debate, will be hers alone.

As she knew he would, Jim has two pints rather than one, and over an hour has gone. When he finally arrives, she makes no comment about the time, but quietly insists on driving home. Her easy tolerance warms Jim's heart, but also disquiets and warns him: something's up.

She has achieved what she wanted: a quiet hour in the dark, watching the lake's molten waters turn black as coal, lights come on in the few houses across the bay, the emergence of a sliver of moon and the glittering canopy of stars across a cloudless velvety sky. Now only an occasional car or truck can be heard from the highway nearby, a dog's bark from the Maori fishing village further down the shoreline. The only insistent sound is that clean, sweet water flopping gently onto the shallows of grey shingle, softly percussive like a drummer's wire brush.

She knows some history from a faded tourist poster in the kitchen of their rented bach: here was once the world's most violent explosion whose dust-laden clouds could be seen in China before they fell to earth, covering the central plateau with a thick crust of pumice. Later, but well before the days of government taxes and introduced trout, Maori tribes put up palisades around their lakeside whare, grew kumara and caught eels.

Behind her, in this Year of Our Lord 1962, lies a scarred wound of mother earth that she and Jim will heal and transform. Not since she yearned for that London scholarship has she wanted anything for herself so badly. Winning the scholarship, the only one awarded in the country annually, she had then been cruelly denied taking it up. While battles raged, while Jim was away in northern Africa and Crete, she hadn't played her piano for five years; it held no comfort for her soul, only a bitter, dull pain. Coming silently to terms with her lost dreams of long northern twilights and immersing herself for a good few years in all the music London had to offer, she took her girls to their music lessons, encouraged their practice, while it lasted, of violin, trumpet, flute, waited for grade exam results and went to their school orchestra concerts, but knew herself secretly relieved neither showed enough talent for a career in music. Anna had reached a respectable Grade 8 violin; she had been second desk in the secondary schools' orchestra. They had played duets together, Beethoven and 'lollipops', for a time.

Now, twenty-two years of genial, devoted wifehood later, her job with the children largely done, grandmother of one, the mortgage of the city house paid off and a neat suburban garden which is starting to get her down, she would commit herself to this bare scab of pumice. To the comfortable little house that would stage by stage be built, the roses that she would plant, the grass that would be persuaded to grow thick and green — oh, the wonderful abundance of water just under the earth's crust! — to the mature, grand trees and the windbreak sheltering her grandchildren from the westerlies. To the songbirds that would return.

She regularly does the family accounts, and in a quiet moment after lunch she had put down enough sums on a piece of paper to know: on Jim's salary until he's sixty, on their various expected pensions, and Jude away south to university next year, with hard backbreaking work, doing most of it themselves: it is possible.

She will plant every tree to its own music, water it from the endless supply beneath the pumice, and the seasonal energy of each one will sing to her of God's glorious spirit.

She would die here, and her ashes would be buried under a tree of her choosing, here.

'They had a television set,' Jim slurs in the darkness of the car. 'Some cricket was on. I think it was Northern Districts versus ... somebody.'

'Good-oh.' She can smell the beer on his breath, and cigarettes on his clothes. 'Canterbury, actually.'

'How do you know that?'

'Roger's damn radio.'

He grunts. 'Actually the rabbit's ears didn't do much good, people kept twiddling with them. Drive you berko. Mostly it was snow and flickers and stripes.' A small belch escapes. 'Pardon, dearie me. The radio is better any day. Did you get bored?'

'No.'

'Scared in the dark? I told you there was nowhere to sit.'

'I sat by the lake. And no, I wasn't scared. Far from it.'

'Got yourself a numb bum, woman, I bet. Sitting by that lake in the dark — crazy. Anyone think you're a mad lady.'

'Maybe.' She quite liked the idea. She suspects people find her boring.

'Might've been a Maori burial ground once. They might've cooked up a missionary or two there.'

She smiles in the dark. 'I didn't get any ghostly visitors or smell something like pork cooking.'

'But you knew I'd come back — I hadn't had an accident or anything stupid?'

'Yes. Of course.' Finding second gear with some difficulty, she turns the Morris Oxford off the main highway up a long wide street that leads away from the lake to the less expensive part of town, and smiles at the very attractive passing thought of driving into the courtyard of a lakeside house. She, Ellie Johns, who can remember going hungry in the Depression, teaching piano day and night to help her parents make ends meet, a war bride counting every penny . . . now, she and Jim, being careful, cutting their cloth, able to even consider buying a lakefront site, the front row of the dress circle.

'You knew I'd come back?'

He sounds anxious, even meek. It is one of those quite frequent moments when she wonders about the things that went on in Crete and Libya, for young soldiers barely out of high school. Did he get left behind by some mates, or perhaps worse, found himself forced to betray some others expecting to be rescued? When he finally came home in 1945, he was not the same man she'd married. Some of the stuffing had been knocked out, he was easily irritated, often morose and disliked his routines being altered; the stress of high-school teaching, about all he could contemplate with his arts degree, simply wasn't an option.

'Of course I knew you'd come back. Don't be silly,' she says fondly. She takes her hand off the steering wheel and briefly squeezes his large paw.

He doesn't mention the section on the way home. Ellie is not sure whether the twin novelties of two pints and a television set have caused him to genuinely forget, or whether he's just waiting, as he often does, for her to make a move. She knows it is too late to find a callbox to ring the land agent, and that she's in for a sleepless night of exquisite uncertainty and probably, before her restlessness starts to disturb Jim, some hours' stargazing. A rich Auckland property developer or Hawke's Bay farmer has surely moved in with an offer. Overnight, sure as eggs were eggs, the chance will slip out of their grasp.

But if, as the good-looking land agent's jolly cliché goes, if this purchase is meant to happen, it will. She tells herself sternly, it *will*. They should have faith, and courage.

She is quite glad that they unlock the front door to find Anna and Roger have not waited up. Peeping round the door, she smiles to see them entwined like children in the lower of the narrow bunks, naked under the rumpled sheets. In his travel cot parked on a wicker chest in the corner of the room, the baby is sleeping peacefully after his last bottle. There will be no further inquisition tonight.

Not quite. At four, untangling her naked limbs from Roger's and the wooden frames of the narrow bunk, Anna is required to give her teething son a bottle and discovers the front door ajar and her mother sitting in the moonlight, on the steps down to the coarse grass. If Anna had but known, she was soothing herself with a Schubert sonata, a favourite.

'Couldn't sleep?' Anna enquires softly, for she knows of her mother's insomnia. Ellie moves over to make room on the step for her daughter and the restless child. Even though it's a heated bottle rather than breast, the child smells richly of milk and baby.

'I know, he needs changing,' says Anna. 'And I'll do it,' she adds quickly. 'Pooey naps at four in the morning are not for grannies, however doting.'

'I don't mind.'

'I do.' She looks up at the blaze of stars, the crescent moon and the black-on-black silhouette of the old macrocarpa in the corner of the section. You could squint and make that into a monster, if you tried, one about to pounce. A distant cat yeowls, maybe that's a hedgehog snuffle, a distant baby's hungry wail — otherwise it's an almost complete silence. A city is never as silent as this. 'Gosh, it's almost worth getting up for, baby or no baby.'

'Yes.'

'I hope Jude's enjoying herself on that awful black beach. All the crowds and boys and their beer and surfboards. Their awful hot rods, and Elvis full blast. Personally, I can't think of anything worse.'

'It was natural she'd want to go off with her friends. That's what sixteen-year-olds do.'

'I didn't. I wasn't such a tart. Did you see her shoes? Dad should have a talk to her.'

Ellie sighs at her daughter's motherly scorn, her early slide — she was only twenty-one, for heaven's sake — into responsible parental thinking. Sometimes she could be taken for a starchy thirty-year-old. 'A little unkind. She's a good kid.'

'She's becoming a real tart. I *know*,' she added darkly. 'And she liked it here as much as anyone, once. Remember how we used to bury her in that gravelly sand, up to her neck, with shovels. Great big ice-creams, triple headers, at that American soda parlour place? And going to the hot pools to get boiled, get absolutely cooked. I think she even quite liked doing that annual walk up Tauhara, really. She just made a fuss out of habit, to keep Dad on his toes.'

A little grieving for childhood here, perhaps, thinks Ellie wistfully. Don't we all? She lets a little silence develop before she asks, 'When you were younger . . . did it make any difference that we rented, not owned something?'

'I love this little place,' protests Anna, surprised. 'It made no difference, Mum. After a few days, filling it with our stuff, it always felt like ours. You let us bring our friends. And you never put a piece of sandpaper into our hands the minute we arrived.'

She hears her mother chuckle softly.

'Anyway, you always said you couldn't afford to buy a bach. Not on Dad's salary, anyway. If you'd done a bit of teaching . . . then . . .?'

The supposition lingers, unanswered. Anna has never quite asked outright why her piano-playing mother has never used her one saleable skill and taken pupils. It would have been so simple: easy work from home, her own hours, choice of two pupils or ten or twenty — Christ, she could have done it under the counter, Roger had once said, exasperated by his in-laws' measured approach to life, the orderliness but complete lack of spontaneity. Since their impeccably organized wedding two-and-a-half years ago, Anna had withstood his occasional accusations of growing as unadventurous and bourgeois as her parents. She knew she sometimes used Andrew as an excuse, when she was tired, which was often.

'Are you thinking you might retire here?' Anna asks astutely. 'Lots do. The place is full of senior cits.'

'That's years away,' murmurs her mother, thinking she must watch her step with this daughter. 'I suppose it's possible.'

'You'd miss your concerts, though. Oops!' Although Andrew was snuffling back to sleep, the odour has suddenly got worse, indicating a leak. She's still not sure which is the best shape for nappies, kite or triangle; both have their advocates among her friends and both still seem, in her fumbling inexperienced fingers, prone to allowing disasters.

'Little beast,' she says, getting up gingerly. He had spoiled the moment when she might have hinted to her mother, to soften the eventual blow, that Roger was mulling over a move to a paper in England, and that she might again be pregnant.

Anna wearily cleans her baby's bottom on the plastic travel pad thrown down on the stained lino of the living-room floor. Dad doesn't like change and Mum's worse; she's going to miss Andrew like hell, and the new one. She pricks her finger with the Plunket-approved safety pin and swears mildly, acknowledging to herself that she doesn't fancy having a baby in Manchester, under the National Health, and no doting granny for support like last time. She's been told they have their babies at home in England; they don't believe in hospital deliveries for everyone. They don't have Plunket, either.

Perhaps it was better to wait to break the news, just a few days, on both counts.

Anna has inherited something of her mother's natural caution and staying power; with both generations back in the city, the silly season over, the schools settling down, she lets the days go by. Her pregnancy is confirmed, and Roger has virtually had the offer of a job in Manchester. They have looked at travelling by sea, which is still cheaper, and would be pleasurable, but decide in the end, with the job not quite in the bag, to fly.

It's time, she tells him brightly, but her heart already sinking, to give them the bad news and the better news.

They invite her parents for a Sunday roast, lamb and all the trimmings, hinting at exciting news to be shared. Jim says on the phone that the timing is great, because they've also got a bit of news of their own.

'No, my love,' he chuckles, 'it'll wait until Sunday. Yes, I think you are going to be surprised. No, we're not doing a world cruise and no, I haven't been given a promotion.' Anna instantly regrets her light-hearted prodding; people like her conscientious, loyal father kept the huge Department of Education going — he never took a day off sick, brought work home occasionally, and was, she believed, much respected by the teachers he dealt with — but her mother had confided in her a year or so ago that he'd stopped applying for more senior positions.

'So you won't tell me, whatever it is? I'm going to have to wait until Sunday? Come on, Dad, you and Mum never have news. Not world-shattering news anyway.'

'This isn't world-shattering. It's just . . . look, I promised your mother. My lips are sealed.' Anna's face is contorted with exasperation as Roger looks up from changing the baby and rolls his eyes at her. 'Wait till Sunday. Don't press me again, love. Your mother wants to tell you herself.'

It is Ellie who suggests that they keep revealing their momentous news, whatever it is, for later: until after their drinks and the roast leg of hogget that's been sizzling in the oven since ten o'clock, and the pavlova and bottled golden queen peaches to follow.

'A good meal makes good news even better,' she says cheerfully. 'Businessmen always do their deals and hard talk over coffee, I believe, not over the soup. A little bit of waiting never did anyone any harm.'

But Anna is feeling irritated by such truisms and Roger sleeping in late when he promised he'd go down to the dairy and get the cream for the pavlova; she's weary after another bad night with Andrew and a mite nauseous. She is rather dreading the moment when her mother realizes that for a few years anyway she is going to be bereft of both this grandchild and the next, and maybe even a third, which Roger keeps saying he wants. With Jude probably going down to university in Dunedin next year, both daughters and grandchildren gone, what will her mother do with herself all day? There are only so many edges to be trimmed, weeds to be extracted, dead-heads to be cut off. The garden is always impeccable; the house gets vacuumed every second day, the sheets washed every week and the windows once a month. Good works will have to be encouraged. She wishes yet again that her mother had some deflection from her dutiful drudgery, like the routine of pupils coming to the house for their weekly lessons, the beautiful Broadwood grand being used more. Duets, a piano trio — surely she could find some kindred souls somewhere?

Roger, having got the cream, is irritated to come back and find Ellie suggesting that they flip a coin for their after-dinner revelations. 'Oh for heaven's sake,' he mutters at the sideboard, pouring his mother-in-law's dry sherry, Portuguese rather than the neat vinegar that passes for local Dally product.

'Tails we go second,' he answers brusquely to Jim's request. Whatever their news is, it can't be anywhere near as adventurous as going to live in Manchester for three years, maybe more, maybe elsewhere. England has a great many newspapers, and each one of them needs chief reporters, various varieties of editors and managers.

'Tails it is,' says Jim, grinning conspiratorially. He thinks Roger is a selfish young fellow lacking a sense of humour and is quite looking forward to the look on his daughter's face.

In the kitchen, Anna gets out the hand beater and whips the cream, the little green handle going round and round. Distracted and nervous, she doesn't quite stop in time; the soft peaks have started to turn buttery. 'Damn,' she mutters, hoping a few swipes with the rubber scraper will undo some of the damage, and knowing they won't.

She simply hates dishing up roasts. Easy enough to throw one in the oven, a real challenge to dish up and serve without something going cold and getting a mess in the kitchen. She mashes down the gravy's lumps with a fork and wants to get this meal over.

But the roast and mint sauce and accompanying veges are hot and well received with a background of the Chopin waltzes she knows her mother likes and now, Anna can hardly believe her ears, and also her good fortune. The weight of her guilt lifts like an old sack from her shoulders. Roger is simply dumbfounded.

'We've bought a section in Taupo,' Ellie is saying. 'Round near the Maori village and the picket fence, that long sweep of beach. It's a new subdivision and ours is the pick of the bunch. Lakefront.'

She smiles benignly around the living room, where they are now sitting over proper perked coffee. Anna cooks a good roast, she thinks proudly, feeling a little too replete. She rarely has the pleasure of genuinely astonishing either of her daughters.

Anna says, 'You crafty . . . ! *Bought* it? How long has all this been going on?'

'Well, we looked at it in January, just before we came home.'

'Anything to do with that mysterious night you went out?' says Anna.

'Everything to do with it,' says Ellie. 'I sat on the beach and listened to what the lake had to tell me. I decided that's where I'd like to end my days.'

'Mum! You're only forty-seven, for heaven's sake. You're strong as an ox.'

'And I plan to be around for at least twenty-five years. I have a thirty-year plan.'

'The next day,' continues Jim, 'we found it had gone. Sold overnight. Some Auckland stockbroker had put in an offer and scraped up the money. If stockbrokers ever stoop to scraping up money. I think the agent was genuinely sorry, wasn't he, Mum?' He is jiggling Andrew up and down on his knee and being rewarded by ecstatic smiles and gurgles. 'Your mother didn't want to look at any others.'

'That or nothing,' says Ellie. 'We could afford it, just. But I had a feeling.'

Jim says, 'Five weeks later we get a ring from the agent. The deal's fallen through, and it's going back on the market. We said hold everything, offer ten thousand less than the stockbroker. We got straight in the car and drove down to Taupo. Two days later, a little bit of fancy footwork, a few anxious moments, it was ours.'

'The agent was very helpful. Nice young man, not as flashy as he looked. I think he quite liked us,' says Ellie.

Anna remembered not being able to get her parents for a couple of days. They always seemed to be out when she rang, even first thing in the morning. The rotters were down in Taupo buying land! She is still reeling.

'Why didn't you tell me?'

'Dearest one, much as we love you, we don't have to tell you everything,' says her mother mildly, gazing down at her gurgling grandson. 'We wanted to be sure. Jim's got some photos — here.'

Ellie takes Andrew and allows him to play with her azure glass pendant, the only one she ever wears. Anna thinks she has never seen her mother look so radiant, and even a trifle smug.

In a brand-new photo album, colour pictures have already been neatly stuck in. Anna and Roger see a grey patch of bare ground, fenced with torn barbed wire, beside a grey featureless lake.

They know that sweep of bay well; sometimes they have all taken their chilly bins and sun umbrellas — there aren't many shade trees on the lakefront — for a picnic a hundred yards or so along from the one unmarked public access. On calmer days, all except the real westerly blow, it's known as the best swimming beach on the entire lake shore, the water crystalline, no rocks underfoot, just soft rippled sand visible until reaching thirty feet or more of purest indigo, against that backdrop of mountains with Ruapehu's everlasting snow sparkling even in late January. On summer days when the lake is completely still and the mountains and western bays clear, the swimming is sublime. Diving down through the top sun-warmed layer, swimmers feel their limbs caressed by ice, a reminder of the lake's unknown depths, the bottomless craters left by those explosions sighted in China.

The photos show the section from the road, from the beach, diagonally across; some with smiling Ellie, others with waving Jim, and, rather sweetly, three with both of them, hand in hand, courtesy of a passing English tourist. 'We told him to come back in ten years time and if we're there, say hello,' says Ellie, giggling slightly at Anna's expression. She knows this sort of gesture with strangers seems uncharacteristic of her.

'That's going to keep you busy,' murmurs Roger, wondering how much they paid for it but knowing that Anna will find out and tell him later. Ellie's father, a widower and owner of a small, struggling bookshop, had died the year before they got together; there might've been some money, but Anna had never mentioned it. It would be so like Ellie and Jim not to splash out on a world tour or a new car but to invest it solidly for a few years, for that hypothetical and extremely bourgeois rainy day. Jim's parents were long gone; his job would be solid, and a pension at the end of it, but money-wise, unspectacular. Once, Ellie would have been able to earn as much, or more, teaching piano. Roger is acquisitive and calculating enough to look into his crystal ball . . . give them twenty years, Jim less probably . . . and see a lakeside property, worth a great deal of money, passing down the line . . . though there's Judith to consider, of course.

'We're looking at those pre-built kitset sort of houses,' says Jim. 'Two bedrooms at first, and we'll build on more later.'

'Something very simple,' says Ellie. 'Meantime, we're getting a second-hand caravan, just so we can go down at weekends, clear the weeds and start thinking about the garden.'

Anna and Roger look at each other: a garden on that pumice wasteland seems far beyond her parents' capabilities or resources. They are nearing fifty, not old, but not young either. And they haven't the money, surely, for hiring graders and other heavy equipment, never mind the *mountain* of topsoil for anything to grow there. They both look again at the pictures in the album and try — unsuccessfully — to imagine something like a Lockwood house there, a garden similar to the one Ellie looks after in the city. Shade trees, roses, a lawn for Jim to mow.

Anna, recovering, jumps to her feet.

'Right. Let's break out the champers, Roger; that bottle someone gave us. Toast the twenty-year plan. The thirty-year plan. Gosh, what a challenge. You old dark horses. I'm impressed!'

'Now?' asks Jim. 'I'm full of roast lamb and pav.'

'You can drink champers any old time, Dad,' huffs Anna. 'Or we've got that Dally port if you'd rather.'

'No, no, champers is fine,' says Jim hurriedly.

'It won't be cold,' says Ellie.

'Put ice in it!' says Anna. 'No, that's a lousy idea for French champagne. Put it in the freezer for twenty minutes, Roger. Then we can toast both our moves.'

'You're moving?' asks Ellie, her face shutting down as Anna knew it would. Her grip around the baby tightens slightly. Despite the just-announced challenge in Taupo, Anna's guilt comes roaring to the fore. She is momentarily paralysed, helpless.

'Yes . . . ah . . . to . . . well, to Manchester,' says Roger.

He has a job, good as, on the *Manchester Guardian*, Roger explains to his nodding in-laws. He'd been feeling increasingly stale in Auckland. Sure the *Star* was a good paper, it could run rings round the opposition, but the juicy assignments, especially on the investigative side where it's all starting to happen, hadn't been coming his way. A mate already at the *Guardian* had suggested he think about it. He'd had a phone interview with one of the top brass and more or less been offered a job on the paper. At least, the assistant editor he'd spoken to had been sufficiently encouraging, pending receipt of his CV, for them to believe it was worth going, and sooner rather than later, so that meant going by air. They liked Kiwi reporters in Britain, apparently, considered them well-trained, tough and enterprising.

'Time for a change of scene,' says Anna stoutly. She has been taught by both her parents that loyalty is one of the cardinal virtues. Manchester, she says, being honest, is not where she would have chosen; however, Roger says it's not far from some lovely English countryside: the Yorkshire Dales, the Lake District of his boyhood hero Arthur Ransome and the pretty box of those colour pencils they all used at primary school. More, the whole Continent lies just beyond the English Channel; they have talked of camping holidays in France and Italy, how they could manage with babies. She has been reading her mother's face through all this. Resignation is what she sees, more than anything else. Andrew, clutching at the azure pendant as he mouths at a small bottle of orange juice, has grown drowsy in Ellie's arms.

'Are there management possibilities?' asks Jim. He knows his humourless son-in-law to be more than a touch ambitious.

'Sure. If not on the *Guardian*, there are plenty of other papers, if I stick around long enough. You have to do the legwork; there's a lot of competition.'

'Are you seeing this as a long-term thing, then?' asks Ellie, her voice even and quiet.

'Three years, Mum,' says Anna, too quickly. 'See how we like it. You know, settle down for a bit. I suppose, now, with Taupo, you won't be able to even think of a trip to . . . to see the new baby.'

'The new baby?' asks Jim.

'A little sister for Andrew we hope, or perhaps brother. I don't care as long as it's healthy, ten fingers, ten toes,' rushes Anna at the fence. She's over: her mother's expression has initially softened, broadening to a genuinely delighted smile.

'Oh Anna, I am so pleased for you both. When is it due? Is everything alright? Come here, give me a kiss.' Careful not to wake the sleeping child in her arms, she tilts her face upwards. But Anna, when she gets close, can also see the rigidly controlled anguish in her eyes, the glint of a suppressed tear.

'Due late October, Mum,' she says. 'And yes, everything's fine, absolutely normal.'

'Will you be gone by then? Or will you stay until after . . .'

'They want me immediately, Ellie, more or less,' Roger interrupts, knowing he is not giving the preferred answer. 'And Anna will be just fine with the NHS. You can have your baby at home, if you want. That's standard practice, apparently. She'll be fine.'

'Of course she will,' says Ellie briskly. 'She could have her baby on the kitchen table if she had to. So when are you going?'

Roger says, 'We're flying out in a month. The airlines won't take you after five months, something like that. It's academic really; they said the sooner I can get there the better.'

Ellie nods. She is still smiling, but Anna thinks the smile now has a forced quality. Her father is gazing at Andrew, his craggy face expressionless. He hasn't said a word. Anna feels a rush of compassion for them both. They are not going to see this baby. Maybe they will never see this baby. They will not see Andrew's first steps, the baby smiling, the baby sitting up, walking. First days at kindy.

She tells herself not to be melodramatic, or unduly pessimistic. Millions of grandmothers all over the world, since time began, have farewelled or never even seen their grandchildren, and for lesser reasons than hers. Families have upped and left, made their lives elsewhere. They go where the work is, the prospects, a new life outside the tribe.

She tells her parents, there are airplanes, there are ships, and it will not be for ever. Just a few years, while Roger gets some experience in England. Then he'll be able to think about coming home to a really good job here, chief reporter or assistant editor or something. It's their overseas trip, you know, like all her university and training-college friends are now doing because they've finished their degrees and courses and their two-year bond teaching in awful rural three-teacher schools, and they've saved their money and they're all up and away to London, free as birds.

She's just doing it slightly differently, with a husband in tow. Or rather she's in tow. She means this to sound light-hearted but realizes it merely sounds odd, a little demeaning, and Roger isn't smiling.

The champagne is not really cold enough, and they don't own proper champagne glasses, but Roger pours out four scrupulously equal measures and they drink it anyway.

'Here's to Taupo,' cries Anna, raising her glass. 'You'll send us *lots* of photos.'

'Of course,' says Jim, who has rallied so far as to shake his son-in-law's hand. 'And you will send us photos of the baby.'

'Both babies,' says Ellie firmly. 'You must make sure about that. First children need extra love when a new baby arrives.'

'Yes, Mum,' smiles Anna. With the amount of babysitting and general support she's enjoyed with Andrew, she knows she's in no position to object to any maternal advice her mother cares to give her. Although Roger had. At one stage, when Andrew was about two months old, she'd had to tell her mother Roger was feeling a bit, well, sidelined. He was the father, after all. She thought Ellie had been a little hurt, but she'd not made an issue of it and subsequently treated Roger in his father role with elaborate courtesy; to the point that Anna sometimes wondered if there was an element of mockery.

'I remember one friend; it was priceless,' Ellie is saying. 'She told her little boy of about, oh five or six, I think, that Mrs Johns was having a new baby, and her little boy said, "Why, what's wrong with the old one?"'

She looks down at the sleeping child so they won't see her tears. She hums the Brahms lullaby she first learnt as a precociously gifted young music student, and still plays on babysitting nights, when the little travel cot gets parked in the downstairs bedroom and Roger and Anna go off to a movie. No more Brahms, she whispers to the cherubic little face.

Outside it is a bright autumn day. Inside Anna and Roger's rented flat, now that these momentous plans for the next few years have been shared, the mood is optimistic. The champagne is quickly finished, Andrew wakes hungry and later, tea is drunk.

A career is being advanced, babies born and raised; a house will be built and a garden will be planted. Though none of them actually articulates the thought, they are all canny enough to imagine the time — a decade? They would not want it to be too much longer — when all these elements will joyfully again come together.

~ TWO ~

Anna and Roger, and their three children, are away for eleven tumultuous years — those of Vietnam, the student uprisings in America and Europe, old values found wanting, new rights and freedoms asserted. The Beatles. It's some years later before battle-weary survivors recognise the sixties as truly a time of momentous upheaval.

As a journalist, Roger is in the thick of it. As the mother of three, in a strange country, Anna feels the sixties pass her by.

For those eleven years, Ellie sits down after tea every Tuesday night and writes to her daughter; sometimes an aerogram, or more usually, several pages of a letter if there are pictures or newspaper clippings to include. She always uses a pad of lined paper; her handwriting is well-formed, legible, typical of her generation's early schooling when teachers meant business and pens meant nibs dipped into squat little bottles of blue-black Indian ink. When they used blotters. She still prefers a fountain pen to a ballpoint any day.

She writes on Tuesday nights because she allows Monday as a day of rest and music after the weekend. She and Jim return from their labours in Taupo usually late Sunday night, although an early Monday-morning run through the mist lying across the Hauraki Plains is sometimes preferred. If they leave at 4 a.m., she can drop Jim to work by nine.

These Tuesday letters usually take a week in transit. For some of the more testing periods of Anna's eleven-year absence, they are her lifeline.

'No flies on them,' says Roger, handing back the packet of photographs.

A month into their time in Manchester, pictures have arrived showing an oval-shaped un-roadworthy caravan parked in one corner of the Taupo section, and a small box-like structure, which the accompanying letter says houses the water pump. The water gushes up icy, sweet and crystal clean, writes Ellie, an endless supply since the water table is not all that far down. A taller box houses a temporary long-drop.

Ellie has taken pictures of Jim with a heavy-duty shovel digging the pit for the long-drop, bare to the waist even though (she writes) it's a bright June day, with a biting autumn wind blowing in. They made him out of the same mould as Ed Hillary, thinks Anna fondly. Jim's picture of Ellie shows her in scruffy brown slacks and thick orange rubber gloves, balancing a giant steel wheelbarrow half-full of rocks. With that unflattering scarf around her head, that determinedly cheerful air, her mother looks like something out of her primary-school history books: the war-torn forties, those land girls in their gingham shirts and dungarees. She looks happy.

What no-one knows is that she's cheerfully shifting those rocks to her internal orchestra playing the 'Radetsky March', Berlioz. Marches are good, Tchaikovsky, Elgar; she's not above a Sousa or two. Polkas, too, 'Schwanda the Bagpiper'. And then, for a contrast, the waltz from 'Sleeping Beauty'. This and other waltzes; she likes their swaying sense of movement. Tchaikovsky reigns supreme here, also Beethoven, Brahms, Verdi, Richard Strauss. She can adjust the tempi to suit the rhythm of her lifting, barrowing, placing. With such an accompaniment, a morning's work beside the lake can go very quickly.

She has to sit down for the piano repertoire, above all her beloved Chopin nocturnes, be still and alone and dreaming under the stars. Beside a lake. One day she will be able to play her own 'Moonlight Sonata' with the lake lapping audibly nearby.

*   *   *

'Still think they're crazy,' says Roger sourly, over a late breakfast. 'They'll run out of money. And steam. That section will be back on the market within two years, you'll see.'

'Five pounds, you're on,' says Anna, irritated. Her parents are not fools. Look at the pictures just arrived in the morning's post, what they've achieved already.

'Done. That child is smelling like a drain again.'

'Have you rung up about the job?'

'Look, just . . . I'm going to, right? After I've read this?'

'You said that yesterday. And you haven't, right?'

'Get off my bloody back.'

'No, I won't. Those people, they're doing the dirty on you.'

'God, it stinks in here,' says Roger, throwing down his *Guardian*. 'For Christ's sake, open a window.'

'Thank you for offering.'

Roger gets up and leaves the dark three-roomed Manchester flat they took the day after arrival. He doesn't open the window before he goes (probably) to the local pub, which, at eleven on a weekday morning, irritates Anna profoundly. She is left to finish Andrew's bottle, change him, put him down for his nap. An unstructured but obligatory day of cleaning, washing, shopping and the playground lies ahead. She is frequently feeling sick these days, but whether from worry or the baby is hard to tell.

There is shopping he could have done to be helpful, had he asked or she been quicker.

Roger's promised job has not quite happened. A staff position, sorry; work as a stringer, certainly, until something comes up. He is welcome to look around, submit features, case the joint. They are sympathetic to the fact that he came 12,000 miles for a job, and has a pregnant wife and nine-month-old baby in tow, but not quite to the extent of clinching a salaried job. Come back in a month, they said.

For the first time in her life, with her parents, Anna dissembles. Roger's settling down well, she writes; it's stimulating work, without specifying what or where. She sends photos of Andrew taken at a local playground, Roger pushing him on a baby swing. England, she writes, once you get outside industrial old Manchester itself, is just so *pretty* in summer. Country lanes and harvest activity, stone walls and great stacks of golden hay; geraniums in the windows of country pubs. Not that she gets to the pubs much.

Ellie knows the time the postman comes by on his bike. This Thursday she is waiting at the gate and is rewarded by a fat package containing pictures of Andrew's first birthday ten days ago. They have had a formal portrait done, Anna sitting, chubby curly-haired Andrew on her lap, Roger standing behind, the protective Victorian father pose. Anna has that ripe secretive look; her face is fuller, hair longer.

'Is this what he went to England for?' asks Jim when he's home and they settle down over a sherry to read the enclosed cuttings from the *Guardian* with Roger's by-line. He's in Sports, writing about pampered soccer stars, local road cyclists training for next year's Tokyo Olympics, fencing contests. 'Fencing? What does he know about fencing, this fancy stuff, foil and épée? I thought he was a rugby man. What's all this soccer?'

'Even I've heard of Manchester United,' says Ellie. 'And he's got to be versatile. Newspapermen have got to be able to write about anything, Anna says.'

'That's the problem; they write about things they know nothing about. Any wonder they get it wrong.'

'Give him a chance, Jim.'

'Hmm,' grunts Jim. 'I hope she's happy. Tomorrow night I can get away a bit earlier.'

Ellie reaches over the tray of chocolate thins on the table and squeezes his hand gratefully. On arrival in the dark tomorrow night they should find the first evidence of their future lakeside home, the wooden frames for the concrete pad on which it will sit. North-facing, kitchen with a view, a sheltered courtyard, two bedrooms, bathroom with a shower, French doors from living room onto a veranda to come later.

A floor plan will now be etched into the pumice, after which a truckload or three of topsoil can be considered. Then, the backbreaking job of spreading it around the section; this will take months of barrowing, spreading with the steel rake, more raking with the bamboo one. Preparing the bare pumice and carting away the rocks was bad enough; despite several pairs of rubber gloves, they both had callouses on the palms of their hands to prove it. But the topsoil, rich and loamy, albeit a bit lumpy, will mean real progress. She can't wait to get her hands into it, bed in a few shrubs, draw up plans for flowerbeds, start her compost going, choose and place her trees. Each one will have its significant special name. The first will be a copper beech, which for some reason always makes her think of Richard Strauss: bold, bronze, brassy, his 'Don Juan' tone poem, but also, where the leaves at the tips of the branches are young and plum-coloured, his waltz suite from *Der Rosenkavalier*.

'You owe me five pounds,' says Anna smugly. She has savoured this moment till after tea and Andrew is read to and bedded down. Roger is writing some feature about the Olympics; he often works at his portable Olivetti on extra pieces at home and has his eye on going to Tokyo. 'Five pounds, please?'

'What for?'

'Five pounds you said Mum and Dad would have given up and sold the section by two years. Well, look at these!' She triumphantly waves some pictures in front of Roger's face. 'House frames! Topsoil!'

And there it is: the frames of the simple U-shaped house sitting squarely on a section now partially covered with a layer of lumpy brown soil. In one corner sits a massive hill of topsoil still to be spread, Jim leaning on his long-handled shovel, wheelbarrow waiting nearby. He's wearing a white floppy hat, shorts and gumboots, and grinning up at the camera. White horses on the wind-tossed lake can be glimpsed through the wooden frames. Anna hesitates before handing the picture over to Roger. Those strong blues of the lake and sky, the snowy cumulus above, the purple of the distant hills, even the straight, sharp, golden lines of the pine-wood frames and the glowing orange of the wheelbarrow — all so foreign to eyes grown used to soft pastel English land-scapes — have unexpectedly brought a lump to her throat.

She bends over Sarah's bottle. How easy it had been, just a straight run to Taupo for those family holidays together, to arrive at the rented bach, no parking problems at whatever beach they chose and, compared with England, remarkably few people.

In two years, Roger's work has allowed them a week in the Yorkshire Dales with some friends and a weekend in the Lake District just before Sarah was born. Pretty, but hard work, even in a hotel for two nights. English people don't seem to like young children in restaurants. She will never get used to having to catch trains for any decent escape from the city — Roger had thought it best not to buy a car just yet. He gets about by train to sports events all over England and a few in France and Germany; Anna, pushing Sarah's little pram, trailing Andrew by the hand, gets to the playground and the new supermarket and sometimes doesn't see Roger for days, even weeks, at a time.

'Five pounds,' she says, adamant.

'I don't remember that.'

'I do. You said they'd've sold up within two years. I said, bet you five pounds.'

'I never.' The shrewd eyes looking over the portable Olivetti typewriter give lie to the words. He reckons he's going to tease me out of it, Anna thinks.

'You did too. You owe me five pounds.' They bat back and forth for a bit, but she's only got energy for two babies, not a third, and in the end, for a quiet life, she withdraws (as, she believes, he knew she would) thinking wistfully that if her younger sister could hear this conversation there'd be no doubt about the outcome. Jude would have had her five pounds out of Roger faster than he could draw breath. She would have pinned him up against a wall and physically extracted his wallet from his hip pocket. Jude has nearly finished her Phys Ed course in Otago and from what few clues Anna has to go on, has a reputation in Dunedin as a wild woman.

For some days she can't bring herself to look at her parents with their shovels, the golden house frames against that intense blue, white-crested water.

Ellie, sitting beside the lake, is succumbing to a rare moment of despondency, and tonight no drifting Chopin nocturne nor stately Bach sarabande is able to help. There is no moon, and the spring wind is chilly. She is tired of backbreaking work with her rake and spade and little hand tools, tired of the incessant wind and tired of her weekends spent in a scruffy twenty-year-old caravan with cheap, rock-hard mattresses.

The builder is having trouble with his subbies and it doesn't help that they are absentee owners, only getting down at weekends. So the house is still to be wired, the windows and doors installed. She thinks of the painting and varnishing to do, wallpapering; the whiteware still to be bought, the light fittings, later on the curtains; later again the third and fourth bedrooms, more furniture for when the family comes home, or by some miracle Jude gets herself married off. And then there's the projected boathouse for the aluminium dinghy Jim has bought for them to go trolling for trout, and her plans to grow trees from seed. The paths to be laid, the fencing still to be done . . . a nice letterbox one day . . .

And still no birds.

Tonight, while Jim sleeps in the stuffy caravan, she sits miserably by the lake, allowing herself to embrace a wave of self-pity. She wonders if really, she has the strength. Underneath all this is her instinct that her daughter's marriage is in deep trouble. Anna's letters are not explicit but clearly she is lonely and stressed with two very young children in a crowded industrial city; she seems to have made few friends and now Roger has gone with the *Guardian* team for a month to the Olympics in Tokyo. Nice for some, she thinks. Anna is sometimes too placid and easy-going for her own good. Ellie fears for her future.

Rarely, she gives in to her deep-seated grief for her lost grand-children and allows tears to drop into the clean beach gravel. Andrew, dear little three-year-old chap who has no memory of her, and Sarah, never once cuddled, a year now and the spitting image of Jim. Only photographs, anxious voices across 12,000 miles of crackling phone line (a waste of time and money), mail containing occasional 'works of art' in crayon and poster paint from Andrew's playgroup, parcels of clothes and toys sent off for birthdays and Christmas, her never-once-missed Tuesday letters. She would swap the half-finished house behind her for one hug, one moment of recognition in either child's eyes of her special significance to them.

This grief she cannot share with Jim. Roger had his career to think of, Jim would say gruffly, he had to go where the work was; to that brutal, inescapable fact of life she would have no answer. There were relatively few newspapers in New Zealand, many requiring good reporters in England; Roger may equally well have gone to work in Invercargill or Perth and then what? Men understand these imperatives better; to them, grandchildren mean less. Since time immemorial, he would imply, grandmothers have simply had to accept these things. Families split up, replicate themselves. Life goes on.

Under the moonless vault of sky, while Jim snores gently in the caravan, and halfway round the world, Anna is at that very moment steeling herself to tell Roger that unfortunately she is pregnant again, Ellie weeps.

With four years gone, of the eleven that the young family are to be away, time starts to bring its own acceptance, understanding, even a measure of forgiveness.

Ellie has filled many photograph albums with pictures of her three absent grandchildren, and of the progress over the years on the lakeside property.

Here is Andrew on his first day at school; little Jane's first birthday; holidays in the Lake District; another when they got a campervan and all went to Brittany. Their new rented two-storey semi-detached house in a suburban street of nearly identical houses; its small oasis of garden behind with the children's plastic bikes, a small swing, a sandpit. Here is Andrew playing drums in a school band; Sarah's first day at school, Jane's first day at kindy. Here is Roger beside their new second-hand car, and many cuttings with his by-line as he progressed from everyday sports reporting to having his own twice-weekly sports column with some editorial responsibility, Ellie is not quite sure what. Anna growing maternal and somewhat dumpy, changing her hair, looking sadder (Roger had ruled out any trip home on grounds of the finance required for a family of five) and always, bone weary; tolerating (Ellie gathers) Roger's strange working hours, his drinking, his increasing girth and receding hairline, his possible affair (she has hinted) with a smart junior on the women's pages, his frequent assignments away from home; but through it all, enduring. She is her mother's daughter.

And here, in many albums, are the originals of the pictures she has faithfully sent to Anna: the house exterior basically finished, the interior walls and windows going in, the sparkies at work, the new whiteware in large cardboard boxes being wheeled into the house.

Here is the master bedroom, freshly wallpapered (by them, of course — they learned on the job and make a good team), the caption noting this was the first time they were able to forego the hard bunks in the caravan, and make up the new blissfully comfortable beds with fresh new sheets. Jim lying on his new bed, arms behind his head, smiling like the Cheshire cat. Here is Ellie with paintbrush, only a few photographs covering the interminable hours she has spent sanding and painting walls, cupboards, ceilings, beams, window trims. Priming and undercoats and topcoats: she has become an expert. Here is the kitchen, the day they first used the new stove; here is Jim up a ladder hanging light-fittings, hanging curtains. There's even a picture of the post-office man installing the telephone.

And the garden! Even more albums, just of the garden, to record growth and progress. Here is the day they finally raked over the last clods of the mountain of topsoil and declared that job once and for all, finished. Here is Ellie raking, and again raking, and again raking, Jim sprinkling fertiliser, Jim and Ellie sowing grass seed. Here are the first shoots, the rather patchy new lawn, the lawn being watered by sprinklers (all that wonderful water below!), the established lawn; Jim's first mowing with a new electric mower. Ellie standing beside the copper beech on its third birthday, its fourth, and now, twice as high, leaves glossy bronze, carefully pruned to an attractive shape, its tenth. Ellie shovelling compost into the barrow, beside the tables of the workspace she has established at the back of the house for germinating seeds and taking cuttings. Ellie setting in place the egg-sized stones that they brought up twenty at a time from each swim to make an attractive border around the house, at the foot of the white weatherboards.

Here is the birdbath, for the tui that are now coming to feed on the kowhai, the sparrows and blackbirds who know there'll always be generous breakfasts of crumbs.

Here's Jim beside the concrete mixer they rented for the paths, and Ellie on her knees smoothing over the concrete with her paddle of wood. Jim standing proudly beside his new tin boat, and later, its low shed and the winch he installed to pull the dinghy single-handedly up and down to the lake; their first rainbow trout, and a monster brown of twelve pounds once caught by Ellie in a November twilight.

Many shrubs are now growing there: assorted natives like hebes and many handsome flaxes; more trees, the fast-growing silver dollar for immediate shade, the slower-growing blue atlas cedar, mountain ash, beeches, a golden ash, the kauri and puriri and rimu for long-term pleasure. Ellie keeps even from Jim that each of them has been planted to the drifting sounds of a carefully chosen piece of music: the mountain ash with its scarlet berries is the 'Carmen' suite, the blue atlas cedar, Beethoven's 'Leonora' overture. The kauri, stern Elgar, the kowhai a sparkling Mozart concerto.

A rock garden has gone in, and a bed prepared for the twenty or so roses that one day, when they are living there permanently, will be planted. From instructions in a house and garden magazine, Jim carefully constructs a classic letterbox of heart rimu, and carves a strutting cockerel weathervane for the roof.

*   *   *

Jim is nearing retirement and now there is no doubt, when that happens, they will quietly sell the house in Auckland, pay off the mortgage on the Taupo property and move Ellie's baby grand piano to its new lakeside home.

They have made a few friends in Taupo: the faithful and sympathetic builder, others from Wellington and Hawke's Bay building cottages on sections nearby (though none nearly so assiduous in their tree-planting, nor keeping lawns so tidily mown and green).

They should still have enough money to build that long-promised veranda along the front, the pergolas for the bougainvillea and climbing white Iceberg rose; after that, they can start planning the new bedroom wing should the family come home — and of course for Jude and her boyfriend, and others, mostly Jim's teaching friends, who ask to come for the night or weekends en route to somewhere else and who express astonishment and admiration when shown the pictures of the flat bit of scorched earth they had started with only a decade earlier.

~ THREE ~

In the eleventh year, ringing the Taupo number, Anna tells Ellie (with Jim listening on the other phone) that Roger has just heard he's been offered a good senior job on the paper in Auckland, and they will be home in three months, in time for Christmas. He is not starting until mid-January, and of course they've got to get a house organized and a car, but they would love to spend Christmas at Taupo, in the new house which they are just dying to see — is that possible?

That night Ellie and Jim work out how they can get the new bedroom wing (with second bathroom and two small bedrooms each with two bunks) open by Christmas.

Of course, they can always fall back on pitching a tent — the two older grandchildren are old enough to sleep out — but if the builder can accommodate their urgency, and Jim takes some of his sick leave and a week's unpaid leave to work as extra builder's mate, it is just possible.

The cup of joy runneth over that Christmas, from the moment (to Ellie's profoundly felt relief) the little family's Air New Zealand flight lands safely at Auckland's airport and the three children walk shyly through the gate to meet their grandparents for the first time. After two days together in the family home in Auckland, Ellie and Jim go off tactfully to Taupo, partly to give the family some time to adjust, but principally to put final touches — some paint, the light fittings, the curtains — to the new bedroom wing.

Roger, who recognises from the moment of greeting at the airport that he has some fences to mend with his in-laws and wonders how much Anna has actually told them over the years, buys a good second-hand station wagon. Two days before Christmas they set off to join Ellie and Jim in Taupo.

No photograph could have prepared Anna for the moment when Roger stops the car on the road beside the house and its garden.

As if to celebrate, it is a brilliant December day, the mountains to the south clear, the lake every bit as calm and blue as Anna has remembered all these years and told her children about.

They have parked in the shade of a towering silver dollar beside the front gate. Behind it is a burgeoning forest shading the lawn, two rock gardens, one with a small fountain, and a simple one-storey house of white painted wood with brown trims. It has open French doors, a long veranda and a leafy courtyard sheltered from the westerlies. A birdbath sits among the trees, a weathervane wavers gently on the roof, and in the courtyard are an outdoor table (set attractively all-white for lunch for seven) and chairs surrounded by potted geraniums, chrysanthemums, flaxes and hebes. In a terracotta pot stands a precious lemon tree, which Ellie hopes can be sheltered from the wind and winter cold and if she talks to it nicely, can be persuaded to prosper.

Joyful music is playing, which Ellie later tells them is her favourite pianist, Solomon, playing some Chopin mazurkas.

In years to come, Anna will remember the two-week run of perfect weather, the sunshine burnishing her English-raised children's porcelain skin, the beam on her father's craggy features, her mother's radiance. Not a single voice is raised, not a grumble heard; by some unspoken pact, in honour of the past eleven years, tolerance and harmony prevail between the three generations for this whole two-week period. The chores of shopping, cooking, pegging out the washing and bringing in the beach towels are effortlessly shared out.

Ellie hears the children laughing and stops whatever she is doing, in wonderment. Even Roger can be seen regularly drying dishes and helping put suncream on the children, and Anna senses her parents' attitude softening. She will long remember the simple joys, harmony and goodwill of this Christmas homecoming.

With Anna and the family back resident in Auckland, putting into operation the plan to sell up in Auckland and move to Taupo is not, for Ellie and Jim, without its share of pain and doubt.

Luxuriating for this brief period in the relative proximity of her grandchildren and the frequent opportunities for babysitting, Ellie is well aware that after the move she will see much less of them. She only has to remind herself of those eleven years of their absence to count — as a still fit and capable sixty-three-year-old — her many blessings.

Taupo is only four hours away, she tells Jim, as they put the

Auckland house on the market. The family will be down for long weekends and the school holidays, Anna and the children if not Roger. She and Jim will be travelling to Auckland occasionally for the concerts they subscribe to.

She is confident that a happy balance can be struck, the future secure as can be expected.

It is eighteen months since Jim's retirement and the baby grand was trundled through the French doors and Ellie, now that she is *in situ* and can water her young trees daily, has begun her programme of really serious planting and propagating.

In the classical sense, the property is in danger, as the trees grow bigger, of becoming almost too luxuriantly populated. But the new roses seem to love this climate, with generous blood and bone sprinkled round their roots; the climbing rose, that lovely single Iceberg with its lemony centre and fragrance, is now to the top of the pergola. Tui, wood pigeons, blackbirds, sparrows and gulls come frequently to drink and splash in the birdbath. The lawn is in splendid shape, the copper beech in its robust thirteenth year. Even the slow-growing blue atlas cedar, which for many years stubbornly refused to put on any height at all, has notched up a few inches. Of all her trees, this is perhaps Ellie's favourite.

When Jim gives instructions to visitors he simply says, as you come down the main road from the airport, you'll see a small jungle just beside the lake. Turn right at the bottom of the hill and head for the jungle. That's us.

He is very proud when cars come (he believes specially) to turn at the end of the street and when people walking to the beach linger a minute or two, all to admire their trees and the simple white house they shade and protect.

After the daily chores, and the later part of the morning spent in the garden, Ellie is playing her piano rather more often these days.

She likes to play in the early afternoons, after lunch. This pleases Jim, who finds he needs an afternoon nap more than he used to. In the winter months, when rains batter the house and they can't get outside, it feels like a pleasant, snug sort of hibernation.

There is only one way their life in retirement could be more perfect, and that would be if Anna and the family lived in Taupo. But Ellie knows very well Roger's job rules that out and he's firmly said he can hardly see himself as editor of the local paper. She considers the balance satisfactory, all things considered, and herself to be truly blessed.

She is even able to send away to New York for these new tapes just available of just the orchestral parts of some of the Mozart concerti, the Schumann, the Chopin No 1, the Greig, two Beethovens. She practises hard at those sections her now-thickened fingers find difficult; when she feels ready and daring, she joyously plays a complete movement with the volume as loud as she dares, knowing that, although the pleasure of a real audience was long ago denied to her, outside the open window her trees are listening.

In Auckland, Roger and Anna have bought a large house with a small garden, in Meadowbank. Anna thinks herself not much of a gardener, compared with her mother, and Roger neither. He grumpily mows the lawns, and that's about all; Anna is grateful for a day's help with weeding and general tidying up when Ellie and Jim come up for a concert.

A year into his new job, Roger seems happy enough. The move away for all those years appears to have paid off, thinks Anna, as he tells her of another small but significant shuffling of desks representing for him another step up the ladder towards chief reporter. She is glad of that, for him and for her own part in his success. She is happy with the children's local schools, and has little time — either real time or sympathy — for the newly loud voices of strident women calling themselves feminists, calling for equality, burning their bras, swearing in public, holding conventions where they talk of centuries of tyranny and repression, betrayal and revenge. On television, they wear dungarees and headscarves, spurn bras and lipstick, talk of men as oppressors, tyrants, bullies, rapists. According to the most belligerent, all men have the capacity to be rapists. It is an uncomfortable thought.

Sister Jude, still aggressively single, returned from two years' hated teaching in East London at a tough co-ed school, now calls herself a feminist and talks like one. She thinks Anna dull, placid and oppressed and tells her so; she further asks when her big sister is going to go back to real work so that she gets out from under Roger's thumb and has some money and therefore choices of her own.

Anna, still locked into a full daily round of domesticity, servicing three children and a husband who likes his shirts ironed and a hot meal at whatever time he chooses to come home, cannot see this happening.

'You could stop being a doormat and go back to primary teaching,' says Jude, drinking coffee in the kitchen on one of her rare visits to her sister's house. 'Perfect job with kids, finish at three, all those holidays, no marking.'

'I'd have to retrain. Anyway, they've got too many teachers at the moment — I might not get a position,' says Anna, deciding to ignore doormat and the untruth about finishing at three. In truth, she's terrified at the thought, and though some money of her own over and above the Child Benefit would certainly be nice, Roger earns enough for the mortgage and bills and extras, like petrol to Taupo and his golf. 'Except in some country school, and that's no use.'

'You're young enough to retrain,' persists Jude. 'You could just about teach violin to little kids.'

'Don't talk rot, Jude. I haven't played a violin in years. Anyway, they're all on Suzuki now.'

'And look at Mum.'

'What about Mum?'

'Shouldn't she have been a real musician? Concert pianist, all that. She was given a talent for music, not for shifting rocks in Taupo and ironing Dad's knickers and even his bloody pyjamas all her life. Just like you do. Tell Roger to do his own, I would.'

'When I think of Taupo I think of Mum's trees,' says Anna stoutly. 'And Mum talking to them, willing them to grow. And you should too.' Jude's cynical, superior smile irritates her. She tips the rest of her coffee into the sink. 'Do you have to wear those god-awful trousers?'

'You're going to be frustrated as Mum one day,' says Jude. 'Get yourself a life.'

'I am not frustrated,' says Anna forcibly, 'whatever you or your "sisters" might think. And neither is she. She loves that garden, and hell's bells, she worked for it. Created it just about with her bare hands. So did Dad. They're happy, isn't that enough?'

She goes quickly out into the garden to bring in the washing, and ignores Jude's final riposte about a tragic waste of hands which should have been playing a keyboard, not grubbing round in the dirt, an absolute waste of a talent in a male-dominated system which won't last much longer, you'll see. The world is about to see a revolution! The age of women has begun!

Gritting her teeth, wrenching the underpants and shirts from the line, Anna tells herself she has no time for all that feminist male-hating stuff, and never will. Her children still need her, and so, when it comes to the point, does Roger, for all his selfishness and constant putting her down and his journo girlfriends who he may or may not sleep with; single Jude, the way she's gone, would never understand any of that.

Yet — remembering sometimes going to sleep as a child to the sound of the piano, remembering the wistful, far-away look on Ellie's face when she listened to her favourite pianists on some radio broadcast — Anna knows in her heart that, about their mother, Jude may be right.

She hangs on grimly to her picture of Ellie watering the roses, serenely gazing out at the lake through the trees. A happy woman.

'You *can't*,' says Anna, aghast. She had thought the midday call from Taupo was for her thirty-ninth birthday, not this bombshell.

'Anna, we can't keep going here. Since Jim's stroke . . . I just can't cope any more. The garden . . . it's all just got too hard.' Ellie's voice over the phone is flat, desolate.

'I'll come down,' says Anna desperately. 'For a month. Roger and the kids can manage.'

'Anna, that'd be just a band-aid, putting off the inevitable.'

'Just till Dad gets stronger.'

'He's not going to, Anna. We had a long talk after the doctor came yesterday. It's the only sensible thing to do. He's going to need more care than we can get here and . . .' her mother's calm voice falters for the first time '. . . I won't want to live here, not on my own.'

'Are you telling me it's that bad?' Anna cries. 'What are you saying?'

'I'm just saying I can't cope any more. And I need to be closer to my daughters.'

Daughter singular, thinks Anna sourly. The other one has gone totally weird and into some sort of a witchy commune, maybe lesbian, maybe into pot; Anna wouldn't know and doesn't particularly want to. Jude is now working for a women's gym, and is a spokesperson for some coven, writes for a feminist magazine, and appears occasionally on television in her mannish suits and foul paua-shell dangling earrings; the only positive thing that Anna can say about her younger sister is that she certainly has the courage of her convictions.

'Are you there, Anna?' Ellie is enquiring. 'Anna?'

'Mum, isn't there . . . look, we'll help pay for a cleaning lady, a gardener. Two gardeners. I can come down weekdays, while the kids are at school. They're old enough to manage for a night even without Roger. '

'Anna, it's the only sensible thing to do.' She plays the card she knows will silence Anna. 'And it's what Jim wants. Now he's virtually bedridden . . .'

'Is he?' cries Anna. 'Bedridden? Has something happened? You haven't told me! What haven't you told me?'

'If we get a little flat nearish to you,' says Ellie implacably, 'then occasional visits from his grandchildren will be welcome. And yes, he had another small stroke two days ago. I can't . . . now . . . the left side . . . and arm . . . his speech isn't . . .'

'Mum, don't cry,' says Anna desperately. 'Please let me come down.'

'The land agent came this morning,' Ellie says dully. 'The house is on the market. She thinks it will sell quite quickly.'

~ FOUR ~

This call marks the beginning of Anna's nine years of filial worry.

Her father improves only a little from that third stroke, just enough to join Ellie in the apartment back in the city that Roger and Anna hurriedly help Ellie to buy.

Roger, deprived for ever of his vision of the house passing to Anna, makes it known that he thinks that Ellie lets the Taupo house, with its magnificent trees and garden, get sold by a too-slick, fast-talking bitch of an agent far too quickly and for far too little. Later, he swears he could have got time off work to go down and sort the land agent and a few things out, but, as Anna acidly reminds him, her mother didn't ask for his help and anyway he would simply have been too late.

Anna is simply appalled at the whole thing; all she can do is ensure that the living room of the apartment they choose is spacious enough for her mother's baby grand and that it has a small terrace where she can grow pot plants. She fills the flat with groceries and flowers the day that Ellie arrives with the furniture van.

Her mother, she thinks, has aged.

Ellie nurses Jim for four years before the stroke which carries him off, mercifully at home. After the large funeral, attended by many of the older teaching fraternity, Ellie tells Anna that he wanted his ashes to be sprinkled on the lake, just out from the house. When the time comes, she adds, that is also her wish.

This first task they drive to Taupo to carry out — just Anna, Ellie and a singularly quiet Jude. Anna can hardly bear to watch her mother's anguish as they drive down the road past the house. One glance is enough to see that the trees are not being well attended to, the garden looks unwatered and neglected. She reminds them impassively: if she remembered correctly it had been sold to a company for use as their executive holiday home; clearly no one capable woman was looking after it properly.

A brisk autumn onshore wind is blowing; the day is sombre and overcast. Ellie looks helplessly at the lake and asks how on earth are they going to scatter ashes in these conditions.

'I never thought — we should have got a boat,' she says. 'I don't know anyone around here to ask now.'

'Can't we just wade out a bit?' says Anna.

'The lake's pretty high at the moment,' says Ellie, looking along the foreshore. Her knowledge of the lake's physical features and behaviour is considerable. 'It gets deep quickly. You'd only get about two yards out before it's over your waist. I don't want to see Jim as scum on the shoreline.'

'Oh, for God's sake,' says Jude. 'If we're going to go paddling let's do it properly. Off with your clothes, Anna.'

'What?'

But Jude is already stripping. 'There's absolutely no-one around. You and me, we're going swimming.'

Anna, conscious of the roll of child-bearing fat that not even her sister should see, looks at her mother for help, but Ellie is smiling slightly.

'Forgive me if I don't come too,' she says. Anna's face is a picture! And, sitting on the same spot where twenty-two years ago she had first listened to the lake's inviting message, Ellie finds a certain curious, sad amusement in seeing her two middle-aged daughters strip naked, get themselves with grim determination into the chilly May water, and take the square tin canister from her. Knowing Jude is the stronger swimmer, she wonders how far they will go, and is surprised to see Anna lead Jude to a yellow offshore buoy.

Hanging onto the buoy, which is about fifty yards distant, they seem to have some trouble opening the canister; oh, Jim, she should have thought to check this, as you who were always so methodical about these things would have done. Then she hears a shout carried on the wind, sees them raise the canister and with some difficulty above the chop, pour out the contents. The stream of ash is thin, barely discernible from the shore. She's relieved that they have the wit to do this with the wind, not into it, and to circle round the spot as they strike out back for the shore.

The last of Jim is absorbed into the lake's deep waters. Ellie sings him the Chopin sonata, the funeral march with its unearthly, cruelly beautiful middle section that played at his graveside.

Anna and Jude choose to repeat this exercise three years later, even though it is September when the lake is absorbing snowmelt from its rivers and is at its coldest.

Ellie's final years have seen her retreat from life, gently deflecting Anna's worries and insisting that she needs no special help or attention. To the end she shops and manages herself well enough, tends the existing plants in her terrace garden but does not buy any new ones. She listens extensively to her beloved long-playing records. In what turns out to be her last year, Anna is not sure if her mother plays the baby grand or not; the lid is often down when she visits. Andrew, Sarah and Jane call in dutifully, but she seems to take less pleasure from their visits. She doesn't ever tell Anna that all things considered she is glad her marriage has survived, though it was clearly through no great effort on Roger's part. There may be unexpected rewards later on; she hopes this will be the case.

Ellie exits gracefully, dying one winter night in her sleep. As she cleans out the flat, Anna cannot help think of her mother as a tree, transplanted and surviving, but simply failing to thrive. She takes comfort from finding the many photograph albums of the Taupo property and late at night, over a cup of tea and Roger who knows where, turns the pages to remind herself of the backbreaking labour that had rewarded Ellie with so much pleasure.

Even if the Taupo house is not, at the moment, being so well cared for, it is still there, she reassures herself, along with its surrounding jungle. It is safe. Surely one day in the future it will again belong to a family, to a woman who loves trees as her mother did. There will be the sounds of a lawnmower, a radio on to catch the midday news, grandchildren making a play hut inside the skirts of the macrocarpa or climbing the sturdy arms of the copper beech, while granddad brings the boat in from a morning's fishing.

After the sale of the flat, Ellie's estate, divided equally between her and Jude, is enough for Anna to consider selling the large house with the small garden she has never much liked and buying a new, smaller one in Parnell. Roger, naturally, needs little encouragement for this move to a 'better' address. A few years more, she and Roger will be — incredibly — on their own.

The sprinkling of the ashes in September is tough, but it remains unspoken between Anna and Jude that they want to do it promptly, and not delay until the summer. The chosen weekend, the lake is bathed in hard spring sunshine, the mountains are still coated heavily with snow, the water calm but a steely deep blue and uninviting. They drive past the house. It looks unloved, rather more than last time, with the rimu letterbox hanging by a screw, broken chairs in the courtyard and the trees undisciplined, taller than ever.

Remember how Dad used to talk about their jungle, murmurs Jude. The blue atlas cedar has about doubled in size these past few years, thinks Anna; it was her mother's favourite.

Though Anna has brought her swimsuit, Jude insists they are naked.

'Think of it as an ancient female ritual,' she says, throwing aside her bra. She picks up the canister and wades out. 'Fuck,' she gasps. 'I wouldn't do this for anyone else. When you go, swear to God, I'll hire a boat.'

'I don't want to be sprinkled here,' says Anna, already shivering and trying to cover the waistline which she knows has thickened further since the earlier occasion. 'Oh, maybe I do. I'll think about it.'

'Well, just do me a favour and cark in summer, will you?'

This time Anna plunges in running. The coldness of the water is literally breathtaking, actually painful. This time there is no buoy. Quickly numb, they swim out to where Ellie could see her beloved blue atlas cedar and sprinkle her gently into the deep.

Anna and Jude grow a little closer in the next few years.

Anna has the curious experience of seeing her assertive, now quite famous younger sister put herself up for a city council, get elected, and read Roger's subsequent column about the new wave of feminism bringing women out of the kitchen and into the council chambers. The tone of it, she felt, was more than slightly patronizing, everything that Jude had complained about for years. And should he be writing about his sister-in-law at all? When she mentions this over breakfast, and is provoked into describing his piece as snide, he finishes the conversation by saying he simply doesn't know what she's on about.

Jude, when she reports this conversation, is scathing. 'And that, dear sister, is why your chubby oaf of a husband has been passed over for higher things. Chief Reporter, forget it. He's the world's worst listener — among other things. Very strange for a journo.'

Or perhaps it's just me, thinks Anna.

Quite often, Anna simply feels lonely and bereft — of her parents' comforting presence, of her children's company as they inevitably move into their own adult worlds. The pleasure of Roger's company hasn't been too great a feature of her daily life for years; working late shifts, his time at home is mostly spent sleeping behind drawn curtains or watching the television, for work reasons, of course. Andrew has gone flatting, Sarah will be going next year and little Jane, so like her grandmother, too soon after that. Anna has heard about the empty-nest syndrome and realizes dully that it seems to have crept up on her.

Jude, of course, is hardly sympathetic. 'I told you, you should have gone back teaching when you could,' she says nastily. 'Too late now, probably.'

Anna doesn't tell her that she has applied for several teacher-aide jobs, so far without success. Clearly she is quite as pathetic as her clever sister thinks she is, a dumpy, dull, middle-aged woman, just on the wrong side of fifty, unemployable with a recession in full swing. Running her eye down the Situations Vacant columns in the local tabloid, she doesn't see much else she can do. Deliver brochures, becoming one of those people who walk round the streets with little satchels? Sell something on commission? Fuck, woman, Jude would impatiently say, volunteer for something. Meals on Wheels, hospital visiting; run a Brownie pack, whatever they call it these days. Auckland City Mission is desperate for volunteers. Go back to university. Get out your violin. *Get out of the house.*

Anna pulls the weeds out of her garden, irons shirts, and keeps her biscuit tins full for the diminishing number of people to eat them. Reading the morning paper, she feels increasingly that she's been washed up in the wrong age. The irony that she once worried about what her mother was going to do all day doesn't escape her.

One Friday afternoon in March she is driving back from Napier. Roger has allowed her the car to drive down for the funeral of an old friend, the first of her classmates to go. Eight from that year had travelled to Napier; fifty-three was too bloody young, they agreed, and breast cancer a terrible thing. There'd been some enjoyable moments, catching up, reminiscing about their schooldays, the riots and revolutions of the sixties which not all of them had completely missed through child-rearing. Their reactions to the assertive new doctrines of feminism ranged from hostile to enthusiastic. Anna saw herself as somewhere in the middle, and had taken on board one barbed comment about those who support the cause in theory but in practice remain cowardly locked into tyrannical marriages and unsatisfactory job situations.

She stays overnight in a little B and B on Marine Parade. She isn't used to solo travel, the unusual freedom to turn out her light when she chooses or take herself for a long walk beside the sea before breakfast and visit the kiwi house before setting off for the five hours' drive back to Auckland. She is more used to fitting in around other people's preferences and agendas.

On a sudden impulse, after the taxing, winding drive over the ranges and at the lakeside junction with the main highway north, Anna turns not right to go north, but left onto the road that winds around the eastern lakeshore towards Turangi. She's feeling a little sombre but quite relaxed, and in no particular hurry, and she will visit the old family house. Check out the trees, and even perhaps find some happy evidence of new owners. It's a pleasant autumn day. If there's no-one around, she might even have a swim, for old time's sake.

The car rolls down the highway incline, easily reaching 105 ks. The expanse of lake on her right shimmers under the low sun, which perhaps explains a flicker of surprise, for her memory is of a concentration of somewhat higher trees comprising the jungle, as her father always called it. Memory and light play tricks, she says to herself; it's nearly three years since we sprinkled Mum's ashes. (What have you done with those three years, Anna?) It'll be nice to say hello to the blue atlas cedar.

She brakes, and turning the car into the street leading down to the lake, drives slowly down to stop outside the front gate, just as she has countless times in the past. This time of course she'll not turn into the driveway, but as a stranger will park here, outside. She looks briefly at the lake fifty metres away, turns off the ignition, and heaves a large sigh.

The shock is actually physical. Afterwards, she remembers feeling as though every vein and capillary in her body are coursing with a liquid fire that is igniting her from within.

And the fire is anger and disbelief and outrage in about equal parts; she is incandescent with a pure, elemental, primitive fury.

As she sits in the car and looks at the empty desolate space where the house and trees once stood, she wonders if this is after all a time-slip. She has seen many photos of the section taken from about this spot, the section just after purchase when it was a pad of bare pumice punctuated with outcrops of rock and thistles. It was just like this in the pictures of thirty-odd years ago, before the wheelbarrows and the people in rubber gloves moved in.

Anna closes her eyes, shakes her head in the hope that it is merely a mirage, this empty space. When she opens them, surely, the house (however neglected by its corporate owners) will be there, the trees will be there, the huge macrocarpa and the copper beech, the blue atlas cedar, surely will be there?

Please God, when I open my eyes, for my gentle mother's sake, so that her spirit can rest in peace, let her trees, at least, be there.

She gets out of the car, not noticing limbs usually made stiff by long-distance driving, but now propelled towards the torn and crushed fencing by a molten energy for which words are completely inadequate.

How dare they? How *dare* they! The house is gone — houses get taken away, whole houses and even cathedrals get put on trailers and carted off to new sites, it's a Kiwi thing — but worse, most of the trees are gone.

Three decades of love, growth and nurturing are gone. Just gone. *How dare they!*

Besides the flattened, crumpled front gate, she stands breathing heavily, and tries to take stock of what she is seeing.

The house is gone. And in its going, hoisted onto a trailer and extracted from its foundations like a strong healthy tooth, to get it out onto the road and begin its journey to wherever it's gone, it's apparent most of the trees had to be removed: the silver dollars and the macrocarpa, the beeches, the laburnum which dripped golden pendants every September, the mountain ash with its red berries, the bronzed hebes and other native shrubs in the courtyard, the fruit trees, the flowering cherry and the apricot, the lemon in its terracotta pot . . .

The thousands of lake stones lovingly placed around the foot of the house, the concreted pathways, the rock gardens and the little water feature, all the living gifts gratefully given by family and visitors over the years: all gone. Of the grass that once grew around the house, lovingly watered in late afternoons by the everlasting supply from below, even grass in the far corners one might have thought out of the reach of contractors' invasive machines, there is barely a trace. The roadside fence has been completely flattened; along the lakefront, the scarlet pittosporum hedge, like a mocking smear of blood, remains.

Aren't there rules against this sort of thing, she thinks? Town-planning protections for mature trees? Isn't there legislation against greedy, ruthless developers and bone-headed contractors laying this sort of waste?

Did no-one care? Or did they just do it in the dead of night without any council awareness of what moving the house entailed, and smugly pay a wrist-slapping token council fine?

Remaining — she ticks them relentlessly off, thinking *there will be a price for this* — are one silver dollar, not in the house's destructive outgoing path, unharmed. One copper beech, also out of the line of fire, also unharmed. The rimu letterbox, tossed as rubbish into a corner. Against the far fence, behind where the house once stood: her mother's rose bed, but the roses leggy, unpruned, diseased; travesties of roses, horrible. The pittosporum hedge, though still standing, shaggy and untrimmed.

And worst of all, one blue atlas cedar, all its seaward branches hacked off, a mutilated wreck of a tree. They'd actually wanted to keep that one, she thinks grimly, imagining the house trailer being inched past the straight standing trunk. They think it will grow back. They think my mother will just gracefully grow back and smile on whatever ghastly fashionable glass edifice, a chilly bin of a house, that some property developer builds here, just as though nothing has happened.

If I had an axe, I would be carrying out a mercy killing, right now. Willingly and gladly.

She debates whether to set foot on the section, whether such an act will be a further violation or somehow help to contain the primitive, violent fury that still threatens to overwhelm her, to lift her bodily off the ground.

She walks over to the lopsided blue atlas cedar and strokes one of its remaining prickly blue branches. Such a beautiful colour, this soft grey blue; once such a graceful tree, stately, uncomplaining, serene, confident, accepting, generous and enduring. Everything her mother was.

After this physical touch, during her further tour of inspection, she doesn't know where this feeling comes from, either: this primitive female rage, full of raw vengeance. Very well, it is saying to the perpetrators of this mutilation, this wanton destruction, this violation of nature — I can also wreck devastation. Watch me. Be warned, I am ancient woman, a wronged daughter of a dead mother whom you might call, for want of a better word, witch; I can make sure that your laying waste can be matched, nay topped, by a force greater than any of yours.

On the floor of the car she finds a ballpoint and in the glove box, by a miracle, several sheets of plain unused paper. Roger, who likes to refer to himself as a simple scribe, has some uses.

To those who have destroyed a garden, felled lovingly

planted trees and thus shattered a dream; to those who
with your machines have cancelled out thirty-five years'
hard backbreaking work — as a daughter of those who once
laboured here, whose loving act of creation for themselves
and their children you have cynically, wantonly destroyed,
I desire that any future efforts to grow another garden on
this enclosed square of earth remain barren.

    May any shrub or flower that you plant on this violated
ground wither and die. May any tree that you plant here
fail to take root. May birds and insects and butterflies shun
this place. May you who did this terrible thing, and this
sacred ground itself, consider yourselves to be cursed for ever.
My name is Anna and it is Friday, March 10, 1995.

    So be it.

With a trembling hand, Anna writes *To the ungrateful and undeserving owner of this property* in large letters on the back of the paper and grimly inserts the paper into a plastic bag she finds under the back seat, smoothing down the shiny surface to make it flat and weatherproof. She feels absurdly powerful, as powerful as witches have presumably always felt when taking a suitable vengeance on some terrible, unacceptable act of greed and destruction.

She places the flat package under the broken wire gate where it will be noticed. Someone connected with this destruction will, some time in the near future, bend down to pick up the gate; he will see the writing and hopefully read it, no doubt for a good laugh. With any luck it might get passed on to an agent, or preferably to the owner himself.

And even if you laugh, she thinks, or even if the short note is screwed up and tossed away as the ravings of a madwoman and never actually gets read at all, you will nevertheless know the consequences of my anger and my power.

*   *   *

Back in Auckland, she rings an incredulous Jude and tells her that before she left the section that morning, she spoke to two of the permanent residents in the next street.

They told her that the house had been taken away about two months' earlier, to a site they thought was somewhere up near Tokoroa. They had been woken one morning by the noise of the chainsaws and watched the trees falling one by one and the bulldozers nudging and wrenching the house from its foundations. It had taken two days to prepare the house and lever the sections onto the trailer. The trees didn't stand a chance. The new owner was apparently a grazier from Queensland who wanted to build a lakeside retirement home for himself, but this could be Aussie bullshit, since (one of her informants told her) an inside source had learned that the new owner was trying to get the local council to agree to dividing the land into two smaller titles, giving two premium lakefront sites. Then he could put two townhouses there, no doubt to sell each for a good fat profit on his original purchase. The council was being a bit difficult. Good, Anna had replied.

'Poor Mum,' says Jude. 'All her lovely trees. It must look awful.'

'It does,' says Anna. She doesn't tell Jude about the note she left, but she does say, quite calmly, 'I put a curse on it.'

She is pleased when Jude doesn't laugh, nor question her further.

'I understand,' Jude says quietly. As a feminist who is reading books about the late twentieth-century renaissance of goddess culture, she understands about women rediscovering their ancient strengths and the power of their curses.

~ FIVE ~

You want to know whether Anna's curse worked.

Surely, you are thinking, she got over it, poor Anna, with her misplaced old-fashioned loyalty to the past and to her parents, her sentimentality, her delusions about that peculiar nonsense they call witchcraft. Sometime or other, she 'moved on'.

Simple wooden houses, even in once egalitarian New Zealand, always get taken away in the end, always sooner rather than later if they sit on premium lakeside properties worth an increasing amount of money, as premium properties worldwide get scarcer and the rich, richer and more ruthless look for second or third homes in communities they will ultimately help to destroy. It's happening right throughout Europe: old farmhouses and quaint villages and whole medieval townships falling to the prosperous and romantically inclined offshore buyer; why should it not happen on the unpolluted, very desirable shores of Taupo-nui-a-tia?

And if a few nice trees get in the way? People — men — like Roger simply shrug their shoulders and say pity, but there it is, m'dear, these things happen, and you've got to move on. Can't live in the past — rotten old wooden houses have to make way for progress — what's done is done. And what's for tea?

With stunning insensitivity, Roger adds, you know I always thought Ellie should've got in a landscape gardener, paid for some proper professional advice. The house design was inappropriate really, they should never have gone for that cheap architectural draughtsman fellow. The section was severely undercapitalized and the trees pretty enough but in all the wrong places. She was an amateur, when it was all boiled down, and Jim might be good enough at DIY but he didn't really have much of a clue, did he? And they should never have sold in the first place. You don't let a property investment like that go out of the family if you've got any sense. (He'd blown smoke into the air above the dining table, despite her request that he only smoke outside.)

'They were pretty stupid really — they let it go for a fucking song.'

It is this last comment which decides Anna. With a sizeable

resurgence of the enraged energy she had felt beside the lake, she sits on, trembling, for an hour at the breakfast table after Roger has left, then rings up Jude and asks if she and her partner would mind giving her their spare room for a week or so, just until she organises a flat. She stands, weeping, for a moment in front of the open wardrobe containing Roger's seven English-tailored suits, his racks of ironed handmade shirts and Italian shoes, and savagely swiping her sleeve across her face, sets to work.

That night she rings up her children to tell them what's happening, and that the house is on the market, and later, near midnight, when Roger gets home from work, shows him the packed suitcases and piles of English suits carelessly tossed in the garage and throws him out.

With the help of a particularly aggressive woman lawyer, she begins proceedings to screw the best possible settlement out of the nonplussed Roger. With Jude's help to effect an introduction, she begins work as a volunteer for the Royal Forest and Bird Society.

Within a year she is on the payroll, in a nice office where she will give eleven years' devoted and enthusiastic service. She helps plant trees in the campaign to restore Tiritiri Island as a bird sanctuary, and always gives trees as birthday presents for her children's gardens.

If she's a witch, thinks Anna, she's a happier witch than she might have been had she not seen the light.

And the property by the lake? Two years later after her separation, on a greyish spring morning, out of a lingering curiosity, Anna draws up beside the Taupo property.

She is pleased to see that the blue atlas cedar, mortally wounded earlier, has gone. A new house, grander but to her eye undistinguished, stands on the section. Maybe the owner didn't win his fight with the council, but nevertheless the house has been sited well back against the far boundary so that perhaps one day another can be profitably rammed between it and the road.

The new house is two storeys, and painted an unappealing stony grey, the window trims dark green. It looks transplanted, alien to the surroundings. The architect clearly meant there to be an Australian outback homestead feel, with a long veranda facing the lake.

And where the lawn and garden once stood is a barren courtyard of beige paving stones surrounding an assertive circular sweep of concreted driveway. No lawnmower is needed here; no-one to keep the edges trim.

Apart from two scraggly eucalyptus in a far corner, just one of Ellie's beloved trees remains. The copper beech stands alone, now about four metres high and looking healthy enough. Anna can summon up a smidgeon of forgiveness to be quite glad about that. She can remember the day it was planted, Jim and Ellie taking turns to dig the hole, refusing Roger's help, dropping in some sort of fertiliser, the piano music drifting from inside the house; in the dusks that followed, her mother standing with the hose, willing the knee-high but perfectly shaped little tree to take strong root and prosper.

The combined effect of the courtyard, driveway and house, Anna decides, is drab, without charm. Well, all those sterile, man-made surfaces, and the lazy-gardener's bark chips put down where good honest weed-growing soil should be: they have just about ensured for themselves that nothing will grow there.

She makes two further visits. The first, next July, on her way back from a trip to Wellington and with a strong westerly blowing, she finds the house is up for sale.

So much for an owner the neighbours had said loved the lake, who lived for the pleasure of fly fishing along at the world-famous picket fence at Waitahanui and planned to retire to that house for the rest of his natural life. Hah!

A high fence and solid gate now stand between the house and the road, forming a palisade against any visual contact with the street or passers-by. No wall will be high or strong enough, my friends, thinks Anna, walking past the lurid red 'for sale' sign and down to the lakeside reserve, where, looking back, she can now get a glimpse of the house. From this angle she can see the long veranda, unprotected by Ellie's shoulder-high pittosporum hedge, fully and foolishly exposed to the westerly. The architect, probably Australian, had clearly never visited the site. Who would ever sit on a veranda lashed by such winds? Did no-one tell him?

The whole property — the new house, the stunted shrubs in the bark chips around the boundaries — appears more than ever unloved, abandoned. The branches of the copper beech, most of their leaves gone, bend to the ferocious wind. It does not look a healthy tree.

Anna did not intend to return, but the following spring, she is travelling to an environmental conference in Napier with her younger daughter, now thirty-four and also pursuing a career in what is now known as the 'environmental sector'. They stop for a coffee in Taupo, and out of the blue Jane asks to drive down to where Granny Ellie once lived.

'The house is gone, remember,' says Anna. 'Last time I was there, the new one was for sale. It looked unloved, so sad.'

She'd really prefer not to run the risk. She believed she had 'moved on'.

Jane reasons that the view and beach are still there; and photographs have kept her early memories of Jim and Ellie's house quite vivid. Anna agrees, reluctantly, to drive past. What if the house remains empty, the garden, such as it is, even more neglected, the copper beech dead? It would give her, now, little satisfaction, only a profound sense of unease.

She notes that the 'for sale' notice is gone. The tall gate is open; there are two vehicles, a station wagon and a small white car, in the courtyard. Neither are particularly flash. She decides to stop and park. They walk down to the grassy reserve. It is a calm spring day, completely windless, and the mountains to the south are clear as a bell. Anna sees a trout jump, disturbing the glassy surface of the lake. Out there both her parents' ashes lie, full fathom five. She cannot bring herself to look back.

But Jane does. 'Look, Mum, a baby under the copper beech, sleeping in a pram.'

'Is it looking . . . healthy?'

'What, the baby?'

'No, my love, the tree.'

'It looks fine. Lots of new leaves. Gorgeous colour, aren't they?'

Before she turns around, Anna notes something else, which makes her smile and reach out for Jane's hand. Tears come to her eyes. Something of Ellie has lasted here after all, her spirit greater than any other.

The two women listen.

A sound is coming from inside the house, a pianist playing scales. From their tentative nature, a child.